GROUNDED

What Reviewers Say About Amanda Radley's Work

Humbug

"*Humbug* is the Christmas cuddle we all want and need this festive season. Once again Amanda Radley has given us characters we can love, a gentle romance and a setting we never knew we needed." —*Kitty Kat's Book Review Blog*

"This is a classic Christmas rom-com, with holiday cheer and a predictable storyline. I would vote for *Humbug* as my favorite Christmas novel of 2021."—*The Lesbrary*

Under Her Influence

"Light, sweet, and remarkably chaste, this sapphic love story will make as enjoyable a vacation pick as it is an armchair getaway." —*Publishers Weekly*

"My heart is just…filled with love and warmth! Finally, I have found an author who does not rely on sex to make a book interesting!! I'm probably going to go on an Amanda Radley read-a-thon." —*Periwinkle Pens*

"Since I'm a big fan of Amanda Radley's romantic comedies, I had no doubt that I'd enjoy *Under Her Influence*. And I did! Her trademark dry wit and family-centered, low-angst romance always satisfies and this was no different. I always seem to learn something about a new industry, too, so that's a bonus."—*To Be Read Book Reviews*

Detour to Love

"If you're on the lookout for well written sapphic romance with stellar characters, wonderful pairings & outstanding plots I whole heartedly recommend any of Amanda's books!!"—*EloiseReads*

Flight SQA016

"I'm so glad I picked this book up because I think I've found my new favourite series! ...The love brewing between these two is beautifully written and I was onboard from the beginning. I had some laugh out loud moments because this is British rom-com at its best. The secondary characters really added to the novel and the rollercoaster ride that is this book. The writing is tight and pace is perfect..."—*Les Rêveur*

Lost at Sea

"A.E. Radley knows how to write great characters. And it's not just the main characters she puts so much effort into. I loved them, but I was astounded at how well drawn the minor characters were, especially Elvin and Graham. The revelations are perfectly paced in this story. We find out more about their backgrounds as they get to know each other. The reader can so easily believe everything A.E. Radley writes because she is so observant and makes the world so real in her books. ...The writing was beautiful—descriptive, real and very funny at times." —*Lesbian Review*

"Absolutely amazing, easy to read, perfect romance with mystery and drama story. There were so many wonderful elements that gave twists and turns to this adventure on the sea. I absolutely loved this story and can't rave about it enough."—*LesbiReviewed*

Going Up

"I can always count on this superb author when it comes to creating unforgettable and endearing characters that I can totally relate to and fall in love with. A. E. Radley has given me beautiful descriptions of Parbrook and the quirky individuals who work at Addington's." —*Lesbian Review*

"This story is a refreshing light in the lesfics world. Or should I say in the romance lesfic world? Why do you ask me? Well, while there is a lot of crushy feeling between wlw characters and all, but, honestly that's the sub-plot and I've adored that fact. *Going Up* is a lesson in life."—*Kam's Queerfic Pantry*

"The author takes an improbable twosome and writes such a splendid romance that you actually thing it is possible…this is a great romance and a lovely read."—*Best Lesfic Reviews*

Mergers and Acquisitions

"This book is fun, witty and adorable. I had no idea which way this book was going to take me, and I loved it. Each character is interesting and loveable in their own right. You don't want to miss this one, heck if you have read any of A.E. Radley's books you know it's quality stuff."—*Romantic Reader Blog*

"Charming and quick witted, I think A.E. Radley is an author to watch."—*Les Rêveur*

The Startling Inaccuracy of the First Impression

We absolutely loved the way the relationship between the two ladies developed. There is nothing hurried about relationship that develops perfectly organically. This is a lovely easy to read romance."
—*Best Lesfic Reviews*

Huntress

"The writing style was fun and enjoyable. The story really gathered steam to the point of me shirking responsibilities to finish it. The humor in the story was very well done."—*Lesbian Review*

Bring Holly Home

"*Bring Holly Home* is a fantastic novel and probably one of my favourite books by A.E. Radley. …Such a brilliant story and one I know I will read time and time again. This book has two ingredients that I love in novels, Ice Queens melting and age-gap romance. It's definitely a slow burn but one I'd gladly enjoy rereading again."—*Les Rêveur*

Keep Holly Close

"It was great to go back into the world of the Remember Me series. The first book in the series, *Bring Holly Home.* is one of my favourite A.E. Radley books. I love Holly and Victoria; they tick all the boxes for me when it comes to my favourite tropes. Plus, Victoria's kids are adorable, especially little Alexia. She melts my heart."—*Les Rêveur*

Climbing the Ladder

"Radley has a talent for giving us memorable characters to love, women you wish you knew and locations you wish you could experience firsthand."—*Late Night Lesbian Reads*

Second Chances

"This is an absolute delight to read. Likeable characters, well-written, easy flow and sweet romance. Definitely recommended."—*Best Lesfic Reviews*

The Road Ahead

"I really enjoyed this age-gap, opposites attract road trip romance. This is a romance where the characters actually acknowledge their differences and joy of joy, listen to each other. I love it when a book makes me feel all the feels and root for both women to find their HEA. Hilarious one minute, heart-tugging the next. A pleasure to read." —*Late Night Lesbian Reads*

Fitting In

"Writing convincing love stories with non-typical characters is tricky. Radley more than measures up to the challenge with this truly heartwarming romance."—*Best Lesfic Reviews*

By the Author

Romance Novels

The Flight Series

Flight SQA016

Grounded

Journey's End

The Remember Me Series

Bring Holly Home

Keep Holly Close

The Around the World Series

The Road Ahead

The Big Uneasy

Mergers & Acquisitions

Climbing the Ladder

A Swedish Christmas Fairy Tale

Second Chances

Going Up

Lost at Sea

The Startling Inaccuracy of the First Impression

Fitting In

Detour to Love

Under Her Influence

Protecting the Lady

Humbug

Reading Her

Mystery Novels

Huntress

Death Before Dessert

Grounded

by

Amanda Radley

2022

GROUNDED

ISBN 13: 978-1-63679-241-5

This Trade Paperback Original Is Published By
Bold Strokes Books, Inc.
P.O. Box 249
Valley Falls, NY 12185

First Bold Strokes Books Edition: April 2022

Credits
Editor: Cindy Cresap
Production Design: Susan Ramundo
Cover Design By Tammy Seidick

Dedication

For the readers.

CHAPTER ONE

Olivia Lewis leaned her head back on the plush leather headrest of her first-class seat and looked out the window to her left. The approach to John F. Kennedy Airport in New York looked much the same as it did every week, but this time felt different. This was the first week that Olivia had changed her schedule, no longer flying the route she had become comfortable with over the past ten years. The reason for her change was quite simple: Emily White.

Olivia let out a sigh; she still didn't quite understand what had happened with the young cabin assistant. However, she knew whatever it was, the blame sat squarely on her own shoulders. It always did.

"Can I get you anything before we land, Miss Lewis?"

Olivia looked up at the flight attendant, her new Emily White. Except this one was actually called Steve, and instead of long, flowing blond locks, he was completely bald.

"No, thank you," Olivia replied politely.

Steve smiled and continued his way around the first-class cabin serving other passengers.

Olivia returned her attention to the window and gazed down at the ocean. The deep midnight-blue waters were making way for lighter shades as the aircraft got closer to land. The sun was setting, and the strong red glare produced an interesting reflection on the waves that rippled below.

Despite the beautiful sight that had other passengers enthralled, Olivia could only concentrate on the fact that she was landing five hours later than her usual flight would have. Emily would be home by now, spending time with Henry.

Henry. Olivia closed her eyes as her breath caught in her throat at the mere thought of the little boy, Emily's son. She allowed herself a moment to reflect on the time they had spent together while Henry was recovering from his heart operation. When she had first met Emily, she'd had no clue how their lives would suddenly become so entwined. Having Emily and young Henry stay at her hotel suite in London while Henry recuperated had changed everything. She missed them, missed the things they had done together. She quickly reopened her eyes and chanced a glance at the seat opposite hers, mentally noting that her seat was actually not hers at all; hers had landed five hours ago. This new seat was a poor replica. The lower back felt different, and the left-hand armrest gave the slightest of wobbles. She looked at the seat opposite, the one that would in her mind always be Henry's, and sighed. It was currently occupied by a young woman who was practically dripping in diamonds and high fashion. She'd spent the entire flight on the satellite phone making small talk with friends about various parties.

Olivia let out another sigh. She knew she had been doing more of that lately, ever since her last conversation with Emily more than three weeks ago. Changing her schedule had been difficult. Olivia was a creature of habit, and despite the enormous discomfort she felt over the change of schedule, not to mention the wobbly armrest, she knew it had been the right thing to do. Her social awkwardness, absence of thought, and general lack of finesse had caused Emily pain, so it was up to Olivia to correct the situation by taking herself out of the equation. But knowing that didn't make it any easier, and she still found herself thinking about Emily and Henry often, wondering what they were doing at any given moment.

She didn't know how long she had been lost in thought, but suddenly the ocean was gone and the coast of Long Island came into view. The aircraft banked heavily from right to left as the pilot straightened up to the flight path. Olivia picked up some paperwork from the storage netting beside her and placed it on her wobbly armrest. She considered whether it would be worth changing to another seat in the future but quickly decided that none would be as perfect as her previous seat, the one that had already landed at JFK and was presumably about to return to London again.

She tried to distract herself by looking at the company accounts Simon had printed for her before her departure that morning. Unlike many of her other clients, this company had become something of a success story. The restructuring and new financial bailout she'd secured from the bank had saved the business. She pushed aside memories of Henry imploring her to save a similar business a few weeks before. She hadn't managed to then, but since the distraction of Emily and Henry had left her life, she had been able to focus more on work.

The cabin lights dimmed, and a small reading light above lit up her workspace. She ignored the gentle sway of the aircraft banking from side to side and focused on the figures in front of her as the cabin crew took their seats for landing.

Everything seemed completely normal, like any of the hundreds of landings she had experienced before. Right up until the aircraft touched down on the runway. Olivia knew something wasn't right but had no idea what it was. She looked up from her paperwork and frowned as she looked out the window for a clue as to what was wrong.

As the aircraft started to slow down on the runway, Olivia realised that it was the noise that was unusual. A screeching sound from beneath her got louder and louder, and she gripped the armrests tightly. The aircraft lurched forward, passengers screamed, and it went dark.

many of her other clients, this company had become something of a success story. The restructuring and new financial [illegible] from the bank had saved the business. She pushed aside memories of Henri Pomeroy [illegible] similar [illegible] weeks before [illegible] [illegible]

Then [illegible] work.

[illegible] light [illegible] her workspace. She [illegible] of [illegible] from side to side and [illegible] out of her as the [illegible]

Everything seemed completely normal, like any of the hundreds of [illegible] she had [illegible] until the [illegible] down on the subway. Olivia [illegible] she had [illegible] She [illegible] up from her [illegible] looked [illegible]

As the [illegible] Olivia realized that [illegible] was [illegible] her [illegible] and [illegible]

Chapter Two

"Em, wake up."

Emily blinked and looked up at the concerned face of her best friend.

"Lucy? What? Is it Henry?" Emily sat up quickly. She looked to her side to see Henry sleeping soundly in the bed they shared.

"Henry's fine," Lucy assured her. "It's the news. You have to see this."

Emily let out a relieved sigh. After years of caring for a sick child, it was hard to keep fear at bay, especially when just waking up. Emily quietly stood up, wobbling slightly. She was still in a daze from being woken from her nap, and still exhausted from a busy week's worth of flights. She followed Lucy out of her bedroom and into the living room, where Tom sat in the armchair, leaning forward and staring pensively at the television.

Emily moved to stand beside him, looked at the news broadcast, and let out a surprised gasp.

"What happened?" she whispered.

"Landing gear failure," Tom explained grimly, and then held up his hand to silence any further questions as the news reporter began to speak again.

"Crown Airlines Flight SQA084 has suffered a catastrophic front landing gear failure at JFK airport. The Boeing 777 from London Heathrow landed at approximately eight o'clock this evening and touched down normally. However, a few seconds later the pilot declared an emergency," the news anchor explained as the camera panned over the downed aircraft.

Tom muted the television, stood up, and ran his hands through his hair. He let out a long sigh. "They're just repeating what little they know."

Emily took his seat, reading the scrolling ticker tape and watching the footage. The front of the aircraft was crushed into the tarmac, the front wheel nowhere in sight, the giant craft seemingly swallowing the enormous landing gear. Chutes were deployed from all doors, and emergency service vehicles surrounded the area.

"Do we know who was on the flight?" Emily started.

"Matthew was first officer. I don't know about the rest of the crew on that flight," Tom answered despondently. "This is bad news, Em. Real bad."

"Were there any injuries?" she asked, examining the screen again for any information.

"They're not saying much yet," Lucy replied. "But there have been a few ambulances back and forth. And there was footage of people being brought out on stretchers."

The news footage cut to an older man in a suit getting out of a chauffeur-driven car, and Emily instantly recognised him as Bob Mercury, the chief executive of Crown Airlines. Tom saw him too and snatched up the remote control to unmute the television. He sat on the edge of the coffee table to listen to what the man had to say.

Emily tuned out as she realised that Bob had no new information to give. While his calming voice carefully explained the strenuous safety procedures to the reporter, the camera panned back to the aircraft and Emily felt a cold shudder creep up her spine. The nose of the plane was lying shattered on the tarmac, and dark scorch marks charred up the paintwork on either side.

"Are you okay?" Lucy asked softly as she sat on the arm of the chair. She looked down at Emily, placing a comforting hand on her shoulder.

"Yeah, it's just, seeing it like that is really scary. I mean, I work in the nose section," she whispered back, shaking her head. "I can't imagine what that must have been like."

"It's terrifying. I've always been scared that you or Tom would be involved in something like this," Lucy said.

"I know we're trained for it, and I know my training would have automatically kicked in, but just thinking about being strapped into my jump seat and suddenly feeling the wheel collapse…" She shivered at the thought even as a trickle of sweat ran down her back. "That's a big drop down to the ground, and at the speed they were travelling…" She shook her head again, trying to dislodge the images taking root in her brain.

"Apparently people saw it happen. It was just a few seconds after they touched down. They could see the landing gear rattling, and then it went up into the plane and the nose came down."

Emily licked her suddenly dry lips. She found she couldn't stop thinking about what she would have done in that situation, and wondered if she would have had time to order passengers to brace for impact, if the power would have gone off, or if a fire might have started in the cabin.

"Mommy." Henry entered the living room with his cuddly toy giraffe, Tiny, clutched to his chest. He stopped dead and stared at the television with a confused expression. "Mommy, what happened?"

Emily didn't want to lie to Henry, but she also didn't want to frighten him, especially when he was already sad about her spending so much time at work.

"There was a little accident," Emily explained, patting her knee for Henry to come and sit with her.

Henry padded over, not taking his eyes off the news report, and shuffled himself onto her lap.

"There was a wobbly wheel and it broke," Emily said, pointing to the screen. "You see how the front of the plane is touching the ground?"

Henry nodded. "Why are there fire trucks and ambulances?"

"To help anyone who might have got hurt."

Henry looked thoughtfully at the screen before turning to look at Tom and then Emily. "But, that wasn't your plane?"

"Oh! No, no, baby, that wasn't our plane," Emily said. Henry's youthful view on the world sometimes still surprised her as she realised it would be hard for him to understand the number of planes and airlines in the world.

"Our plane's much better," Tom said with a wink.

"It is now," Lucy muttered under her breath as she got up and went into the kitchen to prepare some drinks.

"Did people get hurt?" Henry asked, craning his neck to look up at her.

Emily paused before answering. Henry was at the awkward age where a mother had to walk a fine balance between truth and protection. "We don't know yet," she said, opting for a softer version of the truth. "The news channel is telling us more as they find out."

Henry looked at her thoughtfully before turning back to look at the television. "Why did the wheel break?"

Emily looked at Tom with pleading eyes. He nodded his understanding and took up the challenge of explaining a complex situation to a five-year-old.

"Well, buddy, there are lots and lots of pieces in a plane, and even though they are looked at and checked all the time, sometimes things go wrong. But it's really, really rare. Did you know that there are around five thousand planes in the skies right now? And that's just over America."

Henry turned back to Emily with a confused look on his face. "What's five thousand?"

Tom looked apologetic, and Emily grinned. "Lots and lots and lots," she replied as she kissed his hair and held him a little tighter to her body.

"Is your plane going to break?" Henry asked, turning to face the screen again.

"No, our plane is special," Emily replied, a pang of guilt hitting her as she lied. But she knew she couldn't explain the truth to him.

"Time for cookies and milk," Lucy said as she entered the room with a tray.

Henry excitedly shuffled off Emily's lap, sat in front of the coffee table, and waited for the tray to be placed in front of him. As soon as it was down, he picked up a cookie and started to eat it while still staring suspiciously at the television.

"This will damage Crown," Tom said.

"Are you sure?" Lucy asked, handing him a mug of coffee. "Such a small incident?"

Tom nodded grimly. "Yeah, people are scared because there have been so many incidents lately. Crown operates a competitive route, customers have other options, and if they think maintenance isn't up to scratch they'll vote with their feet. And God forbid there have been any serious injuries."

"Mommy, did you see Olivia today?" Henry asked.

Lucy and Tom looked at Emily, and she let out a small breath as she prepared herself for what was about to happen. Henry asked about Olivia at least once a day, despite Emily's standard response about how busy Olivia was. The hope was that he would soon stop asking and Olivia would become a distant memory, but it seemed less and less likely that he was simply going to forget about her.

"No, sweetie, I didn't," Emily answered truthfully.

Henry turned to look at her. "Why?"

"Henry, finish your cookie and then it is time to go to bed," Lucy said.

Henry jumped to his feet and stared at the television silently for a moment. Emily could tell that his young brain was attempting to piece together the facts. Then he turned, walked over to Emily, and started to reach for the pocket in her jeans.

"Henry, what are you doing?" Emily asked as Henry's small hands pulled out a tissue and an old receipt.

"You need your phone, Mommy. You need to call Olivia!"

"Sweetie, I can't call Olivia." Emily gently took his hands and held them still. "I'm sorry, Henry. I can't."

"But—" Henry yanked his hands out of hers, took a step back, and glared at her.

"Henry," Emily said in a low, warning tone.

"You hate me," Henry said bitterly, then turned around and stalked from the room.

Lucy gave Emily a compassionate smile. "I'll talk to him."

Emily nodded her gratitude, pinching the bridge of her nose in frustration.

"Maybe it's time to explain to Henry what happened?" Tom suggested. "Or at least a child-friendly version?"

"He hates me enough as it is," Emily sighed.

"He doesn't hate you. He's just a kid. He's frustrated with things. He thinks you're keeping Olivia away from him."

"I messed up, Tom. I brought Olivia into our lives and I didn't think enough about the repercussions for Henry if it didn't work out. On top of that, I hardly ever see him with this schedule, and when I do see him I can't take him anywhere or treat him like I want to. Like he deserves."

"Things will get better," Tom said kindly. "Like you said from the start, a few months on this schedule and you'll get back on your feet."

Emily tilted her head towards him. "You're right. I'm just tired. I should be grateful that Henry's heart problems are fixed and that I have a job that pays as well as it does."

"And Henry is bound to forget about Olivia soon. It's been three weeks."

Emily nodded. Her next shift after they'd fought, Emily had begged to be moved to the upper deck so she could avoid Olivia. She'd remained up there until she noticed that Olivia's name was no longer on the passenger manifest.

She'd told Henry that Olivia was simply too busy and she hadn't seen her. It hurt to lie to him, but he was too young to understand the complexities of adult relationships. All he knew was that he wanted Olivia in his life, and unfortunately that wasn't going to happen.

"You're right, things will get better," she said with a forced smile, hoping it was true.

CHAPTER THREE

Simon Fletcher was very pleased with himself. It wasn't every day that he found himself sitting in the best seats, watching a top London musical with the woman of his dreams, but today was such a day. It was the end of the first act, and the very moment the musical crescendo finished, the audience were loudly applauding and making their way towards the bars.

"Can I get you anything?" he asked Sophie. "Overpriced ice cream? Alcohol in a plastic receptacle? A booklet of advertisements pretending to be a programme?"

Sophie laughed. "Simon, you're so funny."

"I know." He grinned happily. "Seriously though, can I get you anything?"

"No. I'm going to use the ladies' though." She turned and looked at the enormous queue. "I'll be back in about a week," she added with a wink.

Simon watched her edge along the row and towards the back of the theatre. Sitting back in his chair, he let out a happy sigh. Realising he was in for a long wait and realising he could easily master a few levels of his favourite new app, he reached into his jacket pocket and got out his phone. As the screen sprung to life, he frowned to see that he had seven missed calls from his boss. He quickly dialled and brought the phone up to his ear.

"Simon, at last," Olivia's weary voice answered.

"Sorry, I'm at the theatre. Are you okay?" he asked.

"I'm in hospital. I think I'm going to die." Olivia responded calmly.

Simon jumped to his feet. "What? What happened?"

"They won't tell me anything, and I have this ridiculous thing on my arm and my leg. I demand that you come and get me out of here."

Simon sat back down as he understood the situation maybe wasn't as dire as Olivia had first led him to believe. "What's happened?"

"The plane crashed," Olivia said simply.

"Crashed? What do you mean crashed?" Simon jumped to his feet again.

"Into the ground, Simon. Crashed." Olivia clearly had no desire to explain herself.

Simon quickly plugged his earphone and microphone in and accessed a browser on his phone to see if he could get some information on what had happened.

"I'm never flying again," Olivia said. "You'll have to move to New York."

Simon found a breaking news story and quickly examined the text and photographs. "Okay, so the landing gear collapsed I see," he said calmly. "Are you hurt?"

"I presume so. I'm in a hospital," Olivia replied. "Did you hear what I said? I'm never flying again."

Simon flopped back into his chair. "Is there a nurse or someone I can speak to?"

"I don't know; I've been left in the room to rot."

"Okay. Where are you? I'll call them myself." Simon looked apologetic as Sophie returned to her seat and looked questioningly at him. He took the information from Olivia and promised to call her straight back.

"I'm sorry. Olivia's in hospital," he said. "There's been some kind of crash and I need to see what's going on."

"Is there anything I can do?" Sophie asked as he searched online for a switchboard number for the hospital.

"Yeah." Simon looked at her with a wince. "Could you check for the next flight to New York?"

❖

As soon as Olivia hung up with Simon, she scrolled to her second most frequently contacted person and held the phone to her ear as she waited for the international call to connect. She half-heartedly wondered why all her go-to people were on the other side of the world and why New York to London suddenly felt so far away.

"Hello, darling," Nicole answered brightly.

Olivia snorted a bitter laugh. "I'm crippled. And no one will tell me anything."

"I'm afraid I have no idea what you're going on about," Nicole said. "Hold on."

Olivia waited impatiently while Nicole mumbled an excuse and apology to whomever she was with.

"Okay, start from the beginning," she said.

"I'm never flying again."

"Okay. Lunch will be more difficult, but we can Skype," Nicole joked softly. "You said you were crippled?"

"I'm not joking around, Nic. The plane crashed!"

There was silence for a moment while Nicole's brain caught up.

"I'm sorry, what?"

"The. Plane. Crashed," Olivia said clearly into the mouthpiece of the phone.

"What do you mean crashed?"

"Have you been drinking?" Olivia sighed.

"Liv, what do you mean crashed? Explain to me what happened," Nicole demanded.

Olivia silenced the sarcastic remark that was about to leave her mouth and took a moment to consider her words. "We landed at JFK, but there was a problem with the front wheels. It must have collapsed, because the next thing I know we're falling to the ground with an enormous crash but the plane was still moving, so there were sparks coming up the windows and people were screaming—"

"Where are you now?" Nicole interrupted.

"I'm in hospital."

"What have they said to you?"

"Not a lot. I have this thing on my arm and my leg, so I can't move, and no one is telling me anything. I don't know what's happening."

"Okay, so you've hurt your arm and your leg. Is that what you mean by crippled?" Nicole asked kindly.

"Yes!"

"Darling, I'm sure you're scared and in pain, but they wouldn't leave you on your own if it was serious. They must be attending to other people."

Olivia let out a deep breath and looked around the busy ward. Doctors and nurses were rushing to attend to various patients. People filled the halls of the accident and emergency department. Some held makeshift bandages to bloodied wounds, and some sat on the floor looking pale and exhausted.

"I suppose that might be the case," Olivia said.

"Do you know how bad your injuries are?" Nicole asked.

Olivia looked down at her leg, which was encased in a hardened plastic cast, and tentatively flexed the muscles, wincing when a shot of pain rushed up her leg and took her breath away.

"My leg hurts." She'd never been good at diagnosing her own injuries; often she continued on as if nothing had happened, with no realisation that she was even in pain.

"Remember when you broke your wrist that time in Blackpool?" Nicole giggled.

Olivia laughed at the memory. "Yes, on your birthday, and you'd insisted on taking me to that awful seaside resort."

"I didn't have to twist your arm that much!" Nicole said. "And you were the one who wanted to have your fortune read. Don't blame me for what happened."

"I was horribly drunk, and I'd never seen a fortune teller before."

"To be honest, you probably still haven't. I don't think someone in a tent on a pier in Blackpool charging two pounds fifty to read your palm is really legit. Although, she was spot on with that last piece of information." Nicole's laughter grew, and Olivia shook her head with a rueful grin.

"I didn't see the step!"

"Not five seconds after she tells you to mind your step, you trip and break your damn wrist!"

"Who has a step down from a tent? It's really quite ridiculous." Olivia sniffed.

"Do you remember when you were in hospital explaining to the doctor that your wrist hurt, but only when you did a certain movement, and you proceeded to continuously flip him the bird to demonstrate your pain?"

"As drunk as I might have been, I can assure you I remember that evening very well," Olivia said. "And if you've finished laughing at my expense?"

Nicole let out one last laugh as she attempted to calm herself down. "I'm not laughing at your expense, darling. Just trying to calm you down and make you smile."

Olivia grumpily attempted to smother a grin.

"You'll thank me later."

"Miss Lewis?" Olivia turned to see a nurse approaching her with a clipboard. "We're ready for you now."

"I'll call you later," Olivia said, terminating the call as she looked nervously at the nurse. She hated hospitals.

CHAPTER FOUR

Emily heard Henry shifting and knew it wouldn't be long before he crawled over to wake her up and force her to start the day. The previous night had been hard work. Henry steadfastly refused to acknowledge Emily, stating that he would only agree to talk to her again once she'd called Olivia.

Lucy had put a screaming Henry to bed, and he'd eventually cried himself to sleep with no bedtime story to soothe him. Now he'd decided only Olivia was allowed to read to him at night.

"Mommy?"

Emily kept her eyes tightly closed and pretended to be asleep. She hoped that today would be a new day, and Henry would have forgotten about the plane crash and his desperation to hear from Olivia. She also hoped that if Henry thought she was asleep he would crawl up to her and hug her as he did most other mornings. After the difficult night, she needed to feel close to Henry—not as if she'd failed him somehow.

"Mommy?" Henry repeated sleepily. "Wake up, silly."

Emily barely managed to keep her expression neutral. A few moments later, she felt him crawl over to her, shifting around in the bedding. She knew he was lying in front of her, nose to nose by the loud sounds of his breathing and the warm air hitting her face.

"Good morning, sweetie," she mumbled softly, keeping her eyes closed and enjoying the moment.

"Mommy, I dreamed."

"What did you dream, sweetie?"

"I dreamed you were a giraffe."

Emily grinned. "Wow, were you a giraffe too?"

"No." Henry sounded as if he thought she was being ridiculous. "I was me."

"Oh, of course." Emily smiled and opened her eyes. She reached up and smoothed down his unruly brown locks.

"You ate all the leaves on Mrs. Lipton's tree and she was very angry with you."

"All the leaves?" Emily asked with mock wide-eyed wonderment.

Henry nodded slowly and seriously. "Yes, all of them, Mommy."

"Well, no wonder she was very angry. That's a lot of leaves."

"What are we doing today?" Henry asked as he reached out and played with some strands of Emily's hair that lay on the pillow.

"How about we go to the park?" she suggested.

Henry's eyes glowed with excitement. "Really?"

"Really." Emily was relieved that he could be excited by such simple and inexpensive things. Guilt washed over her as she considered that he simply didn't know any better because she had never been able to treat him to extravagant surprises like she so desperately craved. "And how about a picnic?"

By way of response, Henry slipped out of bed and padded over to the wardrobe to get clothes.

Emily watched him excitedly pluck out clothes and winced when he picked up his favourite giraffe hoodie and turned back to her with a thoughtful look. He looked at her and then looked at the hoodie, his mind obviously whirring with unspoken questions.

"Can we have ham sandwiches at the picnic?" he finally asked.

Emily let out a breath of relief. "Of course!" She got out of bed and stretched. "Why don't you ask if Tom and Lucy want to come too?"

Henry's eyes and mouth opened in joy; he adored Lucy like a second mother, and Tom was his idol. He dropped the giraffe hoodie to the floor, calling out their names as he ran excitedly from the room and down the hallway.

Emily bent down, picked up the hoodie, and let out a sigh as she folded it and placed it on a top shelf where he wouldn't easily find it. She reached into the wardrobe and picked out some alternative clothes for him, placed them on the bed, and hoped that his excitement over the picnic would be enough to distract him.

❖

Simon was exhausted as he approached the hospital reception desk and dropped his hastily packed holdall to the floor. "Hi. I'm here to see Olivia Lewis?"

The nurse typed the name into the computer and read the details from the screen. "Are you family?"

He smiled politely, too exhausted for red tape and bureaucracy. "Yes, I'm her son."

"Oh, I see. Well, she's in room thirty-four, just down the corridor on your left," the nurse replied with a kind smile.

"Thank you so much." Simon picked up his bag. He walked down the corridor, poked his head around the corner of the correct room, and smiled to himself. It was a relief to see Olivia alive and well, and also amusing to see her dressed in a floral hospital gown and grumpily eating a yoghurt.

"Hello, sunshine," he said.

Olivia looked away from the television and glared at him. "Don't say a word."

"About the lovely gown?" Simon walked in and placed his bag next to the visitor's chair. "Wouldn't dream of it."

"When can I leave this…this…"

"Beacon of modern medicine?" Simon finished. "I don't know. I need to speak to someone."

"The food is dreadful," Olivia complained. She placed the half-eaten yoghurt on her bedside table.

"It's supposed to be. You're not meant to like it here," Simon said as he walked around inspecting the room. "It might encourage you to stay. Before they know it, people will be staying here just for fun."

Olivia ignored him. "And the nurses are awful."

Simon turned around and regarded her with a frown. "Why are they awful?"

Olivia shuffled in her bed, pulling herself into a higher seated position with her one good arm. "They are all so, well, happy. Smiling."

"How terrible," Simon drawled.

Olivia shot him a glare. "You may mock, but there is absolutely nothing worse than being in pain and surrounded by unnaturally happy people."

"Yes, nothing worse," Simon said. "I'm glad you've managed to maintain a sense of perspective."

At that moment a nurse entered the room, smiling brightly at the two of them. "Good afternoon, Miss Lewis. I heard that your son is here. Isn't that lovely?" She and Simon shared a smile in greeting.

"My—" Olivia stared at Simon in horror.

"She's a bit overcome with emotions," Simon cut in, smiling wickedly at Olivia from where he stood behind the nurse. "Aren't you, Mum?"

"Mum?" Olivia gave him a furious look.

"Are you from England?" the nurse asked, obviously detecting Simon's accent.

"Yes, flew in from London," Simon explained, then turned to Olivia. "I literally dropped everything and got on the first flight to be here, slept in the airport on a cold bench, so she's very happy to see me. Aren't you, Mum?"

Olivia had the grace to blush as she silently inclined her head. "Yes, thank you, Simon."

"What are children for?" Simon asked with a grin before turning to address the nurse. "Though I know she is itching to get out of here. Do you have any idea when she can be discharged?"

"That will be up to the doctor. He's doing his rounds now and will be here soon. But hopefully we'll be able to release her in a few days."

Simon heard Olivia's quiet but distinctly horrified intake of breath. "Is there any chance she can be released today? She gets very anxious in hospitals, and I don't think it will do her much good being in here for too long." Simon looked at the name tag on the nurse's uniform. "Is there anything you can do to help, Sandra?"

Sandra looked at him, then at the chart she was holding, then back at Simon. She smiled. "I'll go and see if I can get the doctor to see you both next."

"That would be wonderful. Thank you so much. We really appreciate it." Simon smiled politely as she left the room to seek out the doctor.

"Thank you, son," Olivia joked softly.

"No problem." Simon sat in the visitor's chair and gestured at Olivia's leg. "So, what's the damage?"

"Some broken something or other in my leg and a fractured thing in this." Olivia twitched her arm, which was in a heavy-duty sling.

"Oh, so you really listened and paid attention when they told you?" Simon rolled his eyes.

Olivia shrugged before wincing at the pain and letting out a sigh.

CHAPTER FIVE

Tom sat wedged at the bottom of the children's slide. He pouted up at Henry.

"I'm stuck, buddy!"

"No, you're not!" Henry giggled, knowing full well that Tom was joking.

Emily watched the scene with amusement from a bench at the edge of the playground. Lucy hadn't been able to come, but Tom had jumped at the chance. He'd spent the last hour and a half running around the park exciting and exhausting not only Henry but all the other children as well.

As soon as they arrived at the park, Henry had mentioned Olivia's name again, and Emily and Tom shared a terrified look before Tom decided to distract Henry. Emily had played, too, until exhaustion started to overtake her, and then she'd bowed out to sit and watch.

The ever-present niggle at the back of her mind resurfaced. How long would she be able to keep up the punishing schedule? She was back and forth from London to New York so much that she barely knew where she was anymore. And Tom had been right, the jet lag and the exhaustion were building and building.

She looked up as he sat on the bench beside her. "Wow, kids have so much energy."

Emily chuckled. "You kept up with them for a long time."

"They beat me in the end." Tom grinned.

They watched as Henry and a couple of other children stood in a circle watching a worm in the grass. Emily could hear them debate how many teeth it had and what kind of snake it was.

Tom's phone rang and he looked at the screen. "It's work."

He answered, and Emily listened to his side of the conversation with interest. The call only lasted a couple of minutes, and Tom hardly said anything other than to agree with what he was being told.

He hung up and nervously licked his lips. "We've been grounded."

"What?" Emily exclaimed. "Why?"

"Mass cancellations after the landing gear crash." Tom looked over to check that Henry wasn't listening. "Our flight's been cancelled, the earlier flight's taking our passengers, and we're grounded."

"But..." Emily trailed off, knowing there was nothing she could say to change what was happening. Cold dread crept up her spine. She simply couldn't afford not to work. She regretted admitting her earlier exhaustion, suddenly wishing she could double her shifts.

"Maybe Iris will move you onto the earlier shift?" Tom suggested hopefully.

"Iris hates me. She's convinced I did something wrong when I begged her to let me take the upper deck. I know she was snooping. And I'm last in, so I'll be first out."

"You don't know that," Tom said.

Emily chuckled. "Yeah, I do. Just because we're thirty thousand feet in the air doesn't mean we don't have office politics."

"Well, whatever happens, you know Lucy and I are here for you." Tom put his arm around her and pulled her in close.

Henry approached, clearly unaware of any tension in the air. He pointed at an older boy who had been playing with him earlier. "That boy says the worm tasted funny."

❖

Emily unlocked the front door and stood to one side as Tom carried a sleeping Henry into the house. Lucy looked at the sight with a fond smile and kissed Tom on the cheek as he passed by to put Henry down for a well-deserved afternoon nap.

"Someone's tired," Lucy commented.

"He's not the only one. I don't know how Tom has so much energy. Just watching him made me want to sleep." Emily took off her scarf and coat and hung them in the closet. She turned to look at Lucy, who had a pensive look on her face. "What's wrong?"

"We had visitors while you were out," Lucy said grimly.

"Shit, bailiffs?" Emily immediately concluded. "They sent a threatening letter, but I paid their minimum payment! Oh, God, Lucy, I'm so sorry—"

"No, not bailiffs," Lucy interrupted. "But you better sit down."

"I don't want to sit down. You're frightening me," Emily said as Lucy grabbed her arm and gently guided her to the kitchen, where a pot of coffee was waiting.

"The Brennans have been here," Lucy said as she sat down.

Emily stared at her as she dropped herself onto the waiting dining room chair. "What? Henry's grandparents? They came here?"

Lucy nodded and poured them each a coffee. "They wanted to speak to you, but I said you were out. They've asked that you meet them for dinner this evening."

"Did they say what it was about?" Emily whispered. Her breathing was shallow and she could feel the panic rising in her gut.

"No, but it didn't seem like a pleasant social call."

Tom entered the room and clapped his hands together. "Right. Henry's in bed, so I thought I'd…" He looked at them. "What's up?"

"Joe's parents have been here," Lucy said.

"What? Why?"

"To speak to Emily. They wouldn't tell me what it was about, but, well, knowing them, it can't be good."

Tom looked at Emily. "Have you had any contact with them since the custody case?"

"No." Emily shook her head, staring at the coffee cup in front of her. "Nothing. They kind of vanished."

"So what the hell do they want now?" Tom asked no one in particular.

"For me to meet them for dinner, apparently." Emily let out a long sigh. "Great timing."

"Is any time a good time with them?" Lucy asked. Emily and Tom looked guiltily at each other.

"About that," Tom started. "While we were out, we both had calls from Crown."

Lucy paled at the news. "And?"

"We're grounded," he said.

"For how long?"

Tom shook his head. "We don't know. They told me that they were cancelling Sunday's flight and that they'd be in touch soon."

"And they told me that I'm grounded until further notice," Emily added. "You need pilots more than you need cabin crew."

"Oh, Emily, I'm so sorry!" Lucy gasped.

Emily shrugged. "Hey, it never rains, but it pours. That's what they say, right?"

"And that things come in threes," Tom added.

Lucy looked up at him. "Not helping. Go and play with your car or whatever you were going to do."

"I'm going to clean up the spark plugs and then—"

"Tom." Lucy gave him a meaningful look.

He nodded. "Right. I'll, yeah, I'll just be out there." He gestured his thumb towards the door and then left the kitchen.

Emily let out a long sigh.

"Are you okay?" Lucy asked.

"Not really." Emily chuckled ruefully. "What did they say, exactly? Was it both of them?"

"Yes. They asked for you, and I said you were out. Then they introduced themselves. Asked when you would be back, and I said I didn't know." Lucy stood up and fetched a slip of paper. "They want you to meet them here for dinner tonight. They said around seven."

Emily took the note. "Hope they don't expect me to pay," she mumbled.

"What do you think they want?"

"No idea. If it was anyone else, I might think they wanted to connect with their grandson. But they made it very clear after the court case that they would never be in his life. From what Joe told me about his parents, I think that's probably a good thing."

"Does Henry even know about them?"

Emily shook her head. "I didn't see any reason to tell him. He doesn't have an understanding of a traditional family. You know, mom, dad, grandparents. It's always just been me and him. And then you and Tom. So he's never asked. And I've never offered."

"Maybe it has nothing to do with Henry," Lucy suggested.

"Well, I'll find out tonight." Emily looked at the piece of paper again. "I'm going to have to dress up for this place. Do you mind watching Henry?"

Lucy smiled. "It's not a problem. I do it most nights."

"I know. That's why I hate to ask. Although if the situation with Crown doesn't resolve itself quickly, I might be spending a lot more time here."

CHAPTER SIX

Emily walked along the dimly lit street with her winter coat pulled tightly closed and ducked her head to avoid the heavy drops of rain that had started to fall. The weather had taken a dramatic turn, along with her mood, as she'd fought heavy wind and rain to get to the restaurant.

She'd considered not going, but she knew that Irene and Sebastian Brennan were not the kind of people who would be put off so easily. She shuddered at the memory. She'd been struggling to figure out how to be a single mother with no support network around her and a week-old baby. Suddenly receiving a letter from a law firm was the last thing she'd needed. Her sleep-deprived mind had read the letter five times before she could believe what she was reading; they wanted Henry. The ensuing court case had been long, painful, and expensive, but Emily had won. Since then, a Christmas card addressed to Henry was the only thing she'd ever received from the Brennans. Until today.

She paused outside of the expensive-looking restaurant and sighed. Of course they would pick somewhere that Emily would feel out of place. The rain was picking up, so she didn't have much time to think about it as she walked up the steps and opened the grand-looking door. The floor manager looked at her suspiciously, and Emily wondered what kind of a state she must have looked. She pushed down her fear, walked over to him, and put on her best smile.

"Good evening. I'm here to see Mr. and Mrs. Brennan," she said, refusing to show her discomfort to the man.

"And your name is?" He looked her up and down.

"Emily White."

He raised an eyebrow and inclined his head. "Very well, if you'll follow—"

"Actually, I'll be using the restroom first," Emily told him. "In case you're unaware, the weather is atrocious, and I would like to make myself somewhat presentable."

The host looked at Emily with surprise but nodded his head as he gestured towards the restroom across the lobby.

As soon as Emily entered the plush restroom, she realised she had made the right decision. She was a mess. She put her handbag on the vanity unit and pulled out her small make-up kit and hairbrush. A year ago, she never would have thought she'd be carrying around the sheer volume of make-up supplies she did these days. Working in the first-class cabin at Crown had altered her views on personal appearance. She looked in the mirror at her running mascara and her messy hair and let out a sigh.

❖

Ten minutes later, Emily strode from the restroom, having used the hand dryer to dry her clothes, hair, and hands. She'd reapplied her make-up and now felt ready to confront her ex's parents.

She approached the host again and looked at him silently; he knew why she was there, and she wasn't about to ask him a second time. She'd worked with first-class passengers long enough to have seen them use this tactic—attempt to take the high ground by treating the other person like they were somehow unworthy. It wasn't a tactic Emily would normally have employed—she much preferred to treat everyone with respect—but in this instance she was willing to bend a little.

"Ah, Miss White," he finally spoke, as if only just noticing her despite the fact that he couldn't have missed the sound of her heels clicking across the marble foyer. "Please, follow me."

He snatched up a leather-bound menu from the station where he stood and smartly marched down a small corridor lined with various awards and into the main part of the restaurant. It was exactly what Emily had pictured in her mind, an old-fashioned, high-ceilinged, palatial room with golden details on the ceiling as well as the pillars.

The sound of a piano playing some soft, repetitive tune and the murmur of voices was almost deafening to her as she followed him across the room, passing numerous rich, and mostly older, diners.

When they had arrived at the Brennans' table, the host spun around, pulled out a chair, and indicated for Emily to sit opposite Sebastian, with Irene to her right.

"Bon appétit," he said as he laid the menu down and made a quick exit.

Emily remained standing and looked at the two people before her. In the last five years, they'd changed little; they just looked older than when she'd first met them. Both were in their late fifties, with full heads of grey hair, age lines across their foreheads, and no laughter lines around their mouths. Emily remembered all the stories Joe had told her of his stern and humourless childhood with these people. Judging by their expressions, nothing had changed.

"Emily." Sebastian stood in greeting and politely held his hand out to her.

For a moment, she hesitated, wondering if she'd gotten it wrong, if this was just a social call and nothing untoward was about to happen. Then she remembered their surroundings, realized this was probably a frequently visited establishment for the Brennans, and understood that they were keeping up appearances. She reached across the table and shook his hand.

"Mr. Brennan." She tried to smile.

"Please, call me Seb," he replied. "You remember Irene, of course."

Emily turned to the woman, who was looking her up and down with an unreadable expression. She held out her hand, and Irene returned the lightest of handshakes.

"Please, sit." Seb gestured to her chair.

Emily sat down and gently pulled the heavy chair in.

"It's been a while," Seb began as he pulled a bottle of white wine from an ice bucket beside the table. He poured himself a glass and gestured the bottle towards Irene, who shook her head. He looked at Emily and gestured at the glass in front of her.

"No, thank you," she said politely. "I can't stay for long."

"How is Henry?" The question burst from Irene suddenly, as if the faux politeness of the situation was eating at her.

"He's doing well. Very well, actually," Emily replied, unable to keep from smiling at the thought.

"I suppose I should cut to the chase." Seb returned the wine bottle to the bucket and interlaced his fingers in front of him. "We have concerns."

The anger hit Emily quickly, but she remained calm. "Oh?"

"We have reason to believe that you are suffering financial hardship," Seb confessed. "We also know of your relentless work schedule, and we don't believe it's the best environment for our grandson."

"Excuse me?" Emily couldn't believe what she was hearing. "Firstly, my financial situation and my work schedule is no business of yours. Henry is doing very well, and he is surrounded by people who love and care for him. He doesn't even know who you are, so calling yourselves his grandparents is, quite frankly, laughable!"

"Please, don't get defensive. We're trying to help." Seb breathed out a sigh, clearly unhappy with Emily's outburst.

"What makes you think I need help?" Emily folded her arms and glared at him.

"Do you deny that you're in debt?" Seb asked.

"A great deal of debt," Irene added.

"I don't see what it has to do with you," Emily answered curtly.

"What about your work schedule?" Seb continued. "You see Henry on Saturday and Wednesday, two days per week. Do you really think that's appropriate? You leave him with your housemate the rest of the time. Is that right, for a young boy to see so little of his real family?"

"Lucy is his family. She may not be connected by blood, but she's more family to him than you are!" Emily hissed. She paused. "And how, exactly, do you know all of this?" Emily looked at Seb, who glanced at Irene, who steadfastly refused to look at anyone. "How do you know about any of this?" Emily repeated.

"We checked up on you," Irene said, still looking down at the pristine white tablecloth.

"Checked up? What does that mean?"

"We hired a private investigator," Seb explained without emotion. "We wanted to check that Henry was being cared for in the best possible way, as he would have been if he had been living with us."

"You…you…" Emily stopped, speechless.

"We know about the credit cards, the loans, the debts," Seb continued.

"Wait a minute, how do you know all of that?" Emily demanded, swallowing down the expletive that was on the tip of her tongue.

"I believe that information came from the trash can. Maybe you should invest in a shredder, Emily." Seb sipped at his wine. "Not that anyone would want to steal your identity. I can't imagine it's worth much at the moment."

"Seb," Irene hissed.

"You—" Emily started.

"We want to help with Henry," Irene interrupted.

Silence fell over the table as Emily stared open-mouthed at Irene, unable to come up with anything to say.

"You know that we have the funds to support him better than you can," Irene explained.

"And we'd be willing to pay off his medical bills and any debts incurred over the last five years," Seb added.

"Of course you could see him whenever you wanted," Irene continued.

"Or not at all, if you wish. You could be a free woman." Seb smiled at her. "No more debts, no more working an almost illegal number of hours per week, and no more threats from bill collectors."

"You're asking me to give up my son!" Emily hissed angrily. "You want to pay me off for my son!"

"We're doing no such thing," Seb said calmly. "We are simply giving you an alternative."

"You are out of your minds if you think I'm going to trade Henry for a clean credit score. And why now? If you cared so much about Henry, then why wait until now to get in touch? Where were you when he was in and out of the hospital these past few years? Would looking after a sick child be too much for you? Is spying on us from your mansion all the commitment you're willing to make?"

Seb opened his mouth to speak but paused when Irene placed her hand on his forearm. She turned to Emily. "I understand that our methods were wrong, but they were born out of a desire to do good. You were very young when you had Henry, and we, well, we never got the chance to know you. We didn't know if Henry was planned, if it was your choice to be in the situation you're in now."

Emily opened her mouth to speak, but Irene delicately held up a hand to stop her.

"Of course you love him. I know that a mother's love for her son is unbreakable, no matter what. And I'm sorry that we weren't around before, when you both needed us. After all the history between us, it took us a while to decide to try to cross that bridge and get back in touch with you. The main thing is, we want to help. We want to help lift the load a little. If that's financial, or babysitting, or whatever. We want to help."

Emily regarded Irene silently for a moment. She didn't know much about the woman except the few horror stories Joe had told her. But then, people changed, and Emily wondered if the loss of her son and the subsequent years had brought about a transformation.

"I won't accept financial help. Things are tight, but we can manage." Emily didn't know how much they knew and didn't want to provide them with any further ammunition.

Seb unfolded a newspaper, reached into his inner jacket pocket, and removed his reading glasses. He put them on and looked at the page with his mouth open while he searched out what he was looking for.

"Here we are, Crown Airlines." He looked up at Emily. "Your airline, I believe?"

Emily slowly nodded.

He looked back to the paper. "The timing of the crash was terrible. Friday evening. That gives the markets all weekend to get nice and shaken up before trading opens again on Monday. Estimates are that share prices will fall by up to twenty-five percent." He folded the paper and put it to one side, then placed his glasses on top. "Do you know much about large corporations?"

"No," Emily said.

"They are like a giant house of cards. Built on assumptions and trust. They assume that a certain number of people will purchase a certain number of products over a certain amount of time. As long as those assumptions look correct, everyone is happy. But when there's a glitch and those assumptions are found to be incorrect, the whole thing comes crashing down."

Emily reached for the jug of water on the table and poured some into the empty wine glass in front of her. Her nerves about the Crown situation were already high. Seb's analysis of the impending disaster was not helping.

"People will get scared. They will cancel their bookings, transfer them to other airlines. Many people are under the illusion that airlines are highly lucrative businesses, but in truth they're very risky. Operating costs, fuel, aircraft maintenance, staff." He waved his hand towards Emily.

Emily drank the water in two gulps and quickly filled up again.

"I'm not privy to the finer workings of Crown's balance book, but I would say it's a risky business for you to be in at the moment," he continued. "Look, Emily, a friend of mine is opening a new office in New York, he's looking for staff, and I'm sure I could get you a comfortable office job. Nine to five. Medical, dental. Think of it as a gesture of goodwill."

Irene cut in. "You wouldn't be working for us or anything."

"Absolutely," he confirmed. "I'd just be linking together two people, one who needs a secure job, close to her family. And one who needs a reliable, hardworking employee."

"And what do you get from this?" Emily asked.

"Nothing," Irene assured her. "Like I said, we want to help lift the load. If you won't accept money, and I can understand that, then at least accept the possibility of a safe job that allows you to earn more and spend more time with Henry."

Emily didn't know if she could turn down such a good offer, especially since Crown had grounded her. Getting out seemed like a good option, and to have an office job handed to her—to be able to tuck Henry in every night—was too good an opportunity to pass up. While Irene may have had a personality adjustment over the years, Seb was still the unreasonable bully she remembered. The short interaction had left her in no doubt that he was using her as an unwilling pawn in his game of chess. The idea of making a deal with him left a bitter taste in her mouth, and she felt certain he would soon be calling in the favour, but she had very little choice.

"I would look at any offer seriously," Emily said. "It's very kind of you to do that for me."

"These five years without Joe have been hard. There's been a lot of time to reflect," Irene said softly.

Emily understood; she would never truly be over Joe's death herself. She didn't think you ever recovered properly from losing someone important. But the loss of a son—she couldn't imagine it, and a shudder went up her spine at the very thought.

"I can't even begin to—"

"It's in the past," Irene cut in. "And now we're looking to the future."

Emily nodded. "I'm not going to give up Henry."

"I wouldn't expect you to," Irene replied. "Seb spoke out of turn. Ignore him."

Seb let out a sigh and took a sip of his wine.

"Our methods are wrong, I understand that. But our intentions are good. We want to help. Henry is five now; he'll be starting school very soon. These are important points in his life, and he needs stability." Irene licked her lips nervously. "How is he? Is he well after the surgery?"

"If I knew you cared, I would have left a note in the trash for you to find," Emily said spitefully.

Irene winced at the barb but straightened her shoulders and nodded. "I deserved that," she acknowledged. "As I said, I know our methods are flawed, but I assure you that I do care for him. Very much."

Emily could see the sincerity in Irene's eyes and licked her lips. "He's doing great. Recovering really well. The difference in him is like night and day."

Irene smiled. "Thank you."

"School can be an expensive business. Bags and shoes and whatnot," Seb interjected.

Irene rolled her eyes. "We just want you to know that we're willing to help. To start again."

Emily considered the words for a moment. In her heart, she would have liked nothing more than to storm from the restaurant and never see either of them again. But in her head, she knew that it would be better for Henry to have a connection to Joe. Once he started school and started to talk to other kids, he would invariably ask more about his father.

Here she had a real chance to give Henry family, blood relations. In her mind, she pictured him growing up, spending time with his grandparents—but she wondered if that was sentimental and idyllic. Based on what she'd heard from Joe, the reality would not be as joyous as her imaginings. Seb was cold and manipulative; she could see that clearly from her few dealings with him. She didn't want Henry exposed to that kind of person, even if the man was his grandfather. Just as quickly, she wondered if it was truly fair to judge Seb based upon such little evidence. She certainly wouldn't want anyone to judge her so quickly.

The truth was, she had to try. She wouldn't want to have a conversation with Henry several years in the future where she admitted that she didn't even try. She also knew that it would be prudent to keep the Brennans happy.

"I'd like that. To start again, I mean," Emily said softly.

Seb got a business card from his pocket and slid it across the table. "Here's our contact details. If you're interested in the job, give me a call, and I'll set up a meeting. But don't delay too much. The positions are being snapped up."

Emily picked up the card and stood. "Thank you."

"Are you sure you can't stay for dinner?" Irene asked.

"No, I'm sorry, I need to get back."

"I understand," Irene said kindly. "Please, stay in touch."

"I will." Emily said goodbye to the both of them and walked through the restaurant lost in her thoughts.

❖

"That went better than expected."

Irene nodded. "I think she's in more trouble than she's letting on."

"Good." Seb smirked. "If she is in trouble, then she'll need us all the more. Once she's reliant on us, it'll be even easier to get what we want."

"Like I've said from the start, I'd rather do this with her blessing," Irene said. "You bulldozed your way through that conversation, just like I asked you not to."

"I know, my dear, I know," he said, unrepentant. "But the chances of her willingly giving up Henry are very, very remote. If you want any control over the boy's life, then there's a chance we'll have to file for custody again. I'm just ensuring that if we do take that route, everything will be in place."

Irene remained quiet. The last thing she wanted was to start a second custody battle with Emily. It'd been over five years since the last failed attempt, and she still had reservations about those actions. In the past, no one would have described her as a good mother to her own son. But she would have fought tooth and nail for him to stay with her, had she ever been unfortunate enough to be in Emily's position.

Five years was a long time, especially when your estranged grandson was growing older each day, presumably with no knowledge of your existence. She hoped that they would be able to forge some kind of relationship with Emily. More than that, she hoped Seb would be able to keep his temper and controlling tendencies under control.

Already, Seb's selfish schemes, private detectives, and marginal threats were turning Emily against them. Even after thirty-five years of marriage, Irene still didn't know if Seb actually wanted Henry in his life, or if he just had to win.

"What makes you think she'll even take that job with Marcus?"

"She will. I checked the departures on the Crown website. Her scheduled flight was cancelled this afternoon. If she has any sense, and she does, she'll be scrambling to get fixed employment."

Irene picked up her wine glass and took a small sip. "We're doing the right thing, aren't we?"

"Of course." Seb nodded. "She can't look after the boy. She's in debt up to her eyeballs. No, this is best for Henry. And, in the long run, it will be better for her too." Seb reached out and covered Irene's hand with his. "And you'll be the grandmother that Henry deserves."

CHAPTER SEVEN

Simon shivered as he walked along the New York street. He couldn't believe the audacity of Americans complaining about British weather. Okay, so it rained a lot in London, but at least there wasn't a permanent bitterly cold wind blowing.

Unfortunately, he understood that he was going to have to get used to it. He knew Olivia well enough to know that she was unlikely to budge on her decision to not fly again. He'd made arrangements to stay in New York for a couple of weeks, at least. He might not be her son, but he knew he was the closest thing she had to family. He also knew she'd be useless looking after herself, so he'd need to step up and help her.

He walked in through the main hospital entrance and made his way down a number of corridors.

"Good morning." Simon approached the reception desk. "I'm here for Olivia Lewis."

The nurse looked up from her work. "Oh yes, you're her son, aren't you?"

Simon smiled politely. He'd hoped they'd have forgotten that, but apparently not. "That's right. Is she ready to be discharged?"

"Well..." She looked at him with a small smile. "That kinda depends on you."

❖

"Simon!" Olivia cried out enthusiastically. "Have you seen this show?"

He entered the room, staring at Olivia in shock. Her pupils were blown wide open, and her usual stiff manner had vanished.

The nurse had warned him about her reaction to the pain medication, but he was still surprised to see her in such a state.

"It's about these six friends who are really good friends. And they're extremely funny. It's so lovely. The show is basically about their friendship."

Simon looked briefly towards the television. "Yes, they're very funny."

"They're so lucky to have each other. I don't know what it's called, but it's been on all morning. I've watched nineteen of them in a row. Do you have any chocolate?"

"Um, no, I don't. Sorry." Simon spotted Olivia's belongings in a bag beside her bed.

"And today I go home," she told him excitedly. "I just need to wait for my son to get here."

Simon blinked and searched Olivia's expression for any sign that she may be joking. She wasn't. It was surreal to see her so relaxed and oblivious to her surroundings. In the years that Simon had worked for her, he had only ever seen her looking absolutely professional—her dress, her hair and make-up, and her manner always precise and exact.

Olivia giggled at the television. Simon had never heard her giggle. It was disconcerting, but gave him unexpected insight into what he presumed must be the real Olivia.

"About that. He asked me to come instead. Is that okay?" he asked carefully.

Olivia looked relieved. She held out her hand, and as Simon stepped closer, she grasped on to his hand tightly. "Thank goodness. I would much prefer you. He's been so distant to me."

Then she released his hand and looked back at the television screen with childlike curiosity. Simon watched her with interest. Just when he thought he knew everything there was to know about her, he saw a whole new side to her.

"My son also flew over from London, like you," Olivia told him without looking away from the screen.

Simon smiled, wondering what kind of fantasy world she had constructed in her mind. He could easily imagine Olivia as a mother;

her interactions with Henry had proved beyond a doubt that she had parental skills she didn't know about. Despite her difficulties in communicating with adults, she seemed to settle into talking to children immediately. He suspected that was due to Olivia's refusal, or inability, to treat people differently. She didn't make exceptions for people, and therefore she spoke to Henry as she would anyone else, regardless of age.

He remembered being sent out for gifts for Henry. In true Olivia style it was over the top and the boy was showered with more presents than necessary. Later, he was organising a private behind-the-scenes tour of the giraffe house at London Zoo at Olivia's request. All because Olivia wanted to make Henry happy and to ensure that his recovery and remaining time in London were perfect. Yes, he could easily imagine Olivia as a mother.

"Are you sure you're ready to go home?"

"Absolutely, I don't even know why I'm in here. Do you have any chocolate?"

"You're in here because you have a broken leg, remember? And a sprained wrist?"

Olivia pulled back the sheets to look down at her leg cast. "Oh, so that's what this is about."

"I'll be back in a moment," Simon said.

"Bing is a silly name." He heard Olivia announce as he exited the room and sought out a nurse.

"Ah, Mr. Lewis." The nurse smiled warmly. "Ready to take your mom home?"

Simon opened and closed his mouth, pointed towards the door, and then let out a sigh. "Is she going to be like that for long?"

"Some people do react strangely to pain medication. It will wear off in the next twenty-four hours."

Simon stared at her. "Twenty-four hours?"

"She'll probably tire herself out at some point."

"Probably?"

"We could keep her in another day, but I don't think she'd like that."

Simon sighed. "You're right." He heard more giggling from Olivia's room.

"You might want to invest in a box set of Friends so she can see a different episode," she suggested.

"Another episode?"

"Yes, she's watching the previews on the hospital paid-for channel. There's only one episode available."

CHAPTER EIGHT

"Marcus, it's been too long!" Seb Brennan looked around the executive office and smiled. "I see things are going well?"

Marcus stood up and walked around his desk to shake hands. "Seb, it's been ages. How's business?"

"Good, although I'm practically retired these days."

"I don't know how you can stand it." Marcus gestured for them to sit on the comfortable sofa that faced the New York skyline. "I'd be bored out of my mind."

Seb sat down and examined an expensive looking ornament on the coffee table. "Hobbies, Marcus. Hobbies."

"But surely when you enjoy work this much it is a hobby." Marcus spread his arms out to indicate the room.

"Is it work that you enjoy or the challenge of taking down your old boss?" Seb asked with a knowing grin. They'd worked together a few times in the past, thankfully on the same team, and Marcus was just as competitive as he was. Business was about taking out your opponents and appearing loyal to the people who would be useful to you in the future. You never knew when you might need them to do you a favour.

Marcus let out a laugh. "Well, I'll admit that it focuses the mind when you have such a long-sought-after prize at the end of the working day."

"It's good to have you back in New York," Seb said. "There's no challenge left at the club without you."

"It's good to be out of London. It's an okay city, but I always felt like I was imprisoned there."

"Well, you practically were. After your little coup failed," Seb began.

"Don't call it that." Marcus bristled. "I couldn't stand to see Applewood being run into the ground by the snivelling wreck and then his daughter. Once they built up the New York client base, they went to London to do the same, but they took their eyes off of the prize. Completely ignored the opportunities in the New York market. Honestly, Seb, the American arm of the business was left to rot over here while they focused on Europe."

"So, now you're taking back New York?"

"Damn right I am. I've had enough of Olivia's Europe-centric-business bullshit. If she can't identify that there are real business opportunities here in America, then I'll do it on my own."

"And take Applewood's clients while you're at it?" Seb asked.

Marcus crossed over to his desk. He moved aside some archive boxes before picking up a file and waving it towards Seb. "Two of Applewood's top American-based clients are already on board. I didn't even have to ask. They approached me."

"I'm not surprised. You've not even been open three days and already word of your pricing structure is out. But, tell me, Marcus, how on earth are you making any money?" Seb already knew the answer, but it didn't hurt to give Marcus his moment in the sun. Let the little upstart think he was telling him something he hadn't already worked out for himself.

"Volume." Marcus slammed the files back down onto the desk. "If we generate enough business and take on enough retainer-based clients, we can get by."

Seb pursed his lips. It was almost too easy. He waited for Marcus to react.

Marcus rolled his eyes. "Go on, out with it."

"It's none of my business, but are you sure you're not allowing this agenda with Olivia to cloud your judgement? With the margins being so thin, you're playing a risky game. I'd hate to see you lose everything because you focused more on toppling Applewood than building a sustainable business."

Marcus inclined his head. "I appreciate your concern. I really do. But I know what I'm doing and I won't allow my desire to see Olivia crushed get in my way. Besides, what seemed like a gamble is already paying off. We're even making headway into taking over some of the bigger London accounts."

"That's great news." Seb smiled. Having suitably appeared to be looking out for Marcus's well-being, it was time to get to the real point of his visit. "And thank you for agreeing to help me with my little problem too."

"Not a problem. We're expanding rapidly, and we need the new staff. What's her name again?"

"Emily White."

"And, remind me, she's your…?"

"The mother of my grandson. And a damned nuisance." Seb bristled. Ever since his son had met the woman, she'd been nothing but trouble. He had finally been getting through to Joe, convincing him to get a real job and leave the foolish notion of a career in music behind. And then Emily had come along, and her influence had Joe on a crash course towards failure. No real job, no prospects, and an unwanted child.

In the back of his mind, he had always known—and hoped—that he would get the opportunity to revisit the battle with Emily. She was an unfit mother; it was as clear as day. And this time he would win. With a little help from Marcus.

"She was a stewardess with Crown, probably about to be laid off after that crash. It seemed like a good opportunity to…how shall I put it? Keep an eye on her." He winked.

Marcus chuckled. "God bless Crown."

Seb frowned questioningly.

"Olivia was on that flight. Broken leg, I believe. Either way, it's kept her occupied."

"Crown's misfortune seems to be serving us both."

"Indeed it is. See? Everything is coming together nicely." Marcus grinned. "Well, I'll put Miss White on reception for corporate finance. Should keep her occupied. I'll have HR call her for a brief interview, just to dot the i's and cross the t's."

"I do appreciate it. We need to seem willing while we build a proper case against her. We want custody of the boy."

"Hmm, so you mentioned. Aren't you a little old for that?" Marcus joked.

Seb swallowed down his reply. He needed Marcus's help, and he wasn't about to let years of relationship-building go to waste.

"It's Irene. She wants to be a part of his life. But that will never happen as long as Emily has her way. Joe poisoned the girl against us. The boy is five, and time is running out if we're to get him away from her before she does the same to him."

It was partially true. It was certainly Irene's truth. For Seb, it was about settling old scores. Emily had made a fool of him during the first custody battle. Everyone was aware of his very public loss of the case. Now, he would take everything away from her that she held dear, just like she'd done to him.

"Well, I'll help in any way I can."

"It should be fairly simple. We help her to get this job, and with the goodwill that brings, she will allow us to see Henry. Then we can insist on seeing him more, and when she pushes back, we'll produce our ace."

"Which is?" Marcus asked.

"Debt. She's dirt poor and up to her eyeballs in the stuff. Lives in a house with some friends, no lease, no savings, just debt. She can't even afford her minimum payments."

"That's no environment to raise a child."

"Precisely," Seb said. "It'll be best for everyone when we take him. Of course it'll be hard on the girl at first, but in a few months she'll realise it was the best thing that could've happened to her."

CHAPTER NINE

Emily hung up the phone and looked at Lucy. "I got the job. Trial period of one week, and I start tomorrow."

"Shouldn't you be jumping for joy?" Lucy asked with a smile.

"I feel as if I should, but this all seems so weird. I suppose I'll feel better when I'm there, when it all starts to feel a bit more real. I kind of feel as if I'm waiting for the other shoe to drop."

"I understand, but maybe Seb and Irene really are trying to help?"

Emily looked at Lucy with a raised eyebrow. "Suddenly, after all this time, they want to help? I don't know."

"Well, I'm naturally optimistic, so I think it's a good thing and something to celebrate." Lucy's smile brightened.

Emily chuckled. "Well, I'm naturally a pessimist, and I'm reserving judgement."

Henry walked into the room with Tiny tucked under his arm and looked at Emily suspiciously. He brought Tiny's head up to his ear and listened intently.

"Mommy, Tiny wants to know if you're sure you're staying home all day?"

"Tiny is doing a lot of talking lately," Emily said.

Henry shrugged and looked at her silently.

"I promise I'm staying home all day," Emily confirmed. "How about we do some drawing together?"

Henry raised Tiny back up to his ear and quickly shook his head. "No, Tiny doesn't want to draw."

"What about you? Do you want to draw?" Emily asked.

Henry shook his head.

"Okay, how about we go to the park?"

For a moment he looked interested, but then he listened to Tiny again.

"No, Tiny wants to go and do a jigsaw," Henry said.

"Can I play too?" Emily asked.

Henry shook Tiny's head and then turned around and left the room.

Emily let out a sigh and turned to Lucy. "This is getting out of hand. More and more of the time he only speaks through Tiny."

"Something must be bothering him," Lucy said. "I just wish he'd talk to us."

"I'm sure he's picked up on the changes at Crown. My suddenly being home, and Tom flying out on a different day." Emily shook her head. "I did some research online; I know some kids go through phases where they use a toy as a voice. And Henry did that for a while before, but…"

"It's quickly becoming the norm," Lucy said.

"I'll go and talk to him, see if I can get through. Wish me luck."

❖

Emily opened her bedroom door to see Henry curled up on the bed they shared, whispering to Tiny.

"Hey, Henry."

He looked up at her with a confused expression. She sat on the mattress beside him.

"Henry, I wanted to talk to Tiny about some things. Is that okay?"

He clutched Tiny even closer to his chest. "Like what?"

"Nothing bad," Emily reassured him. "I just think that Tiny might be a bit upset about things, and I want to make sure he's okay. I want to make sure he's happy."

Henry slowly nodded his head. He remained lying down but held Tiny as if he was sitting up and listening to her.

"Hi, how are you, Tiny?" Emily asked the cuddly toy.

Henry leaned Tiny towards him and listened intently for a long period. "He says he's fine."

She tilted her head. "Really? Because I think there might be something wrong. Maybe you could ask him again?"

Henry pulled Tiny in close for a few seconds and then nodded. "He says he wants to go back to London and stay with Olivia."

Emily closed her eyes for a moment to steady herself. She had been worried his behaviour was related to missing Olivia and silently cursed herself. In her heart, she'd known that getting closer to Olivia would end in heartache for all involved.

She'd been especially careful with who she dated since her last breakup. Henry had taken the sudden absence of her ex very hard, and Emily didn't want to put him through that pain ever again. But then there was Olivia and the very stressful and unique set of circumstances that continued to push them together.

Olivia had been their white knight, saving them from Emily's poor planning and financial mismanagement with the offer of a hotel room and no expectations of repayment. Olivia had charmed both of them with her generosity, kindness, and unexpected humour.

Everything had been going so well. Emily had managed to ignore the niggling feeling of doubt that haunted her, right up until the flight home. When Olivia had freaked out at the change in seating arrangements. During two tense standoffs on board, Emily had been convinced that Olivia would do or say something to reveal their relationship and put her job at risk. Even all this time later, she shuddered at the memory of Iris catching them talking in the galley when Olivia should have been in her seat.

Olivia had seemed unconcerned about Emily's employment, and in her eyes, the only safe place for Henry was the first-class seat she'd booked for him. She refused to see that Henry was perfectly fine in the economy section being watched by a colleague.

It was an insight into her worst fears. The miscommunications she'd had with Olivia before had been nothing compared to that flight. She'd had to end it. Henry had taken it hard, as she'd known he would. But she comforted herself in the knowledge that the longer she'd allowed the doomed relationship to go on, the more distraught Henry would've been. At least she'd nipped it in the bud quickly.

"Tiny really liked Olivia, huh?" she asked carefully.

He nodded. "Tiny and Olivia are best friends, and he misses her."

"I see." Emily considered the conversation for a moment. "The thing is, Tiny, Olivia is really busy with work. And that means that she doesn't have a lot of time to spend with anyone, not even her best friend. But I know that she still loves you very much."

"It's not fair!" He sat up. "You get to see her all the time!"

"Me?" Emily shook her head. "No. Henry, I've not seen Olivia since we all flew home together."

"Liar!" Henry shouted. "You see her at work all the time."

"Henry, I promise you that I haven't seen or spoken to Olivia since then."

Henry pulled Tiny into his arms and rolled over, showing his back to her.

She placed her hand on his back softly. "I'm sorry you miss her."

"I don't," he mumbled. "Tiny does."

"Well." Emily took a deep breath. "I miss her too."

Henry turned his head and regarded her with suspicious eyes. "You do?"

"Yes, of course. Olivia is a very nice lady and she did a lot for us. But sometimes people go away and we have to remember the good times we had with them rather than be sad about not seeing them."

"But why can't we see her?"

"Because sometimes life doesn't work out the way we want it to."

"That's not an answer," Henry grumbled. "Tiny hates you."

Emily bit her lip and closed her eyes for a moment. Logically, she knew that Henry was at an age where he was starting to lash out. She also knew she'd done the right thing to protect him, even if he was too young to understand that. But logic didn't stop the pain of his words, even if he didn't really mean them. "I'm sorry Tiny feels that way, because I love Tiny. Very much."

Henry remained still, and she knew there was nothing else to be said, so she stood up and quietly left the room. She walked downstairs to the kitchen, where Lucy was filling the dishwasher.

"How did it go?"

Emily released the sob she'd been holding in and Lucy quickly pulled her into a hug.

"Oh, Em, it's okay."

"He says he hates me; I know he doesn't mean it, but it still hurts."

"He doesn't know what it means," Lucy reassured her.

"I never should have gotten involved with Olivia. This wouldn't have happened if I'd just kept my distance. I knew it couldn't work, and I knew that Henry was getting too close to her."

"You did what you had to do. Don't worry. Henry'll get over this."

Emily wrapped her arms around Lucy and held her tightly. "I hope so."

CHAPTER TEN

Olivia limped into the hotel suite sitting room. Her right arm lay loosely in a sling, and her left arm leaned heavily on a crutch as she attempted to look as though she was not in pain.

"You're up." Simon stood up from the sofa, ready to spring into action in case she fell.

"I'm not spending another minute in that room," Olivia grouched. "It's Tuesday morning."

"It is," he said.

She turned away from him and made her way into the kitchen. Simon followed.

"Where did Monday go?" she asked.

"Well." Simon gently guided her into a dining room chair. "You spent most of Sunday talking about, well, everything. You were so exhausted you slept through all of Monday, aside from when I brought you meals."

Olivia shook her head. "I don't remember any of that. Where's my phone?"

"The pain medication hit you pretty hard. But don't let that discourage you from taking it. It will be better than the pain."

"Having two days wiped out is better?" Olivia asked doubtfully. She looked around the room with a frown.

"Yes, trust me," he said. "Can I get you something to eat?"

"Where's my phone?"

"I'm charging it for you," Simon said. "Toast? Cereal? How about some coffee?"

"Maybe some toast." She regarded him suspiciously. "What's going on?"

"Nothing." He opened a cupboard and got a loaf of bread out. "How are you feeling? Any dizziness? The hospital said we should go back if you felt dizzy or nauseous."

"You're…edgy."

He turned around, and Olivia studied him, frowning as she attempted to focus.

"Are you sure you're not feeling dizzy?"

"Simon," Olivia said slowly in a warning tone.

Simon lowered two pieces of bread into the toaster. He turned to lean his back against the worktop and folded his arms across his chest. "I have some work-related news, and you're not going to like it."

"Go on."

"Maybe have something to eat. Get some coffee inside you first," he suggested.

Olivia glared at him. "Don't make me ask you again, Simon."

He blew out a nervous breath. "Okay, we've lost Techtrix, Maddison's—"

Olivia blinked. "I'm sorry, what do you mean lost? Is the database acting up again?"

Simon took a deep breath. "No, I mean lost as in they've left us."

"They…they've terminated their agreements with us?" Olivia struggled to understand and started to adjust her crutch so she could stand up again.

"Yes."

"Both of them?" she clarified, pushing herself up from her seat with her good hand and grabbing the crutch.

"Yes, and more."

"More?" Olivia gave him a panicked look.

"Holder and Son, Grants, RRG, and YSA have all filed notice. And others are asking about the terms of their contracts."

"Why? What's happened? I don't understand…" Olivia's strength started to give way. Simon caught her and lowered her gently back into the chair.

"Marcus." He knelt in front of her chair, effectively preventing her from getting up.

"Marcus?" Olivia paused. "He finally set up on his own?"

"Yes. He has established a company here in New York."

"I…" Olivia's voice faded as she attempted to catch up.

"I'm sorry I didn't tell you before." Simon looked up at her apologetically. "You needed time to recover. Physical injuries aside, you were pretty fuzzy-headed because of the pain medication."

The battle between Marcus and Olivia had been going on for years. Marcus had always assumed a senior partner position would be his when Olivia's father left the firm. But Olivia had ended up being instated as managing partner despite her lack of experience, which was outweighed by her talent as a mathematician, and her public speaking skills. Not to mention her aptitude for memorising and rationalising complicated legal documents.

One thing Olivia couldn't do, though, was understand the rules of office politics; games Marcus constantly initiated. And excelled at. It was well known at Applewood Financial that they despised each other. A huge sigh of relief had sounded throughout the offices when Marcus had left two weeks ago.

"I wish I'd realised what was happening sooner," Simon said. "I knew something was up. People were suddenly handing in their notice, and stopped talking in the breakroom whenever they saw me come in. But I had no proof. And I never in a million years thought it would be something like this." He sighed and shook his head. "Then, on Monday, I was woken up at four in the morning New York time. A ton of people had suddenly quit and not shown up for work over in London. When the New York office opened five hours later, it was clear that something was seriously wrong."

Simon continued to look up at Olivia, who was still coming to terms with the news, her woozy mind taking a while to piece everything together.

"But why…how has he managed to get so many clients to leave so quickly?" she finally asked.

"He's slashed his rates; he is literally charging half of what we charge for a set time. Word spread quickly. He's taken most of corporate finance with him, so clients are basically getting the same work done by the same people, for half the cost."

"But, how? How can he afford to do that?" Olivia furrowed her brow, unable to grasp what was happening. Her business, her father's business, was unravelling at the seams. Everything she'd worked so hard for was being taken away.

She started to replay previous conversations with Marcus in chronological order—always her go-to response when something went wrong. When you had a knack for saying the wrong thing, you quickly learned to analyse interactions to see if the root of the problem could be found.

But she found she couldn't accurately recall what had been said. Confusion, hurt, and loss clouded her memory as she struggled to comprehend what was happening. Her first thought had been that Simon was mistaken. What he was telling her was simply unthinkable. It wasn't long before it became clear that it wasn't a mistake or a joke.

"I don't know," Simon said. "But clients are leaving in droves. And resignations in the London and New York offices are flying in quicker than Human Resources can process the paperwork. Some people just haven't shown up. Those who are handing in notice, I made the decision to ban them from the office and remove their access."

"Good." She nodded. "He's always been gunning for me."

"I didn't want to tell you yesterday. You were too out of it," Simon repeated.

She looked at him. The remorse in his eyes was unmistakable, even to her. She took his hand and gave it a gentle squeeze. "You did the right thing. Who knows what mess I'd have made of things yesterday."

Simon breathed a sigh of relief.

"But today's a new day. And we need to take stock. I want a list of accounts, worldwide. We need to see who has left, who may leave, and who we can rely on. And staff; I need to know who's gone, who's working notice, and who's staying."

"And who can be trusted," he added.

"But…"

"It's dog eat dog now, Olivia. I know you hate office politics, but we have to assume that there are people in the office who will send sensitive information out to their former colleagues."

"You're right." She sounded beaten. She felt beaten. When was enough, enough? Emily, Henry, the plane crash, and now this. What next? She shook off the maudlin thoughts and focused again on what needed to be done. You couldn't fix a problem by lamenting over it. "We need to have an accurate picture of events."

"It'll be okay." He didn't sound certain.

"We'll see," she replied distantly.

Chapter Eleven

Emily looked at her watch and tapped her foot impatiently. When she'd left her job at Crown, she'd hoped, and assumed, that her days of serving beverages were behind her. But standing in a long line at the local coffee shop with a list of the company director's requests proved that was not to be the case.

She'd been in her new job for a week, and, on the whole, it had been positive. Crown had called her the evening after she'd started to tell her that her services were no longer required. Normally such news would have devastated her, but all Emily could feel was relief that she had swallowed her pride and taken the position Seb had helped to set up.

The job wasn't exactly demanding. Answering phones, fetching files, getting drink orders, and so on. Nothing that she couldn't do in her sleep. The pay was better, the benefits were great, and the working hours were amazing. Finally, she was working a nine-to-five job in the city, where she could be home within an hour.

Usually, that would have meant spending more time with Henry. But, as soon as Emily had started working, Seb and Irene had pounced.

Just two days after starting the job, she saw Seb in the office, chatting with Marcus as if they were best friends. Before leaving, Seb had stood in front of Emily's desk and requested that he be allowed to come see Henry the next day. She'd wanted to decline, but Seb had made it impossible by asking in front of Marcus. Knowing that her employment was somewhat dependent on Sebastian Brennan's satisfaction, she'd decided not to rock the boat just yet. With Marcus watching her, she'd begrudgingly invited Seb and Irene to dinner the following evening to meet Henry.

As expected, Henry hadn't taken to them at all. Emily had attempted to claim that it was simply a matter of a lot of changes in a short space of time. But of course, she knew that wasn't true. If Henry had been younger, then maybe he wouldn't have picked up on his grandparents' awkward interactions and lack of social skills. But Henry was five and easily saw that the new interlopers were trying too hard, offering him sweets and toys in exchange for cuddles and smiles.

After an uncomfortable meal, Seb and Irene sat side by side on the sofa in the living room. On the opposite sofa, Emily, Henry and Lucy faced them. The atmosphere was charged.

"Why are you wearing that tatty old thing?" Seb asked Henry, pointing to his giraffe hoodie.

Henry screwed up his face, clearly displeased with the negative comment on his favourite item of clothing. He brought Tiny up to his ear, wiggled the giraffe's head and listened intently.

"Tiny says it isn't tatty."

Irene sighed. "I don't think that's healthy."

Emily knew Henry's recent insistence on speaking via Tiny wasn't ideal, but she wasn't about to be criticised by Irene for it. The woman hadn't been a part of Henry's life and didn't know him.

"A lot of children his age do it. It's perfectly normal," Lucy interjected.

"There's an easy way to stop it," Seb said, watching Henry with a calculating look and obviously debating the best way to snatch Tiny from his grasp.

"It's just a cuddly toy," Emily said firmly, smoothing her hand through Henry's hair to soothe him. Henry tensed and turned away from Seb and Irene to lean into Emily's side. He seemed to have made up his mind instantly, as children often do. He didn't like them, and he didn't want anything to do with them.

Where many adults would have changed their approach and attempted to curry favour, instead they pushed him further.

"Come now, Henry," Seb said. "We've come a long way to see you."

"You've hardly spoken to us," Irene added.

Henry silently fidgeted against Emily, moving his head to avoid eye contact with them. She could understand both points of view. Henry was obviously uncomfortable with the Brennans, and they were clearly trying to make a connection. They weren't being malicious, just clueless.

She knew it would be up to her to attempt to fix the rift. It was obvious that the Brennans wouldn't be giving up anytime soon, so it was in everyone's best interest to get along, or at least project the impression that they were getting along.

"Do you still have dogs?" she asked them.

"Yes, two Labradors." Irene seemingly picked up on Emily's tactic. "Bertie and Max."

"Wow, did you hear that, Henry? You love Labradors, don't you?" Emily said with as much enthusiasm as she could.

Henry didn't say anything, instead burrowing farther into Emily's side.

"We have horses too," Irene tried.

"You love horses! Maybe you could go and see them sometime?" As much as she hated running a publicity campaign for the Brennans, Emily knew it was necessary.

Henry held Tiny up into the air and slowly blew out a raspberry. Lucy excused herself to the kitchen to get more coffee, clearly trying to not laugh at Henry's staunch refusal to participate.

Knowing space would be the best way to move forward, Emily announced that it was time for Henry to go to bed. The Brennans agreed and quickly left, relief visible on their faces.

Later that evening, Emily had mulled over the events. She hoped—and assumed—they would understand that time and space would eventually win Henry over.

Sadly, Seb seemed uninterested in that tactic, and the very next day he'd returned to the office and pushed for more time with Henry. In front of Marcus, he'd suggested taking Henry to the park without Emily, to force Henry to interact with them without the security blanket of his mother. When Marcus approved of the scheme, Emily felt she couldn't say no.

So, some days while she worked, they took him to the park, with Lucy's supervision. They bought him lunch and attempted to buy his love and trust with toys, which Emily really hated. She'd worked hard to have Henry understand the true cost of things, and now that was being torn down in an attempt to buy him.

The real challenge had come over the weekend when they had suggested taking him for the night. Emily had pushed back against the idea.

"I really don't think Henry is ready," she had whispered, hating that the conversation was, yet again, taking place in the office.

"If we wait for him to be ready, it will never happen," Seb had argued. "Sometimes children need to be pushed outside their comfort zone."

"It seems too soon." Emily had shaken her head.

"Nonsense." Seb had waved at one of the finance directors as she passed, then turned back to Emily. "How are you settling in here? Well, I hope?" He'd smiled, but the question was anything but friendly. "Fortuitous that the role was available so soon after Crown terminated your employment. Especially with employment being so hard to come across at the moment," he added.

It was a thinly veiled threat; one Emily couldn't afford to allow him to follow through on. So she'd caved to their wishes and kept her head down. She'd resolved to work hard and gain much-needed experience. When she had a few months of employment under her belt, she'd be able to look for other work. It wasn't an ideal plan, but it was all she could think to do.

She'd hoped that the weekend with Henry would cause Seb and Irene to realise that it wasn't as easy to change the mind of a five-year-old as they thought. She'd hoped it would be enough to make them back off.

Henry had returned on Sunday afternoon more quiet and distant than before he left. Even Tiny didn't have anything to say, a silent testament to how awful the overnight stay must have been for him.

As Emily took his bag from Irene, Irene had suggested that they make it a regular thing, dressing it up as an opportunity for Emily to have Saturday nights to herself. There was even a suggestion of going out and meeting people.

Emily had forced down her anger, smiled, and left the answer deliberately vague. But she knew beyond a shadow of a doubt that Seb would soon be on the case.

CHAPTER TWELVE

Olivia hobbled through the office. Despite her crutch, she managed to skilfully dodge the various secretaries who attempted to prevent her from her goal. She threw open the door to the large office and marched in.

"Olivia!" Marcus looked up and smiled at her. "Do excuse the mess." He indicated some unpacked archive boxes. "We've only been open a week. Still finding homes for everything."

"Marcus," Olivia said tightly. "We need to talk." She wasn't interested in fake niceties.

Marcus looked at Olivia's crutch with a frown. "Did something happen?"

"I'm sure you're already aware that I was unfortunately involved in a plane crash, but that's not why I'm here." She turned around to see one of the secretaries lingering in the doorway, awaiting guidance. Olivia pulled out the chair in front of Marcus's desk, purposefully sat down, and waited silently.

"It's fine, Tina." Marcus dismissed the young woman and walked around his desk to take his chair. He regarded Olivia again and pointed to her forehead. "Nasty bruise you have there."

"Nothing compared to the knife in my back." She'd had enough beating around the bush. Pretence wasn't her thing at the best of times, but now she desperately needed to get to the facts of the matter.

Marcus chuckled. "Now, now…"

"I get that you hate me. You always have. Even I couldn't miss that. But are you so willing to destroy the business that you helped to build? You'll be putting hundreds of people out of work. You'll—"

"Be doing nothing of the sort." Marcus leaned forward and interlaced his fingers on the desktop. "There is a place for everyone, right here."

"Everyone of your clique," Olivia said with a nod towards the main office. She'd seen them as soon as she'd walked in: the obvious traitors, the opportunity seekers, and the odd surprise deserter. Most had looked away from her, busying themselves with sudden phone calls or emails.

"Oh, you've seen the new corporate finance team?" Marcus drawled.

"You mean my corporate finance team?" Olivia asked. "The one we spent years perfecting—internal promotions, training, headhunting, internships. Why are you doing this?" Olivia had promised herself that she would remain calm and collected, keep the conversation professional. But Marcus had worked with her father; he knew how important the company was to her. This wasn't just a business decision; it was a personal attack, and Olivia felt it keenly.

Marcus let out a sigh and leaned back in his high-back leather chair, regarding Olivia analytically. She held his gaze, not willing to back down from his scrutiny.

"Your father," Marcus began, "was a kind man. But he was not a business man."

Olivia opened her mouth to argue, but Marcus held up his hand to silence her. She closed her mouth, waiting to hear what he had to say before launching her counteroffensive.

"Your mother was the business brains, and I regret my decision to go with your father to London to set up the European office. Yes, he was a brilliant accountant, but he had no business acumen."

"That's not true," Olivia argued, unable to stop herself from defending her father.

"I'm sorry, but it is." Marcus shrugged. "The man was a fish out of water without your mother. I mean, she convinced him to anglicise your name, eradicating every sign of your Puerto Rican roots because she knew L-E-W-I-S would be easier to present than L-U-I-S. And he let her. He was spineless, Olivia. Spineless."

"How dare you!" Olivia got to her feet, grimacing slightly at the jolt of pain that rushed from her ankle all the way up her leg.

Marcus tilted his head indifferently. "It's the truth. I made the business what it is today. He handed you that company like giving car keys to a toddler. And now I've had enough of playing the underdog."

"The underdog? You were a senior partner. You managed three departments without a scrap of interference from me. You were given everything you wanted." Olivia knew that they had never seen eye to eye, but she had always made sure to put personal feelings aside. For the sake of the business, she'd given Marcus power and autonomy, which he was now using to destroy her and the company. The company her father had entrusted her with. She couldn't help but feel an enormous sense of guilt. She knew someone else may well have seen the signs and been able to stop Marcus long before things got to this point.

"Not exactly."

"My father…" Olivia felt her voice falter and took a breath. "My father built that business up to an international, well-respected firm. You can't take credit for that."

"I can, and I will." Marcus shrugged. "You were a child when the business was set up. You know nothing of the decisions we made, the long nights, the unpaid overtime, hell, the unpaid anytime! That business grew from blood, sweat, and tears, and not just your father's."

"Oh, please, you think I don't know that?"

"I deserved more," Marcus said fiercely.

Olivia stared down at him, hit by the sudden realisation that she had no idea how to communicate with this man. She never had. He was a shrewd operator, and he had always known how to get under her skin and say exactly the right thing at the right moment. Marcus knew her inside out. He'd been manipulating her for years. But what bothered her most of all was that she'd let him.

The truth was, she had always been afraid of wrecking her father's legacy. Despite her reservations, her father had believed in her ability to learn the skills needed to be a strong leader. Of course, he knew of her social difficulties, but he'd always had faith that she would overcome them. She never had.

And Marcus had always been on hand to remind her of her weaknesses, to point out any and every mistake she ever made. He'd served as a physical reminder of her fear of destroying everything her father had achieved. She'd known him practically all her life, and she knew with certainty that attempting to appeal to his sensitivities would be pointless.

"This isn't over, Marcus."

"I'm sure it isn't, Olivia. But it will be." He grinned. "Soon."

Olivia picked up her crutch and leaned heavily on it as she quickly left, waving away the young secretary and making her way towards the elevators at the end of the office. She glanced at the desks to either side and shook her head as she recognised countless people from both the London and New York offices. As she passed by, heads dipped in focused silence to avoid eye contact with her.

She stabbed her finger onto the button to call the elevator and pursed her lips in irritated silence while she waited.

"Olivia?"

Olivia turned and looked at her with a sigh. "You too, Kathryn?" Kathryn Morgan had been an office manager in New York for many years.

Kathryn looked apologetic. "I'm sorry, I really agonised over it, but Marcus made me such a good offer, and with both boys struggling after the property crash, I just…"

Olivia held up her hand. "I understand. I do. I just, well, I just wish it wasn't this way."

Of course she understood the practicalities. People needed to earn money; they needed to live. She just wished that it didn't feel as if she was losing members of her own family.

"It's nothing personal, from any of us." Kathryn gestured to the rest of the staff. "He simply made us offers we couldn't refuse. Once one up and left, it was like dominoes falling down. As I say, it was nothing personal."

The elevator pinged to signal its arrival, and Olivia stepped to the side to avoid blocking the door. "I appreciate you saying so. I would hate to think everyone was unhappy."

Kathryn nodded a greeting to whomever had exited the elevator. Olivia kept her back to them, unwilling to identify any more of her staff who had left her. She pushed down the small internal voice that berated her for not seeing the signs. Signs that must've been there. A company couldn't fall this quickly without visible indicators.

Kathryn turned back to Olivia and looked at her seriously. "No one was unhappy. It's just the economic climate at the moment. You were a wonderful leader." Kathryn leaned forward and quietly whispered, "Despite what he might say."

Olivia knew exactly what Marcus had to say about her leadership skills. There had been many a phone call and email regarding the subject when he'd worked for her. She wasn't normally one for emotional turmoil and doubt, but the last few hours and days had seen her go from crying in despair to throwing things in anger. The kind words helped her keep it together, something she desperately needed until she could escape the lion's den.

Never before had she been so caught up in the emotion of a situation, nor felt so down and defeated. There had been many times when everyone around her had thought their position hopeless, but she had refused to give up. Her relentless determination had seen her through so much. Now she was struggling to find that drive.

"I should go," Olivia said, not knowing a better response. They said farewell to each other and Olivia stepped into the elevator with her head down to shield her face from the eyes she could feel upon her.

❖

Emily stepped out of the elevator holding the stack of empty archive boxes, hoping they didn't topple over. She couldn't see over them, so she walked slowly. She could hear Kathryn saying good-bye to someone and hoped she wouldn't bump into whoever it was as she inched closer to her desk.

As she sat down, she saw a piece of paper standing between the keys of her keyboard with an instruction to call Seb Brennan. Emily let out a sigh and picked up the phone, quickly dialled the number she'd already memorised, and waited for the call to be connected.

"Hello, Emily," Seb answered politely.

"Hi," Emily replied, not in the mood for small talk.

"A friend of mine is on the board of the Children's Theatre, and we've managed to acquire some tickets for a wonderful show tonight. I thought we'd take Henry. If you don't mind, of course." His tone was friendly, but it was clear to Emily that the decision had been made in his mind and the call was just for the sake of etiquette.

"What show is it?" Emily hoped to hear something she could use as a reason to say no.

"It's a show for under-fives, about a little girl who goes on safari. There'll be giraffes, so I know Henry will enjoy it."

Emily closed her eyes and let out a small sigh. "Sounds great," she lied and hoped it was convincing.

"As it's across town, it'll be a little late for him by the time we get back to yours. So we thought he could stay overnight again. Best for everyone."

Emily shivered at a sudden chill and licked her dry lips. She felt as if she was losing control of the situation. It had quickly gone from occasional visits to daily calls to arrange outings, trips, and overnight stays. But she was trapped; she still suspected that a word from Seb would cause her job to vanish into thin air. There was no easy way out. "I suppose—"

"Wonderful. I'll call Lucy and make the arrangements. I'm sure you'll be glad to get the night off."

Emily continued to hold the phone to her ear despite the fact that Seb had hung up. She silently fumed at the insinuation that he was doing her a favour when he knew full well that she was reluctant to let Henry stay with them.

CHAPTER THIRTEEN

Olivia stood on the edge of the sidewalk with her hand raised in the air. She let out a sigh as another taxi sped by her. It was Friday afternoon, and New York was starting to get busy. Well, busier than the usual. She'd been attempting to flag a taxi for the last twenty minutes, but they were all occupied.

She lowered her hand and turned to regard Marcus's new office building, rolling her eyes at the ostentatiousness of it all. The glass and metal high-rise disappeared up into the sky, and Olivia knew that it was all to satisfy Marcus's desire to boast. Style over substance. Much like the man.

Unable to stand being so close to him, or his pretentious building, she walked farther down the avenue to see if she would have more luck of getting a taxi at the crossroads.

At the junction, another ten minutes went by before Olivia lowered her hand and wearily looked around. Behind her was the cheesiest faux Mexican bar she'd ever seen. After the day she'd had, she needed a drink. With a sigh, she swivelled on her crutch and walked in.

Inside was no better. She looked around at the tacky sombreros hanging from the ceiling and raised an eyebrow. But she was beyond caring as she limped her way over to the nearest bench and sat down.

She fidgeted in the booth, attempting to get comfortable on the worn, leather-clad bench. She shifted her cast-laden foot around under the table searching for a tolerable position but eventually gave up when she realised it was impossible. She'd clearly over-exerted herself, and her leg was paying the price.

She looked down at the paper placemat that was also a menu, picked it up between her thumb and forefinger, and regarded it with a grimace. When a bored-looking waitress came over, Olivia ordered a couple of small tapas dishes and a glass of wine. She was about to clarify that she wanted a chardonnay when the waitress simply asked for her colour preference. Despondent, she shrugged, and the waitress left to place her order.

Her phone rang and she answered it, thankful for the distraction.

"Hello, Simon."

"Hey…is that flamenco music? Where are you?"

"Madrid." Olivia plucked a napkin from the metal dispenser on the table and mopped up an unidentifiable pool of liquid.

"Cool. I prefer Barcelona, but to each their own." Simon played along. "Just checking everything is okay. You know, seeing if you need bail money or anything?"

Olivia smiled. Simon could always cheer her up. "No need for bail money. I was unsuccessful."

"Unsuccessful in what? Killing him?"

Olivia paused. "No. Unsuccessful in reasoning with him."

"You didn't actually think that speaking to him would do any good, did you? Like I said before, he's made his choice, and he won't go back now."

"I hoped I could reason with him," Olivia explained. She scrunched up the damp napkin and looked around for a convenient place to put it.

"I don't think there is any reasoning with him. A very smart person once agreed with me when I called him a dick."

Olivia laughed. "Yes, well, he is certainly living up to that moniker."

"So, what's the plan?"

Olivia had known that was coming. Of course Simon would assume that his all-seeing boss would have a plan, but sadly, she didn't. It had been a week. Things were getting worse, and she was running out of options. "I don't know."

"Are you going back to London?" Simon asked unexpectedly.

After a quick check that no one was looking, Olivia hid the napkin in a pot containing a decidedly un-Mexican conifer. She considered Simon's question and blew out a long breath. The truth was, she didn't know what the best course of action was, but she knew she certainly didn't want to fly anymore.

"No."

Simon paused. "No, not this week? No, not this month? No, not ever again?"

"I…" She cleared her throat and started again. "I don't wish to fly again. Not for the foreseeable future."

"That's understandable. It really is."

"I'm not sure that the London side of the business can be rescued; not as it stands now," Olivia admitted. "The staffing situation is critical, and we simply don't have the cash flow."

A comfortable silence fell between them until Simon spoke again. "May I make a suggestion?"

"Of course."

"Think about cancelling your reservation at the hotel in London."

Olivia considered the statement for a moment. "Yes, that makes sense. The cost is hardly one the business can stomach at the moment."

He sighed. "Yes, there's that, but I was thinking more about you."

"Me?"

"Yes, you," Simon replied. A long pause followed before he continued. "I know you're busy with work, but I really think that you need to consider looking for a home. If you're not going to be travelling all the time, then there's no need to stay in hotels. And, as you say, it's a cost that the business can't really sustain at the moment. It's a good time to think about moving."

She panicked at the very notion. "But…I…I—"

"I know it's a big step," Simon said. "But I think it's the right thing to do now. Maybe I should call an estate agent? What do you guys call them? Realtors?"

She knew why Simon was pushing the point. He'd been doing so for years. They'd once discussed how he thought living in hotels was holding her back, stopping her from putting down roots and living her life. She supposed he was right. But she didn't know if she was ready for such a big step. Change wasn't something that Olivia ever approached willingly, especially when it came to her personal surroundings. She felt comfortable and safe in the hotel.

"Let me think about it."

"Okay. But, seriously, why can I hear a mariachi band?"

"I'm in a Mexican…" Olivia struggled to bring herself to use the word restaurant, "…place."

"Right. Can I ask why?" Simon asked, laughter in his tone.

"I couldn't hail a taxi."

"That really doesn't explain anything."

"I'm just going to have some food and wait until it's a little easier to get a taxi. Really, Simon, I'm fine."

CHAPTER FOURTEEN

Simon stepped out of the taxi and looked at the run-down bar with a tilt of his head. To say it was dilapidated would be kind. To say he was surprised that Olivia had even stepped foot in the place was an understatement.

He shouldered his mobile phone as he paid the driver.

"Well, I'm at the address she gave me."

"You don't sound too sure?" Sophie replied.

"It's a dump."

She chuckled. "It can't be that bad, Olivia doesn't sound like the kind of person who—"

"It's a dump," Simon reiterated. "The sign is a cartoon cactus winking and wearing a sombrero." He checked the street and the bar name to be absolutely sure he was in the right place.

"Maybe it's ironic?"

"We'll see." He walked into the bar and peered around the dimly lit room. "Thanks for joining me on the 'find my boss adventure.' I'm sure you have better things to do."

"Never." Sophie laughed. "You're saving me from tedious studies. I'm intrigued."

Knowing she couldn't see his face, he indulged in a sad smile. He missed her terribly but didn't want to say so and make the pull to go home even greater. He continued to scan the room until he finally found Olivia. At first he didn't recognise her. He blinked a few times in shock.

"Oh shit," he mumbled.

"What's up?"

"Simon! Come and meet my new friends!" Olivia waved excitedly to him.

"Everything's fine," Simon whispered into the phone through a clenched smile. "I'll call you back later."

He hung up and looked at the two Hells Angels bikers who sat opposite Olivia in a corner booth. Both men were in their forties, muscular, tattooed, and covered in leather. Simon licked his dry lips nervously as he approached the table. He had nothing against bikers—not that he'd met any. His entire knowledge of them was drawn from works of fiction, but he was sure that they were perfectly nice people. His concern was for Olivia, who had a tendency to speak her mind and not consider the potential outcome of her words.

"This is Crazy Weasel." Olivia pointed to one of the men, then the other. "And Butcher. Boys, this is Simon."

"Hello," Simon said, wondering how he was going to safely extract Olivia.

"Your friend's pretty drunk," Butcher told him.

"We thought we'd stay with her until you turned up," Crazy Weasel explained. "Pretty lady in a place like this. Bad leg as well."

"They signed my cast," Olivia told him excitedly. "Look!"

She edged her way to the end of the booth and swung her cast out for him to see. He'd seen Olivia drink before, but he'd never seen her drunk. He made a show of looking at her cast with interest.

"Oh, yes, that's lovely," he said. "Maybe it's time to go home now, though."

"She's been downing margaritas like there's a shortage," Butcher explained with a gesture towards the empty glasses on the table.

Simon looked at the glasses and hoped that some of them belonged to the two men, but he somehow doubted it by the way Olivia was swaying. "Have you eaten anything?" he asked her seriously.

"Who can say?" Olivia shrugged.

Crazy Weasel unfolded a slip of paper and handed it to Simon, who picked it up and frowned towards Olivia and then Crazy Weasel. "What's this?"

"She said that's the name of the man who upset her. Is it right? She's drunk and all, and we don't wanna get the wrong—"

"Whoa, whoa, no!" Simon pocketed the paper. He turned to Olivia. "You're setting bikers on him? Are you out of your mind?" Of course he knew that the situation was hard on Olivia, but he never thought she would resort to violence.

"Oh, Simon." Olivia reached up, cupped his face in her hands, and squeezed his cheeks. "Of course not." She let him go and flopped back into her seat. "Butcher was just asking about double-taxation laws because his wife is from China and they want to sell their second apartment. And I happened to mention that Marcus has an apartment in China. That's all."

Butcher looked at Simon seriously. "You have to plan ahead and make sure you have an effective tax wrapper when investing overseas."

"Y-yes, you do," Simon said. "So...you're...not going to, like, kill Marcus?"

The men looked at each other and roared with laughter.

Olivia snickered. "No, I wanted to make sure they didn't get financial advice from him." She swigged from her glass. "Because he's a poopie head."

Simon reached forward, grabbed the glass, and put it out of Olivia's reach. He was worried for her state of mind, not to mention her liver. But on the other hand, he was happy to see her finally let her hair down—even if that did entail getting drunk in a bar and making friends with bikers. Still, it was time to leave.

"Okay, right, let's go." He looked around, saw Olivia's crutch speared through a piñata hanging from the ceiling, and turned back to face her. "Don't move and don't drink anything else."

Olivia attempted to smother a giggle and gave him a half-hearted mock salute.

He walked over and started to remove the crutch from the paper donkey when a member of staff appeared next to him.

"I'm sorry. I'll pay for any damage she's caused," Simon told the man before he had a chance to say anything.

"No damage." He handed Simon a card. "Just wanted to make sure she gets her loyalty card. She's a premium member now, just like she asked, and she's got enough stamps for a second nacho hat."

"Second nacho hat?" Simon asked as he finally freed the crutch from the piñata.

The man pointed towards the table, where Olivia was clapping her hands with glee at a nacho hat with a rim filled with guacamole that was being placed on her head.

❖

Emily walked along the street towards the subway station, her mind distracted as she thought about Henry sleeping at Seb and Irene's for another night. He was already withdrawn and even talking through Tiny was starting to wane. It was obvious that he was depressed, or whatever the term was when five-year-olds suffered from it.

She was so caught up in her thoughts that she barely noticed two people standing in front of her until one was falling to the ground. She instinctively reached out and grabbed the woman by the arm, catching a glimpse of a crutch falling to the ground. Luckily, the man who was with her caught the other arm and, between them, they stopped the woman from hitting the sidewalk.

She looked up and her breath caught. "Simon?"

If he was surprised, he didn't show it. In fact, he looked weary, and as if his day couldn't get worse. "Hello again," he said with an attempt at a smile.

Emily looked down at the woman she was holding; as she feared, it was Olivia Lewis—with a cut on her forehead, her leg in a cast, and a nacho hat with guacamole falling out of the rim on her head.

"Simon…I'm dreaming that Emily is here. Lovely Emily," Olivia declared as she looked up at Emily reverently. "She's just as beautif—"

"Okay, let's try standing on your own legs again now," Simon cut in. He put his arm around Olivia's waist and heaved her to her feet.

Emily reached down, picked up the crutch, and handed it to Olivia, who leaned all of her weight onto Simon and held the crutch out, spinning it like a baton. "Thank you, Fairy Lady."

"Is everything okay out here?"

Emily turned around and found herself facing a leather-clad chest. She looked up, and then up some more into the face of a well-built man with a shaved head, a long grey beard, and a tattoo of dashed lines across his neck with the words "cut here."

"Crazy Weasel!" Olivia shouted.

"Olivia!" Emily admonished her.

"That's his name," Simon said.

"This is Emily. She's a fairy, and I'm dreaming her."

"We're fine. Just a little slip," Simon assured the man.

Crazy Weasel looked them up and down for a moment before shaking his head and heading back into the bar.

Emily let out a relieved breath. She took the crutch from Olivia's hand and placed it on the ground, gently adjusting her arm to hold it properly.

"Oh." Olivia smiled at the improvement and leaned some of her weight onto the crutch, allowing Simon to let go.

"What…" Emily looked around. "Just, what?"

"Do you have any chocolate?" Olivia regarded her seriously.

Emily stared at her for a moment in shock before reaching into her bag and handing over a bar of chocolate. Olivia's eyes lit up as she hurriedly ripped at the wrapper and started to eat.

"She's drunk as a skunk." Simon gestured to Olivia.

"Obviously. Why did you let her get like this?"

"I didn't," Simon said. "I'm picking her up from making friends with Hells Angels and drinking herself into a coma."

Emily looked at Olivia and lifted the nacho hat off of her head.

"No, I won that fair and square by slaying the bonkey deast!" Olivia reached for it. "Donkey beast," she said.

"Nacho hat or chocolate, not both," Emily said.

Olivia considered it for a moment, then bit into the chocolate bar. Emily looked around and found a trash can to put the leaky hat in.

"What happened to her leg?" Emily asked as she wiped her hands clean with a tissue from her bag. Suddenly she realised she had the answer already. "She was on the flight?"

Simon nodded. "Yes, broken leg. Sprained wrist. She's on the mend, though."

"I think you'd called her plastered," Emily said.

Simon walked to the curb and held up his hand. A moment later, a yellow taxi came to a stop by the side of the road. "I know this is awkward, but can you please help me get her to the hotel?"

Emily looked at Olivia and then at Simon. She'd often wondered what she would say to Olivia if their paths ever crossed again, but she'd never managed to answer the question.

She looked at Olivia, drunk and broken, smiling at her and calling her a beautiful fairy. The anger that Emily had thought would never fade was already ebbing. Seeing Olivia so vulnerable was strangely captivating, and she knew that she couldn't walk away.

She handed her bag to Simon. "Open the door," she said.

She turned to Olivia, who had her mouth full of chocolate and was smiling at her. She held out her hand, and Olivia placed the empty chocolate wrapper in the palm of her hand.

She pocketed the wrapper and took hold of Olivia's elbow. "Come on, time to go home."

Olivia thrust her cast-covered leg into the air. "Did you see my cast? Butcher signed it."

"That's nice." Emily pushed her leg down gently.

"I'm sorry," Olivia slurred.

"Don't worry about it."

"Sorry about what I said." Olivia was staring at her with unnerving clarity.

"It's okay," Emily said. And in that moment, it was. The sincerity of Olivia's apology hit Emily hard. The anger she'd been holding on to had already slipped away like grains of sand sliding through her fingers. "Now, mind your head." She reached up, placed her hand on Olivia's head, and guided her into the back of the taxi.

CHAPTER FIFTEEN

Emily opened the hotel suite door and stood to one side. Simon had parked Olivia against the wall while he took a second to get his breath back. While Olivia could hardly be described as heavy, it was also true that Simon couldn't be labelled muscular. That, coupled with the fact that Olivia had a cast on one foot and was making literally zero effort to walk sensibly, meant that Simon had been manhandling her all the way from the cab.

Simon draped Olivia's arm around his shoulder and helped her into the room. She seemed oblivious to the trouble she was causing, happily rambling on about the taxation system in the Middle East. Now, finally, exhaustion was starting to set in.

Simon edged towards the sofa.

"What are you doing?" Emily asked.

"Putting her on the sofa."

"She needs to go to bed."

Simon pivoted around and raised an eyebrow at her. "There's not much that's out of my job description, but that is."

Emily gave him an exasperated look. "Fine, help me get her in there and I'll get her to bed."

Simon let out a short sigh, stood a little straighter, and twisted his neck from left to right before continuing to walk Olivia towards the master bedroom. Emily edged around them to hold the door open. As she did so, she noticed the door to the guest room was open too. The bed was unmade, with men's clothes strewn across it. Simon passed her while she stood dumbly staring at the guest room.

"Are you…staying here?"

"Yup." Simon pivoted Olivia around and sat her on the bed. "She doesn't have anyone else. And there've been problems with work." He nodded towards Olivia. "She needed me."

Olivia flopped backward onto the bed and let out a long sigh.

"Could you get her some water?" Emily asked.

Simon quickly left the room, seemingly happy to escape the situation.

Emily looked at Olivia, who was dressed in a crumpled, black skirt suit. She looked nothing like the smart and elegant woman Emily remembered.

"Olivia, you need to get ready for bed. Do you need help?"

"Sometimes I say the wrong things," Olivia mumbled.

Simon returned with a glass of water and handed it to Emily. He looked at Olivia, still spread-eagle across the bed. "Good luck," he whispered.

Emily glared at him. "You owe me for this."

Simon shrugged before leaving the room, closing the door behind him.

Emily looked back to Olivia. "I think you should drink some water before you go to sleep. It will help to get the alcohol out of your system." Emily held out her free hand and waited for Olivia to take it.

After a moment of debate, Olivia grabbed the offered hand and pulled herself up into a sitting position. She took the glass and looked at Emily as she took a sip.

"Are we in London or New York?"

"New York."

"Oh." Olivia took another sip. "I find it hard to tell. My room's the same."

Emily looked around. "Yes, the suites are identical, aren't they?"

"Nearly identical," Olivia said. "The faucets, sockets, and light switches are different. I checked."

Emily grinned. She'd missed Olivia's precise ways. Among other things she didn't want to think about right now. "Drink some more water."

Olivia swallowed another small mouthful. A frown graced her features and Emily could practically hear the mental cogs turning.

"I think I'm a little bit drunk," Olivia declared.

"Really?" Emily smiled.

"Yes. Don't tell Simon. He'll just tell my son. They're thick as thieves."

Emily frowned but decided not to question the statement. There were more pressing matters at hand. "Drink some more water, and then we need to get you into bed."

Olivia took a small sip, but Emily knew she wasn't going to get much more down her. She took the glass and put it on the bedside table.

"Do you need help getting undressed?"

Olivia looked at her, glassy-eyed.

Emily sighed. She bent forward, removed Olivia's suit jacket, and placed it on the end of the bed. Straightening up, she gestured for Olivia to take her hands and stand up too. Once she was on her feet, Emily undid the zip on her skirt and pushed it to the floor, doing her best not to look. She helped Olivia step out of the skirt and, when she stabilised again, released one hand and pushed back the bedding.

Olivia sat on the edge of the bed again, quickly undid the buttons of the white blouse, and pushed it from her shoulders. Her eyes chanced a peek downwards, and she swallowed at the sight of the expensive silk bra. She silently chastised herself, instinctive though it was.

She knelt on the floor and removed Olivia's shoe from her good foot and then the protective pad from the cast. She stood and picked a piece of stray nacho out of Olivia's hair, and then helped her into the bed. By the time she pulled the bedding back up, Olivia was thankfully almost asleep.

Emily picked up the abandoned clothes and placed them over the sofa in the corner of the room. She looked at Olivia again and wondered what had happened to drive her to drinking herself into a stupor in a run-down bar. Emily hadn't known her long, but she knew Olivia rarely drank. She took one last look at her as she slept and then left the bedroom to find the man with the answers.

Emily found Simon sitting in the living area looking at his phone. When he saw her, he jumped to his feet.

"Is she okay?"

"Asleep," Emily replied.

"Thank you so much." He pointed to the kitchen. "Can I get you a drink?"

"No thanks. I should go." Emily hadn't been in contact with Simon since the fight with Olivia. To be fair, he hadn't contacted her either.

"Okay." Simon fidgeted with his hands. Clearly, she wasn't the only one affected by the awkward atmosphere in the room.

"She mentioned her son?" Emily wasn't sure why she asked. It was none of her business. Except she somehow felt as if it was. She thought she'd been close to Olivia, and she had never mentioned a son. It seemed like a strange omission.

Simon chuckled and rubbed his face with his hands. "Oh, man, that's never going to go away."

"What?"

Simon gestured to the sofa opposite and Emily sat down. He took a seat and said, "When I arrived, it was outside visiting hours. I'd slept overnight in the airport in London, flown for hours, and rushed to get here. And I didn't want her to be alone—you know how she hates hospitals—so I told the reception desk that I was her son."

Emily stared at him. "You didn't."

"I did."

"And they didn't question it?"

"Nope." He shrugged. "Anyway, the next time I saw her, she was high as a kite on pain medication and the nurse had told her that her son was coming to take her home. And Olivia is just like, 'Oh, okay, I have a son.'"

She laughed. "Pain medication is a weird thing. When I was younger, I fell out of a window—long story—but I was on pain meds in the hospital." She shook her head at the memory. "It was so surreal. I was watching some kids' show on television, and I thought it was real. I thought puppets were real and that I was a puppet. So, when I saw the nurses, I thought they were weird. As if I couldn't fathom what a human was."

He smiled. "I thought she might have forgotten by now, but it's clearly buried in there somewhere."

"Yeah," Emily said. "I'm sorry I never got in touch."

"Me too. I…well, Olivia said that things ended badly. I didn't know if you'd want to hear from me again."

Emily nodded. "I felt the same way. I didn't know if I should contact you or not. Did she explain what happened?"

"No, she just said that she made a mistake."

Emily lowered her head. It was true; Olivia had made a mistake. But she wasn't blameless either. She'd broken her promise to Olivia. Her promise to try. And while the anger of the argument was still a little raw, it was dissipating. Even if she didn't want it to.

"I should go." She got to her feet.

"Okay." Simon stood up too. "Well, you have my number. If you want to stay in touch, I can never have enough friends."

She smiled. He was putting control in her hands, and she appreciated it. She'd missed Simon almost as much as she'd missed Olivia—and she had missed her. Being reminded of Olivia's unique and endearing ways certainly complicated matters. She wanted to be angry at her. She wanted to keep her distance, to protect herself and Henry. But she somehow knew that she'd be back. "Me too. I'll call you."

CHAPTER SIXTEEN

When Emily returned home, she quietly closed the front door and slowly turned the lock, wincing at the loud click it made in the silence of the dark house. She shucked out of her coat and shoes and tiptoed across the hallway towards the stairs. Reminded of the times she used to break out of foster homes as a teenager, she mentally congratulated herself at not having lost any of her skill.

She placed a foot on the stairs and looked up to see Lucy standing halfway up, looking down at her, arms folded.

"Out with it."

Emily glared. "Don't do that," she whispered.

"You're trying to avoid me. Something's happened." Lucy walked down one step. "You crept up the garden path like a ninja, snuck in, closed the door, softly." She took another step. "You're avoiding me. Which means it's juicy."

"I don't know what—" Emily began.

Lucy folded her arms, raised an eyebrow, and Emily let out a sigh.

"Okay, in the kitchen." Emily turned and walked that way. Lucy followed, and they both sat down. Lucy put her elbows on the table and cradled her head, leaning forward with a smile. She waited.

"I saw Olivia."

"Olivia?" Lucy blinked in shock. "First Class Olivia?"

Emily snorted a laugh. "The one and only. Although she wasn't very first class when I saw her."

"Where? How? No, never mind that, just tell me everything. Right now."

Emily chuckled at her exuberance. “I was walking to the subway when I saw this man and woman leaving a bar. The woman trips and I catch her. Then I look up, and the man is Simon.”

“Her assistant?”

“Yup.”

“And the woman was Olivia?” Lucy squeaked.

“Yeah, and she’s drunk. Like ‘she has a nacho hat on her head and she’s barely able to walk’ drunk. Oh, and get this, she was on the plane that crashed.”

“No!”

“Her leg is in a cast; she has a bruise on her face. And I’m just standing there, holding her up, wondering what the hell is going on.”

“What happened then?”

“Well, Simon’s absolutely useless. He’s supposed to be looking after her, right? But she’s drunk, making friends with bikers, nachos in her hair. So, I help him to get her back to her hotel and into bed.”

“What did she say?”

“She thought she was dreaming. She called me a fairy.”

“And?” Lucy pressed.

“She called me beautiful.” Lucy opened her mouth, but Emily cut her off. “But she was very drunk.”

Lucy squealed with excitement. “Are you going to see her again?”

“I don’t think so.” Emily shook her head.

Lucy pouted.

“After what happened last time?” Emily looked at her. “Henry’s still depressed, missing her. I can’t just bring her back into our lives, because who knows what he’ll be like if she leaves again.”

“She didn’t technically leave,” Lucy murmured.

Emily could feel her defences rising. “You think I was wrong?”

“No, no.” Lucy reached out and took her hand, giving it a supportive squeeze. “I just know that it was a really weird situation and emotions were running high. And, as much as you talk about Henry missing her, I know you miss her too.”

Emily opened her mouth to reply but stopped and closed it again. It was true. She did miss Olivia. She’d known that before seeing her again, and now the feeling was even stronger. Henry’s mood was understandable. He missed Olivia as much as she did; he just didn’t know how to process the feeling.

"Maybe I overreacted," Emily said softly. "Maybe I didn't. What's done is done."

"Not always."

Emily paused. Lucy was right, but she had spent so long being angry that it was a struggle to see reason.

"Even so," she finally replied. "It's probably better to just forget it. I don't want to go through that again. And I certainly don't want to put Henry through all of that again."

"You assume the worst. What if it all works out?"

Emily gave a bitter laugh. "I don't have the best luck. I find it best to assume the worst."

"Whatever you think is best," Lucy conceded. She stood up, walked over to the counter, and picked up a letter. "This came for you. I had to sign for it."

Emily took the envelope, surprised to see a British return address. She ripped open the seam and pulled out a letter, immediately noticing the check attached to the top of it. She skimmed the words, and her mouth dropped open in surprise.

"What is it?" Lucy asked, seemingly only just managing to keep herself from pulling the page from Emily's hand.

"The journalist." Emily waved the paper in front of her. "She sent me a check. For three thousand dollars," Emily whispered as she read and reread the note. "It's a royalty payment for Henry's story. Apparently, a lot of magazines picked it up across Europe."

Lucy snatched the letter and quickly read it through herself. Emily reached forward and removed the check, reading it again and again to reassure herself that it was what she thought it was: a check, addressed to her, with the correct date, and signed.

"I've never seen a check for this much money made out to me. I've only ever seen bills for this much." She chuckled.

"Looks as if your luck is turning." Lucy handed back the letter. "New job, check for three thousand dollars, Olivia back in your life…"

Emily shook her head. "Henry's depressed, the ex-in-laws from hell are making my life miserable, my job feels like a house of cards, and Olivia is most definitely not back in my life."

"We'll see," Lucy singsonged.

CHAPTER SEVENTEEN

Emily didn't sleep much that night. Her mind was whirring with information and questions. The check had been a welcome surprise, but now she wondered what to do with the money, how to put it to best use.

On top of that, she missed Henry. Although it wasn't ideal that she shared a bed with her son, she'd become used to his company, and sleeping alone was difficult. She missed the snuffling sound of his breathing and the occasional thwacks to the face he delivered while dreaming. Knowing that he was likely miserable where he was did nothing to calm her.

Then there was Olivia. She wished she could say that seeing Olivia again hadn't affected her. But it had. And while sleep eluded her, everything came pouring back. She lay awake and examined every interaction, every conversation.

She was still angry at Olivia's behaviour on the flight back from London. But once the initial rage had subsided, it had become clear to Emily that Olivia's reactions were rooted in caring for Henry and an overwhelming desire to protect him. Lucy was right; Olivia hadn't left. Emily had pushed her away, and in her heart she regretted the decision—one she'd made out of fear.

Now Henry was suffering for it. Henry, who couldn't understand Olivia's absence. She felt the heavy burden of allowing him to become so attached to Olivia.

Going forward she had two choices: continue to avoid Olivia, and hope that Henry would ride out his misery and return to the happy-go-lucky boy she knew and longed for. Or reconnect with Olivia, see if they could somehow mend fences and move beyond the incident. Of course, the latter option ran the risk of upsetting Henry all over again if another falling out was to occur.

When morning came around, Emily wondered if she'd found a third option, or if she was just sleep-deprived. As she brushed her teeth, she stared at her reflection in the bathroom mirror, hoping for a magical solution to all her problems.

In the kitchen, she habitually placed two cereal bowls on the table before shaking her head and putting one back. Henry wouldn't be home for breakfast.

After eating, Emily picked up her phone and scrolled through to Simon's number. She took a deep breath, pressed the contact, and waited for the familiar dial tone to sound. She owed it to Henry to try for the third option, no matter how crazy it might sound.

"Good morning," Simon answered cheerfully.

"Good morning," Emily replied. "How are you both?"

"One of us is responding to the fact that it is morning better than the other."

Emily laughed. "I bet." She licked her lips nervously. "Is she okay?"

"Yeah, she's fine. Hungover, regretting her life choices, swearing off alcohol. You know, the usual. Well, usual for anyone else. I think she believes she's the first person to ever say these things."

Emily was relieved to hear confirmation that this wasn't normal behaviour for Olivia.

"Not one for hangovers?" Emily asked.

"Definitely not," Simon answered. "Don't think I've ever seen her hungover. Don't think I will again. She wasn't happy when I unloaded the dishwasher in front of her."

"On purpose?"

"Of course!" Simon chuckled. "I might have been a little heavy-handed with the cutlery."

"Cutlery's the worse." Emily smiled at the mental picture of Simon noisily slamming knives and forks into the drawer while Olivia held her head in suffering.

"You should come see us. I'm sure she'll want to thank you for the chocolate."

Emily smiled. "I was going to ask to come over. I know a place that does the best hangover croissants in the world."

"Is that a thing?" Simon asked jovially.

"Hangover croissants? Of course. You don't have them in Britain?" Emily joked.

"Nah, we don't like the French. We're more a full-cooked-breakfast nation. I offered it to Olivia; she went a bit green. Maybe she should try these croissants."

"Agreed. See you in around an hour?"

❖

"She's coming here?" Olivia asked, knowing full well that blind panic was apparent in her eyes.

"Yep."

"Why didn't you tell me?"

"I am telling you," Simon said with a puzzled face.

"When did she call?"

"An hour ago." He shrugged. "You were washing your hair. She's bringing croissants."

Olivia was on her feet and reaching for her crutch immediately. "I need to get changed."

"Why?"

"Because I'm wearing sweatpants, Simon." She indicated her lower half with a wave of her hand.

"You have a broken leg," he replied.

"I'm well aware of that, but I need to get changed."

Simon stood and held his hands up in an effort to calm her. "Look, I know you feel a little scruffy."

She bristled—at the word and the suggestion.

"But she will literally be here in five minutes or less. You don't have time. And, to be honest, she didn't exactly see you at your best yesterday, and she's still coming to see you this morning, so I think you're okay."

Olivia levelled her most forceful glare at him, ready to tell him, for the third time in half an hour, that the previous night was not to be mentioned again. Ever. But a quiet knock resounded, and Olivia knew she was out of time. Emily had arrived. Terror set in, and she looked pleadingly at Simon.

"I'll get it," he said. "You sit down."

She did as she was told, looking down at the pink sweatpants Simon had bought her the week before. She couldn't decide if her crisp, black blouse elevated the sweatpants or simply made her look utterly ridiculous.

"Hey," Simon said. "Good to see you. Come in."

Emily walked in, and Olivia glanced up. Of course, she looked perfect in blue jeans, a cream sweater, and a fashionable black coat.

As soon as Emily was in the suite, Simon said, "If you'll excuse me, I just have to run an errand."

"Simon," Olivia warned him.

"I'll be back soon." He grinned at both of them before grabbing his coat from the back of the chair by the door and hurrying out into the hallway.

The door closed, and Emily turned around to regard Olivia. "It's almost as if he wants to give us some time alone," she joked.

"Yes, smooth, isn't he?" Olivia replied.

Emily held up a box. "I brought freshly baked croissants. Not the ones that have sat there since they baked them at five o'clock this morning. These are straight out of the oven. Can I tempt you?"

Olivia slowly nodded. "I'd like that."

"I'll grab a plate." Emily headed into the kitchen. Olivia could hear the sound of plates and then Emily calling, "Coffee?"

"Y-yes." Olivia cursed her awkward tone. "Please," she added.

She attempted to fluff up her hair, glad that she'd washed it that morning after her comb had come to a stuttering halt in some green mess. Her memory of the previous night was absent, and the small amount of information she did have had come from Simon. He'd only mentioned a few selected highlights, no doubt with the intention of drip-feeding the rest at a later date to ensure maximum embarrassment.

She looked at the cartoon picture of a Harley Davidson on her cast and assumed it had been drawn by her new friends with the terrifying names. Apparently, she was now a card-holding member of the bar where she had disgraced herself. And at some point, she had been undressed for bed by Emily White. Not just some random person, or even Simon. No, Emily White—the one she wanted to be her

Emily—had seen her embarrass herself. When she'd learned that, she'd been somewhat pleased with her failed memory.

"Here you go. Coffee and croissants." Emily placed a tray on the coffee table and sat down on the sofa opposite. "How are you feeling?"

"Why are you here?"

Emily laughed, smiling as she shook her head. "I missed your bluntness."

"You're here because you missed my bluntness?"

"No." Emily poured herself coffee from the pot on the tray. "I'm here because I was worried about you last night and wanted to check how you're feeling."

"I feel as if I drank too much and made a fool of myself."

"You rocked the nacho hat."

"The what?"

Emily picked up her mug. "Never mind. Probably best you don't remember."

Olivia took a croissant from the box and placed it on a side plate. "I-I hear you helped to get me to bed?"

"I did."

"Thank you."

"You're welcome. I didn't think either you or Simon would want him to do it."

Olivia prickled at the notion. "True." She bit into the croissant. It was delicious: flaky, warm, buttery—everything a croissant was supposed to be. They sat in silence for a few minutes, Emily drinking coffee while she ate. Olivia's mind raced with questions, scenarios, and, mainly, fear. She wondered if this was a second chance or just a friendly gesture. Completely unprepared for Emily's presence or conversation, she found herself floundering.

"I'm sorry," Olivia blurted out.

Emily looked surprised.

"For what I did, the things I said on the plane," Olivia clarified. "I wanted to tell you before, but I assumed that you didn't want to hear from me."

Emily lowered her mug to the coaster on the table and bit the inside of her cheek, her eyes down as she thought.

"I'm still angry," she finally said. "I don't know if I'm ready to forgive what happened. And that's my fault; I struggle to let go of anger. I understand that you are sorry, and I accept your apology. But it doesn't fix everything."

"So, you're just here to enquire about my health?" Olivia asked, but it was more of a statement. Unable to read the situation, she wanted to be certain so she didn't make a bigger fool of herself.

"Not just that." Emily looked up. "I have a favour to ask. And I have no right to ask you this, but I'm hoping you'll—"

"Yes, anything," she replied quickly.

Emily chuckled softly, and Olivia realised how much she had missed that sound. "You don't even know what it is."

"What is it?" Olivia didn't really care what it was. She knew there and then that she'd do anything to fix her mess. Or, more precisely, anything for Emily.

Emily let out a small sigh. "It's…well, it's Henry."

Fear rushed through her. "What about Henry? Is he ill?"

"No, no. He's fine," Emily reassured her quickly. "Well, physically he's fine. But…" She swallowed. "He misses you. Desperately."

Olivia knew she was staring, but she couldn't help it. "Me?"

"Yes. Like I feared, he took to you very quickly, and now he misses you a lot. He's not been talking much, and when he does, he talks through Tiny. I know things didn't end well between us, but—"

"What can I do?"

Emily's relief was palpable. "I've been telling him that you've been busy with work. But he doesn't believe me. Maybe you could call him? Tell him you're very busy, but that you miss him too, maybe? I don't want to put words into your mouth, but I know that he would—"

"I do miss him. Even though it's quite impossible to have a proper conversation with him." The truth was that their bizarre conversations were what she missed the most. Henry came up with the most random topics and never judged Olivia on her responses.

Emily's eyes met hers for a moment before she stood up and ran a hand through her hair. "I don't want this to mean anything, and I know this is really shitty of me. I just…for Henry. You know?"

Olivia's eyes flicked around the room, and she swallowed the lump of disappointment in her throat.

"I understand," Olivia assured her. "He's a child, and there were a lot of things happening, a lot of things for him to try to process. I'm happy to help."

"Are you sure? I feel as if I'm taking advantage of you."

Olivia's hands drew together, and she nervously pinched the skin between her thumb and forefinger. "How about, and feel free to reject this idea, but how about a trip to the park? I need to get out of this suite, and I'm supposed to be walking to exercise my leg. Maybe seeing him face-to-face will have more effect?"

"You'd do that?"

"It's the least I can do. Think of it as an apology."

"I usually wouldn't ask, but Henry has been so despondent. I just want to make him happy, and this was the best I could come up with."

"I'm offering," Olivia said seriously.

Emily regarded her for a few moments before nodding. "The park sounds great."

A beep from Olivia's phone sounded, and she picked up the device from the coffee table and swiped the screen before wincing.

"Everything okay?" Emily enquired.

"My actions from last night are making themselves known."

"Drunk call?"

"Drunk purchase," Olivia said.

"Anything nice?"

"A ten-series box set of something called Friends."

Emily laughed and sat back down. "Well, that'll keep you busy."

"Indeed it will." Olivia sighed. "I am sorry that my actions caused Henry pain."

"They were my actions as much as yours," Emily confessed. "I'm sorry, for how we left things."

"So am I," Olivia added readily.

Emily hesitated. "You were out of order. But so was I."

"I know. Really, I do." Olivia placed her phone back on the table, lining it up so it was parallel to the edge of the table. "I became panicked, and I wanted to fix things, but I know I acted appallingly. I saw that straight after the event. I don't respond well when my schedule is changed, or when something is out of my control. I'm working on it. I wanted to apologise, but, as I said, I assumed you didn't wish to hear from me."

"It was a very stressful time for both of us," Emily explained. "Our entire relationship had been built on, well, exceptional circumstances.

Henry's illness, the hotel suite, the travel, my job, your position. It was all heading for disaster."

"I suppose it was," Olivia said sadly; she focused on the table and hoped Emily couldn't see through her insincere words. "I'm sorry for it. All of it."

"Well, as I said, it was exceptional circumstances. Maybe we should start over?"

Olivia looked up as Emily walked towards her and held out her hand.

"I'm Emily White. Pleased to meet you."

Olivia smiled. She shook Emily's hand. "Olivia Lewis."

CHAPTER EIGHTEEN

Henry was subdued when his grandparents dropped him off, and Emily was glad to be able to suggest going to the park that afternoon. Any mention of a trip to the park would usually bring a spark to Henry's eyes, but this time he'd simply nodded before going to his room and silently playing. Even now, she watched him as he sat in the wooden fort with Tiny tucked under his arm, watching the other children play. She hadn't mentioned Olivia joining them in case she didn't show. She couldn't stomach the thought of Henry being even more miserable than he already was.

She remembered the days before the operation, when Henry would run around the playground with boundless energy and she would have to race after him and remind him to take things slowly. Trying to slow down a five-year-old sometimes was like trying to push syrup uphill with a stick. But it was the only way Emily could be certain of his safety, no matter how much he'd complained. Hopefully, those days were now well behind them. Even though he was technically still in recovery, the doctor had assured Emily that he would be able to play as other children his age did.

"Miss White."

Emily smiled as she turned around to see Olivia standing behind the park bench, leaning on her crutch and looking over towards Henry.

"Miss Lewis." Emily grinned as relief flooded her.

"Why isn't Henry playing?" Olivia made her way to the side of the bench.

"He's been very quiet today. He got back from his grandparents' this morning."

Olivia looked down at Emily. "Grandparents?"

"Olivia!"

They both looked up to see Henry running towards them with a surprised expression and an enormous grin on his face. Before Emily had a chance to tell him to be careful, he launched himself into Olivia's arms and held her tight.

"Olivia, you're here," Henry yelled breathlessly.

"I am," Olivia whispered as she placed a hand on his back and held him tightly.

Henry pulled back to look at her foot. "You have a funny shoe," he said before turning to her. "You didn't tell me Olivia was coming. Is this a surprise?"

Emily nodded. "Yes, this was a surprise. Do you like it?"

"I love it!" Henry said and grabbed Olivia's hand. "Olivia, come and play with me."

Emily quickly reached out and disconnected Henry's hand from Olivia's before he pulled her over. "Henry, Olivia can't play right now because she's hurt her foot."

"How?" Henry frowned at the cast.

"I brok—"

"She tripped and hurt her foot," Emily interrupted before Olivia could explain about the plane crash and scar Henry for life. "It means we have to be very careful around her foot and we can't be rough with her, okay?"

"Okay, you can watch me play," Henry told them as if granting a lifelong aspiration.

"We will," Emily said, but he was already gone.

Olivia sat on the bench beside Emily and looked after Henry thoughtfully. "So, I just sit here and watch him play?"

Emily chuckled. "Yes. It's his way of connecting with you. He wants to show you all the things he can do."

"Well, he's full of energy." Olivia watched him race back towards the play area.

"Yes." Emily could hear the relief in her own voice.

Olivia smothered a yawn with her hand, and Emily giggled. "Are we keeping you awake?"

Olivia blushed. "Sorry. It's been a few years since I last had to deal with a hangover. And work has been so stressful lately. I've not been sleeping well."

"I'm sorry to hear that. Do you want to talk about it?" Emily said.

"No, I'd rather not think about it."

"Ah."

"Ah?" Olivia asked.

"I was going to speak to you about something, but, well, it kind of relates to your work..."

"Oh?"

"I hate to do this," Emily said, "but I have something I need to ask you."

Olivia nodded, encouraging her to continue.

Emily laughed. "It's funny when you think how pissed I was when you first left your business card. But I kinda need some financial advice."

"Oh." Olivia couldn't hide her surprise.

"If you don't mind, that is?" she quickly added. "I don't mean to put you on the spot or talk about work. But I don't really have anyone else I can talk to, and obviously you're an expert with this stuff, and I'm, well, I'm really not."

"I don't mind," Olivia readily said. "But I know you can be... sensitive, when it comes to these issues. And we both know that's not my strong suit."

Emily nodded and released a deep breath. "Yep, I know what I'm getting myself into, but I'm going to do my best to suck it up."

"Olivia." Henry's voice echoed from across the playground and Olivia looked up. Henry was running towards her with a large smile on his face. He skidded to a halt in front of her, staring at her leg cast suspiciously.

"Did you see me on the slide?"

"Yes, we both did," Emily quickly interjected, knowing full well that Olivia hadn't and would also tell Henry that fact, condemning both of them to watch it over and over. "We loved it!"

"Yes," Olivia said with uncertainty, looking at Emily in confusion. "It was very good."

"Henry," Emily said, "I just need to talk about some boring adult things with Olivia, and then the three of us can play something together. Is that okay?"

"Okay." Henry nodded excitedly and ran back towards the play area again.

"I didn't see him on the slide," Olivia told Emily with a frown.

"No, but if you tell him that, he'll make you watch, again and again and again."

"I wouldn't mind," Olivia confessed.

"I'll hold you to that," Emily laughed.

Olivia grinned. "So, financial advice?"

"Yes." Emily nodded. She could feel her cheeks starting to warm into a blush. "I heard from the freelance journalist, and she's managed to sell Henry's story to a few magazines in Europe. It's going to bring in more money that I thought."

"Okay. What kind of sum are we talking about?"

"Three thousand dollars," Emily explained. "But I don't know what to do with it. I've never had three thousand dollars before. I think I should do something sensible. Maybe invest it?"

Olivia shook her head. "No, you need to clear your debt first."

Emily cringed at Olivia's plain tone.

"Pay debts before you accumulate savings," Olivia explained, as if speaking to a child.

"But," Emily sighed. "It feels like throwing it away into an abyss of debts."

Olivia opened her mouth to speak, and then closed it as she thought for a moment. After a few seconds, she spoke again. "Do you understand the concept of financial interest?"

"Only that my interest in finance is zero," Emily joked, but at Olivia's stern gaze she shook her head. "Look, when you're caring for a sick child and working multiple jobs, you don't exactly have time to check your investment portfolio and the latest currency exchange rates. So, no, I don't really understand financial interest."

Olivia appeared to recognise the tone as a warning to proceed with a little more caution; her expression softened.

"When you are looking at investments, you need to take into account interest figures. Currently, interest being paid on savings and investments is very low. Conversely, interest on borrowing is high," Olivia explained. "Your debts will have a higher rate of interest than any savings account you could find. There wouldn't be much point in putting money aside with one hand and then paying large amounts of interest on your repayments with the other."

Emily scrunched up her face while processing the information. "Okay, that makes sense. So I should pay the money towards one of the loans?"

Olivia frowned. "You haven't consolidated your debts?"

"Should I have?" Emily asked, feeling her blush increasing at Olivia's incredulous tone.

Olivia opened her mouth to speak, but closed it again, her hands snaking together in her lap as she began to pinch her hand. Emily noticed but decided that maybe Olivia needed a little self-censorship at that moment.

"Your debts," Olivia finally replied. "They will have different rates of interest. A good loan company will charge a certain amount, and a bad loan company could charge up to fifty times that. Same with credit cards. You should—and I understand that you don't, and many people don't—but you should know what the interest rates are on all your loans. So you can make decisions about payments in hard times."

"That makes sense," Emily allowed with a nod and a small, uncertain smile.

"When debts are…severe," Olivia continued cautiously, "it is usually advisable to consolidate them into one account. Then you have one thing to manage from an administrative perspective, and you can usually lower your overall average interest rate."

Emily nodded her understanding and looked to the playground to observe Henry playing on the equipment. After a few moments of contemplation, she asked, "Would you help me do that?"

Olivia looked surprised before quickly agreeing. "Yes, yes, I'd like to help where I can."

"Thank you," Emily replied. "I'm quickly starting to realise that if I want to do the best for Henry, then sometimes I need to suck up my pride and do things that are uncomfortable, like face up to my mistakes."

Olivia remained silent, continuing to pinch her hand pensively. Emily smiled, reached for Olivia's hands, and pulled one away from the other. She squeezed gently.

"No need to do that. I think we're learning how to communicate."

Olivia nodded and looked down at their connected hands. "Do you still work for Crown?"

Emily retracted her hand, not wanting to give Olivia the wrong idea. "No, not any more. Literally the day after the crash I got a phone call from Crown saying that they were putting me on standby. A few days later that changed to being laid off. Luckily, I'd already found a new job. Someone I know helped me to get the position. I basically do admin work."

Olivia was silent for a while before asking, "Do you like the job?"

She shrugged. "It's better than being unemployed. But I don't want to talk about that. How are you? What actually happened on that flight?"

Olivia shifted uncomfortably. "The landing gear failed."

"Yes, I know that. How did you get injured, though? Is it bad?"

"I had my foot stretched out, and the chair in front of mine collapsed onto it." Olivia gestured to the half-healed cuts on her forehead. "The ceiling collapsed too."

Emily stared at Olivia, who was watching Henry play on the climbing frame. She had almost forgotten about Olivia's unique way of describing events.

"Are you okay?" she asked directly.

"I had an operation on my ankle. It's improving." Olivia smiled brightly, and Emily looked up to see a happy Henry running towards them.

"Mommy, can Olivia come over for dinner?" Henry wore his best pleading expression.

Emily looked to Olivia. "She's certainly welcome to."

Olivia's eyes tracked from Emily to Henry and back again.

"I understand if you're busy," Emily added. "But we'd both like you there, if you can."

"I'd love to."

"Yes!" Henry cried and ran back to the slide, screaming as he went.

Olivia chuckled at Henry's enthusiasm before addressing Emily. "Are you sure?"

"Yes. If you are?" Emily asked, suddenly nervous that Olivia might have felt bullied into attending.

"If it helps Henry…" Olivia trailed off.

Emily smiled. She knew the situation must be uncomfortable for Olivia. It was certainly difficult for her. But Olivia was selflessly putting herself into a more awkward situation to benefit Henry. Emily coughed softly and looked away, trying to remind herself why she'd ended things with her. Unfortunately, when she looked back, she realised the passage of time had already started to dull the memories.

"I brought some bread for Henry to feed to the ducks," she explained, lifting up a bag of stale bread. "They don't need feeding; they're the fattest ducks I have ever seen, but it beats just sitting here. Do you want to go for a walk towards the pond?"

Olivia adjusted her crutch and lifted herself to her feet. "Sounds lovely. I need to keep walking to strengthen my leg muscles."

Emily felt her cheeks flare at an impure thought about Olivia's leg muscles.

"Right, let's um…Henry!" She called, flustered. "Let's feed those ducks."

Luckily, Olivia didn't seem to notice her agitation, but Emily knew she was fighting a losing battle between her heart and her head.

CHAPTER NINETEEN

Simon removed his glasses and placed them on the coffee table. He rubbed his eyes tiredly and let out a long, heartfelt sigh. He heard a keycard in the door and looked up to see Olivia walk in.

He smiled. "Well?"

She closed the door and removed her coat. "Well, what?"

He rolled his eyes. "How did it go with Emily and Henry?"

She adjusted her crutch, made her way to the sofa, and fell onto it gently.

"I think it went well. It was a little bit of a blur."

"Are you having side effects from the pain medication?"

She shook her head. "No, it was just a little stressful and I found it hard to tell. She asked me for financial advice."

Simon picked up his glasses and cleaned them with the end of his tie. "Emily asked you for financial advice? Emily White? Who was here earlier with croissants?"

She chuckled. "Yes, that Emily White."

"Interesting." He put his glasses back on.

"I'm going over to her house for dinner," Olivia added casually, despite the rattled look in her eyes.

Simon raised an eyebrow and stared at her for a moment in silence.

"Oh, don't do that," she complained.

"I'm not doing anything."

"You're doing that thing with your eyebrow. And you have that face."

"I'm sorry, but it's my face. I can't do anything about it. I don't have a selection."

"You know what I mean," she huffed.

"Nervous?" he asked.

"Terrified. I have to meet Lucy and Tom. Who knows what they've heard about me. It's going to be a disaster."

"Then why are you going?" Simon stood up, interlaced his fingers, and raised his arms above his head to release the tension from being hunched over his laptop on the low coffee table.

"Henry asked me."

"Ah." He noticed the same change in Olivia that he'd seen in London when she spent time with Henry. She was happier, more relaxed. Even with the prospect of the terrifying dinner on the horizon. "Well, you can't really say no to Henry. How was he?"

"Quiet. He perked up a lot when he saw me." Olivia sounded smug.

"Smart boy," Simon joked. "Coffee?"

"Please." Olivia leaned forward and opened her laptop which she'd left on the coffee table earlier.

Simon entered the kitchen and started up the coffee machine. "So, I take it I'm dining alone tonight?" he called out.

"I can bring you as my plus one?" Olivia sounded keen.

"I don't think dinner invitations of that nature include a plus one." Simon chuckled.

"I'll text Emily."

"No, it's fine." He walked into the living room and sat on the edge of the sofa as the coffee machine fizzed to life. "Do you want me to drive you tonight?"

"No, I'll drive, I tested the other day and the cast doesn't interfere."

"Okay. That'll give me some time to Skype with Sophie."

Olivia looked guiltily at him. "I'm sorry, Simon. I'm ruining your private life, aren't I?"

"Not at all. But we do need to talk about the next few weeks. I can't stay here forever."

"I know." Olivia turned away, avoiding his gaze. "But with the way things are at the office—"

"You don't need me here for that," he said gently. "You may have been in London ninety percent of the time, but we worked perfectly efficiently when you were in New York and I was in London."

"You want to go home." Olivia stared at her laptop screen defiantly.

"No, I want us both to know what the plan is. You're working yourself to death trying to find a way to fix the damage Marcus caused. I think we need to cut our losses, take what we can salvage, and start over."

"Absolutely not. I can fix this. I have restructured more complicated scenarios."

"In none of those scenarios was there an evil shit trying to tear down everything you did. In none of those scenarios were you so heavily emotionally invested." He stood up and sat on the sofa opposite, giving her no option but to look at him. "You're working UK hours and US hours back to back. It's been over a week. Marcus has established his new company; he has signed contracts. You know as well as I do that we'll struggle to pay our next wage bill with the clients we've managed to retain."

"I won't announce redundancies."

"You're going to have to," he said firmly.

She opened her mouth to reply but paused. Instead she closed her laptop again and stared at him with tears in her eyes. "Simon, I just don't know what to do. Everything I try he's two steps ahead of me."

"He has been planning this for months. He must've been, to move so quickly."

"I should be able to do this. I should be able to find a solution."

"If this was a normal corporate takeover, founded in greed and money, then, yes, you'd find a solution. It isn't. He wants to make you suffer. He wants to tear down Applewood. You're struggling to find a solution because it's not logical. It's personal. Therefore, there is no logical solution."

Olivia sat silently, staring into nothing as she processed his words.

"I'll go and get that coffee." He walked into the kitchen, arranged cups, saucers, and a china coffee jug on a tray, and took it into the living area.

"Take a step back and pretend you're advising a client." Simon placed the tray on the table and poured coffee for them both. "What is their priority?"

Olivia considered the question and shook her head dejectedly as she replied, "To secure what is left of the business."

"Precisely." He slid a cup and saucer over to her. "It's good advice."

"But if I can convince Signet One and Edison's to move their audit work to us, then I'll be able to cover costs."

"You're trying to achieve something in one week that should take a month, at least. You're exhausted, on pain medication, angry at Marcus—"

"Of course I'm angry at Marcus!"

"I'm not saying you're wrong," Simon said calmly. "I'm saying that he wants you to be angry. He wants you to be upset. You're giving him what he wants. Isn't the best revenge living well?"

"No, the best revenge would have been hiring someone to cut his brakes."

He sniggered but shook his head. "You don't mean that."

She sighed. "No, I don't. I can't even bring myself to want him dead."

Simon laughed. "Good. That's because you're a good person. And good people don't wish bad people dead, even if they are Marcus Hind."

She sipped her coffee and remained silent.

"I think you should take the rest of the afternoon and evening off. Go to dinner at Emily's and don't think about work. Go to bed at a decent hour, get some sleep, and see how you feel in the morning."

While he was pleased that Olivia appeared to be getting something of a second chance with Emily, he couldn't help but worry about the prospect of her getting hurt again. He'd never seen her so emotionally vulnerable and didn't know how she would manage a second rejection. But it wasn't his place to get involved. He was always aware that they trod a very strange line between friendship and employer/employee. As much time as they spent together, and as much as she was more like family to him, she was still his boss, and her private life was not his to comment on. All he could do now was help her to take care of herself a bit better and be there for her. Whatever the outcome.

"But what about you?" Olivia asked.

"About?"

"You going home?"

"Oh." He shrugged. "I'll stay as long as you need me." It was true, he would. That didn't mean he didn't miss Sophie. While the relationship was still relatively new, they had just immediately clicked. Talking via email and video conference was great, but he still longed to see her again in person. But even Sophie had told him that it was right for him to stay with Olivia for as long as she needed him. She understood his unique relationship with Olivia, and that made the distance slightly more bearable.

"It's not fair of me to ask you to stay here."

"You never asked me. I invited myself." Simon smiled.

"You know what I mean. You have to go home eventually."

"How about we talk about that in the morning as well? Once we have a game plan set up for Applewood, then we can decide."

Olivia sipped her coffee and nodded. Simon mentally congratulated himself for finally talking some sense into her, getting her to slow down and take some time to think about her next move. He knew she was desperately trying to fix things, but he also knew what Olivia needed in order to work at peak efficiency. Even if she didn't know herself.

CHAPTER TWENTY

Olivia parked her black Mercedes-Benz E-Class sedan outside the address that Emily had given her. She took a deep breath to try to calm her nerves. She'd spent the latter half of the afternoon changing outfits and foolishly asking for Simon's guidance. Every outfit she showed him, he told her she looked nice, and every time she sighed and went back to her room to change. She didn't want to appear as if she was trying too hard, but conversely she wanted to look as good as she could. Indecision reared its head again now that she had arrived. She looked down at her light grey skirt suit and wondered if it was too formal, even though she knew it had been the best choice considering her foot cast.

She looked at the house, her anxiety rising to new levels, and briefly considered driving away. Suddenly, Henry's face appeared beside her as the boy stood on his tiptoes to look in through the driver's window. His hands gripped the indentations of the car to keep himself upright. This was why she was here. Olivia smiled and gestured for him to stand back a little. When he did, she opened the door with the intention of getting out. Henry, it seemed, had other ideas, as he climbed into the car and hugged her where she sat in the driver's seat.

"I missed you," he declared, adjusting himself on her lap and looking at the interior of the car with interest. "I like your car."

"I missed you too," Olivia said. She brought a hesitant hand up to brush some of his hair away from his face. "You need a haircut."

"Nope." Henry shook his head and frowned.

"No?" Olivia laughed. "You like looking scruffy?"

Henry shrugged and climbed over the central console to the passenger seat, where he continued to investigate.

"Hi." Olivia turned to see Emily leaning gently on the open door. "Sorry. I tried to stop him, but the second he saw you he wanted to come and say hello."

"Mommy, I like Olivia's car," Henry told Emily with a nod of his head.

"Yes, don't touch anything, though, Henry."

Olivia frowned and quietly asked, "Why not?"

Emily chuckled. "Because you have a very expensive and immaculate car, and I have a five-year-old with grubby hands."

"It's just a car." Olivia shrugged, still not seeing the problem.

Emily laughed. "Come on, you two. Let's go and eat."

Olivia got out of the car and retrieved her crutch from the back seat.

"When will your leg be fixed?" Henry asked as he crawled back over the driver's seat.

"Around three months."

Henry looked up at her in shock. "That's forever."

"Yes, it is," Olivia concurred. Once he was out of the car, she closed the door and pointed to the handle. "Can you lock the door, Henry?"

He frowned at her. "I don't have a key."

"You don't need one. Just press the handle and you'll hear it lock."

Henry regarded her suspiciously but stepped forward and pressed his finger to the handle. The doors locked, and a small beep sounded to indicate the alarm had been set.

"Cool! I'm going to tell Tom!" Henry sprinted off up the path.

Emily stood back and gestured for Olivia to follow him. Olivia paused for a moment and took a breath before starting to slowly move.

"Nervous?" Emily asked.

"Should I be?"

"No, but it would be normal to feel apprehensive."

"Then, yes," Olivia said.

As it turned out, she didn't need to worry. Tom and Lucy appeared on the porch, the perfect picture of a friendly young couple without a care in the world. They greeted her warmly, Tom complimented her on her choice of car, and Lucy took her coat.

"I'm sitting next to Olivia at dinner," Henry said before racing upstairs.

"No running on the stairs," Emily called up after him. He slowed to an excited jog.

Olivia watched Henry's retreating form with a frown.

"He has so many things he wants to show you," Lucy explained. "He's been very excited about your visit. We all have."

"Come through." Tom gestured towards the living room.

She walked through the doorway and quickly found herself being given the grand tour.

"I'm sorry about the state of the house," Lucy said. "As soon as I tidy something, Tom messes it up again."

"Hey, I think you mean Henry," Tom said with a grin.

"Absolutely not. Henry knows how to put his toys away." Lucy playfully tweaked Tom's nose.

While the house was small, it was also absolutely charming, and Olivia felt somehow jealous. Every room, no matter how small and tired, exuded happiness. She could tell that Lucy was very house-proud and did the best she could with limited means.

Family photos lined the walls, and run-down furniture was covered with repurposed fabrics. The downstairs consisted of a kitchen, a living room, a small study, and a downstairs toilet. It took all of a minute to see the whole ground floor, but in that time Olivia felt at home and welcome.

Lucy gestured for her to take a seat on the sofa and returned to preparing dinner. Tom offered her a variety of drinks, but Emily returned from the kitchen with a glass of water, already knowing Olivia's preference.

"So," Tom said as he sat in an armchair, excitedly leaning in. "Tell me about the crash."

Olivia opened her mouth to answer, but stopped when Emily crossed the room and thwacked him with a backhand across the arm.

"Maybe she doesn't want to discuss it," Emily suggested.

"Oh, I don't mind." Olivia shrugged.

"Sorry. I didn't mean to be insensitive." Tom rubbed his arm. "I'm a pilot and I'm interested in learning about what actually happened."

"What do you want to know?" Olivia asked, to have something to say.

Tom started to ask a question but stopped and turned his head towards the door. Henry reappeared and, after a moment of staring at Olivia's cast, hopped up onto her good leg and showed her a piece of paper. She put her arm around him to steady him, and examined the drawing.

"It's a monkey factory," Emily helpfully explained.

"Where they make monkeys," Henry added.

"That's very good." She looked at the unidentifiable squiggles and tried to make any sense of them.

Lucy called to say that dinner was ready. Henry hopped down and walked towards the kitchen.

"Olivia is sitting next to me," he reminded everyone loudly, just in case there had been any doubts.

Olivia smiled. Tom offered her a hand and she gratefully took it.

"Maybe we can talk about the crash later, when little ears aren't around?" he asked as he handed her the crutch.

"Absolutely," Olivia said.

"It's good that you came tonight. It spurred Lucy on to make chicken pot pie," Tom said as he walked her to the kitchen. "It's the best you'll ever taste."

❖

Olivia followed Emily up the stairs and looked around nervously. Being shown around the lower level of the house was fine, but upstairs she somehow felt as if she was trespassing. Emily opened the door to a bedroom and gestured for Olivia to go inside.

Olivia looked around with a confused frown. The room contained a double bed with two mismatched single quilts on top, a small chest of drawers, and a tatty-looking wardrobe. A large plastic box of toys was hidden behind the door, and the bare floorboards by the side of the bed were covered by a felt play mat crisscrossed with roads.

"You sleep here?"

"Yes, that's what a bedroom is." Emily laughed lightly. "Henry sleeps here too."

"You share a bed," Olivia commented.

"Yes." Emily reached under the bed, pulled out a plastic box filled with paperwork, and lifted it onto the bed.

"Is that sustainable?" Olivia asked honestly.

Emily took a deep breath. "Well, when he starts dating it might get problematic."

Olivia gasped in shock.

"I'm kidding, Olivia," Emily said with a shake of her head.

"Oh." Olivia realised she'd upset her and looked hesitantly around the room. She understood that Emily didn't want to be reminded that her current living situation wasn't ideal, nor maintainable.

Emily lifted the lid off the plastic box and looked through a few pieces of paper.

"Oh, wrong one," she mumbled, then crouched down to look under the bed for another box.

Olivia glanced at the open box and picked up a stack of papers held together by a rusty bulldog clip. She started to flip through them with interest.

Emily heaved another plastic box onto the bed and looked at Olivia.

"You know that could be considered rude?"

Olivia paused mid-flick. She looked up, confused. "Should I stop?"

Emily chuckled. "Well, it's done now, but for future reference, you should've asked."

"Presumably it's fine; otherwise you would've removed it from my hands by now."

Emily opened her mouth to argue the point but closed it again and laughed. "Yes, you're right. You should still ask, though."

Olivia shrugged. She wasn't about to be drawn into a discussion regarding etiquette when she had something much more interesting in her hands. "You wrote this?"

"Yes," Emily said indifferently. She lifted the lid off the second box and started to sort the various papers that had been haphazardly stuffed inside.

Olivia looked back at the original box, having lost interest in Emily's financial paperwork. "Did you write all of these?"

"Yes," Emily said without looking up. "Just a hobby."

Olivia placed the paper she had been flicking through on the bed. She leaned over the box and started to look through the other papers with interest.

Emily sighed. "I thought we came up here to look for financial papers, remember?"

"Tell me about these?"

Emily frowned, but started, "I used to enjoy writing. When I was pregnant with Henry, I started writing television scripts. There was so much crap on TV, and I knew I could do better, so I thought I'd write my own shows."

Olivia carefully pulled each stack of documents from the box and analysed them before stacking them neatly.

"When Henry got ill, there was a lot of time spent at the doctors', hospitals, and stuff," Emily continued with a hitch in her voice. "And I carried on. It was a good escape. When I couldn't afford a babysitter, and I had to take time off from work to watch him, I would sit beside him and write."

"You either write very fast or Henry was ill a lot," Olivia commented. She took the last couple of documents from the box and placed them in her new pile.

"What are you doing?" Emily asked.

"Stacking them properly. The edges were curling," Olivia explained as she began to methodically place them back into the box.

"Doesn't matter. No one reads them except for me." Emily chuckled.

"May I read one?" Olivia asked.

"You don't have to do that." Emily smiled and shook her head as she returned her attention to the financial documents. "If I'd spent more time on this and less time on that, then maybe I wouldn't be in the mess I'm in now."

"Which one should I read?" Olivia asked, ignoring Emily's deprecating words. "Which is your favourite?"

Emily sighed again. "I don't know; it depends what you're interested in?"

Olivia regarded Emily quietly, making it clear that she wasn't about to be moved on from the subject. Emily shook her head and quickly flicked through the stack, looking for something.

"This is my favourite, but that doesn't mean it's actually any good." Emily handed her a stack of papers held together with string.

"I'll let you know what I think," Olivia said as she flipped through the pages.

"No, I'd rather you didn't," Emily said softly. Olivia frowned and Emily elaborated. "I have this dream, a fantasy really, that I'm good at writing. I don't know if it's true or not, but I don't want to know either. I never did anything with them, because sometimes it's better to not do anything and fool yourself that you're good at something than to have someone tell you you're not."

Olivia bit the inside of her mouth nervously and furrowed her brow.

Emily chuckled. "I don't expect you to understand, Olivia. I know it sounds crazy."

"But…" Olivia sighed. "What if you are good at it? But you never try…to make anything from it…"

"That's the gamble. I can either not show them to anyone, assume I'm a genius, and never be proved wrong. Or I can show them to someone and they'll tell me how bad they are. Personally, I'd rather live in my dream world."

"You're forgetting the third option, where you show them to someone and they agree you're a genius."

"That's not going to happen, Olivia." Emily laughed lightly.

"But—"

"This paperwork," Emily interrupted. "You want bank statements and loan agreements, right?"

Even Olivia could tell that the conversation had moved on.

"Yes, although I might as well take the whole box. It looks as if it could do with some organising."

When the door slammed, they both jumped and spun around. Henry stood there with red cheeks, fury in his eyes.

"I'm not going, Mommy!"

"Henry, I'm sorry, but—"

"Olivia." He ran across the room, grabbed at her legs, and hid behind her. "Don't let them take me."

Olivia looked at Emily helplessly. "What's going on?"

Emily let out a deep sigh and opened her mouth to explain. Then Lucy opened the bedroom door and entered breathlessly.

"I'm sorry. We were playing, and he asked outright when he'd have to see them again. I didn't want to lie…"

"Olivia, can I come and live with you?"

Olivia looked down at his pleading face and then to Emily.

"Henry's staying overnight at his grandparents'," Emily explained.

"But I thought—"

"They want to take him to the zoo first thing tomorrow. It's easier logistically if he sleeps there," Emily explained briefly, her eyes begging for help.

Olivia turned around and looked at him. "Henry, I'm sorry…"

His lip began to tremble, and a little fist smacked painlessly at her thigh.

Lucy crossed the room and picked him up. "We don't hit people, do we?"

Tears streamed down Henry's face, and he attempted to turn away from Lucy.

"I'll take him," Emily said, stepping forward.

"It's fine. I'll give you two time to finish up. This stuff's important, Em."

Lucy left the room and closed the door behind her. Henry's building screams echoed down the hallway as she walked down the stairs with him.

Emily let out a sob and sat on the edge of the bed. She covered her mouth and shook her head. "Oh, God, what must you think of me?"

"I must admit, I'm confused," Olivia said.

Emily bit her lip and regarded Olivia for a moment before taking the plunge. "You remember we spoke about Henry's dad?"

Olivia thought for a moment before nodding for Emily to continue.

"Well, his parents are back in the picture."

"Yes, you mentioned Henry had been with his grandparents. Are these the same people who wanted to take Henry from you when he was a baby?" Olivia was aghast.

"Yes, they…" Emily let out a deep sigh "Look, I wasn't going to talk about all of this—"

"You can talk to me."

Emily looked around the bedroom silently for a moment. "The last thing I wanted to do was tell you how my debts are causing even more problems."

"What do you mean?" Olivia tilted her head inquisitively.

"They hired a private investigator to look into my life. They found out about the debts and the layoff. They said they knew of a job for me, and obviously I couldn't say no."

Olivia was appalled. "They hired a private investigator?"

"Yeah, and now they're using it as leverage to spend time with Henry."

"That's…" Olivia paused, shocked. "That's despicable."

"Yes. And there's not a thing I can do about it." Another sob escaped Emily, and Olivia sat beside her. Uncertain of the protocol, she placed a hand carefully on Emily's thigh and patted softly.

"Crown had suspended me. After the crash, they were in financial trouble. Seb, Henry's grandfather, said he knew someone who could offer me a job. I couldn't say no. I had no choice, Olivia. None. But now they're making more and more demands on Henry's time and Henry hates them. They aren't horrible to him, but he knows something isn't right."

"If staying overnight causes him to react like that, then they should let him stay home."

"It's not the first time he's reacted this way." She chuckled bitterly. "They still take him. He was there just two nights ago. They keep coming up with excuses to have him."

The doorbell sounded, and Emily jumped to her feet. "They're early."

Olivia stood and watched helplessly as Emily attempted to dry her eyes. A loud scream from Henry filled the house.

"They must see that he doesn't want to go?" Olivia asked.

Emily dabbed at her eyes with a tissue and looked at her reflection in a mirror on the chest of drawers.

"Well, apparently, they don't believe in pandering to children."

Henry screamed again, and Emily met her eyes in the mirror. Olivia felt a wave of fury rush over her.

CHAPTER TWENTY-ONE

Emily hurriedly followed Olivia down the stairs. She was surprised at the speed someone with a broken leg could move at, but it seemed Olivia was on a mission.

Seb and Irene stood in the hallway looking very displeased with Henry's screaming, which echoed from the living room. Seb noticed Olivia first; he looked at her curiously but remained silent. Emily stopped on the second to last stair and watched the scene unfold before her.

Tom stood in the doorway to the living room. "Lucy's just getting Henry ready," he explained to Seb.

Seb looked at his watch. "Good. We don't want this ridiculous behaviour to cut into too much of our limited time with him."

Henry appeared in the hallway and edged past Tom, trying to avoid Lucy, who was chasing after him. Tiny was clutched tightly to his chest.

"No, we won't go. Tiny doesn't want to go!" Henry shouted.

"Henry," Lucy said. "We spoke about this before and you said—"

"We won't go!" Henry repeated.

"Hey," Emily cut in loudly. She looked at Henry in astonishment. Her sweet little boy had vanished before her eyes. "Henry, don't talk to Lucy like that."

Henry pouted and sealed his mouth firmly shut. The effort seemed to be immense, and his breath came in short, loud pants. His cheeks flared red, and tears fell from his eyes.

"Is there a problem?" Seb asked irritably.

"Tiny doesn't want to go with you," Henry said loudly.

Seb drew himself up to his full height and looked down at Henry. "Well, then Tiny should stay here?"

"No!" Henry screamed, clutching Tiny to his chest.

Seb made a move to grab at the toy, but Lucy put her hand on his arm to prevent him. "I don't think that's helping the matter," she said carefully.

"And what do you know about it?" Seb scoffed.

"Clearly more than you," Lucy said firmly.

"Seb, you're upsetting Henry," Irene said.

"We agreed on a date and a time," Seb began, raising his voice.

"Seb," Irene warned him.

It was too much. Emily couldn't stand to see Henry so distraught. She had to speak up.

"I'm not letting him go when he's like this."

"Nonsense. We all need to do things we don't want to do. It'll build character," Seb argued. "He'll come with us and realise it's not that bad. If you constantly cave in to him, then he'll learn that this behaviour works."

"Mommy, I don't wanna go," Henry whimpered.

"He clearly doesn't want to go." Olivia stepped in. "Maybe you should reschedule?"

"I'm sorry, who are you?" Seb asked.

"Friend of the family," Olivia explained blithely. "And you are?"

"Sebastian Brennan, Henry's grandfather. And my wife, Irene." He gestured behind him carelessly.

"And as his grandfather, are you not in the least alarmed by the fact Henry is clearly distraught?"

Emily looked on, speechless. She didn't know what to say. While she was rooting for Olivia, she was also fearful of reprisals from Seb.

"He'll be fine when he gets in the car," Seb said.

"I don't think so," Olivia replied. "I think it's abundantly clear that he doesn't want to go, and, as his grandparents, I would have thought you'd respect that."

"Now, just a minute, you—" Seb surged towards her.

"Seb." Irene grabbed his arm in an attempt to calm him.

"Maybe Henry's not fond of you because of that temper?" Olivia pressed on as if nothing had happened.

Henry chose that moment to make his move, with the obvious intention of attempting to flee up the stairs. Seb grabbed Henry's arm and yanked him towards him. Emily gasped, feeling her heart sink. She moved forward but stopped as Olivia raised her crutch straight out in front of her, the end landing on Seb's throat. She pushed him back to the wall and pinned him there.

"Let him go." Olivia's voice was calm, but deadly serious.

Emily stared, shocked at Olivia's quick reaction and composed tone. Olivia had moved immediately while Emily froze in fear and shock. Her feelings were a jumbled mess of relief that Olivia was standing up to the man, and fear for exactly the same reason. She'd never be brave enough to stand up to Seb, and Olivia's protectiveness of Henry was exhilarating. At the same time, the situation was becoming more and more fraught by the second, and Henry was stuck in the middle.

Emily looked across to see Lucy and Tom standing in the doorway, shock written all over their faces.

Seb let go of Henry's arm, and he ran behind Olivia and held on to her skirt, peeking around to look at Seb with trepidation.

"Apologise," Olivia said.

Seb looked furious. Irene edged closer to him, regarding Olivia as if she were deranged. Olivia pressed the crutch forward slightly and applied a small amount of pressure, creating a red circle on his flesh.

"I'm sorry!" Seb shouted.

"To Henry," Olivia clarified.

"I'm sorry, Henry." Seb looked down at him and faked a smile.

Olivia lowered her crutch and glared at Seb, disdain written all over her face.

"Mommy, I don't want to go," Henry whimpered, still holding Olivia's skirt.

"He's staying here," Emily stated firmly.

Seb stared at her silently for a few seconds before looking to Olivia. "This isn't over."

"I think you should leave," Olivia said. She used her crutch to indicate the door.

"You're insane," Seb said. His hand rose protectively to his throat as he edged past her. "She's insane," he repeated to Emily.

Irene opened the door and pulled Seb through it towards safety. Emily rushed down the last step, picked Henry up, and held him tightly.

She looked out the front door, where Irene was rushing towards the car and Seb was taking a photograph of Olivia's car on his phone.

"I'm staying?" Henry asked uncertainly. He craned his neck around to watch them leave while gripping Emily's shoulders tightly.

"You're staying," Emily reassured him. "But you might have to go in the future." She didn't want Henry to go, but she knew she had to prepare him for the eventuality that he might have to. As much as she wanted to protect Henry and stop him from ever having to see his grandparents again, she knew she was cornered. Pressing Seb too far could result in outright war, and she wasn't sure she could win that battle. She squeezed Henry tighter, hating how he was being forced into the middle and knowing that there was nothing she could do about it.

Henry nodded in understanding. "But not tonight?"

"Not tonight." Emily pressed a kiss to his hair.

Tom closed the front door and looked from Emily to Olivia. He held out his hands for Henry. "Come on, champ. I bet I can draw more airplanes than you can draw giraffes."

"Nuh-uh," Henry said, happily falling into Tom's arms.

"Not for long though. It'll be an early night for you now," Emily said as she smoothed Henry's hair. She knew that, after all the stress, Henry would soon be exhausted.

Tom carried Henry into the living room, and Emily turned to face Olivia, who was looking nervous.

"I apologise, I shouldn't have…interfered," Olivia started.

"It was the right thing to do." Lucy put her hand on Olivia's shoulder and gave her a reassuring squeeze.

"Lucy's right," Emily said. "When he grabbed Henry, I just froze."

"That man shouldn't be allowed near children." Olivia shook her head.

"What do you think he'll do now?" Lucy asked.

Emily blew out a long sigh. "I have no idea. He won't give up that easily though."

"Um, sorry to interrupt." Tom appeared in the doorway. "Henry's requesting that Olivia put him to bed tonight."

Tom looked questioningly at Olivia, who in turn looked to Emily.

"Are you okay to do that? I feel as if you've already done so much," Emily said.

"I'd do anything for Henry," Olivia said without hesitation.

Emily felt her heart soar. She knew Olivia was being completely honest; she could never be anything else. The knowledge that someone loved Henry as much as she did and would do anything to protect him was intoxicating. Olivia's openness was another breath of fresh air; there were no games, no pretence. Just a mutual desire to do the best for Henry.

She realised Olivia was still awaiting her response. She smiled as she nodded in gratitude.

❖

Olivia hesitantly opened the bedroom door and smiled at Henry. She'd been offered a cup of coffee while Emily got Henry ready for bed, and had sat in the kitchen making small talk with Tom and Lucy while Henry and Emily thumped around in the bathroom.

Now Henry sat in bed with his back against the headboard in giraffe-styled pyjamas, his damp hair smoothed back and a wide smile on his face. He patted the bed beside him.

"Come here, Olivia," he ordered gently.

Olivia placed her crutch by the side of the bed and then shuffled herself onto the bed. Henry was under the covers, but Olivia didn't feel comfortable in joining him, her memory reminding her that this was also Emily's bed. It somehow felt like an invasion of privacy to sit under the covers.

As much as Olivia longed to be what Emily wanted her to be, needed her to be, she was finding it hard to think of her simply as a friend. The visit to the park and then the wonderful family dinner had given Olivia an insight into a life she had never really considered being achievable for her. Now that she'd had a taste, she wanted more. But she didn't want to put Emily in an impossible position.

Emily had made it clear that Olivia's presence was to soothe Henry. She had to keep reminding herself of that fact and try to keep her feelings for Emily locked away.

"Splat and Ogg Go to Space." Henry picked up a book from the bedside table and handed it to Olivia.

Olivia looked at the brightly coloured book and let out a small sigh. "Don't you have any classics?"

Henry frowned.

She shook her head. "Never mind, of course you don't. Splat and…" She looked at the book. "Ogg…it is."

"Have you ever been to space?" Henry asked. He took the book from her and opened up to the first page.

"No. Have you?"

"Don't be silly, I'm only five."

Olivia smiled and bit the inside of her mouth to prevent a retort from falling out. She'd missed Henry's odd conversations.

"Read," Henry instructed her, tapping his fingers on the words.

"Why don't you read to me?"

Henry looked up at her with a confused expression. "That's not how it works."

"Oh, I see. You can't read," Olivia baited him gently.

"I can." Henry puffed out his chest and easily read the first line of text. He looked up at her with a smug expression.

"That's very good," Olivia acknowledged. "How about I read a page and then you read a page?"

Henry shrugged, seemingly not understanding Olivia's logic, but not minding enough to protest the idea. He started to read, and Olivia tried to follow the words. Within moments, her mind had wandered and reminded her that this would not be a frequent event. She had burnt her bridges with Emily and she was simply invited over as a friend. At this point she was more a friend to Henry than she was to Emily. She needed to remember that fact.

"Now you," Henry said as he turned the page.

Olivia smiled, leaned down, and nuzzled her cheek against the top of his head as she started to read.

❖

"Well, this has been one of the more interesting dinner parties I've hosted," Lucy said. She walked over to the sink and turned on the tap to fill the bowl.

"I think I'm still in shock." Emily folded her arms and leaned against the counter. She couldn't help wondering what Seb's next move would be.

"Olivia's badass." Lucy chuckled.

Despite her nerves, Emily laughed too. "Yeah, I suppose she is. Never would have thought it when I first met her."

"Seeing Henry upset obviously gave her a reason to be. You can see how much she cares about him." She squeezed some detergent into the bowl and stared at the water as it started to bubble.

"Luce..." Emily warned her softly.

"I'm just pointing out what I see. She's hot, devoted to your son, and clearly has feelings for you."

"I know, I know."

"Then why are you keeping your distance? So, she's a little...I don't know, socially awkward, and you had a misunderstanding a few weeks back." Lucy shrugged, turned off the tap, and handed a brush to Emily before indicating the soaking plates. She picked up a towel and started to dry a batch of previously washed dishes.

"It's not just that," Emily said, plunging her hands into the soapy water. "I wouldn't not be with someone because of that."

"Has she..." Lucy paused as she looked towards the door, to check they were alone. "Has she ever considered getting diagnosed?"

Emily licked her lips nervously. She didn't want to have such a sensitive conversation behind Olivia's back, but she needed someone else's perspective on the subject.

"She acknowledges that she sees things differently than other people," Emily said. "So, I think she knows that there is a diagnosis to be had. But she thinks of it as a label, a badge. And she doesn't want that."

Lucy nodded as she poked the end of the towel into a glass tumbler and dried it. "I can understand that."

"You can?" Emily frowned.

"Yes. I mean, if it was something like, I don't know, heart disease, for example, then you would need a diagnosis to get the correct treatment. Hopefully, you can manage the disease or even be cured. This is different." Lucy crossed the kitchen and placed the glass tumbler on a shelf. "A name for her condition would just be a name. She'd be able to tell other people she had it. But she seems very private, so I don't see that she ever would. She'd also be able to meet up with other people who might share her condition, but again, she's so private."

Emily nodded as she absentmindedly scrubbed a teaspoon.

"In a way," Lucy chuckled, "the diagnosis would be for everyone else, not necessarily for her."

"How so?" Emily asked as Lucy plucked the thoroughly cleaned teaspoon from her soapy hands.

"Well, she knows she has a condition, and she knows how it affects her life. She's also developed some coping mechanisms, be they avoidance, bravado, or that hand thing you mentioned," Lucy explained. "She's just getting on with it. Naming the condition wouldn't necessarily help her. Like Alicia, one of the girls in my childcare group, has Asperger's, and we know that's why she acts the way she does. Where we might have thought she was being a brat or having a tantrum, we know there's more to it, so we can modify our behaviour and expectations of her. Her parents are getting her a tutor because she's easily distracted and they don't want her to fall behind when she starts school."

"But Olivia's past all that." Emily understood with a nod.

"Exactly," Lucy replied. "At thirty…whatever she is…"

"Six," Emily finished distractedly.

"Really?" Lucy said with surprise and made a face to show she was impressed. "Wouldn't have guessed."

Emily laughed. "Can we get back on track here?"

Lucy chuckled. "What I was trying to say is that Olivia's an adult, highly successful, and fully able to live her life. She doesn't necessarily need a name for her condition; she just needs to know how to manage it, and surround herself with people who understand her."

Emily washed the final item of cutlery and nodded. "You're right. I hadn't really thought of it that way. I can see why some people would need answers and want a name for it, want to meet other people, but that's just not Olivia's way. She's, well, she's more a problem solver."

"Exactly." Lucy nodded. "And, like I said, she's head over heels for you and Henry."

Emily blushed, smiling as she flicked a few bubbles in Lucy's direction. "Shush."

Lucy laughed as she wiped the bubbles from her cardigan. "She is, and I, for one, think it's lovely!"

"You think everything's lovely." Emily smiled as she pulled the plug and ran a cloth around the edge of the sink. Lucy pulled the cloth from her and took her face in her hands, forcing Emily to make eye contact.

"Don't run away from happiness, Emily. I really think that you two could be great together. You just…work. I don't know what it is, but I see it in both of you, and I really want you and Henry to be happy. You deserve it."

The sarcastic reply died on Emily's lips. She nodded and tugged Lucy into her arms, holding tight while she fought back the tears welling in her eyes. "You're the best friend anyone could ever have." Emily chuckled and took a step back before letting out a sigh. "But I think I may have wrecked my chances with Olivia."

Lucy shook her head. "I've seen the way she looks at you."

"I feel guilty. I pushed her away, now I've pulled her back in for Henry. And she's going to look at the financial mess I'm in. I've told her that it needs to stay platonic. And I'm worried about Henry. What if something goes wrong again—"

"And, and, and." Lucy chuckled. "You know I believe in fate."

Emily rolled her eyes and laughed. "Not this again."

"Things have a way of working themselves out," Lucy assured her.

"Yes, and I have a way of ruining things."

Lucy started to speak, but stopped when they heard Tom and Olivia coming down the stairs. They shared a look before heading out into the hallway.

Tom was carrying the box of paperwork. "I'll just go and put this in your car."

"Thank you," Olivia told Tom, then turned to Emily. "Henry's asleep. I think the excitement exhausted him. We didn't get far into the ridiculous tales of the two unrecognisable blobs from an alien planet."

Lucy smothered a laugh and Emily smiled. "Thank you for reading to him. I know he appreciates it a lot."

"Can I get you a drink? Another coffee?" Lucy said.

"No, thank you. I should be going." Olivia looked towards the doorway nervously.

Emily caught the odd behaviour and wondered what had happened to cause the change in demeanour.

"It's still early," Emily said, hoping to sway her decision.

"I have a busy day ahead of me tomorrow."

Emily knew something was up but decided to allow Olivia to have her escape. "Okay, well, thank you so much for…well, for everything."

"Thank you." Olivia looked at Lucy. "Dinner was wonderful." She turned away, then turned back as if remembering something. "And you have a lovely home."

"Thank you. We'd love to have you back here again," Lucy said.

Olivia smiled and nodded noncommittally before turning and walking out the open front door. Emily walked her to her car. Olivia said goodnight to Tom as they passed him on his way back, and when they reached the car, she stood nervously.

"I'm sorry…for…" She gestured towards the house.

Emily frowned. "Sorry for the part where you agreed to help me organise my finances? Or the part where you were the perfect dinner guest? The part where you defended Henry from that horrible man? Or where you soothed him to sleep?"

"I—"

Emily leaned forward and placed a soft kiss on Olivia's cheek. "Thank you, really. I can't show my gratitude enough. I'm so happy we reconnected."

Olivia blushed and nodded a few times, seemingly unsure of what to do. She pointed to her car, and Emily stood to one side to allow her access to the vehicle.

When Olivia was seated and ready to go, she opened the window. "I'll…call you…about the paperwork."

"I look forward to it." Emily smiled wryly.

Olivia coughed nervously and then gave a small wave goodbye as she drove away.

CHAPTER TWENTY-TWO

The restaurant was one Seb had never been to before, and never intended to go to again. The mismatched furniture and crockery was supposedly charming. To him, it simply gave an air of disorganisation. Irene smiled as her tea was served in a cup and saucer; a teapot with a different print was placed beside it. He huffed and she gave him that look. The one of silent admonishment. Ten minutes later, well after the agreed time, their guest finally arrived.

Donald Smythe was a tall, unkempt man who always wore the same dark trench coat. It appeared as if he had watched one too many 1940s private eye movies and dived headfirst into the culture without a second thought.

He pulled back a rickety chair and sat at the gingham-covered table, looking completely out of place.

"Well?" Seb asked. He was still angry about what had happened the previous evening with Henry. He wanted answers, and the man in front of him was hopefully going to deliver them.

Donald looked up with a smug grin. "All in good time." He tutted before waving down a waitress and ordering himself drinks and a sandwich.

Despite paying the man very well for his services, Seb always seemed to end up footing the bill for his meals as well. Not that he could complain; hiring a private detective was a shady business, and the last thing he wanted was to be on the wrong side of one. Especially the dishevelled and arrogant one in front of him.

"Mrs. Brennan," Donald said with a smirk.

"Mr. Smythe," Irene replied softly, focusing on her tea. Of course, she had no desire to be there; she'd made that perfectly clear earlier. It was only after Seb had complained bitterly at the prospect of going alone that she had finally agreed to come along.

A waitress placed a mug of coffee and a glass of juice in front of Donald before quickly making her exit.

Donald leaned forward and theatrically sniffed the coffee before taking a loud slurp and letting out a satisfied sigh. He lowered the mug back down to the table, reached into his pocket, and placed his notepad on the wrinkled tablecloth. He leafed through the pages, deliberately slowly, and Seb let out a sigh at the continued delay.

He cursed the day he'd instructed Donald to investigate Emily. Just four weeks into working with the man, and he already loathed the cloak-and-dagger in-person meetups. Of course, he'd used private detectives before for corporate reasons, but this was different. He needed someone with less scruples. Someone who was happy to do what needed to be done with no questions asked. Donald was that man, but he was also melodramatic in a way that made Seb want to overturn the table and grab him by the throat.

From the first time they spoke, Seb knew that Donald had the potential to be problematic. But his lack of moral integrity also made him perfect for the job at hand. Seb would suffer Donald's quirks and delays as long as he continued to produce results. The second Donald stopped being of use, Seb would cut him loose. Of course, he had a contingency plan in case Donald became troublesome. It was essential to have blackmail material at the ready when dealing with lowlifes like Donald.

"The car," Donald said, "is registered to an Olivia Lewis."

"What?" Seb asked, shocked. "Olivia Lewis, are you sure?"

Donald looked intrigued by Seb's reaction. "Absolutely. I pride myself on giving correct information. The car in the photograph is registered to Olivia Lewis." He reached into his pocket, pulled out a folded piece of paper, unfolded it, and slid it across the table.

Seb looked at the photocopy of Olivia's driver's license and let out a sigh. "That's her."

"You know her?" Irene asked.

"She owns Applewood Financial, Marcus's old company."

"Will you be pressing charges for assault?" Donald asked.

The waitress returned with a sandwich stuffed with everything the kitchen had to offer, presumably the most expensive thing on the menu. Seb looked at the sandwich and shook his head in disgust. But Donald had provided some information that was worthwhile, so Seb decided to allow him to eat in peace.

"No." Seb shook his head. The last thing he wanted was to go to court for being harassed by a woman with a broken leg. He'd never hear the end of it from the other club members.

"Could be a lot of money there," Donald said. He lifted the sandwich and took an enormous bite, most of the filling falling to the plate.

"Why would she be at Emily's home?" Irene asked.

Seb stared at the photocopied credentials. Things were starting to come together. Surely, the only thing that connected the two women was Marcus. Marcus had effectively destroyed Olivia's life, so why would she now be at Emily's house? Of course someone like Olivia wouldn't be socialising with someone of Emily's class. And that led to one obvious conclusion: she was using Emily to get information. If Olivia wasn't such an unbalanced bitch, he would have shaken her hand. It was inspired. "She's using Emily to get information on Marcus's new venture," he said.

"That seems very underhanded," Irene stated.

"She threatened me. You saw it with your own eyes, woman. She's not a very nice person," Seb bit out.

"Emily was a flight attendant with Crown," Donald said, already two-thirds of the way through his sandwich. "And Olivia used to frequently fly with them. It's not a stretch to assume they met there." He took another enormous bite, demolishing the meal.

"Yes, yes," Seb mused. "I can see it now. Olivia goes to see Marcus—Marcus told me about her turning up there, practically begging, he said. She probably bumped into Emily, recognised her from Crown. Decided to make friends and see what she could find out. Or, maybe she knows of Emily's debts and is paying Emily for information. Hell, I wouldn't put it past her to blackmail Emily. We know how violent and unhinged she is."

Seb leaned back and licked his lips as he considered the situation. "Oh, this is very good for us." He turned to Irene, who was frowning in confusion.

"How so? Should we tell Marcus? Surely this could be damaging to him?" Irene asked.

"Not yet." Seb smirked. "This is further leverage for us."

Irene looked up. "Donald, thank you for bringing us this information. Could Seb and I speak privately?"

Donald nodded. "Absolutely. I'll send you my invoice. Let me know what you want me to do next." He stood up and downed the tall glass of juice in a few short gulps. He looked at the empty plate and then at Seb. "Would you mind? I'll get the next one."

Seb nodded and waved the man away. As soon as he was gone, he turned back to Irene.

"We have to think practically about this. Emily has denied us the opportunity to see Henry, and now that she's done it once, she's bound to do it again. We have no legal right to see him. She could choose to take him away from us."

"I think we should simply talk to her again. She's a reasonable young woman. I'm sure if we could all just talk—"

"No. This isn't the time for talking; it's the time for action." He smacked his palm on the table. Irene startled in her seat and the waitress's eyes darted in their direction. Seb lowered his head a little, and his voice. "At the moment we are in a good position. We know that she is in financial trouble and suspect she is feeding information to Olivia Lewis, a direct competitor to her employer. Both of those things will damage her in court."

"Seb—"

"Think about it. What if she's being paid off by Olivia? What if we try to talk to her and she strings us along for a few weeks while she gets a nice payout? A few weeks down the line and she's no longer in debt, her living situation has improved, and she's no longer in contact with Olivia. We wouldn't have a case."

Irene absentmindedly stirred her tea, a pensive look on her face.

"We want what's best for Henry," Seb said. "You've seen that house. You know the debt she's in. She can't look after him. And now that she's hanging out with violent people? People who are probably paying her to spy? I think you can safely call that a criminal. Our grandson is in a house with criminals."

Irene swallowed and slowly nodded. "Okay. We should speak with our lawyer and see what he says."

CHAPTER TWENTY-THREE

Olivia carelessly tossed her phone onto her desk and sighed. "We've lost Greg."

Simon nodded grimly and stood, picking up a marker from the table. He stood by one of the five large whiteboards that had been set up in Olivia's New York office and swiped a line through Greg's name.

Olivia gently rubbed her eyes, not giving a damn about her mascara. She'd stopped caring what she looked like in the office days ago. The speed at which the crisis was growing and her company dissolving had put such things into stark perspective.

She stared at the whiteboards and let out a sigh. Olivia was gifted with the ability to see the bigger picture clearly in her mind's eye. But she knew that was a trait the few loyal employees she had left didn't possess. So she had put the whiteboards up as a visual demonstration of their wins and losses. Clients were listed from most to least profitable, lines through the losses and green circles around the secured.

It helped morale when she circled a retained client, but having the whiteboards directly in her line of vision all day, every day, had only reinforced how much she'd lost. It wasn't just clients; it was the people. The relationships she'd built up over years of working together had been torn down in just a few short days.

Those clients that hadn't left over pricing had left because of relationships they had forged with Olivia's ex-employees. She'd lost count of the number of clients who had apologetically said they were leaving because their Applewood account manager had left. She didn't understand the breaking down of business relationships. She had shaken hands with these people. Dined with them. Suddenly they were leaving in droves and she felt helpless to do anything about it.

Olivia had a few choice names for Marcus, but even she had to begrudgingly admit that his strategy had been inspired. Pursuing key team members and offering them exclusive packages had enabled him to set up a dream team without any work. The staff and the low pricing had enabled him to do what she would have said was impossible.

Simon smothered a yawn as he stared at the whiteboard. He looked exhausted. Olivia felt guilty about the amount of work she was forcing on him. Not to mention the fact that she was keeping him away from his friends, family, and girlfriend. But Simon never complained. He'd been everything Olivia needed and more. She made a mental note to thank him with an appropriately large gesture, if and when the worst of the situation ever passed.

A phone outside Olivia's office started to ring, and Simon headed out to answer it. Olivia stared at the whiteboard, hoping for a solution to somehow make itself seen in the mess.

Her desk phone bleeped, and she picked up the receiver. "Yes?"

"It's Emily. She says it's urgent." Simon transferred the call without a pause.

"Emily?"

"Oh, thank God, I didn't know who else to turn to. I know you're busy—"

"What happened?" Olivia stood up. The tone of Emily's voice made the notion of sitting down impossible.

"They want Henry. I've just been served with legal papers. They want custody of Henry!"

"Who?" Olivia asked in a confused state of shock.

"His grandparents," Emily explained.

"That's preposterous." Olivia started to pace, only to find the cord tethering her back to the desk. Anger bubbled up inside her at hearing Emily so distraught.

"They're taking me to court. What am I going to do? I can't afford a lawyer. And Henry's living conditions are less than ideal. I mean, he's sharing a bed with his mother. In a house where I have no lease—"

Olivia quickly analysed the situation. She couldn't stand to hear Emily's distress. Something needed to be done immediately. Emily was hurting, and Olivia had to fix it. She couldn't—wouldn't—stand idly by. She beckoned to Simon through the glass partition wall and he hurriedly entered her office.

"Emily, I promise they will not take Henry. There may not be much I can fix right now, but this I can. Simon is going to come and get you, and then we are all going to see a friend of mine. She's one of the best family lawyers in the city, and together we will find a way through this, okay?"

Emily sniffed through obvious tears and Olivia clenched her fist in anguish. She wanted to be there to offer her support. Being on the other end of the phone was maddening.

"I'm sorry. I know you have so much going on right now."

"Nonsense. This is far more pressing. And, unlike the mess I'm in, I can do something about this. Simon will be there within the hour." She nodded at Simon as he grabbed his coat off the rack and headed out of the office.

❖

As soon as Simon's car came to a stop, Emily appeared. She closed the front door behind her, her coat half on, her bag in her hand. Under her arm were a number of documents.

He quickly got out of the car and approached her, taking the bag and papers to give Emily time to put her coat on properly.

"Thank you so much." Her face was red and tear-stained.

"No problem." He gestured towards the car.

Emily got in the passenger's side, while Simon put the paperwork and her bag in the back seat before climbing in again. She started to struggle with the seat belt, so Simon calmly reached out, took it from her, and fixed it in place.

"I'm so sorry. I'm a complete mess," she said.

"Don't worry." Simon placed a comforting hand on her knee. "I can't imagine what you're going through, but we're here for you. Olivia will sort this out."

Emily took a couple of deep breaths and nodded. "Thank you, Simon."

He smiled, started the car, and pulled into the road. "So, was it completely out of the blue?"

"Yes, well, sort of. There was the incident about a week ago, but I didn't think they'd respond like this."

"What happened?"

"Didn't Olivia tell you?"

"No. She's not exactly forthright with these things. Or any things, really."

Emily nodded. "That's true. Well, they were due to take Henry for the night, and, well, Henry didn't want to go. He had a huge tantrum. He's been talking through Tiny a lot lately, and Seb, his grandfather, threatened to take Tiny away—"

"Prick," Simon mumbled.

"Exactly," Emily said. "Needless to say, Henry didn't take kindly to the idea and it just made matters worse. Olivia stood up to him, threatened him with her crutch, and made him leave."

Simon looked at her in shock for a moment before returning his attention to the road. Olivia certainly never mentioned that to him. Of course, he knew why. He'd have given her the look. The one that told her in no uncertain terms that he knew what was going on in her mind, that he could see how deeply she cared for both Henry and Emily, even though she tried to pretend she was unaffected.

Olivia may have been under stress lately, but threatening behaviour was never something Simon would have expected from her. She'd always been calm and measured, never so much as raising her voice, never mind her hand—or in this case, crutch.

Emily's tone suggested that she wasn't entirely unhappy with the developments either. He didn't want to push her considering her current fragile emotional state, but it sounded as if both of them were hopefully, finally realising that they could be good together.

"And then you got the notice?" he clarified.

"Yep."

"Sounds as if they've been waiting for the right moment," Simon said.

"They had me over a barrel either way. If I didn't cooperate at first, they would've done it all the sooner. This must've been their plan all along."

"But they've never been a part of Henry's life, have they?"

"No. But the court won't see it like that. They'll see my situation and that will be it. Olivia said she knows a family lawyer?" Emily asked anxiously.

"Yes, Christine Doherty. She's fantastic."

"Fantastically expensive?"

"She'll see you for free as a favour to Olivia to examine your case," Simon explained. "Don't worry. Olivia won't let anything happen to Henry."

Simon knew that to be an absolute fact. Olivia was extremely protective of Henry, and it was clear she cared for him deeply, even loved him. Simon had never seen Olivia interact with a child before; Olivia had always been the kind of woman who hesitated around children, backed away from them, even. Henry was different, and Simon knew that Olivia would move heaven and earth for him.

"This is my fault. What kind of mother can't provide a suitable environment for her child?"

"Hey," Simon said sharply. "You are a great mother. That is absolutely not in question. Don't let some idiots make you question that. Henry is a happy, healthy, and great kid. And you've been an amazing mum."

Emily pulled a tissue from her coat pocket and wiped away fresh tears. "Thank you, Simon. I really needed to hear that. I just feel so useless at the moment. I can't imagine Henry not being in my life."

"It won't happen," Simon said with certainty. "It can't."

❖

The lawyer's office just screamed money. In a tasteful and understated way, of course. But still…wood-panelled walls, plush carpets, and antique desks made Emily even more uncomfortably aware that she could not afford to be here if not for Olivia.

Emily sat on the very edge of the visitor's chair in front of Christine Doherty's enormous solid mahogany desk. She did this partially because it was an edge-of-the-seat kind of day, and partially because she felt terrified to touch anything in the room.

Olivia sat in the chair beside her. She looked comfortable and at home in the surroundings as she scrolled through messages on her smartphone. Christine had pleasantly greeted them, then taken all of the documents Emily had provided, and was now proceeding to slowly, silently read through every detail. Every single one.

The calm was stifling. Emily was so tense that she wanted to pace the room. She wanted to scream and shout—anything to make her feel as if she was doing something productive. But instead, she sat noiselessly, watching two important women calmly reading while desperately trying not to picture what life could be like without Henry.

"Well," Christine finally said. She turned over the last piece of paper and placed all of the papers back into the file they had arrived in. She took off her reading glasses, put them in their case, and clipped it closed. The snap reverberated off the walls and made Emily jump. "I'm afraid it's not good, Miss White. On the bright side, they are simply attempting to threaten you and the chance of a judge granting custody to them is very slim. However, they have a strong case to request to be a part of Henry's life. And the fact they have tried to establish a relationship will sit well with a judge."

"That's ludicrous," Olivia spoke up. "They are trying to use their wealth to intimidate her. They're not fit to spend time with Henry."

Christine looked at Olivia with a neutral expression. "Not particularly relevant to the court. They are a blood relative."

"I don't want them seeing Henry. Especially now that I know they are lying to me. Clearly, they want him for themselves," Emily said.

"They are being deceitful, but it's tricky to prove. And even then, there's a chance that the judge will still feel they should be allowed visitation rights." Christine turned her full attention to Emily. Her expression softened marginally. "While your situation isn't ideal, you clearly aren't a danger to your son. The possibility of them taking Henry from you is very small. Visitation is highly likely, but I can understand given the circumstances why you would not want that. I'm sure we can find a middle ground you would be happy with. I would be willing to provide you with our services for free, as a favour to Olivia."

"I—" Emily started.

"She'd love to," Olivia cut in.

Emily glared at Olivia, but quickly relaxed and nodded.

"Very well." Christine placed her hand on the file. "I'll keep hold of this and assign your case to my colleague. He'll be able to give this his full attention and be in touch with you in the next few days."

Emily wordlessly nodded. She didn't miss the inference that it would be a colleague dealing with the case—someone more junior, no doubt. And he'd be in touch in a few days. It all seemed to be moving at such a slow pace, but then, Emily didn't really know what she had expected.

Her life was falling down around her, and her instinct was to rush around doing as much as possible; to fight, to be loud and defensive. But the lawyer's office, a place that clearly dealt with these sort of cases frequently, was the absolute opposite. Files were meticulously read, often in silence, notes were made with fountain pens, meetings were set up days in advance. The difference between desire and reality was exasperating.

"Emily?"

She looked up to see that Olivia was looking at her with concern.

"I'm sorry. I zoned out for a moment there." She looked at Christine, who was also looking at her. "I'm sorry."

"Quite all right," Christine assured her. "I know this has been a shock, and I can't imagine how you must be feeling. I promise you that we will do everything in our power."

Emily nodded and stood to leave. She shook Christine's hand and thanked her again before following Olivia out of the room.

"Olivia, I can't thank you enough."

"You don't need to thank me," Olivia stated firmly. "I am going to do everything I can to make this go away."

"That isn't why I called you, you know. I don't expect you to fix this. It's my mess."

"I hope you called me…because I'm your friend," Olivia said.

"I did," Emily said. "I didn't know who else to turn to. But I know you have your own disaster happening right now. I don't want to take your attention away from that."

Olivia opened the door and gestured for Emily to lead them outside. "I could do with some distraction. Especially distraction that reminds me of the priorities in life. Now, let's get you home."

CHAPTER TWENTY-FOUR

Seb Brennan sidestepped a secretary and walked into Marcus's office with a determined stride. Marcus lowered his pen and looked up.

"Seb, good to see you." He stood up and they shook hands cordially.

"Marcus, sorry to come by unannounced, but I've something to tell you and I'm afraid it can't wait."

Marcus gestured to the visitor chair in front of his desk. "Sounds serious."

"It is," Seb acknowledged. "Irene and I have filed for custody of our grandson."

"Ah." Marcus tried to sound interested, but it was obvious to Seb's ears that the latest legal battle of Sebastian Brennan held little interest for him.

"I'm afraid this involves you as well." Seb took a letter out of his jacket pocket and passed it to Marcus.

Marcus opened the letter and quickly read through the contents. He frowned in confusion. "This is a letter from Emily's lawyer?"

"Yes."

"I'm not sure what this has to do with me?"

"It's from Heathcote, Lambert, and Doherty."

Marcus looked at the letterhead, then questioningly at Seb again, still not grasping the significance.

"Emily's broke. There is no way she can afford that firm. I'm sorry to tell you that I suspect that she is being paid off by Olivia."

Marcus balked. "Olivia?"

"We recently went to see Emily, to pick Henry up for a prearranged visit with us. Time which Emily later reneged on, I hasten to add. Anyway, there was a woman there, she had a crutch, and something about her struck me as odd. It wasn't until later that I remembered you'd said that Olivia broke her leg in the crash, and then it all came together."

Marcus stood up and closed the office door. He slowly walked around the room. "So, Olivia was at Emily's house?"

"Yes," Seb confirmed solemnly.

"And you think what? That Olivia is paying Emily's legal fees?"

"There's no way she could afford that firm without some kind of financial assistance."

"Why do you think Olivia would do that?" Marcus sought clarity, like Seb had known he would.

"I think it's obvious. After your successful coup, she wants, no, needs, a mole on the inside. She's getting insider information, and Emily is clearly getting paid handsomely for it."

Marcus turned and looked out the window. Seb watched him with satisfaction. Sometimes manipulating people was all too easy. The letter had been a surprise, a wrench in the works of his otherwise perfect plan to gain custody of Henry. It was obvious that some kind of deal had been brokered between the two women. Emily had to be receiving financial assistance from somewhere. If she wanted to play that game, fine. Seb had been gracious enough to find her employment, but if she was so content to bite the hand that feeds, he'd take it away from her again.

"Do you have evidence that Olivia is paying Emily to spy?" Marcus asked.

"Well, no hard evidence, but it's the only reasonable explanation."

"Emily worked at Crown. Olivia flew Crown frequently. They could have met there; it doesn't mean that anything untoward is happening here."

"I think you're being a fool," Seb said flippantly. Why Marcus was making this more difficult than it needed to be was beyond him. It was obvious what was going on, and Seb had graciously spelled it out for him. What more did he want?

"And I think you are trying to bend me to your will. Again." Marcus turned around and folded his arms as he looked at Seb. "You wanted me to hire the girl and, as a favour to you, I did. Now, you presumably want me to fire her to strengthen your court case against her. I won't do it. I have no proof, and her work has been exemplary. I have no case to fire her, and I won't get embroiled in this."

Seb stood up, regarding Marcus with a cold stare. "Just remember when all of this comes crashing down that I was the one who tried to warn you."

"I think it's time you left," Marcus replied.

Seb stared at Marcus coldly for a few moments before he turned and slammed the door behind him. He stalked through the corridors, seething with anger at Marcus's betrayal. At this point, he hoped Emily was selling secrets to Olivia. He'd love to watch the company burn.

He'd always considered Marcus to be intelligent and pragmatic, but clearly that wasn't the case. And Seb had no time for people who didn't live up to his expectations. He wasn't going to waste another second of his time siding with or aiding Marcus in his foolish new venture.

There had always been the possibility that Marcus wouldn't be able to see reason, so Seb had a contingency plan worked out. He turned to the executive offices, sought out a particular name, and smirked when he found it.

"Michael," Seb said with a smile as he walked into the room.

Michael Underwood removed his glasses and stood up, smiling warmly. "Good to see you, Seb. What brings you here?"

They shook hands. "Oh, you know, Marcus needed some guidance. You know how the youngsters are." Seb knew Michael had invested badly a few years back and couldn't afford to retire. It would be easy to appear as an ally to the older man, using a shared distaste of the younger generation and their new technologies and buzzwords.

Michael chuckled. "Yes, unfortunately, I do. I'm surrounded by them."

"You're a better man than I. How about I buy you lunch? We can swap war stories and remember how businesses should really be run."

Michael's eyes lit up at the prospect of a free boozy lunch. "Sounds like a great idea."

Seb smiled, already planning his next move. He may not have Marcus's help, but that didn't mean he wouldn't get exactly what he wanted.

CHAPTER TWENTY-FIVE

The very moment Simon, Emily, and Henry entered the restaurant, Henry's eyes settled on the children's play area. His head snapped up quickly as he looked at Emily with pleading eyes.

Emily chuckled and nodded. "Go and play for a while. I'll call you when the food arrives."

Henry smiled happily and dashed across the room towards the climbing apparatus.

A waitress greeted them, offered a booth near the play area, and handed them both menus before taking drink orders.

"Thank you so much for this," Emily said as soon as the waitress left. She covered Simon's hand with her own and gave it a grateful squeeze.

"I thought it would be good to catch up." Simon smiled.

"Definitely. And to get out of the house."

Simon looked towards Henry, who was happily using a slide before running around to the stairs to repeat the process. He'd been quiet during the car journey to the restaurant, but the play area had given him a much-needed boost.

It'd been four days since Emily had received the court notice and Simon had driven her to the lawyer's office. He'd sat in the waiting room while Emily and Olivia spoke with Christine, and afterwards he'd driven Emily and Olivia home. Simon had promised to make some time in his schedule for the two of them to catch up, and it was only now that he'd managed to keep that promise.

"Have you told Henry anything?"

Emily shook her head. "Not yet. I'm kind of hoping it will all go away. I suppose I'm burying my head in the sand."

"Have you heard from Christine's office?"

"Yes. I had a call from someone to say that the case had been assigned, that they were looking through the details and would be in touch. They've sent a letter back to Henry's grandparents. But that's it. The waiting's killing me."

"I can imagine." Simon lowered his menu to the table. "I'm sorry we had to leave abruptly the other day. Things are bad at Applewood at the moment."

"It's fine. I was just grateful for the help." Emily smiled, but it was forced.

"It'll be okay. I'm sure of it."

Emily lowered her menu and looked over to make sure Henry was out of hearing range.

"I've been doing a lot of research; they have a very strong case against me. There's…" she took a deep breath. "There's a chance that I will lose the case and Henry will be forced to live with them. I can't live in hope that everything will be okay. I need to be practical, and the truth is that the situation is bad."

Emily paused as the waitress returned with their drinks and placed them on the table. She took their lunch order and disappeared again.

"All of the details of my debts will come out. It won't look good, Simon." Emily shook her head and stirred her drink with the straw. "Which reminds me, I need to ask Olivia for the paperwork back. The lawyer said they'd need it at some point."

"She's not had a chance to look at it yet, but I'll remind her," Simon promised.

"She might be wasting her time at this point." Emily put her head in her hands and took a deep breath.

"Look, things aren't all that bleak." Simon tried to sound upbeat, but he knew he was fighting a losing battle. "Henry's fit and healthy, he's clean…well, aside from that mess he calls his nostrils, which is disgusting. Seriously, it's like a tap or something."

Emily snorted a laugh.

"He has clothes on his back, food in his belly. Despite all the financial problems, you still put him first, and he hasn't gone without. You have a job and—"

Emily chuckled and shook her head. "Oh, don't you worry, that job won't be around much longer."

"How come?"

"Henry's grandfather helped me get it. I'm working for one of his golfing buddies. I'm just waiting to be fired. To be honest, I'm surprised I'm still there."

Simon sighed. "Crap, I'm sorry…this guy is…is…"

"Yeah, I know." Emily nodded. "I should be grateful that Marcus hasn't fired me yet. It's giving me time to look for other jobs, but there's not much around, and I haven't been at the company very long, so it doesn't look good on my résumé."

"Marcus?" Simon asked, his blood running cold at the implications.

"Marcus Hind. He's the big boss. I don't ever talk to him, but he's Seb's buddy."

Simon winced.

"What is it?" Emily asked, clearly seeing his distress.

"Marcus is ex-Applewood," Simon explained. "He's the reason Applewood is in trouble."

Emily swallowed hard. "Oh my God. I didn't know that. There's a lot of secrecy in the office, so I just keep my head down. I try to avoid office politics, you know?"

Simon understood. If he were in Emily's situation, he'd do the same. "He used to work in the London branch. He poached a lot of key members of staff and set up a new practice here in New York. He's pricing us out of business and using his contacts to take clients."

Emily looked horrified. "I had no idea. I'm so sorry. And that's why Olivia is so stressed with work? I realised something big was happening, but she didn't want to talk about it."

"It's pretty bad," Simon said. His mind was racing with the new information. If Marcus had offered Emily a job, then surely he wasn't aware of her connection to Olivia. But that couldn't last. If Henry's grandfather had set up the employment, then it was only a matter of time until the two spoke and Emily lost her job.

"Mommy, when will we see Olivia again?" Henry slid into the booth and reached for his drink. He was panting from exertion.

"I don't know. She's very busy," Emily said, wrapping her arm around the breathless boy and holding him close.

"She told me to say hello," Simon told him and reached into his jacket pocket. "And to give you this." He pulled out a small package and handed it to Henry, who looked at it curiously and tentatively took it.

"For me?" Henry asked.

"For you," Simon said, realising that Henry wasn't that accustomed to receiving gifts.

"Thank you." Henry frowned at the wrapped present.

"You can open it," Emily told him, placing a kiss in his hair.

Henry made quick work of the wrapping paper, uncovering a small, plastic giraffe. He giggled and showed the giraffe to Emily and then to Simon. She smiled and nodded in an effort to look impressed. Henry took another gulp of his drink before heading back to play. Simon watched as he galloped the small toy around.

"Should I tell Olivia that I work for Marcus?"

"No, I'll deal with it. This isn't your mess to worry about."

"That doesn't stop me from worrying," Emily said.

"Okay, no more depressing topics," Simon said. "I invited you to lunch to cheer us all up. I demand cheer. Right now."

Emily chuckled. "You're right. How are things going with Sophie?"

❖

Simon strolled into Olivia's office with a takeaway coffee and brown bag in his hand. "I thought we agreed you'd not work this afternoon?"

Olivia looked up, confused, before glancing at her watch and flinching.

"Lose track of time?" He placed the coffee and paper bag on her desk, in amongst the stacks of files and papers.

"Did you have a nice lunch?" Olivia deflected. "Did Henry like the toy?"

"I did. He did. You were missed." Simon lifted some files from the visitor chair and placed them on the floor before sitting down.

"I ran some new figures," she explained. "I think I can find a way to…"

"To?" he asked as Olivia trailed off, resting her head in her cupped hand and closing her eyes.

"I'm sorry?"

"You said you ran some new figures and you have found a way to…" Simon frowned. "Are you feeling okay?"

"Fine, fine." Olivia jumped up from her seat and crossed the room to the whiteboards. Simon realized she had rewritten them all, condensing the retained clients onto one board and using the others to work out financial projections.

She picked up a pen and started to write some more figures, and Simon waited patiently for her to explain what she was about to say. When it never came, he stood up and walked over to stand beside her.

"Do you remember yesterday?"

"Hmm?"

"Yesterday. The day you hardly ate and promised me, crossing your heart no less, that you would only work this morning and have the afternoon off."

"Yes, yes, I remember." She continued to look at the figures on the board and Simon let out a sigh.

He walked back to his chair, sat down, and started to check his emails on his phone.

"Emily is terrified about losing Henry," he said casually, hoping to pique Olivia's interest.

"That won't happen."

"It might."

Olivia turned around and looked at him. "Has she heard back from Christine's people?"

"Nothing concrete. And something else came up."

"What?" Olivia put her hands on her hips, not enjoying Simon's delaying tactics.

"Henry's grandfather—"

"Awful man."

"—is a friend of Marcus's. And Emily is working for Marcus."

"Marcus who?"

Simon knew that Olivia's brain wouldn't allow her to connect the dots. The idea of Emily working for Marcus was so abhorrent to Olivia that some kind of protective shielding would prevent her from considering it.

"Marcus Hind." Simon lowered his phone and looked up to see her sway slightly.

"Marcus? Marcus the bastard? That Marcus?"

"She had no idea he was ex-Applewood; she also didn't know that most of the staff are also ex-Applewood. She has a junior position and is keeping out of office politics. But now she's worried that Henry's grandfather will attempt to pressure Marcus into firing her. To strengthen the court case against her. You know, add unemployment to her list of problems."

Olivia started to pace the room in a way that Simon had seen countless times before. It was how Olivia took in information and analysed. Simon watched with interest as she silently worked her way through a hundred different scenarios before eventually sitting at her desk.

"If Marcus discovers a connection between myself and Emily, then he may suspect corporate espionage. Did Emily tell you anything about her work or the company? Anything at all?"

Simon thought carefully. "She told me that the head of the company was Marcus and that her role consists of booking meeting rooms and filing."

Olivia licked her lips nervously. "This is a tricky situation, Simon. This could very well affect Henry's court case."

"You think they will claim she's told us secrets?"

"I think there's a high probability." Olivia closed her eyes and leaned back in her chair. "Oh, why didn't I just stay away? It's my connection to all of this that's going to be the issue."

"If you had stayed away, she wouldn't be in touch with one of the best family lawyers in the country. We don't know that this will cause a problem," Simon said.

"We'd be fools to ignore it." Olivia's eyes snapped open, and she leaned forward on the desk. She used her fingers to map out a potential sequence of events on the sparse amount of available desk space. "Sebastian Brennan could put pressure on Marcus to fire her. Which means she will be unemployed going into court. Either Sebastian, who has been known to use a private detective, or Marcus, could discover a connection between us and Emily. Which, again, could cause her to be fired. It could also mean additional charges of suspected espionage. This has the potential to become very serious, very quickly. I should speak with Christine. This is all my fault."

"You can't blame yourself for this." Simon shook his head. "This is just an unfortunate series of events; you did nothing wrong. Neither of you did anything wrong."

"Not deliberately, no. But my presence has only served to upset the balance, and it could cause disastrous consequences."

Simon blew out a breath and nodded. He had considered the possibility himself, but hoped he was overreacting. Now, hearing Olivia lay it out so clearly, he realised how serious the situation could become if left unchecked.

"I'm going to contact Christine, but you don't need to spend your weekend here." Olivia told him as she moved folders across her desk to make more room.

Simon regarded her curiously. Olivia's work schedule had been intense. She hadn't been taking care of herself, and it was starting to show. She was easily distracted, having difficulty focusing, and eating and sleeping had gone out the window. He'd seen her work hard, but the intense stress of the last few days was beyond anything that had gone before.

"Maybe you should take a break?"

Olivia didn't reply as she focused on moving documents across her desk.

"Earth to Olivia?" he asked.

She looked up, her eyes glazed as they had been for a few days now. "I'm sorry?"

"Maybe you should take a break?"

"No time, Simon. Time is essential right now. I'll take a break when things calm down."

Knowing there was no point, he backed down. He'd already argued with her, several times, with no success. He got to his feet and looked around the room. His eyes fell on the box of Emily's financial documents in the corner of the room.

"Emily needs those documents back." He indicated the box with his head.

Olivia looked over and nodded. "I'll make arrangements."

❖

Hours later, Olivia lowered the telephone receiver back to its base and turned thoughtfully to the window. Surprised to see that the sun had set, she stood up from her desk, picked up her crutch, and walked over to look out at the New York skyline.

She couldn't deny that the New York office had better views than her London office. Up on the twentieth floor, she had views of the other skyscrapers that made Manhattan such a visually stunning city. She also couldn't deny that it wouldn't be long before she would have to downsize to a smaller, less grand location. The view was certainly never going to be as impressive. If there was a view at all.

Olivia was rapidly coming to the realisation that there was a real chance Applewood wouldn't survive. At first, she wouldn't allow herself such negative thoughts, but as time went on and things weren't improving, it was becoming a distinct possibility.

She knew she should be devastated by the failure—her failure. Her failure to see it coming as well as her failure to fix it. But the truth was, she was utterly preoccupied with the conversation she'd just had with Christine.

"Frankly, it doesn't look too good," Christine had said with a sigh. "Not for the sake of custody, I think we have that wrapped up. But her debts, as you know, are beyond her ability to pay within her lifetime. Within two lifetimes. It will be a difficult situation for her for the rest of her life. I'm not sure how she's coping or how she will cope in the future. My experience is that children become more expensive as they get older."

Olivia had held her head in her hand, her other hand holding the phone to her ear as Christine explained how dire the situation was.

"Multiple loans, multiple overdrafts, multiple credit cards, all worse than the next. And never a real attempt to do anything about the situation, other than make it worse. You can clearly see the point in time where she is paying off one form of credit with another, and that goes on for months. Until everything is spent and her credit record is torn to shreds."

"But you're sure that they won't decide custody just based upon poor financial management?" Olivia asked, hating even the thought that Henry would be forced to live with his grandparent.

"Extremely unlikely. The child almost always stays with the mother. But, as I say, visitation will likely be granted and then who knows? Emily will continue to struggle with this debt around her neck for years, decades. She has no assets, no savings. It must be an incredible pressure on her. Clearly, the grandparents are aware of her situation and have tried to pressure her before. She'll be constantly subjected to that pressure when they have the right to see Henry more frequently. It's not a situation I think anyone would want to find themselves in."

"That's ridiculous," Olivia had argued angrily. "Emily is a fantastic mother. She loves and cares for Henry, more so than the grandparents could ever do. Its utterly preposterous for them to think they could be a better guardian to him."

"Clearly, they do. Olivia, you know these kinds of people, they think money trumps all. They don't think It's about who would give him the most cuddles. They think it's about who will pay for him to have the latest toys, a private tutor, and eventually go on to the best education."

"It all seems to be coming back to the finances," Olivia had said.

"Doesn't everything?" Christine had asked.

Olivia looked over at the box of paperwork. She'd promised to send it to Christine's office by courier on Monday morning so they could assess the full extent of the situation.

She walked over to a sofa and sat down, pulling the box towards her and lifting the lid. The papers were a mess. Nothing was filed together, or in any kind of order at all. It was simply shoved in the box, seemingly forgotten about until the payment came due. As she leafed through some documents, a child's drawing fluttered to the ground. She reached forward, picked it up, and smiled at the very basic attempt at a giraffe.

She leaned back on the sofa and allowed her thoughts to drift to Henry. From the moment she'd met him, he'd been an absolute joy. Even when he was sad or in a tantrum, she still adored him and his curious ways.

She couldn't let his grandparents take him away from Emily. She was sure that, if that were to happen, he would lose his unique spark. Seeing him pull away from Sebastian Brennan had been terrifying, and Olivia would happily put her body in between the two of them forever more if she had to.

The answer was clear to her. But she knew that Emily would be livid. Without a doubt she would be. Well, Olivia reasoned, it wouldn't be the first time, but it would probably be the last. Emily wasn't likely to forgive her for what she was about to do. No matter; it was the right thing, and she'd do it—whatever the fallout might be.

CHAPTER TWENTY-SIX

Emily knew something was wrong the second she entered the office. Marcus's secretary had left a note on her desk that he wanted to see her the moment she arrived. She placed her coat and bag on her chair and took a deep breath as she approached his office.

She quietly knocked on the open door. He looked up and asked her to close the door and take a seat. She sat and watched as he typed on his laptop, making no move to hurry, clearly ignoring her presence. After a few silent minutes, he finally stopped and looked at her.

"You're friends with Olivia Lewis?" His tone was matter-of-fact.

Emily felt like clarifying that friends wasn't exactly the right word, but she knew that being pedantic wasn't going to help her.

"We know each other, yes," she said.

"Have you spoken to Olivia Lewis, or any of her colleagues, about anything that has happened within this office?"

Emily shook her head. "Absolutely not. In fact, I only found out recently that you used to work with Olivia at Applewood." Honesty was probably the best policy, even though she didn't think it would help her much judging from Marcus's sour demeanour.

"Are you sure that you have mentioned nothing at all?"

"I signed a non-disclosure agreement when I started here, and I have never spoken about anything that I have seen or heard in this office to anyone outside of it. Certainly never to Olivia."

Marcus regarded her for a few moments. "I'm afraid I must suspend you, pending an investigation."

Emily recoiled. "What? Why?"

"We have a leak. An email detailing a contract with a client has somehow made its way to Applewood," Marcus explained.

"You have an office full of ex-Applewood staff, and you're blaming me?" Emily couldn't hold her tongue.

"The email was sent from your computer ID."

"My computer ID is used by anyone who accesses the archives," Emily replied. "Something which I brought up as being odd on my first day here."

Marcus removed his glasses and placed them on his desk. He sighed. "This firm grew exponentially, and I agree that some security measures were badly set up. Which is why I am suspending you pending a full investigation rather than firing you outright."

"I'd like to help clear my name. I've done nothing wrong—"

"The best thing you can do right now, Miss White, is go home. We'll be in touch regarding the investigation." Marcus handed a letter to her. "Here's the official paperwork. Please review it, sign a copy, and return it to Human Resources as soon as you can."

Emily wordlessly took the envelope and left the room. She scanned the office, wondering which one of them had set her up. Everyone had seemed so warm and welcoming when she arrived, and it hurt to realise that there was a traitor in her midst.

She stopped at her desk and quickly picked up the few personal effects she had, suddenly pleased that she hadn't embellished her desk too much. Her coworkers kept their heads down, avoiding eye contact, and Emily wondered if they simply knew what was happening or if they were to blame.

It was obvious no one had stood up for her, despite the friendly words and the promises of drinks after work. Everyone was out for themselves. She picked up her coat and bag and made her way towards the elevators, ignoring everyone around her. Someone had set her up, and she had no idea who or why. She was getting more and more angry and knew she had to leave the office before she snapped at someone.

Once she reached street level, she took a deep, calming breath and walked towards the nearest subway stop. She tried to keep her tears at bay—she'd been crying so much over the last few days that she was surprised the puffiness under her eyes hadn't become permanent.

She wasn't sure how she got home—everything seemed to go by in a daze once she got on the subway—but somehow she was slipping her key into the front door. As she turned the key in the lock, she was surprised when the door flew open, and she was dragged into the house.

"What are you doing home? I've been calling you. Why didn't you answer?" Lucy asked.

Emily only ever had one reaction when Lucy contacted her during the day. "Is Henry—"

"Henry's fine. He's at the park with Tom." Lucy waved away Emily's concerns. "Why are you home so early?"

"I've been suspended. I don't want to talk about it." Emily angrily tugged her key out of the lock and closed the door behind her. "Why did you call me?"

Lucy hurried towards the kitchen. "There was a lot of mail today, and I accidentally opened one of your letters. It was stuck together with one of mine."

"Okay." Emily followed her, not seeing why the accident would warrant a phone call. As soon as she entered the kitchen, Lucy thrust the letter into her hand. Emily looked at the header and saw that it was from a credit card company. Her stomach churned, and she attempted to hand the letter back.

"I don't want to know. I'm really not up for any more bad news right now."

"Read it," Lucy said.

Emily looked down at the letter. She stared, assuming there was some kind of mistake.

"This..." she started.

"It's a receipt! Someone paid off your credit card. All of it." Lucy spun around and started picking up other letters from the table.

"Why would...who would...pay my six-thousand-dollar credit card bill?" Emily examined the letter in shock. "This must be a joke. Or a mistake..."

Lucy held out the other, unopened letters. "I've been dying to know what's in these."

Emily plucked one from the stack and handed Lucy back the credit card receipt. She knew the font and logo on the envelope; this was a statement from a loan company she had seen advertised on television years ago. With a shaky hand, she tore open the envelope and pulled out the statement. She scanned the letter, and she shook her head in astonishment. The balance was zero. Her heart sank. Who would pay off her debts and why?

"Help me open all of these," Emily said, her voice wavering. She should be ecstatic to see the cleared balance, but her heart was pounding and her palms were sweaty. This wasn't the kind of thing that just happened. This wasn't normal. She worried that it was just the next piece of the puzzle in her day from hell.

Lucy immediately started ripping open the envelopes and handing Emily statement after statement. All of her balances had been cleared. She held on to the counter as her legs started to wobble from the shock. Had her debts been bought up by someone else? She'd heard stories about companies selling debt portfolios they couldn't recover to loan sharks.

"What's happening?" Emily whispered. Suddenly she wondered if Seb was behind it. Was this some warped way of attempting to get Henry? Was he going to use this as extra leverage? It seemed unlikely, even for him, but the thought lingered since there were no other reasonable explanations on offer.

"I have no idea." Lucy looked at all of the letters, even holding them up to the light.

"It's not the first of April, is it?" Emily asked.

"You should call one of them, ask who paid the balance," Lucy suggested.

"You're right." Emily turned and looked around in confusion before Lucy picked up the cordless telephone and placed it into her hand.

She looked at the phone and took a deep breath to try to calm her racing heart. Something was wrong—very wrong. She knew she had to make the call, but she also dreaded it with every fibre of her being.

Her life was falling apart, and she felt like a puppet being forced to perform for someone else's perverse entertainment. Debts didn't just vanish. Who was she indebted to now?

❖

Emily walked at a quick pace. She saw Simon at his desk outside Olivia's office, and, through the glass wall, Olivia on the telephone.

"Emily?" Simon stood up as he realised she intended to walk straight into Olivia's office without stopping.

She passed him wordlessly and pushed the door open.

"What the hell, Olivia?" she demanded.

Olivia looked up but didn't seem at all surprised by her presence.

"I'll call you back." Olivia hung up the call. "Simon, please close the door."

"You can't do this. You can't just take over like this. You need to talk to me before you do things like this." Emily waved the papers around. She turned to see Simon close the door but remain in the office.

Olivia looked up and gave a tired shrug. "You wouldn't have accepted it, and this is the only way you can get those awful people off your back."

Emily rubbed her eyes with frustration. "Tens of thousands of dollars, Olivia. How am I ever going to repay you?"

"You don't." Olivia looked down at a piece of paper on her desk. Emily's temper flared and she took a step forward.

"What's happened?" Simon asked.

Emily spun to look at him. "She's paid off all of my debts." She turned back to Olivia. "I asked you to look at my paperwork to advise me. Advise. Not to fix everything. Why didn't you speak to me?"

"Could you lower your voice a little, please? I have a throbbing headache," Olivia said as she rested her head in her hands.

"You have a headache? How do you think I feel? When did you do this? It must have been a few days ago, because I got the statements in the mail. Olivia…I…I'm grateful, of course I am, but this…you invaded my privacy, you didn't tell me what you were doing, you—"

"As I said, you wouldn't have accepted it, and I have neither the time nor the energy to argue with you," Olivia explained with exasperation. "I wanted to avoid this."

Emily shook her head and turned to Simon. "Am I crazy? You see the problem with this, right?"

Simon nodded. "Olivia, you can't pay off someone's debts without telling them or speaking to them about it first."

Olivia slammed her fist to her desk and stood up. "I will not be spoken to like some kind of child! I knew exactly what I was doing and I'd do it again. The Brennans' were using the debts as leverage against Emily. With those gone, their case collapses. It's only a matter of time before Marcus realises that Emily has a connection to me, and then he'll fire her, and that's my fault." She jabbed herself in the chest with her finger to emphasise the point.

Simon took a step forward and put his hands up to calm her, but she refused to be pacified.

"Let's face it; it was only a matter of time before I ruined everything anyway. At least this way I have protected the family unit. Henry will remain with Emily, and any leverage that awful man had is now lost. I fully expected this fallout. I assumed I would never see you again."

Emily balked at Olivia's explanation. In some ways, she was furious and wanted to shout at Olivia for not speaking to her before acting. In another way, the self-sacrificing act let Emily understand just how far Olivia was willing to go to put Henry's needs before her own.

"But, as I said before," Olivia continued, "I'd do it again. I don't expect you to pay me back. I'm in full control of my faculties, and I wanted to do this. It was the right thing to do. It…"

Olivia took a deep breath and started to sway.

"Olivia?" Simon asked, concern clear in his tone.

"I think I need some time alone," she murmured as she started to slip away from the desk. Simon sprinted around and caught her as she fell.

"Olivia? Olivia?" he called to her, but she was unconscious, a dead weight in his arms. He lowered her to the floor, and Emily rushed to his side.

Emily immediately drew upon her first aid knowledge and started to check Olivia's airways and for a heartbeat. For a second she could only hear her own heart pounding loudly in her ears. Then she heard Olivia's and let out a sigh of relief before looking up to Simon.

"She's breathing; I think she's fainted. Call an ambulance."

Simon stumbled to his feet and reached across Olivia's desk. He pulled the phone towards himself and lifted the receiver. His fingers hovered over the keys.

"Shit, I've gone blank. Help a Brit. What's the damn number here?"

"Nine-one-one," Emily told him calmly.

"Of course. I knew that," he berated himself as he made the call, running a hand nervously through his hair as he looked down at Olivia.

Simon's voice faded into background noise as Emily knelt beside Olivia, grasping her hand in an attempt to offer some support. It was strange and alarming to see her so pale and unmoving.

Emily regretted bursting into the office and acting the way she had. If she'd taken a second to look at Olivia rather than shouting at her, she would have noticed that something was wrong.

She gently squeezed Olivia's hand, hoping she was aware of a soothing presence.

CHAPTER TWENTY-SEVEN

Seb heard the doorbell echo throughout the house. He lowered his newspaper to the desk, walked out of the sitting room and across the marble hallway. He opened the door and folded his arms across his chest, levelling a wilting stare at Marcus.

"Yes?" he asked bitterly.

"Can we speak?"

Seb made a show of considering the request for a moment before nodding and gesturing for Marcus to step inside. He closed the front door and watched as Marcus politely wiped his shoes. When he was done, Seb guided him towards the sitting room.

"Can I get you a drink?" he asked.

"No, no. I won't be here long. I just wanted to tell you that you might've been right about Emily," Marcus explained as he sat down.

Seb sat down and raised his eyebrow. "Oh?"

"We found suspicious activity on her computer. And a contract ended up in Applewood's hands."

Seb fought to keep a smile off of his face. He casually shrugged. "Well, I wouldn't want to say that I told you so. But the girl simply cannot be trusted. This actually makes a lot of sense considering what we just heard from our lawyer."

"What was that?" Marcus asked.

"It seems that all of Emily's debts have suddenly been paid off. Our lawyer was looking into her financial records, and, as of this week, she is completely debt-free. Our case has effectively collapsed. We're being advised not to continue seeking custody."

Marcus blinked, clearly shocked. "What will you do? Will you drop the case?"

"No." Seb shook his head. "We'll go ahead. There's still a chance we can win, however remote. I don't back down from a fight. And it will be expensive. If Olivia Lewis is bankrolling her, then I want it to cost her as much as possible."

Seb's plan with Michael Underwood had yielded the desired result. Marcus was back, apologetically at that. As much as Seb hated the way Marcus had spoken to him, he knew the man could prove useful in the future. Carrying a grudge wasn't as useful as collecting favours to be cashed in at a later date.

"So, you've fired Emily?" Seb asked.

"No, not yet. Evidence is scant, but it's enough for me to have severe doubts about her. She's been suspended without pay. I need to do this by the book. We don't want to both be in court with the damn girl."

"Suspension is even better." Seb chuckled. "That won't look good for her in court. We need all the help we can get at this stage. Ideally, I'd like to stop Olivia from funding her, or being able to fund her, but that doesn't seem likely. I don't know what the connection with those two is, but it's clearly of mutual benefit."

"You're sure Olivia is involved in this?" Marcus asked.

"Absolutely, my private detective has told me as much," Seb lied.

Marcus shook his head. "I never thought Olivia would play such a dirty campaign. Of course she's bound to be upset by what's happened, but she's always been professional. Ridiculously so."

"Anger can make women do funny things. She's paid off Emily's debts. What sane person would do that?"

Marcus leaned back and let out a sigh. "How about cutting off the banker?"

Seb looked at him with interest. "What do you mean?"

"As you say, Olivia Lewis is bankrolling her," Marcus explained. "Cutting off the funds would be beneficial to you."

"And what would you get out of it?" Seb asked.

"The joy of seeing Applewood finally sink. It's been floundering for a while now. It's time to put it out of its misery. Olivia won't give in easily. Seems that she needs a little push."

As Seb had always suspected, it hadn't taken long for Marcus to turn and resort to underhanded tactics to get his way. And Seb would be happy to go ahead with whatever Marcus suggested at this point. Olivia's wrench in the works was no small matter—between the physical threat and the interference with the court case, he wanted her taken down a peg or two.

"What kind of push are we talking about?" Seb asked.

"An anonymous complaint about financial irregularities at Applewood. Or, should I say, two complaints. I know just the cases to question. Without key members of staff, they'll have to comb through the archives to find the information. They'll have to respond to the authorities, and it'll take them weeks to comply with court demands." Marcus smirked and chuckled to himself. "It's quite simple, really. A well-worded complaint or two will tie them up in paperwork and red tape for weeks. During that time, they won't be able to maintain the business. We may be using some inside knowledge, but it's no worse than what they have done."

Seb grinned. He'd known Marcus's desire to remove Olivia from the picture would eventually work to his advantage. Marcus had hated Olivia from day one—not a luncheon or golfing day went by without him complaining about the woman. The second the connection between Emily and Olivia was discovered, Seb knew that leveraging Marcus's insecurities would be the key. Driving a solid wedge between the two women was going to help them both.

"That sounds perfect. What do I have to do?"

❖

An hour later, just after Marcus left, Irene approached Seb with apprehension. After she'd realised it was Marcus at the door, she had sat on the bottom step of the staircase and listened to what was being said.

"I overheard every word. Are you sure you want to go down this route, Seb?"

"Of course." He turned and walked towards his study. Irene followed him, not about to let him off that easily. She wanted the truth.

"Did Emily really transfer files to Applewood?" Irene asked as they entered the office.

"No." Seb sat at his desk and looked up at her. "Emily White doesn't have the business acumen to even think of something so enterprising."

"Enterprising? Spying?"

Seb leaned back in his chair and interlaced his hands behind his head. "She's in a unique position. It's very easy to believe that she would and could do such a thing. Just as Marcus believes."

Irene sighed. "You bribed someone?"

"I wouldn't be so careless." He sat forward and turned on his laptop.

This was exactly what she had feared. Seb was consumed with winning—and often his lack of morals meant that he did. That didn't mean that Irene approved of his tactics, or didn't live in constant fear that they would one day turn on them both.

He looked at her with a fixed stare, obviously not wanting to give anything away. Unfortunately for him, Irene knew him well enough.

"Seb…" She sighed again. "What did you do?"

"Does it matter what the specifics were? It worked, didn't it? It brought up questions, Marcus has suspended her, and now I have a way to exact my revenge on that…that violent…woman."

"What kind of example would this set for Henry?" she tried to appeal to him.

Seb rubbed his brow and let out a deep breath. "You'll never be able to set any example for Henry unless we act. Henry won't have anything to do with us if Emily has her way. Trust me, I'm doing this for us. For Henry. Sometimes you have to bend a few rules."

Irene closed her eyes and let out yet another sigh. They had discussed time and time again that they wouldn't resort to any unscrupulous behaviour. They would do everything by the book to ensure there could be no comeback in the future.

But the very second they'd agreed to try to reconnect with Emily, Seb had turned his back on any notion of trying to take the high road. He'd told her that hiring a private detective and going down the legal route was the only chance they had. He'd explained that Emily would never let them have a relationship with Henry unless she was pressured into it.

"We agreed—" Irene began.

"Things have changed," Seb said with finality.

He opened up his desk drawer and rummaged around for something. He wasn't going to see reason, she knew that. Too many times, they had been in a similar situation, and Irene had attempted to speak to him with no success. She shook her head, turned, and left the room. Nothing good was going to come of this.

CHAPTER TWENTY-EIGHT

Simon opened the door and watched with an amused smile as Nicole finished the enormous yawn she was in the middle of.

"Sorry," she said as she walked in.

"No problem. I know it's a long trip. Thanks for coming." Simon took her suitcase from her hand and carried it in.

"How is she?"

"Exhausted, embarrassed, and on strict bedrest." Simon closed the front door behind them.

"So, what happened exactly?" Nicole placed her handbag on the sofa and shrugged out of her coat.

Simon placed the suitcase by the sofa and hung up her coat. "She'd been working all hours, not eating, not sleeping."

"Ah," Nicole said. "Usual Olivia, then?"

"Usual Olivia times ten," Simon explained. "Then she was arguing with Emily and me, and she just collapsed. She was in hospital overnight, and her blood pressure was through the roof. It took me forever to convince them that she'd relax more away from the hospital and to let her finish her recovery here." Simon rolled his eyes. "Not an easy task."

"Is she behaving?" Nicole asked, smothering another yawn.

"Not really, which is why I'm glad you're here." Simon grinned. "I'm technically her employee, so I can't say what I'd like to say to her."

Nicole laughed. "When has that ever stopped you?"

"True. I wanted to play good cop for a while, and that means I need a bad cop," he joked.

"Are you sure you want to call me bad cop after the flight I just had?"

Simon jutted his thumb towards the kitchen. "Can I get you a coffee?"

"Oh, yes, please," Nicole said. "And don't think I didn't notice the change of subject there, Captain Smooth. Is she awake now?"

"She was fifteen minutes ago," he replied as he walked towards the kitchen. "But this has really knocked her out. She drifts in and out easily."

Nicole yawned again. "I know the feeling after that flight. Get me that coffee and we'll go in and gang up on her."

❖

Simon knocked on the bedroom door. Nicole stood beside him with her hands wrapped around her coffee mug as if her life depended on it.

"Come in," Olivia softly called out.

He opened the door and gestured for Nicole to enter first. Olivia was in bed in dark red silk pyjamas, propped up on a number of fluffy pillows. She looked pale and exhausted, her normally luscious hair was dull and lifeless, and she was clearly utterly miserable.

Nicole stepped farther into the room, and Simon closed the door behind them. He watched Nicole give Olivia a disapproving look, and Olivia quietly awaiting her judgement.

After a few moments of silence, Nicole finally sighed. "You are an idiot."

"Thank you for your sympathy," Olivia replied.

Simon winced, knowing that was not going to calm Nicole down at all.

"What were you thinking?"

Olivia remained silent, staring down at her hands twisting in the bedding rather than looking at either of them.

Nicole walked around the bedroom, pausing to look out the window. "I can stay here all day," she said casually. "I mean, I did just fly from London because I thought you were in immediate peril. It's not as if I have anywhere else to be."

"I'm fine," Olivia said, turning a glare on Simon. "Simon shouldn't have called you."

Simon opened his mouth to speak but closed it as Nicole beat him to the punch. "No, he did the right thing." Nicole turned around and looked at Olivia. "Here you are, laid up in bed. You look like death, by the way."

"Thanks," Olivia commented sarcastically.

"Oh, don't be confused, I'm not here to be nice to you." Nicole sat in the chair beside the bed. "You've been an idiot—"

"So you've told me."

"—and idiots need to be told when they are doing too much. And if that doesn't work, then they need to be prevented from doing too much." Nicole placed her coffee mug on the bedside table.

"My business—"

"Is not more important than your life," Nicole said firmly.

Olivia closed her mouth, clearly not wishing to argue with Nicole's fearsome tone. Simon didn't blame her one bit.

"Now, I know things are bad. I know that you're thinking about all the people who rely on you. I know there is more than just a business at stake here. There's your father's memory. I get it, really I do. But that is not a good enough reason to work yourself to death. People need you. Dammit, I need you." Nicole reached into her jeans pocket and pulled out a tissue. "And I'm crying because you're stupid."

"I'm sorry," Olivia whispered.

"Don't be sorry. Just don't do it again."

"I didn't mean to. I didn't even know…"

"Come on, I can't believe for a moment that there were no warning signs. Surely Simon nagged you to take a break?"

"Yes, I did," he confirmed.

Olivia looked at Simon as if he was a traitor before returning her gaze to the bedding, ignoring Nicole's exasperated look. Simon watched as Nicole sat back in the chair and looked at Olivia, whose eyes were starting to flutter from exhaustion.

"Sleep," Nicole gently ordered her. "And when you wake up, we'll be having an in-depth conversation about how to look after yourself. Which clearly you need."

Olivia chuckled softly before her eyes closed, and within minutes, even breathing indicated she was asleep.

Nicole looked at Simon questioningly.

"This is normal," he assured her in a whisper.

"She gave me quite the scare," Nicole whispered back. "After I got your call, I threw some clothes in a bag and headed straight for the airport. I sat in the terminal and panicked about whether or not I'd ever see her again."

Simon glanced at Olivia, who was clearly headed into a deep sleep. "I know the feeling," he said. "I thought I'd never get that promotion."

Nicole chuckled lightly. "I know you don't mean that. You two are like some strange double act. Never one without the other."

She leaned back, turning her head from side to side, and Simon winced at the cracks that sounded.

"We have to keep an eye on her," Nicole told him.

"Agreed."

She picked up her mug and pointed to some bound papers on the bedside table. "What's this?"

Simon shrugged. "It better not be work."

Nicole picked it up and started to flip through the papers, shaking her head. "No, not work."

"Good. Speaking of work, I need to go and make a couple of calls."

Nicole lowered her mug to the bedside table again. "I'll finish my coffee in here," she said distractedly as she began to read. "I'll be out in a bit."

Simon stepped out of the bedroom and quietly closed the door behind him. He was relieved that Nicole had come to help keep Olivia in check. Seeing her collapse and so unwell in the hospital had been a sharp shock to the system.

After the plane crash, Olivia had seemed fine. Disorientated on pain medication, but otherwise well. This was different. It had amplified quickly and turned into something that Simon didn't quite know how to deal with. He'd known Nicole would be his best bet to make her see sense.

He sat in the living room and caught up on calls and emails, quickly losing track of time as he tried to keep what little that was left of Applewood in one piece. It must have been an hour later when Nicole walked back into the living room.

"She's still sleeping. Or doing a great job faking it because we told her off." She sniffed and looked around the room, stretching tiredly. "I think I'll go check into my room and have a rest and come back later if that's okay with you?"

Simon nodded. "Sure. It's been a long journey for you."

"It's been a long few weeks for you. When are you heading back?"

He shrugged. "No idea."

"You can't stay here forever." She picked her handbag off the sofa.

"I know, but I can't leave now either." He stood and walked over to fetch her coat. "It's weird to see her like this."

"I know," she said softly. "But she'll bounce back. She doesn't tolerate being ill; you know that."

Simon laughed, handed her the coat, and picked up her suitcase to carry it for her. "That's true. And I know she'll not be like this for long. I just hope she doesn't try to bounce back too soon."

Nicole opened the suite door and they both exited into the corridor. "Well, that's what you and I are here for. If she won't look after herself, then we'll do it for her."

"That's one of the reasons why I called you. She's not listening to me at all." Simon shook his head in frustration as they approached the elevator and Nicole pressed the call button.

"She'll listen to me," Nicole said firmly. "Anyway, more interestingly, you mentioned Emily before. Is she back in the picture? Please tell me she's back in the picture."

Simon chuckled. "That's a long story. You ready?" he asked as they both stepped into the elevator.

❖

Emily sat in the chair beside Olivia's bed. Olivia had been asleep since she arrived, and she'd spent the time making notes in her script. She'd almost forgotten that Olivia had taken it. That evening had been completely overshadowed by Seb and Olivia's standoff.

Emily had been surprised to see the script beside Olivia's bed and wondered if she'd read it. She decided to refresh her memory on the contents of the script and soon found herself scribbling notes. An extra word here, a pause there. She remembered how much she enjoyed writing scripts and plays. Sometimes the addition of just one small word could completely rejuvenate a whole sentence. It was exhilarating.

It was also a great way to kill time while Olivia rested. She could have edited anywhere else, but she wanted to be closer to Olivia. After the adrenaline of Olivia's collapse had worn off, the guilt had quickly set in.

In hindsight, she could see that Olivia had looked sick and exhausted, and yet she had carried on arguing with her. She wished she could travel back and approach the conversation in a different way, but at the time she had been so angry. Of course she was ecstatic, elated that her debts had been paid off. But the fact that Olivia had done it without talking to her first had been too much for Emily to take in. She'd only recently become comfortable with the idea of accepting more help from others, and she'd felt as if Olivia had played her.

After sitting in the hospital waiting room, waiting for the doctor, she had calmed down and started to think about Olivia and her personality. In a strange way, it made sense. It was such an Olivia thing to do. And she couldn't imagine Olivia blackmailing or bribing her; it just wasn't a part of who she was. Emily's fears had started to float away as she'd analysed what she knew of Olivia until all that was left was remorse.

When Olivia had woken up, Simon had gone in and spoken to her while Emily remained in the waiting room, worried that her presence might further upset Olivia.

Once Simon told her that Olivia was being released back to the hotel, Emily had decided it would be wrong to hide any longer.

She suddenly felt a shift in the atmosphere of the room and looked up to see Olivia looking back at her.

"Hello," Emily said with a smile. She lowered the manuscript and her pen to the bedside table. "How are you feeling?"

Olivia's eyes flicked towards the closed bedroom door before returning to Emily.

"Are you going to shout at me? Because I really don't feel up to it," Olivia said in a tiny voice.

Emily felt her heart clench and edged forward on her chair. "I'm not going to shout at you. I'm sorry I overreacted."

"I understand why you did."

"Do you?" Emily asked uncertainly.

"I think so," Olivia said.

"I can't thank you enough for what you did for me, and for Henry," Emily said with sincerity. "I was so shocked by it, I didn't know how to react. I felt as though you had lied to me, played me. But that doesn't excuse my actions. As I say, I'm sorry."

"Lied to you?" Olivia looked so lost that Emily's heart ached.

"You took the paperwork with the intention of paying off my debts…"

Olivia struggled to sit. "I didn't—"

Emily stood up and put her hand on Olivia's shoulder. "Don't sit up."

"I didn't plan to clear the debts. I only considered it when I realised how…damaging they were to your custody case." Olivia lay back down but looked desperately at her.

"Oh." Emily hadn't considered that possibility. Now she felt even more remorseful for her assumption that Olivia had been lying to her. That Olivia had used her request for help as a way to do what she wanted, even though she knew Emily wouldn't like it.

She shook her head to try to clear the guilt that had settled heavily on her. "Okay, but, still, you should have spoken to me about it."

"I don't want the money back."

"Well, you're damn well getting it back," Emily said with a chuckle. "I'll pay you back somehow. But, without interest. I hear that's how people get into debt."

Olivia smiled. "Now you're learning."

Emily noticed the door opening and a woman walked in. She stood up from the edge of Olivia's bed.

"I'm sorry, am I interrupting?"

"Not at all," Emily replied.

"Emily, this is my good friend, Nicole. Nic, this is Emily, who I told you about." Olivia shuffled up a little so she was sitting up, ignoring Emily's disapproving look.

"I'm so sorry to barge in, but I just went out and got some takeaway. I picked up some of that lasagne that you love," Nicole explained. She held up a takeaway bag and Olivia's eyes flashed with interest.

"I need to head home soon anyway," Emily said. "I'll come back to see you tomorrow."

"You don't need to leave," Nicole insisted.

Emily was already approaching the door. "I have to get back. I hadn't realised the time. It was nice to meet you." She smiled warmly at Nicole before saying another goodbye to Olivia and excusing herself from the room.

On her way out, she peeked into the kitchen, where Simon was plating up food.

"Hey, do you want to stay for dinner? There's plenty to go around," he said as she walked in.

"No, I need to get going. I was thinking of coming by tomorrow, though."

Simon turned and gave her a sad face. "Stay. We haven't had much chance to catch up."

Emily chuckled. "Don't pout. I'll be back tomorrow I promise."

"Are you still angry at her?" Simon asked.

Emily shook her head. "No. I was. Obviously." She leaned against the doorframe and closed her eyes for a moment. "I'm starting to get her. She doesn't always make sense, but I'm looking at her intentions rather than her actions."

Simon beamed. "Good. I can subscribe you to the Olivia Lewis Fan Club. There's a newsletter, stickers, and everything."

Emily laughed. "You're such a brat." She winked as she turned and gathered her things from the living room. "I'll be by around tomorrow at eleven if that's okay?"

"Yup," Simon said. "See you then."

CHAPTER TWENTY-NINE

How is she?" Lucy asked the moment Emily stepped in the door.

Emily looked around for Henry. She hadn't told him about Olivia being unwell.

"He's playing in his room," Lucy reassured her.

"She's okay. Exhausted. Sleeping a lot, which is good." Emily hung up her coat and bag.

"Did you manage to talk to her?" Lucy asked.

Emily nodded. "We're good. I apologised for overreacting."

Lucy bit her lip and Emily chuckled softly. "Out with it, Luce."

"You're accepting the money, right? You didn't do anything crazy like reverse the payments?"

"I didn't do anything crazy," Emily promised. "I'll need to talk to her properly about how the hell I'm going to pay her back. But that's for another day."

"I made a chicken pot pie for you to take to her." Lucy tilted her head towards the kitchen. "I bake when I'm nervous."

"Why are you nervous?"

Lucy looked towards the stairs to check that Henry was out of sight before grabbing Emily and dragging her to the kitchen. She closed the door and started to pace the room, bursting with nervous energy.

"I say this with love," Lucy started.

"Nothing good ever comes from saying that," Emily said.

Lucy leaned against the counter and let out a deep sigh. "Seeing you, Henry, and Olivia together was so wonderful. You just worked like a little family unit. And I know that you are still trying to figure things out, but I can see a perfect image of the future."

Emily pulled out a dining chair and sat down. She had a feeling she knew where this was headed.

"But then she paid off the debts, and I know you, Em. I know that you are proud and determined, and I worried that you would push her away again."

"I nearly did," Emily said softly.

"I was nervous." Lucy hesitated. "I am nervous that you're going to end things with her. Because I honestly think that she is the best thing that's ever happened to you and Henry."

Emily chuckled at the dramatic words.

"No, hear me out," Lucy said. "I'm not just talking about her obvious wealth. She cares for both of you, deeply. I see it every time she looks at you. I've heard about London, and I've seen her interact with you both with my own eyes. Someone who is so willing to open their heart is a rare thing."

"Lucy, I know that she cares—"

"And you clearly care about her."

"It's an awkward situation," Emily said vaguely. "I've pushed her away and now…I don't know if she wants to try again. I think she's given up on me and moved on."

"I don't think so, not from what I've seen," Lucy said. "Just don't overthink it."

Emily rested her head on the kitchen table. "Too late." She let out a deep breath. "Every time I think I have her figured out, I realise that I haven't."

"What do you mean?"

Emily sat up. "The payments. I thought she took the paperwork with the intention of paying the debts off. But she says that she didn't; she only considered it later when the custody case came up."

"So…it wasn't premeditated?"

"No. She didn't lie to me," Emily said. "She just didn't tell me what she was planning to do. And she didn't tell me because she knew I wouldn't agree to it. She expected me to no longer want to speak to her after she did it."

"She knew the risks and she did it anyway, because she felt it was the right thing to do," Lucy said. "If I were in her situation, I may well have done the same."

Emily looked at her in disbelief. "You'd use someone's private paperwork to pay off their debts without telling them? Waiting for them to find out when their statements arrived?"

Lucy laughed and nodded. "Yes, if it would keep you and Henry together, I think I would."

Emily sighed. "Now you're making me feel as if I'm a bad person because I don't want people to pay off my debts."

"Well, it should make you feel like a good person. Because we would all be willing to do it for you."

CHAPTER THIRTY

The next day Emily turned up at the suite with a large dish of chicken pot pie under her arm, feeling slightly ridiculous. She took a deep breath and knocked on the door.

A moment later Simon pulled it open and smiled in greeting. "You come bearing gifts!" he exclaimed when he saw the foil-covered dish.

"A chicken pot pie from my housemate. Apparently, she bakes when she's nervous." Emily handed him the dish.

Simon lifted a corner of the foil and inhaled. "Wow, can she be nervous more often? This smells amazing."

Emily smiled. "I'll let her know you said so."

"Tea?" Simon asked as he walked towards the kitchen. "Coffee, juice, water?"

Emily followed behind him and lightly slapped his arm. "Ha-ha. Tea would be great, thank you."

"Nicole's in with Olivia at the moment," Simon explained as he set down the baking dish and started to make the tea.

Emily leaned back against the counter, trying to look casual. "So…Nicole's?"

"A friend from London. I called her because she's the closest thing Olivia has to family. Well, family she cares about, anyway."

"And she's…" Emily trailed off as she wondered how to ask the question that was on her lips.

"Straight. No competition," Simon answered with a wide grin.

"Simon!" Emily admonished him, looking around to check they were alone.

He laughed. "Oh, come on. You two are dancing around each other, and it's exhausting."

Emily folded her arms and looked away, but she smiled.

"I know a lot has happened between you," Simon continued, "but my last count was that you couldn't be with Olivia because you were focused on Henry's recovery. But seeing him in that play area the other day makes me think he is pretty much recovered."

She picked up the dish and placed it in the fridge. "I do want to…" Emily felt her voice give out at the admission. She coughed lightly and continued, "I just don't know if, well…Olivia's been distant. I know I haven't exactly been fair to her lately, and I don't want to hurt her more."

Simon regarded her seriously. "Look, I think—"

"I need a list of everyone who has visited Olivia in the last twenty-four hours," Nicole said as she hurried into the kitchen. "Sorry to interrupt. Hello, Emily."

"Problem?" Simon asked.

Nicole held up Emily's script. "This is fantastic. What's more, it's been added to since I last picked it up yesterday. And this is only part one. There must be a part two floating around out there. And I need to find it."

"That's mine," Emily confessed.

Nicole turned to her with a wide smile. "Yours? As in, you wrote this?"

Emily nodded.

Nicole opened the script. "And these additions are yours?"

Emily nodded again.

"We haven't been properly introduced. I'm Nicole Blake, theatre producer." Nicole held out her hand, and Emily promptly shook it. "Can I take your agent's contact details?"

"Agent?" Emily spluttered out a laugh. "I don't have an agent."

"Emily's not a professional writer," Simon added.

"Oh," Nicole replied with a shrug. "Do you want to be?"

"Is this a joke?" Emily asked bluntly.

Nicole chuckled. "Not at all. I'm always looking for fresh new ideas, and this is wonderful. And the amendments—it was good before, but the changes are phenomenal. Then I got to the end and realised there was a second part. Please tell me that there is a second part."

"There is," Emily said. "I wrote it years ago. I can email it over to you if you like?"

"Absolutely. Just let me get my card." Nicole left the kitchen.

Emily turned to Simon, silently requesting some kind of an explanation.

"Nicole works for a group of London theatres. She's an award-winning producer," he said.

"One in need of fresh material," Nicole added as she came back into the room, handing Emily her business card as she did. "I'm always on the lookout for new scripts."

Emily looked at the business card and nodded nervously. "I'll send you the second half this evening."

"Thank you so much. I'm dying to know what happens next. Have you been writing for long?" Simon waved a mug in Nicole's direction and she nodded. "Yes, please, Simon."

Nicole took a seat at the kitchen table, and Emily did the same.

"I've always enjoyed writing. When my son was young, he was very sick, so there was a lot of waiting around in hospitals."

"Yes, Olivia mentioned. Is your son well now?"

Emily couldn't help but smile. "Yes, he is much better. Like a different little boy. You wouldn't know he'd been so ill."

Simon placed two mugs of tea on the table and they both thanked him.

"So, you primarily wrote when you were with him in hospital?" Nicole asked.

"Yes. At home too, but that's where I really managed to get a lot done. When there is nothing else you can do, and you're desperate for distraction, it's amazing what you can accomplish."

"Amazing is the word; I don't think I could write that quality under those circumstances."

Emily felt a blush rising on her cheeks. "Oh, it's nothing. It's really not that good."

"I disagree. You're very talented."

Emily shook her head. She wrapped her hands around her mug, grateful for something to hold on to. "Are you sure Olivia isn't putting you up to this?"

Nicole and Simon shared a look and both smiled.

"What?" Emily asked, feeling left out of a private joke.

"Olivia refuses to go to any of Nicole's productions. She doesn't get them. At all," Simon explained.

"Hates them, is more the word," Nicole added. "She frequently tells me that she doesn't get what's happening. If Olivia had liked your manuscript, I would have instantly turned it down. In fact, Olivia will hate this." Nicole flipped through the pages and smiled. "The scene where the main character speaks to the audience? She'd throw a fit at that."

Emily smiled. That did sound like Olivia. Her phone rang, and she lowered her mug of tea. "I'm sorry, excuse me," she said as she stepped into the living room and took the call.

"Lucy?"

"Henry's fine," Lucy replied immediately. "I just had the weirdest phone call though."

"Oh?" Emily asked, sitting on the arm of the sofa.

"Irene Brennan just called. She wants to talk to you and me. She says she only has a short window of time, and she wants to meet us for coffee in the city."

Emily frowned. "I don't understand. Why?"

"I don't either, but she seemed genuine and determined. It's just her, not Seb."

"I suppose we should go, but what about Henry? I don't want to take him. I know I'm being paranoid, but—"

"I know, I know," Lucy said. "I phoned a couple of friends, but they can't take him on such short notice."

"Did you try Angela?"

"Yes, and Caroline."

"There must be someone who can babysit Henry for a couple of hours?" Emily said as she wracked her brain.

"Sorry to eavesdrop." Simon poked his head around the corner. "Can I help?"

Emily looked up at him and smiled in relief. "Would you be okay to watch Henry for a couple of hours?"

"Absolutely."

"Lucy, can you bring him here to the hotel? Simon can watch him."

She gave Lucy the address, hung up the phone, and turned to Simon. "You're a lifesaver."

"Yeah, I know. I am pretty great." Simon winked. "What's going on?"

"Irene, Henry's grandmother, wants to meet me and Lucy. Alone."

"Weird."

"Who's Irene and Lucy?" Nicole asked as she stepped out of the kitchen. "Sorry, I'm dreadfully nosey."

Emily chuckled. "Lucy is my best friend. I live with her and her husband."

"Oh, the nervous chicken pot pie baker." Nicole looked to Simon and pointed her head towards the kitchen.

"That's the one," Emily confirmed. "Irene is my son's estranged grandmother. His grandparents have been trying to gain custody of him. But now she wants to meet us and says she only has a short window of time."

"Interesting," Nicole commented. "Sounds important. Does this mean I get to meet the legendary Henry?"

Emily smiled. "Yes, Lucy will drop him off here. Thank you so much, Simon."

"Does he know about Olivia?" Simon asked.

"No." Emily shook her head. "He would have demanded to come and see her immediately if he knew something was wrong. Probably best to tell him that she's got a cold and is sleeping. Then he'll be quiet and won't try to bother her."

"Cool." Simon nodded. "So, I'll order a curry and we'll have a few pints, play Grand Theft Auto, and you'll be back in no time, right?"

Emily smirked at him. "Lucy will bring him some plain cheese sandwiches, and he'll probably ask you to do some colouring with him. Try not to corrupt my son too much in a couple of hours, please?"

Simon sighed and playfully rolled his eyes. "Fine, have it your way."

CHAPTER THIRTY-ONE

Emily and Lucy sat in the busy coffee shop, nervously looking around at the various people coming and going. It was a generic chain. One where the door was opening every few seconds, and each time Emily turned to see if it was Irene.

"Are you sure she meant this one?" Emily asked.

"Yes. She made me write it down and confirmed the address twice." Lucy angled her head to look around the crowded shop. "She wanted to meet alone, so maybe she has to make some excuse to get away from Seb?"

"Or maybe this is just part of some elaborate plan?"

"Pessimist." Lucy sighed.

"Realist," Emily said.

"She's here." Lucy indicated the door with a nod of her head, and Emily turned around.

Irene was wearing large sunglasses and a scarf that she'd folded up to obscure her face. She looked uncomfortable and nervous, wary even, as she scanned the shop. After a moment, she weaved through the crowds towards the small table they'd managed to secure.

"Thank you for meeting me here," she said softly as she sat down, still glancing around fretfully.

"Is everything okay?" Lucy asked, also inspecting the other patrons more closely. Irene's suspicion seemed to be catching.

"I don't want to be seen." Irene let out a nervous sigh. She looked at Emily. "As you know, my husband hired a private detective to follow you, and now I'm paranoid he's having me followed."

"Why?" Emily asked.

Irene fidgeted with her scarf for a moment before letting out a deep breath. "Because I'm leaving him."

"Oh." Emily couldn't think of anything else to say. While Irene had always been the quieter of the two, she'd been absolutely certain that they were in it together. The news that Irene was at odds with Seb was both interesting and surprising. She briefly wondered if she would now be fighting two separate custody battles before feeling guilty at immediately thinking of herself. But it was impossible not to. This breakup would clearly affect her and Henry; she just didn't know how.

"He doesn't know yet." Irene took one last look over her shoulder. "Well, I don't think he does."

"Do you want to go somewhere else?" Lucy asked. "If you feel it's not safe for you here?"

Irene shook her head. "No. Thank you, but no. Everywhere feels equally unsafe. Seb…he didn't used to be like this…" She took a deep breath. "He's changed a lot over the last ten years. Maybe more. He's never been a saint, that much I always knew. But he used to be kinder, more caring. All that seems to have vanished. Now he'll do anything, absolutely anything, to get what he wants." She lifted a shaky hand and removed her sunglasses. "He's relentless in crushing anyone he sees as competition. It used to be work-related, but since he retired, well, he'll pick a fight with anyone."

"Like me." Emily sipped her coffee.

"Yes. But I can't fully blame him for that," Irene said. "I…I spoke about Henry. Often. I always wondered how he was and what was happening." She reached forward, picked up a spare napkin from the table, and held on to it tightly. "After we lost the initial court case, Seb forbade me from contacting you. I hoped that if I told him I was wondering about Henry, he would relent and allow me to get in touch with you. To see Henry from time to time." She brought her other hand up and twisted the napkin tightly as she spoke. "He's the only thing I have left of my own boy." Tears spilled over her eyelids as she stared at Emily, unblinking.

The sorrow she could see in Irene's eyes cut Emily's soul in two and brought back every tear she'd shed after Joe's death, every moment of worry over Henry's illness. Every time she'd received a call, and the thought that Henry was no longer with her had flittered across her mind. She'd been lucky and never had to live the reality of that pain. Irene had. It didn't matter that Joe was a grown man when he'd died. He was still her boy, her baby. Her only son.

"Instead of what I wanted, he contacted a private detective. That despicable little man found out about your financial trouble, and Seb knew that he could see a way for us to win. To get custody of Henry. I didn't want that; I truly didn't. You're his mother, you've taken good care of him despite the difficulties, and you clearly love him. He should be with you. I hoped that I'd be able to convince Seb of the same thing."

Emily wanted to believe her. She wanted to trust that everything she could see in Irene's eyes—eyes that reminded her so much of Joe—was the truth. But how could she take that chance? It was Henry's future she was talking about. Henry's life. She couldn't afford to blindly trust, to leap without looking, no matter how genuine Irene seemed. She needed more. "I don't mean to be rude," Emily started, "but how do I know you aren't just saying this now that your case isn't going to go your way?"

"I don't expect you to believe me. At least not straightaway. I know that trust has to be earned, but I hope in time I can convince you of my good intentions. Which is one of the reasons why I'm here. I have to warn you about Seb's latest plan."

Lucy and Emily exchanged a concerned look.

"Seb believes that Olivia Lewis paid off your debts in return for information from within Marcus's company, and he's convinced Marcus it's true."

"What?" Emily shouted before quickly lowering her voice again. "What? That's crazy. If I could actually speak to someone and defend myself, I could prove that—"

"I know you're innocent." Irene held up her hand. "I suspected as much and Seb as much as confirmed it. He didn't want to spell it out to me, but I'm convinced he bribed someone in Marcus's office to frame you."

Emily's mouth dropped open in astonishment.

"Why would he do that?" Lucy asked.

"To win. He'll do anything. He's…obsessed and unscrupulous. It was the last straw for me. I've been thinking about leaving for a while, but I stepped up my plans. I don't want any part of this."

"You said Seb has a plan?" Emily asked.

"Yes. Seb knew that Marcus would be livid if he found out that Olivia was getting information about his business. There's a lot of history between them, and Seb knew that convincing Marcus of a connection would push him to take action. He knew Marcus would retaliate, and now they're planning to submit anonymous complaints of financial misconduct at Olivia's firm."

Lucy let out a gasp and covered her mouth in shock. Emily gave her a quick look to silently convey that she didn't want Irene knowing about Olivia's current state of health. Lucy seemed to get the message and gently inclined her head.

Irene continued. "Marcus used to work with Olivia and has insider information. He knows exactly what to submit a complaint about. Seb's playing him too, for his own ends. Seb was furious that Olivia threatened him and wanted to, as he said, teach her a lesson. I'm not sure if there is anything that can be done, but I wanted to warn you."

"Why now?" Emily asked. "You have to agree that this all looks suspicious. Just as your case is losing ground, you suddenly want to help me."

Irene nodded. "I understand your concerns; I'd be the same if our positions were reversed. I was wrong to stay with him, to stand by his side. To be honest, I was too scared to leave him before. But now I see what levels he will stoop to…I don't want Henry to grow up anywhere near Seb."

"That makes two of us," Emily replied.

"Which is another reason I'm leaving him. Once I leave, he'll drop the case. And if he doesn't, it'll be thrown out because there is no way he could care for Henry alone."

"You want to see Henry," Lucy said.

"Yes." Irene nodded. "I…I want a chance to learn to be a grandmother to him. I know I failed Joe terribly. I didn't protect him from Seb and his temper. I want another chance to do right by my son. I don't expect you to trust me, not yet. As I say, I know trust isn't handed out so freely."

Emily let out a sigh. Her mind was spinning; it felt as if the ground was constantly shifting underneath her. She longed for her flight attendant days, the security of knowing what was going to happen and when. Everything ran like clockwork. These last few weeks had been a rollercoaster of emotions. Now she was looking at Irene, a woman with an enormous weight on her shoulders, and thinking she'd misjudged her. She wanted to reach out an olive branch, but knew she had to be cautious.

"I appreciate you coming to us with this, really I do." Emily nervously played with the mug in front of her. "But, you're right, trust isn't something I can give out so easily. Joe told me a lot about his upbringing…"

"I was a terrible mother," Irene said.

"Terrible is a strong word." Emily attempted to soften the blow.

"I'd always been under my own mother's control. She was very strict, and I wanted to get away from her. So I married Seb when I was just eighteen." She laughed bitterly. "Out of the frying pan and into the fire, as they say. I'd hardly even dated before him, and I really didn't have much time to develop into my own person. When Joe came along, I just listened to what my mother and Seb told me and took it as gospel. It was easier than trying to fight them both all the time. I was too young and too weak to be the mother my son deserved." She dabbed at her eyes with the screwed-up napkin. "I won't fail my Joe again by not being strong enough to stop Seb from doing to Henry what he did to my boy." She sniffed and balled the tissue into her fist. "I will not let him steal the light from his eyes too." Irene looked down at her sunglasses on the table. "There's not a day that goes by that I don't wish I could go back and do everything differently. It's only recently, with age, that I'm finally realising there is a whole world out there. A world for me—and not the me that is simply an appendage to my mother or my husband."

"You're really leaving him, then?" Lucy asked.

"Yes, but it needed some preparation. If I tell him…well, I don't know exactly what he'd do."

Emily and Lucy shared a look of concern.

"Please don't worry for me. I'm moving in with my brother, until the worst is over." She smiled sadly. "I'd planned to make contact with you once the dust had settled. But when I heard their plans for your friend, I had to act."

Emily nodded. "Thank you. I really appreciate it. I know you took a risk in coming here."

Irene put her sunglasses back on and made a move to stand up. As she did, Emily reached out and gently caught her arm.

"There's definitely a place for a grandmother in Henry's life. When the dust settles, give me a call." Emily meant it. For the first time in a long time, she could see Henry having a meaningful relationship with a grandparent, a window into the enigma that was his father. When she was young, she'd thought about her future children and always pictured a large, happy family. Now it looked as if she would be able to give Henry what she'd never had, safe in the knowledge that the custody case was well and truly over.

Irene looked relieved and nodded. "Thank you. I really won't let you down."

Once Irene had left the shop, Lucy looked at Emily and asked, "You trust her?"

"Yeah," Emily said. "I'm not sure why, but I do. She was willing to leave; she didn't ask for anything from us."

"True." Lucy sipped from her tea. "What are you going to tell Olivia?"

"I don't know. Nothing right now. I'll tell Simon. Olivia needs time to recover, not hear that I'm causing even more trouble in her life."

"It's hardly your fault."

"It feels like it. I feel as if my shouting fit hospitalised her. Now this." Emily put her head in her hands. "I just don't know if I'm coming or going at the moment. I should be jumping for joy. My debts are cleared. Henry is staying with me. I have a new start."

"I don't think emotions work like that."

"Mine definitely don't," Emily said.

Lucy finished off her drink. "By the way, who was that woman at the hotel? Nicole?"

Emily chuckled. In all the excitement, she'd forgotten to tell Lucy about Nicole and her manuscript. "You might want another drink."

CHAPTER THIRTY-TWO

"So, what would you like to do?" Simon asked.

Henry shrugged as he sat on the sofa in the living room of the hotel suite, staring at Nicole and Simon sitting opposite him.

"Would you like to do some colouring with Auntie Nicole?" Simon suggested, ignoring Nicole's glare.

Henry turned to look at Nicole with a confused frown. "Are you my mommy's sister?"

"No," Nicole replied with a shake of her head. "I'm a friend of Simon's."

"So, you're not my auntie?"

"Um, no, that's just something that adults say sometimes." Nicole looked to Simon for assistance.

"Why?" Henry asked, looking from Nicole to Simon.

"Because…erm…" Simon ran out of steam, unable to explain the custom to a five-year-old in a way that made sense. He offered a smile and tried distraction instead. "So, colouring? I'm great at colouring. I always stay inside the lines."

"Where did my mommy go?"

Nicole stood up, a wicked grin on her face. "Have fun, Simon. I'm going to make a drink."

Simon looked up to her and whispered, "You're not going to help me?"

"You were the one who volunteered. I've never proclaimed to be a maternal sort of person. You're on your own, pal. To be honest, I'm only hanging around to see how disastrously this will turn out."

"Thanks a lot," Simon mumbled as Nicole walked to the kitchen. He looked back to Henry, who was eyeing him suspiciously.

"So, no colouring?"

Henry shook his head.

"Um. TV?"

Henry shrugged, and Simon took that for as close to an agreement as he was going to get. He turned the television on, found a cartoon, and headed into the kitchen to join Nicole.

"Given up already?" Nicole chuckled.

"He's nervous. He doesn't know us very well. I think."

"And here I thought you could charm the birds from the trees?"

Simon smirked. "Clearly my charm doesn't work on five-year-old boys."

"I'm nearly six."

Nicole and Simon spun around to see Henry walking into the kitchen with a giraffe lunchbox in his hand and Tiny tucked under his arm.

"I thought you were watching TV, mate?" Simon asked, bending down so they were face-to-face.

"Tiny wants lunch." Henry walked past Simon and put his lunchbox on the table.

"What's a tiny?" Nicole whispered to Simon.

"I can hear you, you know," Henry said as he pulled out a dining chair. He put the giraffe toy on the table and pointed to it. "This is Tiny."

"Oh, well, nice to meet you, Tiny." Nicole held out her hand to the cuddly toy.

Henry looked at her and shook his head in exasperation. "He's just a toy. He can't do that."

Nicole held her hands up, stepped back towards the work surface, and continued making tea.

Henry sat on the chair, leaned forward towards Tiny, and listened intently before nodding. "Tiny wants to know if he can have a glass of water?" He looked up at Simon hopefully.

"One glass of water, coming right up." Simon turned around and picked a glass out from the cupboard.

Henry opened up his lunch box and started to unfold the foil wrapper around a cheese sandwich. Simon placed a half-full glass of water in front of Tiny. Henry continued to watch Simon as he slowly chewed the first bite of his sandwich.

After an age of slow chewing and a loud swallow, he finally spoke again. "Where's Mommy?"

"She's just running a quick errand," Simon supplied the same excuse Emily had used when she'd left.

"What kind of errand?"

"Yes, Simon, what kind of errand?" Nicole leaned against the work surface and looked at him.

"A very important one. But one that won't take very long," Simon replied through clenched teeth while scowling at Nicole.

Henry picked an apple out of his lunchbox and held it up for Simon. Simon hesitantly took it, frowning.

"It needs to be wet, or I can't eat it," Henry explained.

Simon nodded, turned around, and ran the apple under the cold water tap.

"Do you work with Olivia at the piggy bank?" Henry asked Nicole.

"No," Nicole replied. "I work in the theatre. I make plays."

Simon placed the wet apple on a piece of kitchen paper in front of Henry.

"Is Olivia really sleeping?"

"Yes, that's why we can't have a loud party." Simon sat down beside Henry, who regarded him with a bored expression. Simon reached forward to the water glass in front of Tiny and mimed Tiny drinking from it, making loud gulps as he did.

Henry watched with a stony expression, took another bite of his sandwich, and looked at Nicole. "Do you live in London?"

"I do."

"Why are you in New York?"

"I'm visiting Olivia."

"But she's asleep."

"Yes. I'm hoping she'll wake up before I have to go home and feed my cat."

"You have a cat?"

Nicole sipped her tea. "I do. His name is Muffin."

"Why did you call him that?"

"I'm not really sure. It seemed amusing at the time." Nicole shrugged. "Why did you call your toy Tiny?"

"I made muffins with Lucy last weekend," Henry said, ignoring the question. He reached for his apple, frowned, and handed it back to Simon. "It's dry."

Simon took the apple, stood up, and walked back over to the sink.

"Do you help a lot in the kitchen?" Nicole asked.

"I'm good at stirring."

Simon put the wet apple back in front of Henry on a fresh sheet of kitchen paper.

Henry looked to Simon with interest. "Why are you in still New York?"

"I'm helping Olivia with some stuff."

"Does Olivia live in New York now?" Henry looked excited at the prospect.

"Um. I'm not sure. You'll have to talk to your mommy about that," Simon replied.

Henry huffed. "That's what adults say when they don't want to tell you something."

"Would you like to play a game on my phone?" Simon tried to distract him.

"No. Can you count to twenty?"

"Yes, I can." Simon nodded.

Henry stared at him.

"You want me to do it now?"

Henry took a bite of his sandwich and slowly nodded as he chewed.

"Okay." Simon took a deep breath and then counted to twenty as fast as he could. When he finished, Henry looked unfazed.

"That was silly," Henry told him. "No one could hear the words."

"Can you count to twenty?" Simon asked.

"I can count to a hundred," Henry replied with pride.

"Go on, then." Simon sat back in his chair and folded his arms.

"I don't feel like it." Henry picked up his apple. "This is dry."

❖

After lunch, Simon convinced Henry to do some colouring. He sat beside the boy as they both coloured in various animal shapes from a book Lucy had packed in Henry's backpack. Henry didn't seem in the mood for small talk and was quieter than Simon could ever remember him being. Simon wondered if the situation with his grandparents was still haunting him. He knew that a stressful environment was known to affect children, but he was shocked by the drastic change in Henry's personality.

"Are you married?" Henry's voice shook Simon from his musings.

"No, but I have a girlfriend," he replied, concentrating on the purple stripes he was applying to the zebra in Henry's book.

"Is she pretty?"

"Very pretty."

"Prettier than Nicole?"

Simon looked up at Nicole, who paused looking at her phone to grin at him.

"They are just as pretty as each other," Simon replied diplomatically.

Nicole smirked, nodded, and returned her attention to her phone.

Henry seemed happy with the response and moved Simon's hand to one side as he turned the page, seemingly bored with the pig he was colouring green. He looked at the new page, picked up a new colour, and handed it to Simon, tapping at the outline of a bird for him to colour.

"Is Olivia dying?"

Simon looked at Henry in shock. "No, she's just a little under the weather," he quickly answered. "She'll be just fine in a few days."

"Are you sure?" Henry seemed uncertain.

"Very. But I know that a get-well-soon card from you will make her recover even faster," Simon said.

"No, it won't!" Henry shouted. "That's a lie!"

Henry slammed his pencil down, took the book away from Simon, and closed it. He folded his arms and brought his knees up to his chest. "You lied!"

"Henry…I didn't mean—"

"I want to go home."

"Your mum will—"

"I want to go home now!"

Simon opened his mouth to speak when he saw Olivia appear in the doorway. She looked as if she had just woken up and leaned heavily on her crutch as she frowned at the scene in front of her.

"Henry?"

Henry's head spun around. "Olivia!" He sprinted across the room and hugged her legs tightly.

Olivia put her hand on his head and gently smoothed his hair, looking curiously at Simon and Nicole.

"Simon was practicing being a father with mixed results," Nicole said by way of an explanation.

"Emily had to run an errand, and we said we'd look after Henry for her," Simon clarified.

"Simon said that. I mainly sat here and watched." Nicole grinned.

Olivia looked from one to the other and then shook her head. She adjusted her crutch, took Henry's hand, and started to turn around.

"What are you doing?" Simon asked, standing up.

"Henry's going to sit with me."

"You're supposed to be resting."

"How is one supposed to rest when child abuse is occurring in the next room?"

"Hardly child abuse." Simon sighed.

"I don't know," Nicole started. "Some of the bad jokes Simon has subjected that poor child to…"

"Hey," Simon argued.

"Henry will sit with me," Olivia said. Henry turned around and nodded at Simon before following Olivia to her room.

❖

Olivia got back into bed and adjusted her blankets. She took a deep breath to relax herself after the strain of hurrying out to see what the noise was about.

"Why were you upset?" she asked Henry, who was getting her a fresh glass of water from the bathroom.

"Simon said you were sick and a get-well card would make you better." Henry slowly walked into the room with both hands wrapped around a full glass of water.

Olivia frowned and shook her head. "Why would a get-well card make me better?"

"He's silly." Henry gently placed the water on the bedside table. "He can't even count to twenty properly."

Olivia patted the space beside her, and Henry climbed onto the bed and curled up next to her.

"Can you count to twenty?" Olivia asked as she wrapped her arm around him.

"I can count to one hundred."

"Well, if you can count to one hundred, then you can count to nine hundred and ninety-nine."

"Can I?" Henry looked up at her, confused.

"Yes. You say ninety-nine, one hundred, and then you start again, but you put one hundred in front of everything. And then when you get to one hundred and ninety-nine, you start again and put two hundred in front of everything. And then three hundred, and so on."

"What comes after nine hundred and…" Henry struggled to remember the number.

"Nine hundred and ninety-nine," Olivia finished. "One thousand."

"That sounds hard."

"Yes. We'll leave that until you are six," she told him.

"Are you very sick?"

Olivia thought about the question. The truth was that she didn't know. She'd been told that she had been working too hard and needed to rest, which didn't sound all that serious. On the other hand, her body ached in places she didn't know existed, and her mind felt fuzzy and exhausted.

"I feel better now that I'm with you," she answered honestly.

"Why is this room the same as the other room?"

"The room in London?" she asked, looking around herself.

Henry nodded as he gripped the soft blankets.

"Because hotels are ridiculous."

"Do you not have a house?"

"No." Olivia looked around the characterless room. "But I should get one."

Henry looked up, a hopeful look on his face. "In New York, near me and Mommy?"

"Yes, in New York." She smiled.

"Can you count to a million?" Henry asked.

"Why would I want to do that?"

"To see if you can." Henry snuggled against her tighter.

"I don't think I want to count to a million. It would take a very, very long time," she explained.

"Would I be a grown-up by the time you got to a million?"

She chuckled. "Not quite that long."

"How long would we need to count for me to be a grown-up?"

Olivia considered the question for a beat before understanding that a realistic answer wasn't necessary. "A very, very, very long time," she replied. "Why do you want to count until you are a grown-up?"

"Because Mommy told Tom that I might have to live with Grandpa Seb, and I don't want to. So if we count all the way until I'm a grown-up, then I won't have to."

She pulled Henry a little closer. "Your mommy and I are going to do everything we can to make sure you don't have to live with your grandparents. To make sure you can live with your mommy forever."

"What if I have to live with Grandpa Seb though?"

"Then you'll have to."

"But I don't want to."

"Sometimes we have to do things we don't want to do. It makes you stronger and braver."

"I don't want to be stronger or braver." Henry sat up on his knees and looked at Olivia imploringly. "If I have to go and live with Grandpa Seb, will you beat him up for me? You can hit him with your stick again."

Olivia smiled. "Maybe. We'll see." She lifted her arm and Henry returned to his previous position, snuggled up to her side. "But for now I want to hear you count to twenty."

❖

Emily hurried back to the hotel. She trusted Simon and Nicole to care for Henry, but he'd been in such a strange mood lately. She worried that the atmosphere in the house had been getting to him. As much as she tried to keep upbeat and positive, she knew he could easily see through it.

She felt as if she were swimming through syrup. So many huge changes were occurring at such a blistering rate that she could barely keep up. Even though she knew logically that she was no longer in debt, the suffocating fear was still strong. She imagined it would stay with her for some time yet as her brain continued to process everything.

Of course, she was grateful to Olivia for helping her, but Emily had grown up knowing that people expected something in return for a good deed. It took a lot of willpower to suppress the feeling that Olivia would suddenly ask something of her. And Olivia's unbelievable kindness didn't help the terrible way Emily felt for treating her so abysmally. She'd had good reasons for doing the things she'd done, but that didn't help the guilt.

She knew Olivia had had feelings for her once. In London, that had been very clear. But when Emily had asked Olivia to speak with Henry, she'd made it clear that it was simply for Henry. That she didn't want it to mean anything between them. The problem was, now she was falling for Olivia again. Not for the repayment of her debts—in fact, absolutely not for that. She was falling for Olivia because of the way she'd defended Henry from Seb, the way she was with him generally, and the way she'd dropped everything to help with the lawyer. Olivia, as a friend, had done more for Emily and Henry than any of her previous partners.

She couldn't deny that she had been attracted to Olivia in London. It was hard not to be. Chocolate-brown eyes, dark flowing hair, a perfectly proportioned body. Olivia Lewis was definitely easy on the eyes. But since reconnecting, Emily was seeing another side—the caring side. Her attraction to Olivia now was not founded on looks, but in actions.

She had to make a decision. Right now she was walking a fine line; not in a relationship with Olivia, but not just a friend either. It wasn't fair to anyone. Emily was reluctant to enter a real relationship in case things went wrong and Henry suffered more. But she knew the flip side was that Henry would be ecstatically happy to be a family with Olivia. If things worked out. Emily found herself constantly wondering just how big an "if" that was. She never gambled; she always took the most sensible route, the path that seemed most secure. But a leap of faith would be required if she was going to try to make a go of things with Olivia.

That was, of course, if Olivia even wanted to try again. Had she pushed Olivia too far? Had she come to her senses and realised that she could do better than an unemployed single mother who had no idea what was happening with her life? An unemployed single mother who might have just met a theatre producer who, against all the odds, thought she could write.

The sludge that was Emily's thought process groaned. She knew that she should, in theory, be ecstatic. Her debts were paid, she was away from a job where she was monitored by the man who was trying to take her son, her court case looked better, and she had met a professional who had told her she could write. She should be cartwheeling her way back to the hotel, but she was still in shock. Everything had happened so quickly. In just a few days, her life had gone from absolute disaster with seemingly no chance of escape to something beyond her wildest dreams.

The problem with things beyond your wildest dreams was the disbelief. Emily's brain simply wasn't wired to take so much good news. She was still waiting for the other shoe to drop, for someone to tell her that it had all been a big mistake. For her life to fall apart around her ears again. She stopped dead in the lobby of the hotel as a thought hit her.

She wasn't dancing for joy because she expected the worst, but she wasn't fearful either. For the first time in many years, she had someone in her life who would stand by her no matter what. Despite not being in a relationship, she knew with absolute certainty that Olivia would be there for her. No matter what.

She realised that people were staring at her as she had her epiphany. She shook her head and quickly headed towards the elevators. Her brain struggled with the weight of her revelation as she anxiously tapped her foot on the elevator floor.

At the suite door, Simon welcomed her in. She said hello to Nicole and then quickly scanned the room for Henry. Nicole silently stood and gestured for Emily to follow her. When they got to Olivia's bedroom, Nicole nudged the door open, and they both looked in.

Henry was curled up against Olivia's side, Olivia holding him tightly while they both slept. If Emily had any remaining doubts about her feelings for Olivia, they quickly floated away.

"Simon and I were terrible at looking after him, so Olivia took over. We heard the mumblings of them talking for about half an hour before it went quiet," Nicole whispered.

Emily smiled. "Olivia once told me that she wasn't good with children."

"I think it rather depends on the child," Nicole replied.

"She loves Henry," Emily said with a slow nod of her head. Her eyes were still fixed on the bed.

"Not just Henry."

Emily felt her cheeks heat as she stared at Nicole in surprise. "Maybe she used to. I think I've...well. I think it's too late now."

"Why have you never sent a script to an agent?" Nicole asked.

Emily blinked and blew out a breath, the change in topic taking her off guard. "Um, well, I kind of always thought that if I did, then someone who knows what they're talking about would tell me I'm terrible. I could pretend that I was good in my own little headspace."

"But, due to an extraordinary series of events, I saw your script. And I'm telling you again, it's wonderful. But the problem is that extraordinary series of events are rare. Sometimes you have to take a chance."

"I know." Emily let out a nervous sigh.

"Simon and I are going to pop out for something to eat. I suggest that you two talk properly."

Nicole turned and started to walk away, but Emily reached out and gently held her arm. Nicole turned to look at her, and Emily smiled gratefully.

"Thank you. I needed the pep talk."

Nicole smiled and squeezed Emily's hand. "The most terrible reactions are generally created in our own mind, through fear. You know that."

Emily nodded and watched as Nicole walked into the living room, threw a coat to Simon, and hurried him out of the room. When they'd left, Emily turned to look at Olivia and Henry again. She smiled and stepped into the room, wishing she could preserve the moment forever. It didn't seem right to take a picture, so she stared at the scene, trying to capture every detail and lock it up tightly in her mind's eye.

She sat on the bed opposite Henry, and tentatively reached out to tuck a stray curl of hair behind Olivia's ear. Olivia's eyes flickered open to look at Emily in confusion. Emily softly placed her hand on Olivia's shoulder to keep her in place and gestured towards her sleeping son with her head. Olivia looked at Henry and then back to Emily, fondness and understanding in her eyes.

"How are you feeling?" Emily asked, her voice barely above a whisper; she had to sit close to be sure that Olivia heard her.

"Tired, but better than I was."

"I'm sorry Henry disturbed you."

"He didn't. I fetched him when I heard that he was upset. Where did you go?"

Emily knew that Olivia needed the information, but she also knew that now was most definitely not the time. "Nothing to worry about now. Thank you for looking after him."

"He's a wonderful boy," Olivia whispered, the words so easily slipping from her mouth but so steadfast in their meaning.

Emily leaned forward and placed a soft but firm kiss on Olivia's lips, knowing actions would speak louder than words. Although she was aware that, with Olivia, she would also need to explain her actions in detail.

Sure enough, when Emily pulled back, there was a confused look on Olivia's face. It was up to her to clarify what was happening, what she wanted to happen. Simon's words echoed in her head, and she understood that it was up to her to alter her behaviour because Olivia was unable to, no matter how much she might want to.

"You have become very precious to me, Olivia Lewis."

Olivia's frown deepened, her confusion growing.

"It's not just Henry who missed you."

A spark of recognition and hope shone in Olivia's eyes.

"I know I have no right to ask you this. I've treated you terribly, but I'd—"

"Yes, anything," Olivia whispered.

Emily chuckled. "You don't even know what I'm going to ask."

"The last time you asked me something and I agreed without knowing what it was, we ended up here."

"Everything's happening very fast, and I'm a bit of a mess at the moment," Emily said. She lightly brushed her fingers through Olivia's hair, wanting to feel closer to her but not wanting to kiss her again with Henry so close. "But you've become such an important person in my life, and in Henry's life too."

Olivia looked at Henry, who had started to squirm.

"Mommy?"

"I'm here, Henry."

He crawled from Olivia's embrace and put his arms out to Emily. She reached out and pulled him across Olivia gently and into her own lap, where he cuddled into her.

Olivia looked at them with wild eyes, clearly wanting to know what Emily had been about to say and cursing the interruption. She looked pleadingly at Emily, who chuckled softly.

"What I was going to say is, when you're feeling better, maybe we could go to dinner?" Emily said in a low tone, so as not to disturb Henry.

"Dinner?"

"A date. If you're willing?"

Olivia quickly nodded her agreement. A moment later, her face clouded over and Emily could practically see the cogs in her brain whirring.

"But—"

"A fresh start," Emily interjected. She knew Olivia was replaying every conversation they'd previously had. The mixed messages, the push and pull.

"A fresh start." Olivia smiled.

Chapter Thirty-three

Two relatively quiet days passed for Emily after she left Olivia's hotel room—with reassurances that she'd be back soon. She chuckled to herself as she remembered gently, but firmly, ordering Olivia to focus on her recovery. It was hard to be apart, but Emily knew she needed time. Processing everything that had happened wasn't going to be an easy task, but it was essential. If she was going to embark on a new life, then she owed it to herself, Henry, and Olivia to be sure she was ready.

So while she left Olivia to recover, Emily spent her time organising her life. For the first time in as long as she could remember, she organised her financial affairs. Between the severance payment she'd received from Crown and the money from the journalist, she was actually in the black. For the first time in years, she had money in the bank and no immediate debts to focus on.

She'd taken the box of paperwork back from Olivia, noting happily how meticulously organised it was. Checking every document, she confirmed that everything was paid up before she gleefully shredded them and cut the old credit cards into pieces. The relief was palpable.

The previous day, she'd enlisted Henry's assistance. She'd handed him a piece of paper and watched with a smile as he'd walked over to the electric shredder and carefully fed the document into the machine, keeping his fingers out of the way as he did. As soon as he was done, she gleefully handed him another piece.

"This one too?" Henry asked.

"That one too," Emily confirmed, watching her now-healthy son feed the statement of the card she'd primarily used for food into the machine.

Her hand was already holding the next piece of paper when Henry turned around and regarded her with a sigh. He didn't understand why shredding the papers was so cathartic to her.

"More?"

"More, many more." She leaned forward and kissed his head as he took the next one. "Remember to mind your fingers."

"'Kay," Henry said as he carefully fed the next sheet in. "Why, though?"

"Because these are bills that have been paid, so we don't need them anymore." She knew he probably wouldn't understand, but he'd only learn by asking questions.

It was as if someone had opened the windows in an attic that had been closed up for eons. Emily felt lighter. Every breath she took was fresher. Of course she'd known she was stressed, but she'd had no idea how much it had affected her in everyday life. Now she woke up feeling refreshed, as if she'd actually slept rather than just laid down, and her neck didn't crack every time she turned her head.

Henry had immediately detected and reacted to the change. He was brighter, happier. It hurt to think that her depression had become so all-consuming that she'd unknowingly dragged him down. Suddenly the correlation between her happiness and his was much easier to see.

She was pulled from her memories by her phone vibrating in her pocket. It was a text.

I left Seb this morning and will be out of town for a few days until things calm down. Please send Henry my love, if you think it is appropriate. Irene.

Emily worried her lip. She could only imagine how hard it had been for Irene to leave her husband of so many years, even if he was as bad as Seb. Her heart clenched as she replied.

I'll pass your message on to Henry. I know he'll enjoy having his grandmother in his life. Things went okay?

She didn't know if Irene would feel comfortable sharing those kinds of details with her, but she wanted to offer a shoulder, if not to cry on then at least to unburden herself. The reply was quick.

It was as I expected. I'm glad I was prepared and didn't have to hang around. I'm also glad I'm away from him, even if the next few days will prove to be unpleasant. I have to look to the future. Thank you for letting me see you and Henry as a part of that future.

Emily read the message a few times. Irene hadn't gone into detail, but between her message and Emily's knowledge of Seb, she assumed it hadn't been an amicable exchange. She looked forward to things settling down. Henry deserved some downtime with his grandmother. It wouldn't be easy to change Henry's initial perceptions, but Emily was determined to forge a bond between them.

A few hours later, Emily received a phone call from her lawyer to confirm that Seb had dropped the custody case. She walked into the living room where Henry was playing, knelt beside him, and squeezed him extra hard. Henry happily returned the hug with all his strength.

Despite all the good news, two things still terrified Emily. Her potential relationship with Olivia was one. The other was figuring out what her future held. The money she had in the bank wouldn't last long; she knew that from painful experience. So now she had to figure out if she had what it took to make a leap of faith. The doorbell rang, and she knew it was time to find out.

Lucy gave Emily a confident smile and a geeky double thumbs-up. Emily nodded and opened the front door to greet Simon and Nicole, directing them into the living room.

Olivia was on the mend, which meant Nicole was heading home soon. After Lucy and Tom had encouraged Emily to send a few more of her finished works over, and she had eventually caved and hit the Send button with a shaking finger, Nicole had called to ask if they could meet before she left.

Now Nicole was sitting in her living room, being offered a drink by Lucy, who was introducing herself. Emily shook her head to snap out of her haze.

"Simon!" Henry said loudly when he walked in from the garden.

Simon gave Nicole a smug look before greeting Henry.

"Simon, will you play with me?" Henry asked.

"Absolutely." Simon stood up from the sofa, and a moment later they headed to the garden.

Once they were alone, Nicole reached into her bag and flipped through pieces of paper. "Obviously, I haven't had time to read everything you sent me," she started.

Emily sat on the edge of an armchair and waited nervously for her to continue.

"But I'm loving what I see."

Emily felt a breath of relief leave her body and anxiously nodded, too fearful to speak.

Nicole pulled out some paperwork and rearranged the sheets into the correct order.

"I sent the email copy of the original script I read to my colleagues, and like me, they adore it. We want to produce it. Of course, it will be a small production. We'll try it out on the circuit, minimal sets and overheads as we tour to see how it goes. There will be a lot of work needed on the manuscript to tailor it—"

"You...you want to produce my play?" Emily stammered. She could hear her heart beating loudly in her chest as her heart rate spiked through the roof. She felt flushed and worried that she might pass out.

Nicole looked up at her, and her expression softened, as if suddenly were remembering that she was dealing with an amateur. "Darling, I'd sell a kidney on the black market to produce this play. I love it. I believe in it."

Lucy walked into the room, set three mugs down, and looked from Nicole to Emily. "Should I go?"

"No, please stay. In fact, pinch me. Make sure I'm not dreaming," Emily said hurriedly.

Nicole laughed. "You say that now, but trust me, when you hear about the rewrites, you'll think it is more of a nightmare than a dream."

Nicole handed Emily a piece of paper with a calendar on it.

"As you can see," Nicole said as she gestured to different dates with her pen, "there are a number of large events, and the circuit is getting booked up. If we want to tour with this, we need to get things booked in soon or it will mean waiting another ten months for the next circuit. Theatre is affected by other events in the calendar, summer seasons, Christmas, awards shows, etcetera. We are coming to the end of the window for this term, but we can make it."

"Why do I feel like there's a but coming?" Emily asked.

Nicole smiled. "We need drastic rewrites, and we need them within a very short window."

"What kind of rewrites and how much time?"

Nicole handed Emily another piece of paper. Emily looked through the list of proposed changes and the reasons for them—cutting scenes to reduce the number of sets, removing a background character, adding pages to make up the time.

"I don't make these decisions alone. I have two partners who will need to see a new manuscript, with these changes, in order to approve the go-ahead for this season. They would need to see it soon; I'll have to speak with them about times, but we're talking under a month. Probably less."

"Is that usual?" Lucy asked.

Nicole nodded sadly. "Rewrites are the bane of my life. Most plays have script changes right up until an hour before opening night. After that, many change several times over the first few productions. It's normal for scripts to change a lot while the play is running."

"That's really impressive. I had no idea," Lucy commented.

Nicole sipped her coffee. "If we do a good job, you shouldn't notice. Actors are used to it. It's producers like me who live in fear."

Emily had finished reading. "These all make sense. I can definitely make these changes. I'm not sure how quickly though."

"I can watch Henry," Lucy said.

"He'll wonder what I'm doing. You know what he's like." Emily chuckled.

Nicole handed Emily another piece of paper. "Playwrights aren't millionaires. I'd love to pay you an upfront fee for your manuscript, but as an unknown it would be hard for me to justify. As much as I love the script, we are taking a gamble on it."

"I understand." Emily looked down at the document Nicole had handed her and realised, with some shock, that it was a contract.

"We can offer you a royalty agreement," Nicole continued. "This means you are directly tied to the success of the play. If it makes nothing, you make nothing. If it is a resounding success, well…you get the gist."

The papers shook in her hands as Emily read through the document. The legal tone was confusing, and she wasn't entirely sure what it all meant, but it was a contract for her script. With her name on it, and signed by Nicole.

"So, how does that work?" Lucy asked, clearly sensing Emily's shock.

Nicole turned her attention to Lucy. "Basically, we total the ticket sales from each night, we remove production costs, and then, from what's left, if there is anything left, Emily will receive a percentage as detailed in the contract. Different theatres have different capacities.

It all depends on how many seats we manage to sell over how many nights."

"Do I sign this now?" Emily asked, her voice wavering slightly.

Nicole shook her head. "No. I don't want to pressure you. I know it may seem like a dream come true, but there really is a lot of work and we cannot pay you until the production is up and running. And that's if it even gets up and running. There's always a risk that you'll spend time working on this and it'll never see the light of day. I'll do everything in my power to ensure that doesn't happen, but sometimes, that's how theatre works."

Emily considered the words. She'd never been one to take chances, and the second Henry was in her life, she'd convinced herself that she needed to play everything safe. That clearly hadn't worked out very well for her, despite her best intentions. This was a real opportunity, one that would never come around again, and one she felt she actually had the skillset to do something with.

She'd never been very good at believing in herself, never really had anyone who believed in her. Now she was being handed a chance, an opening that people would kill for.

"I'm never going to get another opportunity like this, so I'd like to go ahead."

"Marvellous." Nicole put her coffee mug down. "Have a look over the contract in your own time and speak with your financial adviser."

"I don't have a financial adviser," Emily explained.

Nicole stared at her for a moment.

"Oh…you mean Olivia?" Emily asked.

"Yes." Nicole chuckled lightly. "She'll explain the numbers jargon. I don't know about you, but that stuff bores me to tears. In the meantime, I'm headed back to London to speak with my colleagues, then I'll be in touch about potential deadlines. How does that sound?"

"Incredible." Emily beamed. She looked out the window to where Henry was chasing Simon in the garden with a water pistol. She'd never thought that those years passing the time beside Henry's sickbed would turn into something so positive. She turned her attention back to Nicole. "How's Olivia doing?"

"Better." Nicole replaced some papers in her bag. "Simon is going to talk to her about the Applewood issue you told him about once I've gone home. We wanted to give her as much time as possible to recover."

"Understandable," Emily said.

"She suddenly took her bedrest much more seriously," Nicole commented with a grin. "Something about wanting to be better as she had a date to arrange."

Emily smiled shyly.

"I'm pleased you managed to sort it out."

"Me too! Took them long enough," Lucy added.

Emily threw her an exasperated look. "It was complicated, okay?"

Lucy laughed, and Emily rolled her eyes.

"It makes it easier for me to head home, knowing that someone is going to be looking out for her," Nicole said as she closed her bag. "Of course, I'll have to maim you if you hurt her."

Emily inclined her head in understanding.

"I'm sorry to dash off." Nicole stood up and looked out the window to where Simon played with Henry. "I hadn't expected a sudden visit to New York, and work's calling."

Emily got to her feet. "I understand. Thank you so much for coming over."

"I'll be in touch once I have a chance to speak with my team. I hope to have good news for you very soon."

"Good news was when you said that you liked my writing," Emily said.

Nicole smiled. "As I say, you'll hate me when you are in the middle of rewrites."

CHAPTER THIRTY-FOUR

Olivia shook her head and lifted the remote control to pause the DVD. She picked up the case and looked at the back to read the season description.

"What am I doing with my life?" She looked up at the sound of the door opening and smiled at Simon as he entered.

"How's it going?" Simon asked, putting his coat in the closet.

Olivia sighed. "I'm up to season four. I've become one of those people who binge-watches television."

Simon chuckled. "Hardly. You've only watched for two days, and you don't have much else to entertain you."

"No." Olivia glared at him. "Not since you stole my laptop and my phone." Olivia looked at the clock on the wall. She picked up the remote and shut off the television.

"On that note…" Simon sat on the opposite sofa and looked at her seriously.

"That's your bad news face. Even I know that."

"I have bad news," Simon said.

Olivia shrugged. "Go on. Might as well get it over with."

"Marcus is filing an anonymous complaint about financial irregularities. He's planning to bury us under paperwork."

"Oh." Olivia pulled herself up and adjusted to a more comfortable position. "Well, that's slightly preferable to tearing down professional relationships built up over a twenty-year period."

"Excuse me?" Simon asked.

"Well, so far his strategy has been to break up professional relationships. I hadn't realised how hurtful that would be. At least this is business. Diabolical and shallow. But just business."

"You seem remarkably calm." Simon looked at her with suspicion.

Olivia looked at the clock again and shrugged. "Collapsing in your office gives you a different perspective, Simon."

"No, it doesn't. You're acting shifty. What's going on?" He turned and looked at the clock. "Why are you looking at the clock?"

"It just…feels…like time for tea." Olivia reached for her crutch. "Don't you think it might be time for tea? You're British. Surely you must want some tea?"

"You're lying." Simon stood and regarded her cautiously. "What are you up to?"

Olivia stood, too, and adjusted her crutch under her arm. "You're so paranoid, Simon. Tea?"

There was a knock on the door, and Simon narrowed his eyes.

"Who's that?" he asked.

Olivia frowned and attempted to look confused, but she knew she couldn't pull it off. "I can't see through wood. You'd better answer it."

Simon gave her one last look before turning around and opening the door.

"Sophie!" He pulled his girlfriend into a hug and Olivia watched in satisfaction as her plan came together. She was very pleased that Sophie seemed to be the punctual type; she wouldn't have lasted long under Simon's cross-examination.

Sophie stepped into the room and Simon closed the door behind her, then ran his hand through his hair as he stared at her in disbelief.

"You're here! I can't believe you're here. Why are you here? How are you here?"

Sophie laughed, put her hands on Simon's cheeks, and angled his head down so he'd look at her. "Breathe, Si. Breathe."

He let out a nervous laugh, ducked forward, and kissed her nose.

"Olivia invited me. It was a surprise. I'm sorry I couldn't tell you."

Simon broke eye contact with her and looked at Olivia with a confused expression.

Olivia stepped forward, regarding him fondly. "You've been wonderful, Simon. You've done more than I ever could've asked of you. You deserve a break. I thought you might like to show Sophie around the city? I organised a suite for you in Midtown so you'll be near Broadway. I thought you might like that?"

Simon continued to stare in shocked silence until Sophie elbowed him gently in the ribs and whispered something to him.

"T-thank you," he stuttered. "Thank you so much. Are you sure? What about—"

"I've monopolised enough of your time. I can survive perfectly well for a few days on my own. In fact, it'll probably do me a world of good."

"Oh, I see. You're sick of me?" Simon joked.

"Thoroughly," Olivia replied with a smirk. "Now, go pack and get out."

Simon laughed loudly and turned to look at Sophie. "Just give me five minutes, okay?"

❖

"Thank you so much for all of this." Sophie placed a hot cup of tea on a coaster on the dining table in front of Olivia.

"Thank you for coming." Olivia straightened the cup on the coaster. "Simon's been extraordinary since my accident. I wanted to give him something back."

Sophie sat opposite, her own cup in her hands. "He'll be so happy when I tell him about the theatre tickets. You're very generous."

"He deserves it." Olivia straightened the coaster in line with the grain of the table. "He's been very good to me."

"He's glad to do it. I know how much he looks up to you."

Olivia chuckled. "Please don't say I'm like a mother figure to him."

Sophie grinned. "No, more like a mentor. You're not that old!"

"I feel old."

"Well, you're not," Sophie said simply. "And I'm sure with some rest you'll feel much better."

"Oh, I already feel much better than I did."

"Just make sure you take it easy. I know Simon was really worried about you."

Olivia smiled. "Oh, I will. I've no intention of ever being ill again. I realise I need to listen to my body, even if I don't like what it's saying."

Soon Simon was ready to leave, and as Olivia stood to see him off, he gave her an impromptu hug and made her promise to call him if she needed anything at all. Only once she agreed did he finally leave, giving her back her phone as he did.

Olivia looked around and let out a sigh. It was the first time since the plane crash that she had been alone in the suite. It was a bittersweet feeling; in some ways she was pleased to have her private sanctuary back, but in others she had gotten used to the sounds of life bouncing off the walls.

She scrolled through her contact list to Emily's name, took a deep breath, and pressed the screen. It only rang twice before the line was connected.

"Hello. Feeling better?" Emily's happy voice put Olivia instantly at ease.

"Much," she said. "In fact, I have a doctor's appointment tomorrow. A check-up following my accident and hopefully a chance to get rid of this damn crutch. If he declares me well, I was wondering if I could take you and Henry out to dinner?"

"Me and Henry?"

"Yes, is that okay?" Olivia frowned, wondering if she'd already make a mistake.

"It's very okay. I just assumed that you'd want it to be just the two of us."

"Oh." Olivia bit her lip as she processed the information.

"But I love that you want to see us both," Emily added sincerely.

"So, it's okay?" Olivia confirmed.

"Of course. I know Henry would love to come out to dinner with us. As long as your doctor approves."

Olivia remained silent; the very thought of going back to the doctor was enough to make her blood run cold.

"Olivia?"

"Sorry. I was distracted."

"Is everything all right?"

"I…" Olivia paused. "I really don't like going to the doctor."

"That's understandable. Would you like some company?"

Olivia blinked in surprise. "You'd do that?"

"Absolutely. If you don't mind, I'd love to come along. I can check up on you and make sure you are fit and healthy again." Emily's voice took on a joking tone.

"I think I'd like that," Olivia said.

"Great. When's your appointment?"

"Four."

"Okay. How about I come over around three?"

Olivia sat on the arm of the sofa and let out a breath of relief. "That would be wonderful."

CHAPTER THIRTY-FIVE

Olivia carefully negotiated rush hour traffic while Emily sat in the passenger seat, pretending to look at the sights around them, but mainly trying to catch glimpses of Olivia. The doctor had performed a few tests and quickly pronounced her fit and well. He'd prescribed rest and relaxation. He'd also suggested that she try to reduce stress levels.

As soon as they'd left the doctor's office, Olivia's mood had lightened, and she'd let out a sigh of relief and thanked Emily for her company. Emily had told her it had been no bother, but the truth was that she'd desperately wanted to be there. To hear the doctor give Olivia the all-clear was a huge relief. And to be able to hold Olivia's hand and soothe her through a stressful appointment had been exhilarating.

"Pull over here," Emily said when they were a few streets away from the house.

"But—" Olivia frowned in confusion.

"I want to say something before we get to the house," Emily explained. "Just pull over here." She pointed to an appropriate spot on the deserted street.

Olivia did as she was told and slowed the car to a stop. She fiddled with the gear shift slightly longer than was necessary, and Emily realised she had spooked her.

"It's nothing bad," Emily said.

"People say that when it's something bad." Olivia turned to face her.

Emily chuckled. "They also say it when it's nothing bad."

"Your nothing bad might not be the same as my nothing ba—"

Emily cut her off by quickly removing her seat belt, leaning forward, and silencing her with a kiss. The moment their lips came into contact, she wanted more. She brought her hand up to hold Olivia's head in place as she deepened the kiss, gently stroking Olivia's cheek with her thumb.

Olivia shucked out of her own seat belt and cupped Emily's face with her hands as she leaned into the kiss. Emily brought her free hand up to hold on to Olivia's arm and softly squeezed through the material of her blouse sleeve.

When oxygen started to become an issue, Emily ended the kiss and rested her forehead against Olivia's. "See? Nothing bad," she said.

Olivia laughed. "Quite the opposite."

Emily placed a small kiss on Olivia's lips as they both attempted to get their breath back.

"If we're having dinner with Henry tonight, we'll have to be on our best behaviour," Emily explained.

"I see."

Emily kissed Olivia softly again. "So we'll have to make the most of now."

"I intend to," Olivia replied. She angled Emily's head and swiftly brought her mouth down onto her lips.

❖

Lucy raised her eyebrow at Emily as she entered the kitchen. Emily frowned. Lucy smirked at her while closing the refrigerator door.

"What?" Emily asked.

"Nothing." Lucy shrugged. "Just admiring that shade of lipstick."

Emily spun around to look at her reflection in the hallway mirror. She could see the remains of Olivia's lipstick smudged around her lips from their hot and heavy session in the car.

She plucked a tissue from the box on the sideboard and cleaned the dark red shade away, mentally damning Olivia for not mentioning it before she exited the car.

"Is she not coming in?" Lucy asked as she ran a cloth under the kitchen tap and started to wipe down the counter.

"No." Emily turned around and put the tissue in the trash. "I'm just grabbing Henry, and then we're leaving again. We kinda lost track of time."

"Oh, really?" Lucy smiled knowingly.

Emily blushed, grinning.

"Don't be embarrassed. It's good to see you happy."

"I am. I know it is really early on, but she really makes me happy."

Lucy let out an excited squeal before covering her mouth with the palm of her hand.

Emily rolled her eyes. "Calm down. No expectations, remember?"

"I know, I know. But you really deserve this, Em," Lucy said as she walked over and pulled her into a tight hug.

Emily smiled. "As much as I'd love to have a long, mushy chat, I have to get Henry ready. Olivia's waiting in the car, and I said I wouldn't be long."

Lucy pulled back, smiling. "I already got him changed. I put him in that adorable suit you got him for Clara's wedding. Without the jacket though. It's a bit warm for that."

"Oh my God." Emily smiled at the memory of the outfit. "Olivia will love it. Bow tie and vest too?"

"Yep. Not a giraffe in sight. I slicked back his hair too. He looks like such a little gentleman."

"You're the best." Emily gave Lucy another quick hug before looking towards the hallway. "Where is he? I can't wait to see him."

"The second you came in the front door, he ran out the back, around the house, and across the garden to see Olivia," Lucy said, pointing out the window. "I watched him, obviously."

❖

"I think you should live in a house with eighty-eight bedrooms," Henry told Olivia as he hugged Tiny to his chest. Apparently, the cuddly toy was his one concession to not wearing anything giraffe-related.

"Why?" Olivia frowned.

"Because then you could have people to stay," Henry said.

"I could have people to stay with three bedrooms," Olivia said sensibly.

"Will you have a swimming pool?" Henry asked.

"Do you like to swim?"

"Mommy does. I'm not very good."

"Well, one of the apartment buildings I looked at does have a swimming pool," Olivia said.

"Then you should pick that one," Henry said. "As long as it has eighty-eight bedrooms. When will you move?"

"I don't know." Olivia shrugged. "I haven't started to look properly yet."

Henry bounced excitedly in his seat as a thought came into his head. "You should build an island in the ocean," he said seriously.

"Why?"

"Then you could be halfway between London and New York."

"But how would I get to either?" she asked. "I'd need to build a runway on the island too."

"You could use magic instead," Henry said as he strained his neck to look out the window and up into the branches of the tree Olivia was parked beneath.

Olivia was about to reply when she saw Emily approaching with Henry's car seat in her hand. Emily opened the front passenger door and smiled at Henry.

"Wow, Henry, you look amazing," she said.

"My hair is hard," Henry said with a smile as he angled his head toward her.

Emily gently touched the hardened gel. "Wow, very cool!"

"Olivia's going to build an island and live there," Henry said.

"I'm not," Olivia clarified.

Emily chuckled. "Right, well, let's get you set up in the back seat, Henry."

Olivia watched as Henry slid out of the front passenger door and waited while his mother fitted his car seat in the back. As soon as she had, he handed Tiny to her and climbed in. He settled himself and reached for Tiny again. Emily clipped his safety belts into place and gave him a kiss on the forehead.

Henry held Tiny up towards her face. "And Tiny," he said.

Emily smiled and gave Tiny a quick peck on the head before closing the back door and getting into the front seat.

"So, where are we heading?" Emily asked.

"I did have an idea," Olivia said mysteriously, grinning widely.

❖

Emily frowned and held Henry's hand tightly as Olivia walked them into an exclusive-looking but bustling bar. As soon as they entered, a man with a scruffy beard came rushing over from behind the bar and held out his arms.

"Olivia!"

"William." Olivia smiled and they hugged. "This is Emily."

Emily shook the man's hand, trying to smile despite her worry as to why Olivia thought it might be appropriate to bring them to a bar.

"And who is this well-dressed gentleman?" William knelt down beside Henry with a wide grin.

"Henry," Henry said quietly, frowning at William's enthusiastic manner.

"Henry. Well, Henry, I'm very glad you came. We need more dapper bow ties in this place."

Henry attempted to look down at his red-and-white-spotted bow tie, and then looked up at Emily with confusion as he gripped her hand a little tighter.

"Right." William stood up and rubbed his hands together. "Follow me."

William walked across the busy bar towards a large metal spiral staircase that led down. Emily followed Olivia despite her reservations about the surroundings. They slowly made their way down the steps, Olivia taking Henry's other hand to ensure he was safe on the tight stairwell.

Henry bit his lip in concentration as he looked at each step. When they got to the last one, he looked up to see where he was.

"Bowling!" Henry jumped up and down and turned to Emily, wide-eyed.

Emily looked around the downstairs room with surprise. The hectic and ultra-modern bar upstairs was a stark contrast to where she now found herself. A handful of antique-style sofas and armchairs were scattered throughout the space. At the end of the room were two bowling lanes. A couple of formal dining tables were set up on either side of the lanes, and a private bar filled one wall.

William turned to Olivia. "If you need anything at all, just give me a yell. A waiter will be down with menus in a couple of minutes." With a look to Henry and then Emily, he continued. "Please, make yourself at home," before he turned and made his way back up the stairs.

"Can I bowl, Mommy?" Henry asked with excitement. He'd never seen a bowling lane in person before.

"Maybe in a little while," Emily said as she tried to catch up. "Is this all for us?"

Olivia seemed confused by the question. "This is a private hire venue. We have it for as long as we wish this evening."

Emily leaned closer to Olivia's ear and whispered, "So, he's allowed to bowl?"

"Yes," Olivia replied quickly. "That's why we're here. Well, that and the food. They do amazing food here."

Henry was already down by the bowling lanes and looking at the brightly coloured bowling balls with interest, his excitement palpable as he tested the slippery floor in his best shoes and giggled as he slid a little.

"This is amazing, I thought we'd just go to a diner or something." Emily smiled.

"Is it okay?" Olivia asked, obviously worried that she had overstepped some invisible line again.

"Perfect. It's perfect. Look, he's beside himself," Emily said with a nod towards Henry.

Behind the bar, a door opened, and a well-dressed waiter appeared.

"Good evening, ladies."

Olivia turned and smiled at him. He guided them to a dining table near the bowling lanes, pulling out a seat for each of them and then handing them both menus.

"Mommy, can I bowl now?" Henry asked, his hand hovering over a bowling ball anxiously.

The waiter smiled at Henry's obvious excitement and addressed Emily. "Would you like me to get the bowling ramp and show him how it works?"

Emily looked from him to Henry and nodded. "That would be great, if you don't mind?"

A few moments later, Henry was lifting the lightest of the bowling balls up onto the bowling ramp with the assistance of his new friend. He let it go and jumped up and down with delight as the ball rolled its way towards the pins.

Emily and Olivia watched as the waiter showed Henry how everything worked and then allowed him to run amok on both bowling lanes at once.

"He'll sleep well tonight," Emily said with a fond smile.

Olivia grinned as she studied the menu, occasionally glancing over at Henry.

"By the way." Emily leaned forward. "The next time I leave your car with your lipstick all over my mouth, could you tell me?"

Olivia bit her lip, her gaze firmly on the menu. "I don't know what you're talking about."

"Oh, you do." Emily chuckled. "I'm beginning to realise you're not as innocent as you might seem."

"I never claimed to be innocent," Olivia flirted, peering over the top of her menu to make eye contact.

With a glance at Henry and a thick swallow, Emily steered the conversation back towards appropriate topics. Before long, they had ordered food and drinks and were letting Henry pull them to the bowling lanes.

Emily's mediocre bowling skills were still superior to Olivia's paltry and Henry's overly excited attempts, so she quickly took the lead, causing Henry to resort to underhand tactics to stop her winning streak. At one point, Emily tried to bowl with Henry clamped to her leg like a koala bear—and still managed to knock half the pins down.

When Henry's excitement began to reach fever pitch, Emily deliberately started to throw poorly to give him a chance to catch up and calm him down a little. Over a few frames, Emily bestowed her strategy to Henry, then gave him some time to practice while she took a breather with Olivia.

"So…" Emily swirled the wine in her glass. "You clearly don't know about this place because of your bowling skills."

Olivia attempted to look affronted, but the laughter she tried to conceal easily spilled over. "No, I know the owner."

"Oh." Emily tried to act casual. "The tall, dark, and scruffy one?"

"Yes, we went to school together."

"Oh, he went to boarding school too?" Emily asked.

"Yes. Clearly, we took different paths."

"Clearly, you're both successful." Emily was impressed. She turned around and called over her shoulder, "Henry, you're going to boarding school."

Henry robotically nodded his agreement, poking his tongue out in concentration while angling his bowling ramp.

"Emily, you can't—" Olivia began, obviously horrified that Emily was considering sending her son away.

"It's a joke." Emily grinned.

"But you told him—"

"He doesn't know what boarding school is, and he isn't listening to a word I'm saying anyway. I could tell him we're going to the moon and he would just nod at me." Emily reached across the table and took Olivia's hand softly.

"So…" Emily said, trying to be casual. "You and William…"

"Yes?" Olivia asked.

"Yes?" Emily wavered.

"Yes," Olivia repeated with a frown.

Emily blinked. She removed her hand from Olivia's and sat back. "Oh." She paused. "So, you and he were, well, more than friends?"

"Oh! No." Olivia shook her head. "No, I've always been interested in women."

"So he's…"

"Just a friend," Olivia clarified.

Emily let out a sigh of relief. She noticed that Olivia was smirking and chuckled at her own jealous behaviour.

"So, new topic," Emily said. "I hate to bring this up, but, has Simon told you about Marcus's plan?"

"He did." Olivia watched as Henry continued to run around the bowling lanes.

"And?"

Olivia shrugged. "There's more to life."

Emily looked at her in shock. "He is trying to destroy you and your business."

"I know. I have a meeting scheduled with him tomorrow. If I can reason with him, wonderful. If I can't, then I can't."

"Are you laid-back or depressed?" Emily chuckled.

Olivia looked at her seriously and smiled. "Certainly not depressed." She sipped some wine. "My little collapse helped put things into perspective. There's more to life."

Emily examined Olivia, trying to ascertain whether or not she truly meant the words. To her surprise, she couldn't detect any hint of untruth.

When their meals arrived, Emily called Henry over. She pulled a wet wipe from her bag and cleaned his hands before allowing him to eat his dinner.

As he ate, Henry explained more about Olivia's island in the middle of the ocean. Olivia played along happily, and Emily smiled as she watched the two of them. Emily's previous dates had made the mistake of either ignoring or talking down to Henry. Olivia spoke to him as she would anyone else and treated him like a valuable third person in the conversation. Even when Henry forced the discussion into extraordinary and bizarre directions, Olivia would honestly consider the points he made and answer seriously.

After dinner, dessert, and a suitable amount of digestion time, they bowled again and Emily returned her game to full strength, easily beating both of them combined.

As they were leaving, William appeared with a T-shirt for Henry, declaring him the overall winner.

Henry looked to Emily with confusion. "But I didn't win," he whispered.

"Bowling has a really weird scoring system," William said. He pointed to the screen above the lanes to where Henry's name was listed. "I think that's the highest score we've ever had."

Emily noticed that all of the practice games and playing alone had indeed given Henry an enormous overall score.

"Look at that, Henry," she said in awe. She knelt down and read out the numbers, emphasising her own score being higher than Olivia's before reading out Henry's. Olivia snorted with laughter behind them.

Henry gratefully accepted the T-shirt from William. "Mommy, help me," he demanded as he started to put it on over his shirt, tie, and vest. As Emily helped get his arms through the T-shirt holes, Henry looked at her seriously. "Maybe if we come back again, you might win a T-shirt."

"Maybe I will, if you show me your tricks of the trade," she told him, kissing his forehead.

❖

When they pulled up outside the house, Emily asked Olivia if she wanted to come in. Olivia declined, saying that she had an early start the next morning.

From the back seat, Henry looked from one to the other and grinned as he giggled. "Are you two going to kiss?"

Olivia looked at Emily and chuckled when she started to blush.

"Henry, close your eyes," Emily said.

"But—" Henry argued.

"Henry, I mean it," Emily said, turning to regard him.

He closed his eyes, and Emily quickly leaned forward and kissed Olivia, their tongues swiftly meeting before she pulled away again. Her intention to leave Olivia breathless and wanting more appeared to be working.

"Tonight was wonderful," Emily said sincerely. She looked deep into Olivia's eyes, softly stroking her cheek. "Thank you for everything."

"You're most welcome." Olivia coughed to return her voice to normal. "I really enjoyed it."

Emily smiled shyly as she undid her seat belt. "I'll call you tomorrow."

Emily heard the click on Henry's safety belt, and a moment later he'd pulled himself through the gap between the seats and was pressing a sloppy kiss on Olivia's cheek.

"Night, Olivia," he said sadly.

"I'll see you again soon, Henry," Olivia assured him.

Emily got out of the car, opened the back door, and helped him out.

"Why did I have to close my eyes?" Henry asked tiredly.

She lifted him up and balanced his weight on her hip, grabbing his car seat with her free hand. "Because," Emily replied as she smiled at Olivia.

"Did you kiss her?" Henry grinned.

"Wave goodnight to Olivia," Emily told him, and he turned and waved.

Olivia waved back.

"I think you did kiss her," Henry said matter-of-factly.

CHAPTER THIRTY-SIX

Olivia looked up and watched as Marcus paused just outside the entrance to the bar. He looked quickly in both directions, presumably checking that no one would see him entering the building. Also probably wondering if it was the right location. It wasn't the sort of place that Olivia, or anyone, would usually choose for a business meeting. But she needed to make Marcus feel uncomfortable and out of place. And a Mexican bar where she was now something of a legend was just the place.

She was pleased that he had agreed to meet her. Of course, she'd been particularly vague about the reason for wanting to see him face-to-face. She assumed he was hoping she'd given up on the idea of saving Applewood and was negotiating some kind of corporate sell-off. He'd be in for a shock.

He finally stepped into the heavily themed bar, grimacing while being careful not to make contact with the stained wall. He took a deep breath and looked around the room, spotting Olivia in the booth and heading towards her.

"Olivia," he said neutrally.

"Marcus." She smiled and gestured to the bench opposite. "Please, sit down. Have you eaten?"

Olivia could tell that her pleasant behaviour was putting Marcus further on edge. She could almost see the cogs of his brain whirring as he tried to figure out why she could possibly be happy.

"Marcus?" she said at his prolonged silence.

He sat down and shook his head. "I've eaten already."

"A drink, then? They do marvellous cocktails, some alcohol-free if you have further meetings this afternoon?"

"Whatever you're having."

Olivia picked up the laminated drinks menu and pondered the available choices for a moment. When a waiter came to the table, she ordered two tequila sunrises, knowing that Marcus would think she had cracked. It was all part of the game.

She hummed softly to herself as she plucked two napkins out of the metal dispenser and started to clean a sticky liquid from the table. Out of the corner of her eye, she could see Marcus shifting uncomfortably, presumably thinking he was watching a broken woman, slumming it in a strange bar, drinking cocktails in the afternoon, wondering what had gone wrong with her life.

Satisfied that the table was clean, and Marcus was suitably unnerved by her behaviour, she placed a folder on the table. He made no move to take it, so she pushed it towards him and opened it to reveal its contents.

"Here is the anonymous complaint that you and Sebastian Brennan attempted to file with the authorities. As well as the additional paperwork that you supplied in order to validate your claims of financial mismanagement."

The waiter returned with two brightly coloured cocktails and placed them on the table.

"Thank you," Olivia said.

She watched as Marcus looked at the papers in horror, clearly wondering how Olivia had managed to get them. She arranged the tall cocktail glass to ensure that it sat exactly in the middle of her coaster, which was shaped like a sombrero.

"Where was I?" She looked back at the paperwork. "Oh yes. Your anonymous complaint." She let out a small sigh and shook her head lightly. "This isn't like you, Marcus. This isn't like you at all. Of course, it's all irrelevant now because I have it."

"How?" Marcus finally managed to ask.

"Nothing gets past me. You know that."

He looked back at the paper.

"Don't worry, none of your staff…my staff…our staff, had anything to do with this. I know someone has been telling you that I have spies in your organisation. That's not the case, I assure you."

Marcus had always complained about her inability to lie, always telling the truth no matter how damning to the business it could be. Telling him outright that there were no spies in his business would hopefully put an end to any notion of corporate espionage.

"The thing is, that's not the only complaint I have in this file." She gestured to the folder and encouraged him to turn the papers.

He reluctantly turned over the letter and accompanying paperwork that he had gathered and sent in anonymously. He turned the last leaf of paper over and found the other letter. As he started to read, his brow furrowed in confusion. Halfway through, he picked the paper up, appearing to skim to the end before starting over and reading the whole document again.

"You're reporting Applewood Financial for financial misconduct?" He looked over the top of the letter at her.

"In a manner of speaking. And I'm not hiding behind anonymity."

He looked at the letter again, his eyes drifting down to the bottom where her signature was.

"You see, Marcus, when I heard about your complaint, I was disappointed. And then I had an idea. I should thank you, really. Nothing gets past me," Olivia repeated. "Though, unfortunately, when I was younger and new to Applewood, I had a tendency to sign things without fully understanding them. I trusted my coworkers a little too much. But I did always look at everything eventually, even after they had been signed and sent off."

Marcus lowered the letter. "You're going to report my old audit files. Have me investigated and barred for financial mismanagement that took place years ago?"

"Well, that's definitely a possibility."

Marcus laughed. "You do realise—or maybe you don't; I really don't know where your head is right now. You do realise that, if you report this, it takes me down but you along with me? It may have been my work, but it was your signature. You were the safety net."

"I'm well aware of how it works, Marcus. I may have been ignorant at the time I signed the paperwork and filed the accounts, but ignorance is no excuse. I know that reporting you will be the end of my career as well as yours."

"You'll never work in the sector again," he said.

"I know." Olivia shrugged. "But I'm happy to shoot myself in the foot if it brings you down with me. Of course, I don't have a business to worry about. Applewood Financial is about to fold, as you well know. I'd hate to be in the situation where I ran a large financial company and would need to find a colleague to take control while I was being investigated and then struck off. Trying to find someone to trust is very difficult these days."

Marcus pushed himself back from the table and stared at her venomously.

"Or, there's another way," Olivia said. She leaned forward and sipped from the straw in her drink.

"You're blackmailing me."

"No, I'm providing you with motivation to listen to my very reasonable solution to all of our problems."

"And if I refuse to hear you out? Or if I do and I disagree?"

Olivia smiled. "Then you'll be left wondering just how well you know me. Would I really send this or is it all a bluff? I know you think you know me so well, but would you stake your career on it?"

Marcus closed his eyes and looked as if he was attempting to control his temper.

"Drink up. It'll make you feel better."

Marcus opened his eyes, snatched the colourful drink, and drank a few big gulps from the rim, ignoring the straws.

"I have to congratulate you," Olivia said. "Sincerely. Your business is exceptional. The slick operation, the people…honestly, I'm impressed at how much you've built up in such a short space of time."

He frowned at her, clearly unsure as to why she would compliment him.

"As you know," Olivia explained, "I analyse businesses for a living. We both know that your new operation is weak in two places, audit and corporate restructuring. Both of these departments sat under my control, and therefore you've not managed to build as strong a team as you would probably like."

"It's just a matter of time," he said.

"Absolutely." Olivia nodded her agreement. "You'll be able to recruit and train in about four to nine months. But, sadly, you don't have four to nine months. Techtrix and Maddison's both have audits coming up next month. PAK is on the brink and will need to be restructured if they're to stay solvent. I give them six weeks before they're in a critical position."

Marcus rolled his eyes and sighed. "What do you suggest?"

"A partnership."

Marcus shook his head and opened his mouth to argue.

"I'm stepping down," Olivia added. "Simon will take my place as managing director of a much smaller Applewood Financial. Now, I know you like and respect Simon, and he is excellent at people management and scheduling. Which is exactly what an audit and restructuring specialist would need. The staff that remain at Applewood are in a perfect position to take on this work as an outsourced provider. It makes sense."

"You're stepping down?" Marcus clarified.

"Yes. You won't be working with me. I won't even be a nonexecutive director. I will be completely removed from Applewood Financial."

"And you're leaving your secretary in charge?"

"He's an executive assistant," Olivia said. "And it wouldn't be as if he replaces me in my current role. He would be the project manager between your team and Applewood's team."

"And Applewood would be our outsourced audit and restructuring partner," Marcus said.

"Precisely. Let's be honest; your problem is with me. I'd be gone. You'd work with people you know, people you trust. But Applewood will stay independent. The people in London will retain their jobs, and the work will not be moved to your New York office." She took another sip of her drink. "Besides, I can't imagine you have much capital left. Expansion at a rate that you have achieved doesn't come cheap. While it would take you four to nine months to create your own team, I can't imagine that you can afford to source or salary that team for at least another twelve months anyway."

Marcus attempted to school his features, and Olivia concluded that her estimates were right. She could tell that he was considering her offer, and she hoped that he would be able to see beyond his hatred of her and realise it was the best option for everyone involved. Yes, she was threatening him, but she had to do that to knock him off his high horse and get him to listen to reason. This solution was one that worked for everyone.

"And if I disagree with this partnership plan?"

"Why would you?" Olivia asked honestly. "You know it makes sense."

"I'll have to think about this."

"Take all the time you need. You're the one with a deadline. I'm happy to walk away from Applewood at this point."

Marcus shook his head and chuckled. "I don't believe that for one second."

"You should," she told him earnestly. "I'm realising that there is a lot more to life. I've been stuck in a terrible rut without ever analysing why I do what I do."

Marcus looked over Olivia's shoulder and frowned. He leaned forward and gestured for her to do the same. "I don't mean to startle you, but I think those bikers behind you are listening to us. We need to—"

Olivia sat back up and waved his concerns away with her hand. "That's just Crazy Weasel and Butcher. They are making sure I'm okay. I told them it would be fine, but they wanted to be sure you behaved yourself." She turned around and smiled at her new friends.

Both men smiled back warmly before looking at Marcus with stony expressions. She turned back to Marcus and watched as he swallowed and tore his eyes from them before returning his attention to Olivia.

"So…" He let out a sigh. "Let's figure out how this might work."

CHAPTER THIRTY-SEVEN

"But I don't wanna sleep," Henry mumbled through a big yawn.

Olivia chuckled. "You may not want to, but I think you need to."

"Can we go to the zoo again soon?"

"Of course." Olivia pulled the bed sheet up around Henry and smoothed his hair from his forehead.

"Really?"

"Really," she confirmed. An idea struck her. "As long as you go to sleep now."

Henry considered the compromise and nodded his agreement. "Night, Olivia."

"Goodnight," she whispered.

"Kiss," he demanded as she turned to leave.

She turned back and kissed his cheek, smiling as he left a very wet kiss on her own cheek.

He closed his eyes, turned to his side, and stretched out. Even at full stretch, he looked tiny in the enormous bed of the hotel guest room. Olivia turned off the lamp and returned to the living room, where Emily was excitedly pacing the room while on the telephone to Nicole.

Emily finished the call and hung up. She turned to Olivia with a large grin on her face.

"You won't believe what she said," Emily said. "Nicole has been looking through my other scripts, and she thinks that there are two that she can easily sell. They won't work for her productions, but she knows a Scottish production company, and she wanted my permission for her to approach them on my behalf."

Olivia opened her mouth in surprise and simply nodded.

"Is Henry okay?" Emily asked.

"He didn't want to sleep." Olivia sat on the sofa and poured herself another glass of wine from the bottle on the coffee table. "But he also wanted to go to the zoo again. I told him he could, as long as he went to sleep."

"And you say you're not good with children." Emily sat beside her, picked up her own wine glass, and took a sip. "Thank you for today. And yesterday. And the day before that."

"I'm making up for lost time," Olivia said through a grin.

"You're spoiling us." Emily placed a soft kiss on Olivia's cheek. She frowned. "Um, Olivia…your cheek is wet?"

Olivia pulled a tissue from the box on the coffee table and wiped her cheek dry. "Sorry, Henry kissed me."

Emily chuckled. "I'll be glad when we're over the wet kisses phase."

"One day he'll be a teenager and won't want to kiss you at all," Olivia said.

Emily put her hand to her heart and shook her head. "Don't wound me. Henry's going to stop growing when he is seven and remain my sweet little boy forever."

"That's unlikely." Olivia shook her head.

"A girl can dream."

Olivia chuckled. "What else did Nicole say? Has she got a date for the rewrites?"

Emily lowered her wine glass and looked apologetic. "Yes. I need to cancel dinner tomorrow."

"Oh." Olivia knew she shouldn't feel disappointed. She'd had so much time with Emily and Henry lately.

"She wants the rewrites for the weekend," Emily continued.

"This weekend?" Olivia asked, surprised.

"Yes, she apologised, but that's the only date one of her partners can look at it before he goes on vacation. I've no idea how I'm going to get through it all, but I'll try my best. I just hope I can keep Henry entertained with something, or that will slow the process down."

"I can watch Henry if you like."

Emily looked at her for a moment. "Really?"

"Of course. He can stay here."

"Are you sure you wouldn't mind?" Emily worried her lower lip.

"I don't have anything else to do. Henry's a welcome distraction."

"You still haven't told me what's happening at work. I can tell something is up." Emily looked at her intently.

Olivia sipped her wine. "There's nothing to say yet. The details are still being arranged. I'll tell you when there's something concrete."

"Okay, but you'd tell me if there was something important, wouldn't you?"

Olivia could feel her cheeks flare with heat. "Of course."

Emily sighed. "What is it?"

"Nothing. It's just the wine. Everything's fine. Absolutely fine."

Emily reached out, took Olivia's glass, and placed it next to hers on the table. She leaned forward and unbuttoned the top button of Olivia's blouse.

"You know how we kinda had an unspoken agreement that tonight we'd finally…"

Olivia swallowed as Emily licked her lips and undid a second button. She didn't trust her voice, so she simply nodded her understanding.

"How we planned to exhaust Henry at the zoo and tuck him up in the guest room so I could finally get a look at the master suite," Emily continued.

Olivia nodded again, her breath catching.

"Well…" Emily looked up. "That's all off the table unless you tell me what you're hiding from me, right now." Emily sat back, picked up her wine glass, and sipped the liquid, looking over the rim at Olivia.

Olivia licked her lips and let out a quick breath, finally remembering how to breathe. "There's noth—"

Emily's gaze turned serious.

"I bought a house," Olivia blurted out.

Emily coughed, choking on her wine. "What?"

Olivia winced. She'd planned a way to tell Emily, and this certainly wasn't it.

"You bought a house?" Emily stared at her in confusion.

Olivia nodded. Sometimes gestures of the cranium better expressed what was happening than words.

"When? Where? Why didn't you say something?" Emily asked.

Olivia realised that no amount of nodding was going to help. "Here, in New York. I close in a few days." Olivia picked up her iPad from the coffee table and unlocked the screen, then brought up details of the property.

Emily snuggled into Olivia's arm, glanced at the iPad screen, and then grabbed it from her and stared in shock.

"Holy shit." Emily stared at the large house and then looked at Olivia with wide eyes. "Is this it?"

"Yes." Olivia nodded, concerned by Emily's reaction.

"It's a mansion," Emily declared as she started sweeping through the photos with her index finger. "Five bedrooms? What are you going to do with…oh my God…it's got a pool? And a gym in the garage. Correction, double garage."

Olivia watched intently as Emily swiped through the pictures and read the property details, desperately trying to ascertain what her thoughts were.

"Wow," Emily finally said. She handed the iPad back. "You'll need to hire a cleaner. It's huge."

A nervous laugh escaped Olivia's mouth. "You like it?"

"Like it? It's incredible. Beautiful. I'm not quite sure why you kept it quiet from me. Or why you need quite so much room…" Emily trailed off as the realisation hit her. She sat up, frowning at Olivia.

"I, well, I guess I was hoping that you and Henry would live there with me," Olivia said before fear rendered her speechless again. "I know it's ridiculously soon. And I don't mean now, of course. But, I want us to be together. And I thought that buying a house with room for all of us would…" Olivia jumped to her feet and started to pace the room. "I'm not really sure what I was thinking. I just did it. Then I didn't want to tell you because I know that it's too soon. But the house was perfect." She let out a shuddering breath and slowly turned to face Emily.

Emily smiled and slowly shook her head in disbelief. "You'll never stop surprising me."

"Is that a good thing?" Olivia asked.

"Well, I certainly won't complain of boredom."

"You're not angry?"

Emily stood and held out her arms as she walked towards Olivia. She enveloped her in a hug. "No, I'm not angry. I'm glad you've taken a step forward and bought a house. I understand why you bought a big house and why you wanted to keep it a secret from me."

"I don't know why I do these things," Olivia said. She nuzzled her face into Emily's blond hair and inhaled the smell of her shampoo. "I know it's too soon to be asking you to move in."

Emily pulled back a little so she could make eye contact. "It is too soon. And buying a house isn't the usual way to ask someone to move in with you."

"I've never been accused of doing things the usual way," Olivia said.

"No." Emily chuckled. "That's definitely true. When do you move in?"

"I get the keys on Friday," Olivia replied. "I need to furnish it, of course. I may need help with that."

Emily loosened her grip around Olivia's waist. "My help?"

Olivia nodded. "I've never decorated a home. Never bought furniture. I don't have a clue what I'll need. What we'll need, if you agree to moving in with me one day."

Emily bit her lip, gently untangled her arms from Olivia, and walked away, deep in thought.

"Emily?" Olivia frowned at the sudden change in atmosphere.

"Olivia…" Emily let out a small sigh. "You know I can't afford a stick of furniture for a house like that."

"I don't expect you to buy anything," Olivia replied softly. She watched as Emily paced the room, arms wrapped around her waist as she contemplated.

Emily let out a sad laugh. "Olivia, you are so very generous. But I don't know if I can accept this. Any of this."

Olivia turned, walked over to the window, and stared out at the twinkling lights. She knew this was an important moment. A time to say the right thing.

"Money," Olivia said, "is such a difficult subject. In my working life, I meet people with enormous amounts of money. I also meet people who have lost enormous amounts of money. Do you know what they all have in common?" She turned to look at Emily questioningly.

Emily shook her head.

"Not a damn thing. Money is an object, a thing. A very important thing, I absolutely understand that, but to me it's just a thing. Some people earn their money, some people inherit it, some people marry into it, some people steal it, and some people win it. A person cannot be judged for their money, only what they ultimately do with it."

Olivia leaned on the back of the sofa and pointed towards the guest bedroom. "Today, you gave me a gift. The gift of Henry's company. A gift that money can't buy. I am not precious about money. I would shovel hundreds of thousands of dollars into a furnace if it meant spending more time with you and Henry."

Emily opened her mouth to speak, but Olivia held up her hand, begging for silence. She didn't know if she was saying the right things, but she was speaking from the heart, and that had to count for something.

"I know I don't always make sense, and I know that sometimes I say the wrong thing and people find it hard to follow my train of thought. But in this I am resolute; I believe that people come before money. I have money, and I wish to share it with you. It's no more valuable than you sharing your life and family with me."

Emily was silent, her expression unreadable.

Olivia chuckled. "I want to buy Henry a bunk bed with a slide. I want to convert a bedroom for you to have an office, with built-in shelves for your scripts. I want to put a trampoline in the garden—away from the pool, of course. I want to be a unit. A family."

Emily quickly walked towards her, arms outstretched. Olivia fell in and gathered her up in a tight embrace.

"I don't always understand your methods, Olivia Lewis," Emily whispered. "But I'm starting to understand your intent."

Olivia frowned as she tightly held to Emily. "Is that a good thing?" she murmured.

"A very good thing," Emily replied tenderly.

"Are we breaking up?" Olivia asked.

"No." Emily squeezed Olivia a little tighter.

"Are we fighting?"

Emily chuckled a little. "No."

"I've not said the wrong thing?"

"Definitely not. You said the most perfect thing."

Olivia nodded and squeezed her eyes shut as she gripped on to Emily.

"Olivia?" Emily said softly.

"Mmm?"

"I love you," Emily whispered.

Olivia tensed up. She hadn't expected Emily to say what she'd been thinking for days, weeks, even. She was used to rushing headlong into things and being in a completely different place than other people. But now Emily had said it, had been the first one to say it. She'd known that Emily cared for her, but love? She'd only dared hope. Suddenly, the weight of holding in her true feelings was lifted.

"I love you," Olivia replied. "I love you so very much. I have done for a long time."

Emily pulled back and looked at Olivia with a wide smile.

"This is crazy, isn't it?" Emily asked with a chuckle.

Crazy didn't sound good, and Olivia felt herself frown.

"In a good way," Emily amended. "I just mean how quickly things have happened and how well we fit together. I never saw this coming."

Olivia breathed a small sigh of relief. She nodded. "I'm very glad that it did."

"Me too." Emily's eyes drifted down and she raised an eyebrow. Olivia looked down to the two open blouse buttons. "Now, where was I?"

Olivia laughed. "I believe you were attempting to seduce me in order to get me to spill my secrets."

"And it worked," Emily said. "I wonder what else I can get you to admit to."

Olivia took a step back, fully aware that Emily was able to see the tip of her red lace bra. "Two can play that game," she said as she brought her hands to the third button of the blouse.

Satisfaction coursed through her as Emily's eyes grew wide in anticipation.

"I'll tell you anything you want to know," Emily murmured.

"Maybe we should take this to the bedroom?" Olivia suggested. She walked past Emily without waiting for a response, happy when she heard Emily right on her heels.

They entered the master bedroom, and Emily closed the door behind them. She looked around the room and let out a low whistle.

"Fancy," she joked.

"Yes," Olivia said seriously as she stared at Emily meaningfully.

"You seem to have forgotten what you were doing," Emily said. In a couple of quick strides, she stood in front of Olivia with her hands on the straining third button. "Would you like some help?"

Olivia found herself momentarily speechless. Not that it mattered, as a second later Emily's lips were tender on hers. Olivia felt a soft moan bubble up inside her as Emily unbuttoned the third button.

She was so distracted by Emily's kiss that she didn't notice Emily pulling the blouse down her arms while the bottom buttons remained done up, effectively trapping her arms behind her back.

"A rookie interrogator mistake," Emily whispered against Olivia's lips.

"I was distracted." Olivia leaned forward and captured Emily's lips again, intensifying the kiss by nipping at Emily's bottom lip with her teeth.

Emily gasped and Olivia took the opportunity to shuck her arms out of the blouse and quickly pull Emily close, revelling in the sensation of holding her against her own bra-clad body.

Emily leaned her body away while maintaining the kiss, and for a brief second Olivia thought that something had gone wrong, that the moment was over. Then she heard the sound of ripping thread and buttons lightly bouncing on the carpet. Then Emily's body was back against hers, and she felt skin against skin.

"I love you," Olivia said into the kiss. She was unsure why the declaration had bubbled from her lips at that exact moment. She seemed to have no control of her voice, her heart taking the shortest route to her mouth and no longer bothering to consult her brain.

Emily's hands started to unbutton the rest of Olivia's blouse. "I love you too, so much I can't even think straight. Let's get this damn top off."

Olivia chuckled as she stepped back to give Emily the access she needed to remove the troublesome blouse. As Emily made quick work of the buttons, Olivia stared hungrily at her. She hadn't known it was possible for tight jeans and a black bra to look so good.

Emily's pale white skin looked so soft and inviting, and she wanted to see more of it. She grabbed hold of Emily's jeans by the waistband and jerked her closer, her other hand holding Emily's face still as she kissed her hungrily.

Emily wrapped her arms around Olivia, her hands slowly working their way down her naked back until they rested on the top of the zip of her skirt before she pulled away and asked, "May I?"

Olivia didn't trust her voice not to waver so she simply nodded. A second later, she felt Emily slowly inch the zip down until her skirt fell away from her body and dropped to the floor.

"Garters?" Emily asked. "Are you a walking, talking fantasy?"

"They're convenient," Olivia said.

"They're something all right." Emily licked her lips.

Olivia opened her mouth to respond, but Emily pushed her shoulders and she found herself falling onto the bed with a squeak.

"You're a squealer," Emily noted with a smirk before straddling her hips.

"And you're very forward." Olivia placed her hands on Emily's hips, wishing she'd had time to rid her of her jeans.

"You haven't seen anything yet," Emily promised.

CHAPTER THIRTY-EIGHT

Olivia looked up from her newspaper to see Henry turning his head from one side to another with a frown. He kicked off his shoes, quickly scrambled his feet up onto the plush sofa, and turned his body around until his legs were sticking straight up the back of the sofa and his head dangled off the edge. With a small giggle, he regarded the upside-down screen, stretched his arms out on the sofa, and took a deep breath as he watched.

"Henry, what are you doing?"

"Watching," he replied without looking at her.

"Why are you sitting like that?" Olivia asked with a confused frown.

Henry shrugged, or tried to, but his current position didn't allow for much movement.

Olivia put her newspaper down and looked from Henry to the television. "I don't think you can see very well sitting like that."

"It's fun," Henry claimed.

Olivia looked at the screen with a frown as she twisted her head from one side to the other, then shook her head as she realised what she was considering.

"So, what toys did you bring with you today?" Henry had only been with her for half an hour, and while he had seemed very receptive to the idea at first, he'd become withdrawn soon after Emily left.

"Jigsaw." Henry looked up at her with a hopeful face.

"Why don't you go and get your jigsaw, then we can both do it together?"

Henry pressed his feet against the sofa and managed an impressive forward roll to the floor. Impressive in that he didn't break his neck while doing it. Olivia reached out to help him a second too late, and he'd already managed to land on his feet and was on his way to the guest bedroom, where he'd left his bags.

She pressed her hand to her heart as violent images of Henry's neck snapping or him rolling straight into the glass coffee table entered her mind. She was beginning to wonder whether or not she was fully prepared to watch him for two days and an overnight stay. It had only been a short while, and he'd already nearly broken his neck. She jumped to her feet to follow him in case of any other potential injury, deciding that the best course of action was to watch him like a hawk.

As she entered the guest bedroom, she saw the abandoned open bag and looked around in confusion until she heard Henry call her name from the en suite bathroom. Peering around the corner, she saw the boy sitting on the toilet with his trousers and underwear hanging off the ends of his dangling feet. He was reaching to the side for the toilet roll holder on the wall, which was just out of reach of his small arms. She entered the room with her eyes averted, pulled off a few sheets, and passed them to him.

"Thank you," he said brightly as he wiped himself methodically and then jumped down from the toilet. He threw the used paper into the bowl, pressed the button behind the toilet, and watched as fresh water rushed down the sides of the bowl.

Once the show was over, he pulled up his underwear and trousers, walked to the sink, and stretched up to use the soap and water. Olivia realised it was a struggle for him to reach and lifted him to sit on the vanity unit.

After pumping too much liquid soap onto his hands, he pressed them together and pulled them apart again, watching the soapy bubbles emerge.

"Are you mommy's girlfriend?" Henry asked as he watched the bubbles.

Olivia felt a wave of heat flush her cheeks. "Yes, I am." She tried to keep the panic out of her voice but didn't think she was having much success. Why was Henry asking such questions? Did he even know what a girlfriend actually was?

Henry turned the tap on. "When are you and Mommy going to get married?"

Olivia was sure her heart stopped, or at least skipped a couple of essential beats. She opened her mouth and closed it again as she stared at him rinsing soap from his hands. She had no idea how to answer that question, nor what Emily would expect her to say or do. In all the instructions that Emily had left for looking after Henry, this had never come up.

"Can Tiny come when you get married? Will you get married in a church like Natalie did?" Henry asked, turning to face her.

She considered what to say and the hundred or so ways that her responses could have serious repercussions. "You'll have to ask your mother," Olivia eventually said. "Let's dry your hands."

Olivia grabbed a towel from the rail, turned off the tap, and gently dried his hands.

"Why do you live in a hotel?" Henry frowned. "Is it because you like towels?"

"Towels?" Olivia asked.

"There are towels everywhere, even in the wardrobes. You must really like towels. And pillows too." Henry decided his hands were dry enough, pulled them from the towel, and pushed himself to the ground.

He stumbled slightly and then tottered into the bedroom. Olivia threw the towel to the floor and quickly followed him, wondering what he might get up to next.

Henry picked up the jigsaw and walked into the dining room. By the time Olivia caught up to him, he was tipping it out onto the table. He pulled out a chair, climbed up, and leaned on the table, sorting the pieces. Olivia decided to sit opposite him and wait for instructions. She'd played with Henry enough to know that you waited for a duty to be assigned to you.

"Find the edges," Henry said, holding up an edge piece to show her.

Olivia nodded and started to search through for edge pieces. She noticed that Henry was quickly grabbing as many as he could and realised that he thought of it as a competition. Feigning a lack of ability to find any, she brushed her hands over pieces as if hunting for elusive edges, often uncovering one for him to see before moving on.

"Did Mommy sleep in your bed the other night?" Henry asked.

Olivia suddenly understood what people meant when they spoke of cold dread. A spark of fear shivered through her spine as she wondered what on earth she could say to that.

"'Cos when I woke up in the night, she wasn't there. But in the morning she was. So she slept in your bed, didn't she?" Henry battled to get two mismatched pieces of the jigsaw to fit together.

"Well…um, yes, she did," Olivia said tentatively. In the back of her mind, she could see Emily folding her arms and staring at her with displeasure for saying the wrong thing. Was it the wrong thing to say? She had no idea. She'd signed up for a night of babysitting, not an inquisition. She tried to remind herself that Henry had no idea of the sensitivity of what he was asking—even if she did wonder if she was unintentionally scaring him for life.

"If you and Mommy live together, will I have my own bed?" Henry asked as he tossed one of the pieces aside, picked up another, and easily snapped them together.

"You'll have to ask your mother about that too," Olivia said as she stood up. She couldn't take any more questions; she was terrified what he would ask next, and concerned that she would bankrupt herself and Emily at the cost of his lifelong therapy bills if she said the wrong thing. "Would you like some juice?"

Henry nodded, and Olivia rushed out of the room, breathing heavily as she wondered what she'd gotten herself into. Were these normal questions for a five-year-old to be asking? And what would normal answers be? Running away from the problem certainly wasn't the right answer, but it was the best one she had at the moment.

Once in the kitchen, Olivia picked up her phone from her handbag and selected a contact. She pressed the device to her ear and waited for a reply, occasionally checking the hallway for Henry.

"Hello, Olivia," Nicole answered. "How's young Henry?"

"He's only been here three quarters of an hour, and he's already asked if Emily and I are sleeping together. And he wants to know if we're getting married," Olivia declared in a breathless panic.

"Aww," Nicole cooed. "Well? Are you getting married? Can I be a bridesmaid? By the way, I hate pink, so don't even think about it."

"Nicole, this is serious," Olivia hissed.

Nicole laughed. "See, kids aren't as easy as you think, are they?"

"Why is he asking these questions?" Olivia asked. "And how am I supposed to answer them?"

"Well, firstly, he's…what…five? Five-year-olds ask about a million questions a day. Secondly, he's five. You don't owe him any answers, and certainly not any detailed answers. By all means, tell him that you sleep with his mother. To him, sleep is sleep. Just remember that he sees things in a childlike way."

"I'm terrified of what he might ask next," Olivia said. She checked the hallway once more before getting a glass out of the cabinet and opening the refrigerator door.

"Then chair the conversation," Nicole said. "Think of it as a board meeting. Guide his thoughts to where you want. Ask him questions. His mind is only wandering because you've allowed it to."

Olivia poured some juice and nodded. "Yes, okay, that makes sense."

"Good, glad I could be of assistance," Nicole replied. "I'd start charging you for these chats, but it's all going in my memoirs anyway."

"One more thing," Olivia said as she placed the juice back in the refrigerator and closed the door.

"Yes?" Nicole asked.

"I might have neglected to tell you that I've bought a house and asked Emily to move in with me," Olivia stated.

Nicole had clearly been taking a sip of something and started to cough wildly. "What?" she spluttered. "That's fast. Even by your standards."

"I love her," Olivia said softly. "And Henry."

"Oh, believe me, I know," Nicole said gently. "I'm really happy for you. Shocked, but happy for you."

"She hasn't said yes."

"Did she say no?"

"She said she would think about it. And said that it was all happening rather quickly."

"But she didn't say no," Nicole added. "I assume you're only telling me this now in case Emily mentions it when I next speak to her?"

"Maybe," Olivia said.

"That's it. We're setting up weekly Skype lunches. The only way I could ever get anything out of you was by sitting you down and watching you slowly crack under the pressure of my gaze."

Olivia chuckled. "I miss you."

"I miss you too," Nicole said. "Seriously, though, we're having weekly Skype lunches. It will be our new thing. You can't get rid of me just by moving to New York."

"Okay, yes, Skype lunches it is. I'd better get back to check on Henry."

"Okay, darling. Best of luck, with Henry and with Emily. And, seriously, about that bridesmaid thing, pink just washes me out."

Olivia laughed. "Goodbye, Nic."

❖

Emily sat in bed with her antiquated laptop, staring at the document Nicole had emailed over to her. She'd hardly made any headway into it, apart from reading it cover to cover at least eight times. How to fix the problems was another matter entirely, and the enormity of the task ahead was starting to panic her.

In the past, Emily had always written for pleasure, for her own benefit. Now she was being asked to edit a script—a real live script—that would be turned into a play that people would pay good money to see. Theatre productions cost hundreds of thousands to put on, and a failure could easily mean bankruptcy. The stakes were high, and the pressure to deliver the right script, immense. If Emily delivered anything substandard, Nicole would ditch the project and that would be the end of it. No second chances.

The biggest problem was that Emily knew exactly what she wanted to do, but it was a risk. It would mean a complete rewrite; more than Nicole had requested. It meant the removal of at least two characters and a plot twist that had Emily giddy with excitement.

But Emily's instructions had been to tweak the script, add some pages, and tighten the plot. Having never worked in the industry before, she was struggling, and had been scrolling the wheel on her mouse up and down for the past hour.

Chewing the inside of her mouth nervously, Emily flicked to another screen and opened her email. She selected Nicole's most recent message and started to type a reply. After spending far too much time on the simple four-line email, Emily hit the Send button and let out a deep sigh.

Her mind wandered to Olivia, and she wondered how she was getting on with Henry. She hadn't dared to call, because she knew she would want to drop everything to go over there and spend time with them. If she ignored her responsibilities, maybe the whole stressful situation would just go away?

Her phone rang, and Nicole's number illuminated the screen. With a nervous swallow, she picked up the phone and took a deep breath before answering the call.

"Hi, Nicole."

"Hi, Emily. I just got your email," Nicole replied cheerfully.

"I'm sorry if it's a stupid question." Emily winced, wondering if Nicole had called to tell her that the deal was off. "I just want to make sure it's all right."

"Definitely not a stupid question," Nicole said. "If I'm understanding what you've written, you want to move the crisis point to the start of the first act, and kill off Meredith and Will?"

"Yes. I know it's a lot, but I kind of think it would—"

"Oh, I love it. It's a departure from the original script, but I understand why you want to do it. It means more work for you, but it would improve the script, it fits in with our criteria for fewer actors, and it removes that complicated scene at the start of the second act. As long as you're happy with the final result and it meets the list of requirements I sent you, I don't see a problem. My primary goal is that you're happy with the script you send us."

"That's what I thought," Emily said.

"Then go for it." Nicole chuckled. "Just bring me the drama. Bring me the passion."

Emily laughed. "Okay, I will. I'm sorry. I was just having a crisis of confidence. I'm really new to all of this."

"Oh, it's fine. I was actually about to call you anyway," Nicole said. "I gave your script about the blind teacher to a friend of mine who runs a theatre company in Edinburgh. He. Loves. It."

Emily felt her body start to shake with nerves and quickly shoved her laptop off her lap and onto the bed.

"You're kidding me?"

"No, he loves it. He wants to buy it and put it on in his shabby little underground theatre." Nicole laughed.

"Wow…okay, how do I sign up?" Emily chuckled.

"Oh, darling, you need a manager," Nicole said. "The very first person I showed it to wants to buy it, and I'm not joking when I say shabby little theatre. It's a dive. We can do better."

Emily's mouth fell open. "Okay," she managed to say. "I really don't know anything about this."

"That's fine. We were all new to the industry once," Nicole said. "I can put you in touch with a couple of managers if you like? Or I could represent you? But I don't know if that may be a conflict of interest?"

Emily quickly replied. "I'd love for you to represent me, if you can? If you have time? I mean. I don't know anything about this industry, and I certainly don't know anyone in this industry, other than you."

"I'd love to," Nicole confessed. "I get to tell everyone how I discovered you."

Emily laughed. "I still can't quite believe this is happening. I keep thinking it's a dream and I'll wake up."

"Oh, you say that now, but once you're up against a script change deadline with some irritating producer breathing down your neck, you'll think it's a nightmare. Oh, wait, that's exactly where you are." Nicole chuckled.

"Still a lot better than my last two jobs," Emily said.

"Olivia told me about your schedule at Crown once. It made my head swim," Nicole said. "Well, as your newly hired manager, here's what I think. Obviously, I'm not in the know on your financial situation, but if you would like me to arrange for the sale of your script to Daniel in Edinburgh, I can, of course, do that. But I'm confident we could get more money by shopping around. However, if you need the money now, then we can make the deal. It's entirely up to you."

"I don't know," Emily said. "What kind of figures are we talking about?"

"Well, Daniel would pay the minimum, which is four thousand pounds. We need your human calculator of a girlfriend to correctly calculate taxes and exchange rate, but let's say that's around five thousand dollars," Nicole explained.

"Five thousand dollars?" Emily's heart felt like it was beating out of her chest.

"Yes," Nicole said distractedly. "I'm pretty sure we could get more like fifteen thousand pounds for it if we find the right producer. Which would be around twenty, twenty-one thousand dollars."

Emily slid from the bed to the floor as her body shook harder. She scooted up so her back was supported against the wardrobe door, not trusting her muscles to keep her upright.

"Right," she said shakily.

"You have other scripts, besides the ones you already sent me, do you not?" Nicole asked.

Emily nodded before realising that she needed to speak for Nicole to hear. "Yes, I…yes, I think I have around nine finished plays and twelve that need work."

"Well, if they are up to the standard that I've seen from you so far, then I'm sure we can sell more of them. If you're interested, I'm sure we could get you some editing work too, if you're up for it?" Nicole asked.

"I…yes, yes, that sounds great. I'd started looking for jobs, but the market is pretty dead here."

"As I said, we could get more for that script, but it's an offer on the table and you may want to take it," Nicole said. "I said I'd get back to Daniel next week, so have a think about it and speak to your financial adviser."

Emily frowned. "I don't—"

"I meant Olivia, darling," Nicole reminded her with a chuckle.

"Oh, oh yes!"

"Emily," Nicole said, her tone suddenly serious.

"Yes?" Emily asked nervously.

"I'm saying this as a friend, and as your newly appointed manager," Nicole said. "You are an extraordinary writer; your plots are tremendous. You have an understanding of the human psyche that most writers would kill for. That, coupled with your comic timing, your ability to weave an intricate tale, well, you're very talented. I just need you to know that."

Emily leaned heavily against the wardrobe with a disbelieving smile and shaky hands. Emily had never had anyone tell her that she was good at anything before. Her foster families had never encouraged any talent, and she wasn't used to receiving praise.

"Thank you," she gushed. "Thank you so much. You don't know how much that means to me."

"I mean every word. Now, I better let you go. Your rewrite means you've given yourself extra work, and you'll need every second if you're going to hit the deadline. I really wish I could give you more time, but you know how it is."

"It's fine. I'll get it done," Emily said.

They said their farewells, and Emily hung up the phone. She lowered it to the floor and stared ahead in shock. Writing had been a way to pass time, an escape from the real world, and a way to have some form of control, even if it was essentially over made-up scenarios. She'd never expected it to amount to anything. She'd never expected anyone to even read her scripts, never mind want to buy them.

She couldn't decide if she was more blown away by the fact that people liked her writing or by the amount of earning potential she now seemed to have. Her mind raced at thoughts of being able to sell her scripts and live off the proceeds, even to save up money and pay Olivia back. She could realistically envision a future in which she could spend her time at home, writing—a time when she could be with Henry all day, every day. A life in which she could afford to take him out and have fun.

Emily put her hand over her phone and paused as she realised her instinct was to text Olivia and tell her the news. Her hand had moved without her even considering the action, like muscle memory. She stared at the phone and smiled.

In her hopeful visions of the future, of course there was Henry, happily running from room to room, playing while she worked—but Olivia was also there. In each and every scene Emily imagined, she saw Olivia with her. The three of them together; a family.

Emily picked up the phone and sent a quick text to Olivia before pulling herself up and sitting on the bed again. She pulled the laptop onto her lap, cracked her fingers, and started to type.

CHAPTER THIRTY-NINE

Olivia heard a text arrive, and picked up the phone up to read, I love you, so very much.

With a wide smile, Olivia typed back a quick reply: and I you.

"What are you looking at?" Henry asked. He stood up from where he'd been leaning on the coffee table, colouring in the outlines of giraffes that Olivia had now mastered.

Olivia angled the phone to show him. "Your mother texted me."

Henry looked at the screen and slowly sounded out the words with Olivia's assistance.

"She loves me." Henry gave her a toothy grin and sat back down.

Olivia briefly considered telling him that the statement was meant for her, but she quickly decided against it.

"What do you want to do tomorrow, Henry?" Olivia asked. "We have all of Saturday to fill."

"Park?" Henry asked excitedly as his eyes drifted to the giraffe scooter she'd given him. He'd attempted to use it several times in the suite, but Olivia had feared him barrelling into something unforgiving and told him that it was only for use outside.

"Okay. The park sounds fun." Olivia smiled. "How about a movie too?"

Henry looked up at the television with a half-hearted shrug. "I suppose."

"I mean at the cinema," Olivia clarified. She'd been busily searching online for ways to fill the day with a five-year-old. Many people agreed that the cinema was a good two-to-three-hour rest for adults. That, and she'd seen a trailer for a funny-looking animated movie that she rather liked the look of.

Henry slowly turned and looked at her, as if he expected her to take it back. "Really?"

"Yes," Olivia said. She opened an application on her phone. "There's a showing at one; I thought we could go after lunch?"

Henry launched himself at her and held her in a tight embrace, his eyes squeezed tightly shut. "Thank you, Olivia."

Olivia put her arm around him and gently held him. "You're most welcome, Henry."

After a few short moments, Henry released her and took a shaky breath before he returned to his colouring. Olivia watched him for a few minutes while she attempted to analyse his reaction. She considered Emily's time away from home and financial situation and realised that Henry probably rarely, if ever, was taken to the cinema.

With insight she hadn't known she was capable of, she realised that her desire to give Henry everything he could ever dream of could be extremely damaging. Clearly, he had become used to a frugal existence, and being treated was something quite foreign to him. While he enjoyed the idea of the indulgence, he was clearly overcome by it as well.

Olivia began to understand Emily's initial concerns, remembering with crystal clarity the gift shop at London Zoo. At the time, she had wanted to buy Henry anything he desired, but now she realised it would've been the wrong thing to do.

Giving Henry a taste of a lifestyle where money wasn't as big an issue as it was in his current world, and then, potentially, taking it away again would be traumatic, for both Henry and Emily. Suddenly, Olivia found that she understood the responsibility she'd taken on and had a greater respect for it. She wanted to get things right with Henry. She owed him that much.

"Will we have popcorn?" Henry asked almost timidly, without looking up from his colouring project, his brain clearly whirring at the prospect of the cinema trip.

"Maybe," Olivia allowed. "A small bag."

Henry smiled and nodded his head in understanding.

❖

A few hours later, Olivia was fed up with being in the suite. It was another revelation when she considered just how long Emily had been stuck indoors while Henry was recovering. She told Henry they'd eat dinner in the hotel restaurant downstairs and left him with the television on while she went to change.

In her bedroom, she removed her dark blue jeans and replaced them with a pair of smart black trousers. She pulled off the cream sweater, picked a crisp white shirt from a hanger, and put it on. As she was doing up the buttons, Henry burst into the room and she quickly moved to draw the shirt around herself. He stood in front of her with tears in his eyes as he clutched a small blue shirt in his hands.

"Henry? What's wrong?" Olivia crouched down, thoughts of modesty gone from her mind at the sight of his tears.

"I don't have nice clothes," he sniffed.

"What do you mean?" Olivia frowned.

He backhanded some falling tears from his cheeks. "You're changing your clothes so you look nice at dinner," he explained. "I don't have any nice clothes."

He held up the blue shirt and pointed to the ever-present giraffe hoodie he was wearing. "I only have these and my T-shirts."

"Oh, Henry. You don't need to wear smart clothes." She smiled at him and stroked his cheek affectionately.

"Then why are you changing your clothes?" Henry frowned with a wobbling lip.

"I…" Olivia looked down at what she was wearing. "You know, you're right. I don't need to get changed. I'll change back to what I was wearing. Go and watch some more television and I'll be there in a moment."

"You sure?" Henry asked, frowning.

"I'm sure." Olivia smiled warmly and stood up. "Off you go."

As Henry headed back to the living room, Olivia shook her head at her own foolishness. She removed her white shirt again and pulled on the cream jumper. Next she removed and hung up her black trousers and put her jeans back on. She looked at herself in the mirror with a critical eye. It had been so long since she'd worn casual clothes regularly that these days she felt more comfortable in smart clothes. But it seemed that was also going to have to change if she was going to ensure Henry's comfort.

After a quick reapplication of make-up—because there were some lines that Olivia wouldn't cross—she and Henry went downstairs. Olivia smiled with pride as she noticed many of the other diners looking at Henry and smiling. Tiny sat on the table, in front of a half-full glass of water and a bread roll on a side plate that the waiter had kindly set up for him. They talked about what they would do the next day, and Henry asked a million and one questions about space, which Olivia either answered from her own knowledge or consulted Google and then explained to him.

At one point, Henry looked at Tiny and started talking to the toy in some incomprehensible language.

"What are you saying?" Olivia asked.

"I'm speaking Chinese," Henry replied.

Olivia speared a piece of pasta and slowly chewed it as Henry continued to talk to Tiny.

"It doesn't sound like Chinese. Why are you speaking Chinese anyway?"

"Tiny is from China."

"Giraffes are from Africa," Olivia argued.

Henry picked up Tiny, turned him over, and thrust his bottom into Olivia's face. He pointed to a white tag. "Tiny is from China."

"Oh, I see." Olivia nodded.

Henry put Tiny back on the table, somehow managing to put his other hand into a pile of uneaten ketchup on his plate.

"Oops." He held his hand up for her to see.

She picked up her napkin in one hand, held his hand in place with the other, and gently wiped at the red mess.

It turned out that wasn't the only mess Henry had managed to get himself into over the course of the day. When they returned to the suite, Olivia realised that there was pen ink and food all over him, including in his hair. Luckily, Henry was happy about the prospect of taking a bath; he had brought his toy boats with him and was eager to show them to her.

Olivia entered the bathroom to find Henry standing on his suitcase to reach the sink, where he was currently brushing his teeth with a giraffe-handled toothbrush.

Henry spat into the sink and looked up at Olivia with a wide, toothy grin. He stepped off of his suitcase, handed her the mucky toothbrush, and started to pull his trousers down. Olivia quickly averted her eyes and washed her hands and the toothbrush under the tap. Then she put the cap back on the toothpaste and rinsed what looked like half a tube of the stuff from around the sink.

When she turned around, Henry was naked and his clothes were strewn around the bathroom. She saw that the scar on his chest from the heart operation was already nicely healing up.

Henry noticed her gaze, looked at his chest, and pointed to the scar with his finger. "It bleeded." He smiled proudly.

"Bled," Olivia said as she frowned. "When?"

"Ages ago." Henry shrugged.

"As in before today?" Olivia clarified.

"Yep," Henry said as he turned, gripped the edge of the bath, and proceeded to try to climb in by himself.

Olivia quickly realised that he would fall in headfirst and she stepped forward to put a restraining arm across his chest. She checked the temperature of the water and once she was satisfied, lifted him up under the shoulders and into the bathtub. She tried to hold on to him while she lowered him into the water, but as soon as he was in the bath he pulled away. He started to swish around the tub, alternating between his front and his back.

"Look, I'm a shark," he said as he swam around.

Olivia laughed. "Yes, you are," she said.

She wet her hands and threaded them through his messy mop of hair, moulding it into a Mohawk, then laughed.

"Let me see," Henry cried excitedly, and Olivia angled the extending shaving mirror so he could see his hair.

He fell back laughing once he caught a glimpse of himself in the mirror. "You're silly, Olivia."

"You're silly," she countered with a smile.

"You're sillier." He giggled.

"Maybe I am." Olivia laughed as she looked at the boats on the edge of the tub. "Now, what about these boats?"

Olivia found that she quite enjoyed bath time with Henry; they spoke about boats, giraffes, school, airplanes, astronauts, hotels, and then back to giraffes. Olivia enjoyed talking with Henry. It was relaxing, so much easier than speaking with adults where there were rules and expectations. If she said something that Henry didn't understand or didn't agree with, he would either giggle, ignore her, or change the subject.

She managed to navigate the rules of shampooing and conditioning his hair with assistance. Under his instructions, she advised him when she had washed the soapy suds away, and it was safe to open his eyes. Eventually the bath water started to cool, she could see the goose bumps appearing on his arms, and she suggested it was time to get out of the tub.

Finally, he agreed, and she pulled a soft towel from the towel rail and placed it on the floor in front of the tub before grabbing another to dry him.

He stood up and shivered a little as she quickly lifted him from the bath, then wrapped the fresh, warm towel around him. As she rubbed it over his back and arms, he leaned in and looked up at her with a smile.

"Love you, Olivia," he whispered.

The simple words took her breath away. She obviously knew that she loved Henry, but she had never really considered that he might feel the same way. She wrapped her arms around him and placed a soft kiss on his wet hair.

"I love you too, Henry," she said.

After a moment or two in the embrace, Henry pulled away. He pushed the towel to the floor and left the bathroom in search of his pyjamas. She watched as he walked away, knowing the grin on her face must have verged on ridiculous. But she couldn't help it. Those three words from Henry changed everything.

❖

Once Henry was in his pyjamas and had climbed into bed, Olivia was struck by an idea.

"Henry, I think we should make a little movie. What do you think?" She waved her phone playfully in front of him.

Henry looked from the phone to Olivia, eyes gleaming. "What movie?"

"A goodnight movie," Olivia explained. "We can record it, and I'll send it to your mom."

Henry fidgeted excitedly while Olivia set up the phone to record them both. She showed him the little picture of them, and they crouched together to ensure they were both visible.

"Think about what you want to say," Olivia said with a smile as her thumb hovered over the Record button. "When you see the red light, you need to speak, okay?"

Henry nodded, and she pressed the button. The red light appeared, and Henry leaned in close, taking up all of the screen with his face.

"Mommy. This is a goodnight movie from me and Olivia. I love you. Goodnight and sweet dreams and I love you. Night, Mommy!" Henry shouted quickly, staring raptly at the screen as he did.

Olivia bit her lip to stop from laughing as she looked to the camera. "Buenas noches, hermosa."

Olivia stopped the recording and put her phone on the bedside table while she picked up a book to read to Henry. It took three passes of the book before Henry's questions about the next day eventually died down and he was tired enough to go to sleep. When they finished reading, he knelt up and gave her a wet kiss on the lips.

"Night, 'Livia," he mumbled before crawling into the bedding. "I love you."

Olivia swallowed back the unexpected lump in her throat. "I love you too."

She slipped off of the bed and pulled the bedding up around him, pressing a soft kiss to his hair, then picked up her phone and headed to the kitchen. She poured herself a well-deserved glass of wine to celebrate surviving the day, and she sent the movie to Emily, hoping she wouldn't be disturbing her too much. As she started to clear up some of the mess in the kitchen—she'd had no idea how much work having a child actually was—her phone started to vibrate loudly on the work surface. Olivia quickly answered it, smiling as she realised who it was.

"Hello, darling."

"I want to be with you two," Emily said tearfully.

"Are you…are you crying?" Olivia started to panic.

"Yes, happy tears," Emily said. "That video was adorable. So perfect. Thank you so much."

"Well, Henry said most of it." Olivia chuckled.

"But you thought of it," Emily said sincerely.

Olivia felt herself blush and attempted to change the subject a little. "I'm sorry, but Henry's asleep…you said not to call you in case he got upset…"

"That's fine," Emily said. "I called to speak to you. How's he been?"

"Delightful," Olivia said sincerely. "I think, well, he's wonderful. Once he stopped asking if we were going to get married."

"Married? What?" Emily sounded shocked, and Olivia laughed.

"I told him to ask you about it," Olivia replied with a grin, practically able to feel the heat of Emily's blush down the phone.

"Right." Emily laughed nervously. "Well, I'll look forward to that conversation, thanks. Everything else go okay? Any problems?"

"I'll admit I'm a little concerned about tomorrow morning."

"You'll be fine. Like I said, just let him come to you. Henry in the morning is a little hard work, but once he wakes up a bit you'll be fine."

"I hope so. How's the writing going?"

"Amazingly," Emily said. "I had a crisis of confidence earlier, but I spoke to Nicole and she really helped. I'll tell you about that later, when I see you, but it's going really well."

"Wonderful." Olivia smiled and licked her lips nervously. "I miss you." She hadn't meant to admit it, but the words just slipped out. Time without Emily now seemed like wasted time. She was surprised by how strong her emotions had become, and so fast.

"I miss you too."

"I should let you get back to your writing," Olivia said reluctantly. "Or I'll start flirting outrageously in an attempt to get you to come over."

Emily chuckled softly down the line. "I love you."

"I love you too," Olivia whispered, her emotions starting to get the better of her.

"And now I'm going to go because I have to finish this," Emily said, a touch of frustration in her tone.

"Speak to you tomorrow?" Olivia asked hopefully.

"Yes, I hope…well, I don't want to jinx it, but if it goes as well as it's been going today then…well…" Emily struggled to verbalise her thoughts.

"And to think you want to be a writer, dear," Olivia said with a smirk.

"I could start to dislike you, you know."

They shared a bittersweet laugh.

"Goodnight, Emily," Olivia said softly.

"Night, Olivia."

Olivia quickly hung up the phone before she blurted out anything else and closed her eyes as she held it to her chest. She bit her lip and smiled as she realised she actually felt like a teenager with her first crush; any time apart from her lover was sheer torture.

With a sigh, she picked up her wine glass and went into the sitting room to watch some television, trying to distract herself from thoughts of Emily.

❖

The next morning, Olivia stood by the coffee maker, patiently waiting for it to do its thing and provide her with the only known substance that would get her through another full day of Henry.

Olivia was hesitant about the morning ritual, but Emily assured her that he did it most mornings with Lucy. The usual play of events was that Henry would run into the kitchen to look for Emily, see she wasn't there, then run back to his bedroom to cuddle with Tiny until he felt more awake. When he came back to the kitchen, he'd silently eat his breakfast and eventually start speaking.

Despite the knowledge that even the exalted Lucy wasn't enough for Henry in the mornings, Olivia still hoped against hope that he would somehow feel at ease with her.

The sound of a door creaking open and the thud of bare feet on the carpeted hallway alerted Olivia to the imminent arrival of her charge. Henry appeared in the doorway, hair mussed, pyjamas in disarray. He squinted as he looked around the kitchen, then turned to examine the sitting room before turning back to the kitchen and regarding Olivia with a frown.

Olivia smiled before turning away to pour herself some coffee. During her own uncomfortable moments of social interaction, she felt more at ease when she wasn't being watched. The gamble worked; Henry paused in the doorway for several moments before he ran back to his bedroom. Olivia took a sip of her coffee, and considered that it was an improvement on what she'd worried would happen. Her biggest fear was that he might cry.

She made herself some toast and jam and sat down to read the morning paper. By the time she reached the entertainment section,

Henry was back and peering at her around the doorframe. Olivia sat stoically, in silence, ignoring his presence even though she monitored his every move.

Slowly, Henry crept into the room. He noisily dragged a chair next to her and sat on it with a tired pout.

Olivia silently reached forward, picked up a slice of toast—Emily had previously instructed her that Henry liked cold toast so the jam wouldn't melt—and placed it on his plate. She opened the jam jar and placed the plastic giraffe knife that Emily had packed in front of him.

He seemed to appreciate the gesture, and the silence, as he applied a generous amount of jam to his cold toast and Olivia poured him some orange juice. He ate while Olivia read, occasionally sipping her now lukewarm coffee.

After a while, she felt him nudge her arm, and before she knew what he was doing, he'd ducked his head under her arm and was making a move to sit on her lap. She uncrossed her legs to better accommodate him and continued reading while he silently snuggled into her. Olivia smiled; she could practically hear the creaking sound of his brain waking up and feeding him the information he needed to function correctly.

After ten minutes, Henry looked up at Olivia with a toothy grin. "Park?"

CHAPTER FORTY

"Why can't you just tell me what this is about?" Emily asked.

Olivia paused and faced Emily, ignoring the other pedestrians on the busy New York street. She'd stopped using her crutch, but her walking speed was still much slower than it had been before, which frustrated her.

"Because then I'd have to repeat myself," Olivia said.

Emily laughed, looped her arm through Olivia's, and guided her to continue walking.

"You know, you can actually say things more than once."

"But to tell you all about it now and then tell them all about it in five minutes' time…" Olivia shuddered. "It would be exhausting."

"Okay, we'll work on that. I'll add it to our list," Emily said.

Over the course of the last week, they had decided to tackle their communication problem head-on. They were both too invested for any silly misunderstandings or fears to destroy what was building between them.

Olivia was modifying her behaviour where needed—but only once Emily had explained why a change might be useful. So far it had been working very well, and Olivia was appreciating the new insight into improving her communication and understanding what people expected from her. And why.

She led Emily inside the Italian restaurant. Simon and Sophie were already seated, but rose to offer Olivia and Emily hugs of greeting.

"Have you two been having a nice vacation?" Emily asked before Olivia could launch into a conversation about work. Olivia shot her a grin, understanding what she was doing, then pulled out a chair for her. Emily sat down.

"Holiday," Simon corrected her. "If you're going to use our language, then use it properly."

"Vacation." Emily grinned at him.

Olivia took her own chair. "Vacation," she confirmed to Simon with a smirk.

"It's been amazing," Sophie cut in. "We've seen so much. I always wanted to come to New York, but now that I'm actually here…wow."

"I need to see more of it," Emily said. "Isn't it always the way that when you live somewhere, you don't appreciate it as much as a tourist would?"

"True. I've lived in London for years and hardly been to any tourist attractions," Simon confessed.

Emily turned to Olivia, who was looking at the menu and attempting to ignore the conversation. "I presume you haven't had time to do many touristy things in either London or New York?"

Olivia looked up. "Me? No." She shook her head, then frowned in thought. "Well, some, I guess. I did get invited to a lot of events in London."

"She's seen everything," Simon told Emily. "During the time I've worked with her, she's been to one event or another at every place you could name. She's even been to Buckingham Palace."

Emily snapped her head around to Olivia. "You've been to Buckingham Palace?"

"She's met the Queen," Simon added.

"You've met the Queen?" Emily stared in surprise.

Olivia swallowed as she looked at the three people staring at her. "Yes. Well, twice. Once at the palace during a garden party and once at the Tate Gallery."

"You've met the Queen twice?" Emily repeated.

"Yes."

"And you never mentioned this?" Emily chuckled and picked up her menu. "This is also going on the list."

Simon laughed at their interaction. "Anyway, thank you for inviting us to lunch."

"Thank you for getting me in trouble," Olivia joked.

"You're not in trouble," Emily sighed with a smile.

"Do I like chervil?" Olivia asked Simon.

"You called it parsley with a French accent, but you ate it," Simon said.

"Oh, yes, now I recall. Oh, and, make sure you don't have the ricotta. It upset your stomach last time." Olivia pointed to the menu item containing the offending ingredient.

Sophie chuckled and looked at Emily. "Anyone would think that they're dating each other." Simon regarded her with an expression of horror, and she was sure that she echoed the sentiment. Emily simply laughed.

A waitress approached, and they placed their orders and made small talk until the drinks and bread basket arrived. Emily gave Olivia a small nod, signalling that enough initial conversation had taken place and she was allowed to talk about work.

Olivia seized upon the opportunity. "I'm stepping down."

Simon coughed into his beer. "I'm sorry, what?" He wiped at his mouth with a napkin.

Olivia turned to see Emily staring at her, open-mouthed.

"I'm stepping down," she repeated.

"You're giving up?" Simon asked sadly.

Olivia picked up a wholemeal bread roll from the basket and placed it on her side plate. "No, I've come to a compromise with Marcus."

"Compromise?" Simon's voice rose, and Sophie placed a calming hand on his arm. "Olivia, you can't trust that man. He—"

"Simon," Olivia said sternly. She knew she was to blame for some of his antipathy towards Marcus, but that had to end now if they were going to work together. There was no going back from the decisions she'd made. Marcus was in agreement with her plan, and it was up to her to make it work. Even if making it work meant standing to one side and allowing the business to continue without her.

Olivia had fought so hard for Applewood to survive that she had forgotten one essential thing: she needed to do what was in the best interests of the company as a whole. When she looked at restructuring other businesses, she was ruthless and pragmatic. When she had initially attempted to save Applewood, she'd been too emotional and too personally invested. Once she'd managed to step to one side, she'd known what she needed to do.

Simon took a deep breath and nodded. "Sorry, go on."

"Marcus is no longer going to file the anonymous complaint with the regulator, and we had a long discussion about a gap in his portfolio: audit and corporate restructuring. We've agreed that he'll partner with Applewood for those projects." She broke open the bread roll and started to layer a small amount of butter on it.

"This means that the London staff will keep their jobs, and the business will survive, even though it will be much smaller. Marcus doesn't have the time or the money to set up his own departments, so this works for everyone."

"But what about you? You're stepping down?" Simon asked. "He's making you stand down?"

"No, I offered." She deliberately hadn't told anyone about the negotiations with Marcus. She felt bad about keeping things from Emily and Simon, but she'd had to do it alone. Applewood's failure was her fault, and at first that knowledge had been almost crippling.

She'd been so caught up in the trauma of what was happening at work that she hadn't had time to really think about what was happening around her. After her collapse, she'd started to think. Staring at the ceiling of her hotel bedroom, she'd come to a few conclusions, the main one being an understanding that she was just going through the motions. Every day, every week, followed a certain structure. A set series of events with no room for change. Once the schedule was broken, Olivia had been forced to stop and think about her life.

And when she'd started to reflect on what she actually wanted from life, she'd been shocked to find that it wasn't even remotely business-related.

Simon ran his hands through his hair in exasperation. "This is a lot to take in," he said. "I'm not sure how I feel about working for Marcus."

"You won't be working for Marcus," Olivia explained. "You'll be taking my position."

Simon shook his head, confused. "What?"

"Pardon," Olivia corrected him. "You'll be managing director."

"I can't be managing director."

"Of course you can," Olivia told him with a roll of her eyes, then delicately took a bite of the bread roll. She'd known that Simon would balk at the suggestion of taking over. It was in his nature to stand behind someone else, rather than put himself front and centre. But she also knew she could teach him.

"I'm too young," Simon argued.

"Don't be silly," Olivia said. "Anyone would think you don't want the job."

"Oh, I want it," Simon said. "I just don't know how you managed to sell it to Marcus."

"No offence," Emily interrupted, "but isn't it a big step up from being a personal assistant to being managing director?"

"Hey, don't get involved," Simon complained with a grin.

"It's not common," Olivia said.

"So," Simon said, "let me see if I have this right. Marcus doesn't have an audit and restructuring team?"

"He doesn't," Olivia confirmed.

"And you've somehow managed to convince him that he can outsource that work to Applewood?"

"I have."

"And he has agreed to this?"

"He has."

"And you're stepping down?"

"I am."

"And I'm replacing you?"

"Well, I would hope so."

"And Marcus knows about this?"

"He does."

Emily, who'd watched the interaction, shook her head. "Well, that felt like watching a tennis match."

Simon sat back and blinked as he took everything in.

"Would Simon be working here or in London?" Sophie asked.

"London," Olivia replied. "There may be some travel to New York, but he'll be based in our current office." The question brought a flashback to the crash, and she shifted uncomfortably at the memory. She'd miss London, but there was no way she'd be able to board a plane again.

Although, despite nearly dying, the crash hadn't been a terrible thing. Without it, she wouldn't be where she was now. She wouldn't have Henry and Emily back in her life. In some strange, twisted way, the crash had almost been a good thing for her. Not that she'd ever admit it as she'd grumbled about walking with a cane, and, for the last week, learned how to walk without it again.

"Unless you decide to move," she said.

"Move?" Simon frowned.

"The office space may be too big. Although you will probably need to hire more staff. Marcus's firm will grow at an extraordinary rate. There will be some redundancies, obviously, but I'll deal with that before I leave."

Emily placed her hand on Olivia's arm. "I think we should give Simon a few moments to digest all of this."

Olivia looked at Simon's terrified expression and realised that the information was probably overloading him.

"Is there no other way?" Simon asked.

"This is the best way," Olivia said.

"But he's forcing you out."

Olivia chuckled. "No, I'm going because I want to."

Simon shook his head. "But, but you love Applewood. You love working."

"I do. I did. But…" Olivia sighed. "Simon, a lot has happened lately, and it's opened my eyes to a lot of things. I wasn't living; I was simply being. I'm making changes—changes that should've happened a long time ago."

"You really want this? To quit?"

"Very much so." Olivia reached out and gestured for him to do the same. She took his hand and squeezed it reassuringly. "Next week, I move into my new house. I don't have to worry about an exhausting commute, and my time will be my own until I decide what I want to do next." She turned to Emily and smiled. "I have Emily and Henry in my life now, and that's worth more than any job." She turned back to Simon. "Of course, Applewood is important to me. Its legacy is important to me, and I want it to survive. But the time has come where I need to separate Applewood's life from my own."

Simon squeezed her hand and nodded.

She retracted her hand and smiled fondly at him. "Besides, I wouldn't trust anyone else to do the job. You've shadowed me for long enough to know every facet of the business."

Simon laughed nervously. "There's a difference between seeing you do it and doing it for myself."

"There'll be a handover period," Olivia assured him. "I've every faith in you."

The heavy words hung over the table for a few moments before Simon joked, "As long as I don't have to do your old commute."

"I wouldn't let you." Sophie gently elbowed him in the ribs. "I wouldn't want you flirting with the cabin crew."

Emily laughed, and Olivia felt heat in her cheeks.

"You have to watch out for these financial sorts," Emily told Sophie. "They'll give their business card to anyone."

Sophie laughed. "You got the business card too?"

Simon and Olivia looked away, blushing, and Emily burst out laughing.

❖

"I can't believe you were planning to quit and have Simon replace you and you didn't tell me in advance." Emily pressed the elevator button and shook her head.

"I don't like repeating myself," Olivia said.

"You thought I might argue with you and wanted to wait until we were with other people," Emily surmised.

"Possibly." Olivia grinned.

The elevator doors closed, and the car started to ascend to the top floor of the hotel.

"Do you know what you're going to do next?" Emily asked.

"No idea." Olivia let out a sigh. "It still feels unsettling to me. I never thought I'd leave Applewood, and now I'm doing that and moving into a house at the same time. I don't mind admitting that I'm quite nervous about the whole thing."

Emily took Olivia's hand and intertwined their fingers. "Nervous?" she asked.

Olivia grinned again. "Terrified."

"I'm so proud of you," Emily whispered softly. "I know you hate change, but you're facing all of this head-on."

"I couldn't have done any of this without you."

"I think we should make a list of things you'd like to do next. You like lists," Emily said.

Olivia's eyes lit up. "I think I'd like that. You know, I've always liked the idea of growing tomatoes."

Emily chuckled. "If that's your dream, then we'll figure out how to grow tomatoes."

CHAPTER FORTY-ONE

Olivia looked at the suitcase by the front door and let out a sigh. She didn't know what made her more miserable, the fact that Emily was going away to London, or the fact that she couldn't stand to be without her for a few days. She'd always been independent and kept her feelings to herself. Since being with Emily, she'd learned to express herself more, which was a good thing—except when expressing herself was moping about being without her girlfriend for such a short period of time.

"Don't pout," Emily said as she pulled on her jacket.

"It feels as if I only just managed to convince you to move in. And now you're leaving again."

Emily turned and cupped Olivia's face in her hands. "I've been living here for a month. I moved in just two weeks after you. It was hardly a long wait. And I'll only be gone four days. I'll be back before you know it."

"Why do people say that?" Olivia grumbled. "You won't be back before I know it. If you were, then you wouldn't be leaving. It's such a bad saying. It would be more accurate to s—"

Emily's lips silenced her. She felt herself being pressed up against the front door, Emily's hands in her hair, her body tight to Olivia's. Emily tore her lips away and started to plant hot, wet kisses down her throat.

"You don't fight fair." Olivia groaned as Emily blew cool air across her wet neck. "You know this won't make me miss you less, don't you?"

"I don't want to go. I have to," she breathed against Olivia's ear, then gently bit the skin below. "I'll call you every day. And when I get back—"

"Mommy!"

Emily sighed and pulled back, quickly checking herself in the mirror. "We're down here, sweetheart."

Olivia looked over Emily's shoulder and fixed her lipstick. "When you get back, can Lucy take Henry for the night, or maybe the weekend?"

"My thoughts exactly." Emily smiled.

Henry ran into the hallway and held out a piece of paper. Emily took it and crouched down to look at it with him.

"Wow, is this a goodbye card? For me?" Emily enthused.

Henry nodded and threw his arms around her neck. Emily returned the hug. "I will be back before you know it, okay?"

Henry nodded again. Olivia turned away and shook her head.

"And you'll be good while I'm gone?" Emily asked.

"Yes," Henry promised, his voice just a whisper.

A car horn sounded outside.

"That's my taxi." Emily kissed Henry's cheek and gave him a final squeeze before she stood up.

Olivia tried not to look devastated, but she knew she was doing a terrible job of it. Emily hugged her and gave her a chaste kiss on the cheek. "I love you both. Be good."

Olivia and Henry walked Emily out to the car and waved her goodbye. They both watched as the taxi disappeared from sight, then turned to each other and slowly walked back into the house. In the hallway, Henry let out a sigh as he closed the front door behind them.

"I'm bored."

"You cannot possibly be bored." Olivia reached around him and locked the door.

"I am though."

"Why don't you play in your room?"

"With you?" Henry asked with a grin.

Olivia chuckled. "Oh, I see. You're bored, so you want me to play with you?"

Henry nodded excitedly.

"Very well. But I promised your mother that I would get you some new shoes, so I think we should go shopping first."

Henry sighed. "Not shopping."

"I'm afraid so. Get your shoes on."

"You used to be fun," Henry grumbled as he passed her.

"Was not. I was never fun. I made you eat cucumber the first time we met," she told him with a smirk.

❖

After an age of getting ready and getting to the store, Henry had complained that he was hungry and would need to eat before starting to look at shoes. The department store restaurant overlooked the busy New York street below, and Henry stared out the window with interest.

Olivia was fairly convinced it was one of Henry's many delaying tactics, which he deployed when asked to do something he found boring. But as she couldn't be sure, she'd allowed him to sit with a sandwich and juice while she drank a coffee.

"Why are people clapping?" Henry asked.

Olivia lowered her coffee cup and looked out the window to where Henry pointed.

"That man's proposed; I assume she said yes."

"What does that mean?"

Olivia thought for a moment. "Well, it's a tradition that when someone asks their partner to marry them, they get down on one knee. Like that man is doing."

"What's prosposed?"

"Proposed," she corrected him. "When you propose to someone, you are asking them to marry you."

"Why is she showing that lady her hand?"

"Because he has given her a ring to wear."

"Why?"

Olivia quickly realised that explaining things to a five-year-old made a lot of things sound utterly ridiculous.

"It's a gift. He wants her to have the ring for the rest of their lives together. If she accepts it, then she is saying yes and that she wants to marry him."

"When will you ask Mommy to marry you?"

"Me?"

Henry nodded.

"I…Henry…it's…"

"Because you love each other, don't you?" Henry pressed on. "So, you should get married."

"It's a bit early to be thinking about marriage."

"How long should it be?"

Olivia picked up her coffee, wishing she had wine instead. "I don't know, longer than it's been."

"Another month? A year? Three years? A hundred years?"

Olivia sipped her coffee. "I, well, there's no set amount of time, Henry."

"Why is it too early, then? How do you know when it's the right time?"

Olivia lowered her coffee and looked out the window as she considered the question.

"Why do you think we should get married?" Olivia asked.

"I dunno." Henry shrugged. "Lucy and Tom are married."

"That doesn't mean that your mother and I should get married."

"Lucy says that people get married to show they love each other and they have containment."

Olivia frowned and thought for a moment. "Commitment," she said.

"That," Henry said. He took a bite of his sandwich. "What is that?"

"A promise. I've made a commitment to look after you. I've promised to look after you."

Henry sipped his juice. His brow furrowed in concentration. "So, Lucy and Tom promise to look after each other."

"In a way, yes."

Olivia waited for further questions, but none arose. As the silence stretched on and Henry continued to look out the window, she thought about the idea of marriage.

She'd been married before. She hadn't hesitated to make that commitment. But she had no idea what Emily's feelings were on the matter. She wished she had taken the opportunity to ask when it had come up before. She looked at Henry and smiled to herself. She'd like nothing more than to solidify their family with the act of marriage.

Essentially, she knew that marriage was a piece of paper and a promise. Of course, she also knew that there were certain tax benefits to being a married couple. But taxation aside, she wondered how much her life would change if she and Emily were to marry. If Emily would even say yes.

"Why are you smiling at me?"

Olivia blinked and shook her head. "I was lost in thought. Henry, do you think your mother wants to get married?"

"Yes." He nodded his head. "She always talks about it with Lucy."

Olivia swallowed and looked nervously around the restaurant. She knew it was wrong to quiz a child about something so personal, but somehow she couldn't help herself.

"Oh, yes?" She tried to sound casual.

"Can we buy my shoes now?"

Olivia looked at him in exasperation. "I thought you didn't want to buy shoes? Now you suddenly want to?"

"Yep." Henry shrugged.

Olivia decided it was probably best that she didn't have the chance to pump Henry for more information. She'd learned early on that Henry was not to be trusted with secrets and would blab them to Emily with no warning at all.

They finished their meal and left the restaurant in search of shoes that Henry liked, that Emily would approve of, and that Olivia felt were ergonomically suitable. Luckily, a sales assistant helped out, and within fifteen minutes they were leaving the children's department and heading to the ground floor.

As the escalator slowly carried them towards the exit, Olivia looked at the huge sales floor. She looked at the perfume, make-up, and jewellery counters, and the people excitedly buzzing around them. An idea came to her, and she pressed down the little voice that told her it might be a bad idea.

"Henry, would you like to help me with an extra-special project?"

CHAPTER FORTY-TWO

Emily used her key to unlock the front door. She was a little surprised that neither Henry nor Olivia was at the door to greet her. But then, her flight had landed early and the taxi journey took less time than expected due to the suicidal driver who had never once dipped under the speed limit.

She put her suitcase in the hall, then closed and locked the door. The sound of Henry's feet running through the house had her smiling as she turned around. The moment she saw him, her breath caught. He wore a tiny, fitted tuxedo, complete with shiny, black shoes and a black bowtie. His hair was slicked back, and a curly black moustache was drawn on his upper lip.

"Welcome to Amor Restaurant. Your chair…" Henry paused and frowned. "Your table is ready."

"Why thank you," Emily said, holding back her desire to scoop him up and hug him tightly. Clearly, there was a plan, and she didn't want to ruin it.

"May I take your coat?" he asked.

Emily shrugged out of her jacket and handed it to him. She smothered a giggle when he opened the closet and haphazardly chucked the garment in before kicking the door shut again.

"Please follow me." He gestured for her to hurry as he rushed across the living room towards the dining room.

As she entered the room, she gasped out loud. The table had been set to perfection with a beautiful candelabra in the centre. Henry pulled out a chair and pointed to it.

"Sit," he ordered.

A loud cough sounded in the other room.

"Please," Henry added with a blush.

Then he rushed out of the room, and Emily was left on her own to appreciate the attention to detail: the finest china, exquisitely shined cutlery, cut-crystal wine glasses. A gentle rumbling noise had her turning around to see Henry pushing a serving trolley into the room.

Olivia appeared behind him and Emily felt the breath leave her lungs. Olivia wore a perfectly fitted black cocktail dress with black heels, her hair and make-up styled as if she had just stepped out of a fashion magazine.

"H-hi," Emily stammered.

Olivia smiled and bent down to give her a soft kiss on the lips. "Welcome home."

Henry and Olivia removed the plates and dishes from the serving trolley and placed them on the table.

"What's this all about?" Emily asked, eyeing them both suspiciously.

"Nothin'." Henry shrugged.

"Nothing," Olivia repeated, pulling out a chair for Henry to sit down. She walked around the table and took the seat on Emily's other side. "Just a nice dinner, to welcome you home."

"We missed you, Mommy."

"I missed you both, very much." Emily was about to ask them what was going on again when Olivia lifted a cover from a dish. "Is that?"

"Yes, duck à l'orange."

Emily reached for a serving spoon. "I will be quizzing you about this right after I have eaten every piece of that duck."

Olivia chuckled. "Just a little welcome home surprise."

Emily looked at the hint of a blush on Olivia's cheeks and noticed that her hands had come together and she was pinching at her skin. Something was clearly amiss, but she decided to wait for Olivia to be ready to tell her.

Dinner was divine. Olivia had arranged for all of Emily's favourite dishes, and Henry kept the conversation going strong with his new career aspirations of being a zookeeper in space. Olivia seemed withdrawn and hardly ate. Emily was desperate to ask what was wrong.

After they'd eaten and Henry was repeating the story of the M&M he'd stuck up his nose for the third time, Olivia spoke. "Henry."

He frowned at her.

"Henry, it…you…it's time for that thing. The thing you can't be here for," Olivia stumbled over the words.

"Okay." Henry slid from his chair. "I'm going to watch cartoons."

He exited the room and Olivia jumped to her feet.

"Olivia? Are you okay?" Emily asked, worried by the sheen of sweat on her forehead.

Olivia opened a drawer in the sideboard and returned with a red envelope.

"Olivia," Emily said, reminding her that she hadn't replied.

"Oh, yes, I just wanted you to have this."

Olivia stood by her chair, reached over, and handed Emily the envelope. Emily took it and smiled.

"Why don't you sit down? Before you fall."

Olivia sat on the edge of the chair and anxiously stared at the envelope.

"Do I get a clue what this is?"

Olivia shook her head. "Open it," she suggested.

Emily slid her finger along the edge of the thick red paper. She looked in and smiled at the familiar sight, then looked up to Olivia.

"What is this?"

"Open it."

Emily reached in and pulled out an origami swan made from a bill.

"Are you tipping me?" Emily joked, remembering the first time Olivia had given her a swan made of money. She lifted it up and realised that it was heavier than the first one had been. She glanced at Olivia, who looked as if she might pass out. Olivia nodded her encouragement, and Emily started to gently unfold the delicate paper.

As she did, she realised that something was within the swan, and, with shaky hands, focused her attention on freeing the item hiding within.

When she pulled out a diamond ring, she let out a gasp. She stared at the intricate engraving around the band and then at the three set diamonds. It was beautiful. Exactly her style. Elegant and understated. She knew what it meant, but her brain wouldn't allow her to put the pieces together just yet. Looking at Olivia, she asked, "Is…is this what I think it is?"

Olivia nodded.

Emily felt her hands shake. "I need you to say it, Olivia. I don't want any misunderstandings. I need to—"

"Will you marry me?" Olivia blurted out.

Emily felt herself sag with relief that she hadn't misinterpreted the situation. She'd often wondered what her future with Olivia might look like, if Olivia would want to get married again. But she had never thought it would happen in such a romantic, perfect way. They'd come full circle. The swan brought back Emily's memories of that first flight with Crown. The first time she'd seen the impressive, beautiful woman who now sat in front of her, watching with nervous eyes. It was only then that Emily realised she hadn't answered.

She quickly nodded, then stood up. The chair fell backwards behind her as she rushed to Olivia, who stood and threw her arms around her. The held each other tightly. In that moment, everything was perfect. Emily couldn't imagine a more apt proposal; she could see how much thought and effort Olivia had put into it to make it perfect. Her eyes filled with happy tears as she realised that she had everything she could ever want.

Emily had never been one to believe in perfect partners. She couldn't believe that even the worst day could fade into insignificance just by hearing the sound of someone's voice. But Olivia was that person.

From the second she'd seen Olivia interact with Henry, she'd known that was what she wanted in a partner. Someone who could love and cherish Henry as much as she did while still gently pushing him to be the best he could possibly be.

"Did she say yes?"

Emily spun around to see Henry peeking around the doorframe.

"Henry, how did you know?" Olivia asked. "I kept this bit a secret," she told Emily.

"I'm not stupid," Henry said. "I'm nearly six."

Emily burst out laughing and allowed the tears to flow freely. She knelt down and held her arms out, and Henry ran into her embrace. "Did you say yes?"

"Yes," Emily said. She looked up at Olivia with tears in her eyes. "Yes, absolutely, yes."

CHAPTER FORTY-THREE

The doorbell sounded, and Henry came storming out of the television room into the foyer.

"I'll get it," he shouted.

Emily exited the kitchen and watched him with a smile. She'd seen the latest arrivals coming up the front path a few minutes before.

Henry grabbed the lock and twisted it several times before grabbing the handle and flinging the door open.

"Simon, Sophie!" he cried out enthusiastically, jumping up and down on the spot.

Simon looked down at him with a wide grin. "What a welcome. You're not sick of us yet?"

"No," Henry said, then reached forward, grabbed both their hands, and dragged them into the hallway. Once they were in, he walked past them and started to pull their suitcases inside.

Emily entered the hallway and hugged Sophie, then Simon. "Good to see you both. How was your flight?"

"Oh, you know. It was okay, but Crown Airlines would be so much better." Simon winked.

"Hey." Emily elbowed him in the ribs while Sophie gave him a gentle smack on the arm. "You know we don't mention that name in this house."

"Simon," Henry said as he tugged on Simon's suit jacket sleeve.

"Yes, Henry?" Simon crouched down and smiled.

"Will you play with me?" Henry asked eagerly.

"Of course I will," Simon said. He looked at his watch. "It'll have to be later because I have boring work to do now. But, I'll totally block out my schedule for playing. How does four o'clock sound?"

Henry smiled and bit his lip with excitement. "Okay."

"Make sure your room's tidy," Emily told him as he ran towards the stairs. "And no running on the stairs."

Henry skidded to a halt, then slowly began walking up the stairs while holding the bannister rail tightly. "Yes, Mommy."

"Can I get you both a drink?" Emily asked.

"I'd love some tea," Sophie said as she followed Emily.

"Tea sounds good," Simon said. "Where is she?"

"In the garden with Nicole," Emily replied as they walked into the kitchen. A set of double doors leading to the garden were wide open, and Olivia and Nicole could be seen walking around outside.

"I'll pop out and say hello," Simon said. He kissed Sophie on the cheek and walked out.

"Is it me, or do they get anxiety if they don't talk to one another at least every day?" Emily asked as she filled the kettle.

"More like every few hours," Sophie replied, settling herself on a stool by the breakfast bar. "It's cute."

"It is," Emily said.

"Thank you so much for the theatre tickets for last weekend, by the way."

"How was it?" Emily asked as she set about getting some cups ready.

"Amazing," Sophie exclaimed. "And of course, Simon told everyone in the bar that he knew the writer."

Emily chuckled. "And what did they say?"

"They all thought he was crazy and ignored him."

Emily laughed. "Well, we're flying over on the twenty-first of next month for the new opening. You should both come."

"That sounds great. We'd love to. How're the plans going? Everything organised?"

Emily rolled her eyes. "Well, at this rate there won't be a wedding because I'll have killed her first."

Sophie laughed. "You're getting married in four days."

"Still time." Emily winked.

"Simon did say that Olivia was likely to fixate on little things."

"I know," Emily said. She leaned across the counter to check that Olivia was out of earshot. "To be honest I don't see what difference it makes whether we give the guests edible favours or mementos of the day, but Bridezilla out there thinks it's a big deal. Like, a really big deal."

Sophie chuckled. "What did you decide?"

"This is Olivia. She decided to do both. Well, she and Henry decided." Emily started to pour boiling water into the assembled cups.

"Henry?" Sophie asked.

"Henry's turning into a budding wedding planner. To be honest, I think he's even more excited than we are. I feel terrible to admit it, but he's been helping Olivia with arrangements more than I have."

"Well, time is sparse when you're an award-winning playwright. Although, I see you finally had time to finish painting the foyer. It looks fantastic, by the way."

Emily looked out into the freshly painted foyer. "Yes, after having little squares of paint samples on the wall for six months, we thought we really ought to just make a decision."

"Hello, Sophie," Nicole said as she entered the kitchen.

"Hey, Nic." Sophie stepped off the stool and crossed the room to embrace her.

"Is Olivia boring Simon with work already?" Emily asked.

"Something about a restructuring in Isleworth." Nicole shook her head as she and Sophie pulled out stools and sat down. "Honestly, she's terrible at retiring."

"Simon's just as bad. He acts as if he can't make a decision without talking to her first. But he knows what he's doing. I think they just enjoy chatting," Sophie commented.

"They are literally on the phone or on webcam all the time. I don't know how he has time to get any work done." Emily chuckled and placed two cups of tea in front of them.

"Oh, tea, marvellous." Nicole happily grabbed the mug.

"Being surrounded by Brits, I'm understanding of the importance of tea at all times," Emily replied. She looked up as the doorbell sounded again. "Excuse me. I'll be back in a moment."

As she walked towards the front door, Henry came hammering down the stairs.

"Henry! Walk, don't run," she called out.

"I am," he insisted. "I'll get the door."

Emily slowed to a stop in the entryway to allow him to catch up to her. She smiled as he wrestled with the locks on the door and threw it open. A second later, he launched himself at Tom and Lucy, who were crouched down and ready for impact. He stretched as much as possible to reach his arms around them.

"Tom," Henry said as he pulled back. "Will you play with me and Simon later?"

"Sure, buddy. But only if it's the most epic water pistol battle ever," Tom told him seriously.

Henry almost hyperventilated with excitement and nodded. "I'm going to practice," he said as he ran back into the house.

"No water in your bedroom," Emily called after him. "And no running on the stairs."

Henry grumbled something unintelligible as he slowly walked up the stairs, gripping the handrail as he went.

Emily guided Lucy and Tom into the kitchen, where they greeted Nicole and Sophie.

"Is that tea?" Lucy asked as she stared pointedly at a cup.

"It can be," Emily chuckled.

Tom looked outside. "I'm going to say hi to Simon," he said.

"No, you're going to ask Simon about that new game you've been playing," Lucy said with a smile.

"Maybe." Tom winked and walked out into the garden.

Lucy sat on a stool and looked outside. "How's Bridezilla? Living to see another day?"

"Barely." Emily smiled. She made another cup of tea and passed it to Lucy.

"You missed the favour debacle," Nicole said.

"Ah," Lucy said. "Good, because I'm telling you, the cake issue was seriously damaging to my waistline."

"Cake issue?" Sophie chuckled.

Emily gave her a serious look. "It's no joke, Sophie. Chocolate or plain sponge? A fruity uplift at the end of a meal or not? What filling? To ice or not to ice? What kind of icing? Seriously, we had cake samples to feed an army."

"I ate most of it," Lucy said.

Emily sighed. "I know she's doing it because she wants it to be the perfect day for me. But I can't get her to understand that I just want to be married. To her. Everything else is just extras."

"Aww," Sophie and Lucy cooed simultaneously.

Nicole laughed. "Well, it will all be over in a few days. You'll be married, and wedding planning will be a distant memory."

"Thank goodness. And I've managed to convince her to cut back on the amount of work she's doing. Because, for someone who is supposedly unemployed, she spends a lot of time working."

"How did you manage that?" Lucy asked.

"Joint attack." Emily gestured her mug towards Sophie. "Sophie and I told Simon and Olivia that they had to spend at least two days a week not talking. Try to break Olivia's need to work and Simon's need for her advice."

"And what, pray tell, is she intending to do with these two days per week?" Nicole asked.

"Well." Emily felt herself blush. "She might be a bit busy in the future. We're kinda hoping to try for a baby."

Nicole, Sophie, and Lucy all screeched in excitement at once and launched themselves towards Emily to hug her. Emily looked out at the garden and saw Olivia, Tom, and Simon all look into the house with confusion before shaking their heads and continuing their conversation.

Nicole put her arm around Emily and leaned in close as she stage-whispered, "You do know that, no matter how hard you try, you won't be able to impregnate her?"

Emily laughed. "Yes, we know."

Nicole laughed, put her arms out, and embraced Emily for a second time. "I'm so happy for you both."

They settled back down onto their seats, all beaming from ear to ear at the unexpected news.

"Thank you. I really can't wait," Emily said. "Olivia's going to be an amazing mom."

"Yes," Lucy said. "Yes, she really is."

"We kinda have to tell Simon soon though," Emily chuckled. She looked at Sophie.

"Why?" Sophie asked.

"The guest room that you're staying in is going to be the baby's room, and, well, you know what Olivia's like. She's painted it already."

Sophie laughed. "Oh, I'm sure it will be fine. A lick of paint won't bother us."

"There's a crib in there, and the walls are covered in teddy bears," Emily said. "And balloons, and of course—"

"Giraffes," they all said at the same time before bursting out laughing.

❖

Simon scraped the mud off the carrot he'd just dug up from the vegetable patch at Olivia's instruction.

"Jesus, Olivia, what are you doing to these? This is a beast."

"You should have seen the marrow from last week." Olivia shook her head. "I needed Tom's help to lift it."

"Clearly, gardening suits you." Simon laughed. He turned to Tom. "Both of you."

Tom held up his hands. "I just do what she tells me in return for payment in food."

"You better not tell anyone in the office about this," Olivia told him seriously.

"Yeah, because your image would be ruined if people knew you grew killer carrots." Simon laughed.

"I don't want people to think I've gone soft." Olivia stepped farther into the vegetable patch and adjusted a piece of garden twine on a wooden stake.

"No chance of that," Simon said.

"Tom, could you pass me that shovel?" Olivia pointed to the tool, and Tom handed it to her. She turned to Simon. "We'll need to talk about Abbots and run through those figures again. Maybe tomorrow. Emily will tell us off if we try to talk over dinner tonight."

"Sure," Simon said. "Although, Abbots is months away. We can discuss it over the phone another day. I speak to you nearly every day."

"From what I hear, you two talk more than Lucy and I talk and we live together," Tom interjected.

"I'm a fascinating conversationalist," Simon said.

"Not what Emily says," Tom joked.

"Well, we may possibly need to—probably, actually, need to cut back on our conversations," Olivia said.

"Yes, Sophie did mention something. Trying to get us to talk about work less?" Simon asked.

"Indeed," Olivia confirmed. "After the wedding, I will, hopefully, be preoccupied."

"You're going to feed America with this ridiculously large vegetable garden?" Simon joked.

Olivia chuckled. "Not quite. We're going to try for a baby. If all goes well, I'll be carrying a child."

"That's fantastic news." Simon gently stepped into the mud and hugged her. Tom was right behind him offering his own congratulations.

"Thank you, both of you. And, Tom, I was wondering if you could do something for me?"

"Sure, anything," Tom answered immediately.

"Obviously, Emily's guest list is a little sparse, especially with her lack of family," Olivia explained. "I was wondering if you would agree to a sort of father-of-the-bride role? I have my uncle Richard to give me away, but Emily really has no one other than you, Lucy, and Henry. Henry has other duties to perform, mainly upstaging the two brides."

"I would be absolutely honoured." Tom smiled.

"Thank you. Keep it a secret for now. We'll tell her over dinner."

"Right." Tom nodded in agreement.

"I know it would mean a lot to her. Well, I assume it would. She's taken to calling me Bridezilla and refusing to talk about the details of the wedding. I'm still waiting for a confirmation on the confetti designs I sent to her. I don't think she knows we're only four days away."

"I'm perfectly aware that we are four days away." Olivia turned around to see Emily behind her holding a tray with three mugs perched on it. "And I replied to you on the confetti designs. Not that I knew what confetti designs were until you started to fixate on them."

"I'm not fixated on them," Olivia huffed.

"You sent me twenty-seven different designs in an email sent at three o'clock in the morning." Emily held the tray out towards Tom, who took a mug.

"They sound like a married couple already." Tom chuckled.

"I feel so proud." Simon took the second mug.

"Proud?" Olivia asked.

"Yeah, without me you two probably would never have gotten together."

Olivia scoffed a laugh. "Well, if we're playing that game, then I'm taking credit for you and Sophie. If you'll excuse me, I'll go inside and say hello to her."

Olivia grabbed the last mug from the tray and placed a kiss on Emily's cheek before making her way inside.

❖

Later that evening, Tom and Simon were manning the barbeque while Lucy, Nicole, and Emily sat at the large patio table enjoying the hot summer's evening. Olivia walked with Sophie around the garden, pointing out new plants and explaining her plans for her vegetable patch, which had taken over a large part of the garden.

"Of course, the problem with growing all this food is that you need to have someone who eats it," Olivia explained. "Henry's getting there, but he'd still rather eat sweets than something that will actually fill and nourish him."

Sophie chuckled. "He's a kid. That's what they do, isn't it?"

Olivia sighed. "I suppose so. He likes cucumbers. That will be my legacy with him."

"I'm sure your legacy with him will be much bigger than that. He told me you taught him how to count to a million."

"I did. Well, the theory of it anyway." Olivia looked at her with a tilt of her head and then over at the other guests. When she was sure they were out of hearing distance, she finally said what had been on her mind. "How far along are you?"

Sophie looked at Olivia in shock, and she worried for a moment that she had said the wrong thing.

"How did you know? Am I showing? Did Simon tell you?"

Olivia shook her head. "No, not at all. You're holding your stomach a lot, and you seem different. I notice odd things."

Sophie smiled and shook her head. "You must do. Good observation." She looked down at her hand, which hovered over her stomach, and quickly dropped her arm to her side. "I'll have to watch out for that."

"Is it a secret?" Olivia asked.

"We didn't want to steal your thunder," Sophie said.

Olivia frowned. "You shouldn't keep your good news a secret for us. We're all friends here."

"Olivia!" Henry shouted as he ran across the garden in wild excitement. "Grandma is here! Mommy, Grandma is here."

Olivia and Emily barely had time to respond as Henry barrelled into the house at speed and the doorbell sounded a moment after.

"Excuse me," Olivia said and made her way into the house.

Once she got there, Irene was already in the kitchen, being dragged through to the garden by Henry.

"Olivia, Grandma is here."

"So I see," Olivia replied. "Why don't you give her a moment to say hello to people before you show her your tree house?"

Henry nodded and let go of Irene's hand. She pulled Olivia into a hug, and when Emily entered the kitchen, Irene pulled her into the hug as well. "Oh, I'm so glad to see the two of you."

"We're glad you could make it. Did you have a good flight?" Emily asked.

Irene pulled back and let them go. "Yes. I travelled Crown." She winked.

"Crown? That terrible outfit?" Simon said as he entered the kitchen and greeted Irene.

"Let's take this outside. We can complain about Crown Airlines where there is alcohol." Emily laughed.

They stepped outside, where Irene greeted everyone and was offered a glass of wine as she sat at the table.

"What's so funny?" Nicole asked Emily.

"We were talking about Crown Airlines," Emily said.

"Oh, I hear the cabin crew service has improved recently," Lucy joked.

Emily feigned horror.

"Technically, you should thank them. Without them you wouldn't be together," Sophie said.

"She's not wrong," Nicole said with a laugh.

"You know, you're right." Emily picked up her wine glass from the table. "Ladies and gentlemen, please charge your glasses."

Everyone picked up a glass of wine or beer, and Irene poured Henry some orange juice. When everyone had a full glass Emily raised hers into the air and declared, "To flight SQA016, where it all started."

Tom, Simon, and Olivia repeated the flight code verbatim, while everyone else replaced the letters and numbers with some yadda yaddas. Henry simply guzzled his juice, ignoring whatever was happening with the adults.

Emily sat down beside Olivia and kissed her cheek.

"So," Olivia said, "I had an idea about the confetti—"

Emily chuckled. "Olivia, darling?"

"Yes?" Olivia frowned.

"I love you." Emily smiled and pulled Olivia in, silencing her with a kiss.

About the Author

Amanda Radley had no desire to be a writer but accidentally turned into an award-winning, best-selling author. Residing in the UK with her wife and pets, she loves to travel. She gave up her marketing career in order to make stuff up for a living instead. She claims the similarities are startling.

Books Available from Bold Strokes Books

Cold Blood by Genevieve McCluer. Maybe together, Kalila and Dorenia have a chance of taking down the vampires who have eluded them all these years. And maybe, in each other, they can find a love worth living for. (978-1-63679-195-1)

Greener Pastures by Aurora Rey. When city girl and CPA Audrey Adams finds herself tending her aunt's farm, will Rowan Marshall—the charming cider maker next door—turn out to be her saving grace or the bane of her existence? (978-1-63679-116-6)

Grounded by Amanda Radley. For a second chance, Olivia and Emily will need to accept their mistakes, learn to communicate properly, and with a little help from five-year-old Henry, fall madly in love all over again. Sequel to Flight SQA016. (978-1-63679-241-5)

Journey's End by Amanda Radley. In this heartwarming conclusion to the Flight series, Olivia and Emily must finally decide what they want, what they need, and how to follow the dreams of their hearts. (978-1-63679-233-0)

Pursued: Lillian's Story by Felice Picano. Fleeing a disastrous marriage to the Lord Exchequer of England, Lillian of Ravenglass reveals an incident-filled, often bizarre, tale of great wealth and power, perfidy, and betrayal. (978-1-63679-197-5)

Secret Agent by Michelle Larkin. CIA agent Peyton North embarks on a global chase to apprehend rogue agent Zoey Blackwood, but her commitment to the mission is tested as the sparks between them ignite and their sizzling attraction approaches a point of no return. (978-1-63555-753-4)

Something Between Us by Krystina Rivers. A decade after her heart was broken under Don't Ask, Don't Tell, Kirby runs into her first love and has to decide if what's still between them is enough to heal her broken heart. (978-1-63679-135-7)

Sugar Girl by Emma L McGeown. Having traded in traditional romance for the perks of Sugar Dating, Ciara Reilly not only enjoys the no-strings-attached arrangement, she's also a hit with her clients. That is until she meets the beautiful entrepreneur Charlie Keller who makes her want to go sugar-free. (978-1-63679-156-2)

The Business of Pleasure by Ronica Black. Editor in chief Valerie Raffield is quickly becoming smitten by Lennox, the graphic artist she's hired to work remotely. But when Lennox doesn't show for their first face-to-face meeting, Valerie's heart and her business may be in jeopardy. (978-1-63679-134-0)

The Hummingbird Sanctuary by Erin Zak. The Hummingbird Sanctuary, Colorado's hottest resort destination: Come for the mountains, stay for the charm, and enjoy the drama as Olive, Eleanor, and Harriet figure out the meaning of true friendship. (978-1-63679-163-0)

The Witch Queen's Mate by Jennifer Karter. Barra and Silvi must overcome their ingrained hatred and prejudice to use Barra's magic and save both their peoples, not just from slavery, but destruction. (978-1-63679-202-6)

With a Twist by Georgia Beers. Starting over isn't easy for Amelia Martini. When the irritatingly cheerful Kirby Dupress comes into her life will Amelia be brave enough to go after the love she really wants? (978-1-63555-987-3)

Business of the Heart by Claire Forsythe. When a hopeless romantic meets a tough-as-nails cynic, they'll need to overcome the wounds of the past to discover that their hearts are the most important business of all. (978-1-63679-167-8)

Dying for You by Jenny Frame. Can Victorija Dred keep an age-old vow and fight the need to take blood from Daisy Macdougall? (978-1-63679-073-2)

Exclusive by Melissa Brayden. Skylar Ruiz lands the TV reporting job of a lifetime, but is she willing to sacrifice it all for the love of her longtime crush, anchorwoman Carolyn McNamara? (978-1-63679-112-8)

Her Duchess to Desire by Jane Walsh. An up-and-coming interior designer seeks to create a happily ever after with an intriguing duchess, proving that love never goes out of fashion. (978-1-63679-065-7)

Murder on Monte Vista by David S. Pederson. Private Detective Mason Adler's angst at turning fifty is forgotten when his "birthday present," the handsome, young Henry Bowtrickle, turns up dead, and it's up to Mason to figure out who did it, and why. (978-1-63679-124-1)

Take Her Down by Lauren Emily Whalen. Stakes are cutthroat, scheming is creative, and loyalty is ever-changing in this queer, female-driven YA retelling of Shakespeare's Julius Caesar. (978-1-63679-089-3)

The Game by Jan Gayle. Ryan Gibbs is a talented golfer, but her guilt means she may never leave her small town, even if Katherine Reese tempts her with competition and passion. (978-1-63679-126-5)

Whereabouts Unknown by Meredith Doench. While homicide detective Theodora Madsen recovers from a potentially career-ending injury, she scrambles to solve the cases of two missing sixteen-year-old girls from Ohio. (978-1-63555-647-6)

Boy at the Window by Lauren Melissa Ellzey. Daniel Kim struggles to hold onto reality while haunted by both his very-present past and his never-present parents. Jiwon Yoon may be the only one who can break Daniel free. (978-1-63679-092-3)

Deadly Secrets by VK Powell. Corporate criminals want whistleblower Jana Elliott permanently silenced, but Rafe Silva will risk everything to keep the woman she loves safe. (978-1-63679-087-9)

Enchanted Autumn by Ursula Klein. When Elizabeth comes to Salem, Massachusetts, to study the witch trials, she never expects to find love—or an actual witch…and Hazel might just turn out to be both. (978-1-63679-104-3)

Escorted by Renee Roman. When fantasy meets reality, will escort Ryan Lewis be able to walk away from a chance at forever with her new client Dani? (978-1-63679-039-8)

Her Heart's Desire by Anne Shade. Two women. One choice. Will Eve and Lynette be able to overcome their doubts and fears to embrace their deepest desire? (978-1-63679-102-9)

My Secret Valentine by Julie Cannon, Erin Dutton, & Anne Shade. Winning the heart of your secret Valentine? These award-winning authors agree, there is no better way to fall in love. (978-1-63679-071-8)

Perilous Obsession by Carsen Taite. When reporter Macy Moran becomes consumed with solving a cold case, will her quest for the truth bring her closer to Detective Beck Ramsey or will her obsession with finding a murderer rob her of a chance at true love? (978-1-63679-009-1)

Reading Her by Amanda Radley. Lauren and Allegra learn love and happiness are right where they least expect it. There's just one problem: Lauren has a secret she cannot tell anyone, and Allegra knows she's hiding something. (978-1-63679-075-6)

The Willing by Lyn Hemphill. Kitty Wilson doesn't know how, but she can bring people back from the dead as long as someone is willing to take their place and keep the universe in balance. (978-1-63679-083-1)

Three Left Turns to Nowhere by Nathan Burgoine, J. Marshall Freeman, & Jeffrey Ricker. Three strangers heading to a convention in Toronto are stranded in rural Ontario, where a small town with a subtle kind of magic leads each to discover what he's been searching for. (978-1-63679-050-3)

Humbug by Amanda Radley. With the corporate Christmas party in jeopardy, CEO Rosalind Caldwell hires Christmas Girl Ellie Pearce as her personal assistant. The only problem is, Ellie isn't a PA, has never planned a party, and develops a ridiculous crush on her totally intimidating new boss. (978-1-63555-965-1)

On the Rocks by Georgia Beers. Schoolteacher Vanessa Martini makes no apologies for her dating checklist, and newly single mom Grace Chapman ticks all Vanessa's Do Not Date boxes. Of course, they're never going to fall in love. (978-1-63555-989-7)

Song of Serenity by Brey Willows. Arguing with the Muse of music and justice is complicated, falling in love with her even more so. (978-1-63679-015-2)

The Christmas Proposal by Lisa Moreau. Stranded together in a Christmas village on a snowy mountain, Grace and Bridget face their past and question their dreams for the future. (978-1-63555-648-3)

The Infinite Summer by Morgan Lee Miller. While spending the summer with her dad in a small beach town, Remi Brenner falls for Harper Hebert and accidentally finds herself tangled up in an intense restaurant rivalry between her famous stepmom and her first love. (978-1-63555-969-9)

Wisdom by Jesse J. Thoma. When Sophia and Reggie are chosen for the governor's new community design team and tasked with tackling substance abuse and mental health issues, battle lines are drawn even as sparks fly. (978-1-63555-886-9)

Watching Over Her by Ronica Black. As they face the snowstorm of the century, and the looming threat of a stalker, Riley and Zoey just might find love in the most unexpected of places. (978-1-63679-100-5)

#shedeservedit by Greg Herren. When his gay best friend, and high school football star, is murdered, Alex Wheeler is a suspect and must find the truth to clear himself. (978-1-63555-996-5)

Always by Kris Bryant. When a pushy American private investigator shows up demanding to meet the woman in Camila's artwork, instead of introducing her to her great-grandmother, Camila decides to lead her on a wild goose chase all over Italy. (978-1-63679-027-5)

Exes and O's by Joy Argento. Ali and Madison really only have one thing in common. The girl who broke their heart may be the only one who can put it back together. (978-1-63679-017-6)

One Verse Multi by Sander Santiago. Life was good: promotion, friends, falling in love, discovering that the multi-verse is on a fast track to collision—wait, what? Good thing Martin King works for a company that can fix the problem, right…um…right? (978-1-63679-069-5)

Paris Rules by Jaime Maddox. Carly Becker has been searching for the perfect woman all her life, but no one ever seems to be just right until Paige Waterford checks all her boxes, except the most important one—she's married. (978-1-63679-077-0)

Shadow Dancers by Suzie Clarke. In this third and final book in the Moon Shadow series, Rachel must find a way to become the hunter and not the hunted, and this time she will meet Ehsee Yumiko head-on. (978-1-63555-829-6)

The Kiss by C.A. Popovich. When her wife refuses their divorce and begins to stalk her, threatening her life, Kate realizes to protect her new love, Leslie, she has to let her go, even if it breaks her heart. (978-1-63679-079-4)

The Wedding Setup by Charlotte Greene. When Ryann, a big-time New York executive, goes to Colorado to help out with her best friend's wedding, she never expects to fall for the maid of honor. (978-1-63679-033-6)

Velocity by Gun Brooke. Holly and Claire work toward an uncertain future preparing for an alien space mission, and only one thing is for certain, they will have to risk their lives, and their hearts, to discover the truth. (978-1-63555-983-5)

Wildflower Words by Sam Ledel. Lida Jones treks West with her father in search of a better life on the rapidly developing American frontier, but finds home when she meets Hazel Thompson. (978-1-63679-055-8)

A Fairer Tomorrow by Kathleen Knowles. For Maddie Weeks and Gerry Stern, the Second World War brought them together, but the end of the war might rip them apart. (978-1-63555-874-6)

Holiday Hearts by Diana Day-Admire and Lyn Cole. Opposites attract during Christmastime chaos in Kansas City. (978-1-63679-128-9)

Changing Majors by Ana Hartnett Reichardt. Beyond a love, beyond a coming-out, Bailey Sullivan discovers what lies beyond the shame and self-doubt imposed on her by traditional Southern ideals. (978-1-63679-081-7)

Fresh Grave in Grand Canyon by Lee Patton. The age-old Grand Canyon becomes more and more ominous as a group of volunteers fight to survive alone in nature and uncover a murderer among them. (978-1-63679-047-3)

Highland Whirl by Anna Larner. Opposites attract in the Scottish Highlands, when feisty Alice Campbell falls for city-girl-about-town Roxanne Barns. (978-1-63555-892-0)